VITAL
LINES

For Nancy + Phil,
    With deep appreciation
for everything you're doing
to help Jacob and
our family.

[signature]

9/27/98

Also by Jon Mukand (editor)

Sutured Words: Contemporary Poetry About Medicine
AIDS and Rehabilitation Medicine

VITAL LINES

CONTEMPORARY FICTION ABOUT MEDICINE

JON MUKAND, EDITOR

ST. MARTIN'S PRESS · NEW YORK

ACKNOWLEDGMENTS

Editing this collection of stories was a pleasure because I was able to read a variety of fine contemporary fiction and work with the people mentioned below. I greatly appreciate the generosity of the writers who allowed me to include their work in this volume. I would also like to acknowledge the encouragement and advice of Suzanne Poirier, Anne Hudson Jones, and Joanne Trautmann Banks. For their comments on the introductory essay, I am indebted to Howard Spiro, George Monteiro, and Giselle Corre. The editorial advice of Stephen Dixon was most helpful at an early stage of this work.

At St. Martin's Press, David Hirshfeld's enthusiasm for this book helped give it the necessary momentum. In the later stages, the editorial advice of Ruth Cavin and the scrupulous attention to detail of Barbara Norton were invaluable. I appreciate the technical assistance of David Stanford Burr at St. Martin's Press and Nancy Egan at the Landmark Medical Center (Rhode Island).

Most of all, I am grateful to my wife, colleague in medicine, and favorite (literary) critic, Giselle Corre, for her tolerance and encouragement of my careers in literature and medicine, and for her sustenance in so many ways.

For Permissions see page 433.

VITAL LINES: CONTEMPORARY FICTION ABOUT MEDICINE. Copyright © 1990 by Jon Mukand. All rights reserved. Printed in the United States of America. No part of this book may be used or reproduced in any manner whatsoever without written permission except in the case of brief quotations embodied in critical articles or reviews. For information, address St. Martin's Press, 175 Fifth Avenue, New York, N.Y. 10010

Production Editor: David Stanford Burr

Design by Judy Dannecker

Library of Congress Cataloging-in-Publication Data

Vital lines / John Mukand, ed.
    p. cm.
    "A Thomas Dunne book."
    ISBN 0-312-05176-X
    1. Medicine—Fiction. 2. Short stories, American. 3. American fiction—20th century. I. Mukand, Jon, 1959– .
PS648.M36V58 1990
813'.0108356—dc20   90-8625
                                       CIP

First Edition: November 1990

10 9 8 7 6 5 4 3 2 1

Contents

Acknowledgments iv
Introduction .... Jon Mukand, ix

THE MEDICAL ENVIRONMENT
The Wrath-Bearing Tree ...... Lynne Sharon Schwartz, 2
Going .... Amy Hempel, 11
In Search of the Rattlesnake
   Plantain .... Margaret Atwood, 14
A Hospital Fable .... Diana Chang, 24
Losses .... Layle Silbert, 29
The Operation .... Scott Russell Sanders, 33

PATIENTS LOOK AT ILLNESS
Only the Little Bone .... David Huddle, 40
This Year's Venison .... Pamela Ditchoff, 54
Wounded Soldier (Cartoon Strip) ..... George Garrett, 57
How to Get Home .... Bret Lott, 67
An Infected Heart .... John Stone, 80
He Read to Her .... Anne Brashler, 84
Solo Dance .... Jayne Anne Phillips, 88

LOOKING AT DOCTORS
Anniversary .... Elaine Marcus Starkman, 92

Three Doctors .... Jim Heynen, 101
Dr. Cahn's Visit .... Richard Stern, 103
Outpatient .... Rosalind Warren, 109
The Discus Thrower .... Richard Selzer, 115
Doctor .... Tema Nason, 119
Tale of a Physician .... Robert Watson, 122
Fathering .... Bharati Mukherjee, 135

FAMILY AND FRIENDS
Roth's Deadman .... Joe David Bellamy, 144
By That I Mean Angina Pectoris .. Gregory Burnham, 149
How to Win .... Rosellen Brown, 150
Some Stories Should Have a Real Hero .. Jeff Elzinga, 166
Stung .... E. S. Creamer, 168
The Signing .... Stephen Dixon, 172
Dying with Words .... Reginald Gibbons, 177
Girls .... Tess Gallagher, 181

WOMEN
What I Don't Tell People .... Kelly Cherry, 200
Sunday Morning .... Pat Carr, 215
Fertility Zone .... Patricia Eakins, 219
The Baby in Mid-Air .... Sandra Thompson, 226
A Story About the Body .... Robert Hass, 230
Mother .... Hilma Wolitzer, 231
Bringing the News .... Ellen Hunnicutt, 244

MENTAL ILLNESS
A Sorrowful Woman .... Gail Godwin, 254
Crazy Lady .... Mary Peterson, 261
Patients .... Jonathan Strong, 266
Hanging .... Steven Schrader, 276
The Prisoner .... Curtis Harnack, 279

DISABILITY
And the Children Shall Lead
    Us .... Irving Kenneth Zola, 292

A Problem of Plumbing .... James M. Bellarosa, 295

Wheelchair .... Lewis Nordan, 301

Old Glasses .... M. Thorne Fadiman, 312

Parting .... Michael Martone, 316

Close .... Felix Pollak, 328

Cathedral .... Raymond Carver, 329

SOCIAL ISSUES

How I contemplated the world from
the Detroit House of Correction
and began my life all over again .. Joyce Carol Oates, 348

If the River Was Whiskey .... T. Coraghessan Boyle, 366

End Over End .... Ron Carlson, 376

Pelicans in Flight .... Sheila Ballantyne, 380

Running on Empty .... Edmund White, 386

Social Security .... Norah Holmgren, 410

Mother's Child .... David Shields, 416

Sinatra .... Susan Dodd, 421

About the Editor and Authors 430

INTRODUCTION

. . . .

An elderly man in a wheelchair, his right arm hanging in a shoulder sling, looks up as I enter the room, and cheerfully greets me, in slurred speech, with "Hi, Doctor." Surprised at this welcome, I recover and respond to his greeting. Only a week earlier I had considered that this patient had a mild dementia in addition to his stroke (although pseudodementia caused by depression was also a possibility). Just yesterday he was tearful as he said, "The therapists keep telling me, 'One more day, one more day. Then you can do this or do that for yourself.' What do you think, Doc?" With his left hand he had lifted his flaccid arm for me to examine, as if I could somehow speed up the process of recovery.

What has happened in the last twenty-four hours? I sit down by him, and we begin to talk. He is starting to recover movement in the right arm and shows me how he can help with putting on his shirt. His entire strength seems to be concentrated in the right arm, which he lifts and places in the correct sleeve. On a quick mental status test, he no longer appears to have dementia, probably because his physical gains have improved his emotional condition. He shows off his weak finger flexion, which allows him to grasp a spoon with a large foam handle, and speaks in poetry: "Look. I can move it. It's better than just a piece of dumb flesh."

Nerve impulses travel from the damaged but recovering brain to the hand; the flesh speaks the language of movement. His words remind me of all the poetry in medical work. I remember a statement by William Carlos Williams that poetry and medicine amounted to the same thing for him. Then I think of my earlier pessimistic evaluations of this patient, of his family's unrealistic expectations from rehabilitation, of his interactions with the nurses and therapists, and I extend the comment by Williams: "Fiction and medicine amount to the same thing." After all, medicine is full of narratives, though often technical language and processes obscure the stories underlying the cases. By acknowledging this basis of medical practice and its various implications, we can diagnose both the harmful and the therapeutic aspects of medical encounters. As with any narrative, we can examine traditional elements such as character, plot, setting, irony. Post-structuralist criticism would consider socioeconomic, political, and ethical aspects of the medical narrative; feminist critics recommend sensitivity to gender biases in medical practice; health care workers should be aware of personal and idiosyncratic reactions (countertransference) to the patient-text, just as reader-response and psychoanalytic critics would recommend.

Before going further, we may consider that the practice of medicine is a form of literary criticism. Dr. Williams once referred to the poem as a machine. I would venture to say that the poem is a patient. This is not to imply that all texts exist in a state of illness and belong in a literary emergency room or intensive care unit. Much of medical practice is preventive and routine, such as immunizations or examinations for sports. (Seeing the patient as existing only in a pathologic state is a not uncommon medical fiction.)

To make a more general statement, the text is a patient and the patient is a text. Contemporary literary criticism occasionally hints at this similarity between patient and text. Allon White, in his book *The Uses of Obscurity,* suggests that "the symptom or the metaphor . . . simultaneously reveals and conceals." The Marxist critic Fredric Jameson obviously draws upon psychoanalytic theory in *The Political Unconscious,* and also refers to an "x-ray process" of analysis. And the critic G. S. Rousseau suggests (in *Literature and Medicine,* 1986) that the model of patient as text is "a vital concern" and "worthy of more attention than the analogy has received."

This concept has ancient origins in medical practice, which looked for "signs." *Dorland's Medical Dictionary* describes signs as "objective evidence of a disease . . . perceptible to the examining physician." There are obvious similarities between diagnosis in medicine and in the literary theory of signs and signification called semiotics. (The seventeenth-century physician William Harvey, near the end of *De motu cordis,* described medicine as consisting of "physiology, pathology, semiotics, therapeutics.") In my work as a clinician and researcher, and fortunately rare instances as a patient, I have found that the medical encounter—when one looks beyond the checklist of symptoms, signs, lab data, and radiologic procedures—often turns out to be similar to the encounter with a poem, short story, essay, or in some long-term cases, such as rehabilitation of spinal cord injury, a novel or epic poem. With all its weaknesses and strengths, the text requires an empathic yet analytic approach; often the process of appreciating the text is a multidisciplinary one, which is usually advantageous for the text just as for the patient. Between the physician-reader and the patient-text lie many layers of imagery and metaphor that contribute to a variety of fictions, which have found their way into the works of many writers.

From Nathaniel Hawthorne to Joyce Carol Oates and Raymond Carver, American fiction writers have found a rich source of inspiration in medical themes. This should be no surprise, for health is inextricably linked to human existence and disease affects characters in literature just as much as in real life. Although American literature has novels such as *The Country Doctor* by Sarah Orne Jewett and *Arrowsmith* by Sinclair Lewis, medical themes probably appear in their most concentrated form in the American short story. Literature has the power not only to illuminate but to create and perpetuate

metaphors and types of characters associated with certain ill-
nesses, as Susan Sontag has imaginatively shown in her book
Illness as Metaphor: "In contrast to the modern bogey of the
cancer-prone character—someone unemotional, inhibited, repressed—the TB-prone character that haunted imaginations in
the nineteenth century was an amalgam of two different fantasies: someone both passionate and repressed."

How do these metaphors and stereotypes come into existence? Very often the medical setting is the source. By "medical setting" I do not mean the "hospital" or "nursing home"
or "rehabilitation ward," but the imaginary space where interactions between patients, families and friends, medical
workers (including physicians, nurses, administrators, techni-
cians, therapists), and the media are held and processed. In this
setting the poetry and the fictions of medicine are created and
injected into our culture. Very often these fictions have practical consequences for the individual and for society.

Since medicine should focus on the patient, let us begin with
fictions created by patients. Perhaps the most obvious example
is that of dementia, where the loss of short-term memory
sometimes leads the patient to "confabulate." The origins of
this word are quite suggestive in the context of medical fiction:
fabula from the Latin for narrative, story. The confabulator
appears as a demented old man in "The Wrath-Bearing Tree"
by Lynne Sharon Schwartz. The narrator's father is dying in
a ward that also shelters this striking character, who asks all
visitors about the location of "Six-two-four Avenue D," and
occasionally exposes himself, "spreading wide the folds of his
white cotton gown with a quick flapping like a gull's wings."
In fact, his fictive world is so convincing that another visitor,
a newcomer, is completely taken in and criticizes the narrator
for not answering his question: "That's the way it is with these
young people. They won't give you the time of day." (As a
junior medical student at the Milwaukee County Hospital, I
once met a patient who appeared quite "normal" until I started
doing a mental status examination, and discovered she thought
the date was "Fall, 1939." It was actually January, 1984.) A
variation of this disorientation occurs with a delirious patient

in a story by Margaret Atwood titled "In Search of the Rattle-snake Plantain." An elderly man, who used to be very active in the outdoors, has had a recent stroke and seems to be getting worse. He neglects his garden, loses his appetite, becomes dehydrated (much like his garden), and this leads to delirium. One day he asks for the car keys. "He wants out, he wants to drive, away from all this illness," the narrator says in trying to make sense of her father's behavior. He says that "The rattlesnake plantain is making a comeback," which the narrator interprets for us: "I understand that, from somewhere in there, from underneath the fever, he's trying to send out some good news. He knows things have gone wrong, but it's only part of a cycle." (As we see here, and will discuss later, family members often create their own fictions to comprehend the traumas and fictions affecting themselves and their relative. One may view defense mechanisms as attempts to create plausible and emotionally acceptable fictions.)

Another instance of delirium, in Bharati Mukherjee's story "Fathering," is complicated by striking cultural differences: the patient is a child *and* is of Vietnamese origin. The invaluable research of Robert Coles *(The Moral Life of Children* and *The Political Life of Children)* has explored the ways in which children differ from adults. From Piaget's work we have learned the various stages of cognitive and social development in children. As any parent or pediatrician is well aware, the symptoms of children are often obscured by problems in communication. A miniature teddy bear attached to one's stethoscope or lab coat serves as an emissary, but in some circumstances there is little possibility for mutual understanding. The child, feverish, caught between two cultures, now in the alien culture of medicine, imagines her dead grandmother can protect her from the doctor and screams, "Don't let him touch me, Grandma! . . . Kill him, Grandma! Get me out of here, Grandma!" Then the child immigrant more pointedly rejects American medicine: "When they shoot my grandma, you think pills do her any good? You Yankees, please go home."

Less dramatic but just as strong examples of how children

respond to illness occur in "The Operation" by Scott Russell Sanders and "Only the Little Bone" by David Huddle. The former story is a brief exploration of a child's response to surgery. In an attempt to reassure his patient, the surgeon tells him the procedure will be "like cutting hair. You'll sleep right through it and wake up a new man." The omniscient narrator suggests that this is not entirely convincing by adding, "His eyes were grey and hard to see into." Back in the ward after the surgery, the boy Reuben inquires about "the kid with the orange peejays" and is told by a nurse, "Oh, they took him away this morning." He is not convinced, and later "he started to think at least *he* (emphasis mine) didn't die." A child's imagination is allowed, by the refusal of adults to describe medical details that "kids don't understand," to wander in who knows what strange ways. At the end of the story, Reuben knows "Something was different beneath the bandages, beneath the sheets, and he wondered what." This is the beginning of a major fiction in a child's life, whether fantasy or nightmare.

David Huddle's story explores how such an event can become the focal point for a complex meditation. The narrator and two other boys have been kept in isolation because of a polio epidemic in the county. On their first day of freedom, the narrator is hit by a car and breaks a bone in his leg. As an adult years later, holding his old cast, he "can almost understand the wacky logic of that accident," which is related to the polio epidemic, his Roy Rogers scarf, his mother's arthritic neck, and another car that didn't have brakes. His old cast serves as a nucleus and stimulus for memory. Disruption of health provokes the formation of layers of memories; excavation and eventual reorganization of these layers leads to the fiction. As I think of my own childhood, some of the most striking memories are involved with illness. For instance, I can still remember hiding in bed when I came down with chicken pox, terribly embarrassed about my disfigured body image when the neighbors came to visit and offer their sympathy.

That incident may have been why I was so affected by Anne

Brashler's short story titled "He Read to Her." Having undergone a colostomy, the woman in this story is repulsed by her own body and projects her feelings onto others. True, there is some justification for this perception, for when her husband enters the bathroom after her accident with the collection bag, he leaves and can be heard gagging in the kitchen. She does her best to push him away, physically and emotionally. But he is like "a person beatified" and does not respond to statements such as, "You creep. That's not going to do any good," when he brings her tea and addresses her as "my beautiful wife." He merely ignores her and begins reading *Moby Dick* to her. At first she is resistant and asks, "Are you going to read the whole damn book out loud?" But by the end of the story, "she lay back and closed her eyes. His voice was music; he became Ishmael, telling her a story." This demonstrates another major fiction in the medical setting: an exaggeration of the patient's self-image. A similar distortion of body image occurs in anorexia nervosa: No matter how close to starvation, the patient sees the body as bloated and repulsive.

On occasion the body is affected in such a manner that the patient resorts to the defense mechanism of denial. Recently I examined a patient with an amputation below the knee. A veteran of the hospital setting because of her diabetes, she had experienced a variety of medical procedures but none as traumatic as this loss. Because of "phantom" sensation, she was able to convince herself that her leg was still present. It took her a week after surgery before she was able to look at her residual limb, and even then a nurse had to apply her Ace wrap because she could not bear to confront her loss. In another case a patient got up at night, thought his leg was still present, tried to walk, and fractured a hip. Some of the fictions created by the body are dangerous. Among the most challenging patients in the rehabilitation setting are those with right-hemisphere strokes, whose body image may actually be hemisected. They "neglect" the left side of their world and, consequently, one sees them veering to the left in their wheelchairs, running into people and the corridor walls, wondering why they cannot go any farther. I will never forget such a patient, an old woman learning to compensate for this problem. She walked into the bathroom without much trouble, but couldn't understand what had happened to the toilet bowl (on the left). "What kind of place is this"? she said, understandably annoyed. Later, I requested that she touch her left hand with her right. After searching her body for the paralyzed hand and finding it, she gently patted it as if for reassurance that it was not lost or forgotten. These problems, of course, have a physiological basis, but are examples of a fictive body image originating from the patient.

In other instances one may see denial of a medical problem as a defense mechanism, as in the ironically titled story "Fertility Zone" by Patricia Eakins. A nurse's aide has been trying to have a child for seven years, and has regimented her life by this wish, checking her temperature each morning for the time of ovulation, creating an imaginary life with her unborn daughter (already named Mary Ellen). Some of this life has already materialized, in the form of clothes: "I've knit seven pair of booties, three receiving blankets, a playsuit, a bunting, a snowsuit, and four kimono sweaters, two with matching hats, all pink though I did knit one blue sweater just in case." In bed she tries to wake up her husband by saying, "It's time to build a dollhouse. . . . Mary Ellen will cry for it soon." An ironic and sad event at the hospital emphasizes this almost psychotic denial of her infertility: a woman in a coma has had a daughter delivered by Caesarean section. The narrator would give anything for a child and to be a mother; the comatose patient has had a child and cannot be a mother.

So far we have seen the patient's varied responses in the medical setting. Family members and friends are not only vital influences on these responses, but also create their own fictions. Sometimes these appear as the primitive defense mechanism of denial. At the most benign level, this may seem to be an attempt to rationalize a patient's erratic behavior, such as we saw in the daughter's poetic interpretations of her father's delirium in the story "In Search of the Rattlesnake Plantain."

Also fairly benign is the kind of magical thinking that occurs in the story by Lynne Sharon Schwartz. When the patient, moaning on the hard stretcher, asks his wife to wheel it herself, she replies "that it is against hospital rules." He goes into a tirade about "Law and order! . . . Rules are made by petty minds, for petty minds to obey." Later, after the daughter has broken the rule, she informs us: "Actually, my mother is not at all a fanatical law-and-order person. Only right now she thinks, hopes, yearns to believe that if she obeys all the rules in life God will look down on her with favor and let my father live. I know that he cannot live, so I can afford to be lawless." This is not just religious faith, but an attempt to act in a rigid, ritualistic manner for the magical effect of a cure.

When a relative denies the effects of illness, serious medical problems can develop. Once I treated a patient whose wife refused to believe that he had had a severe stroke: she insisted he was just feigning paralysis in order to make her feel bad. (His stroke had developed after a violent argument, and she may have been feeling guilty about possibly having caused the hypertensive intracranial hemorrhage.) One day I discovered her forcing him to stand up, which could have led to a fall and a fracture. This "therapy" was, of course, promptly discontinued.

A somewhat similar situation is depicted in "How to Win" by Rosellen Brown. An autistic hyperactive boy is destroying a family, figuratively and literally as he smashes their possessions. The mother, who is also the narrator, recognizes his behavior as being abnormal. But the father is in ambivalent denial. On the one hand he acknowledges that his son is an "exceptional child," but on another occasion, after Christopher has "smashed [his razor] to smithereens . . . and left cobweb tracks in the mirror he threw it at," he wonders "Well, what are other [boys] like"? He even suggests taking his son on a business trip! But the mother, aghast, reports: "Meanwhile I lose one lamp, half the ivory on the piano keys, and all my sewing patterns to my son in a single day."

In the most extreme form of creating fictions based on

medical problems, a relative or close friend may accept the psychotic delusions of a patient. The intellectually and emotionally dominant person "infects" the other with his or her mental illness. Treatment involves physically separating the two people involved in the *folie à deux*, which usually works well for the passive partner. Psychiatrists theorize that the passive partner has become so closely identified with the other (because of similar backgrounds, goals, and emotions) that *not* to join in the psychosis would mean losing the dominant partner.

A variation of this occurs in a story by Gail Godwin titled "A Sorrowful Woman." The startling first lines suggest the nature of the patient's problem. "One winter evening she looked at them: the husband durable, receptive, gentle; the child a tender golden three. The sight of them made her so sad and sick she did not want to see them ever again." Once her depression has set in, the husband and child go to extreme lengths to protect her. The husband fixes her nightly "sleeping draughts" consisting of cognac and a tranquilizing medication, takes care of the son and the house, hires a live-in nanny/housekeeper (until his wife fires her). Finally the sorrowful woman stops seeing her son and husband, communicating with them only through their notes. There has been no attempt to seek medical help for a clearly dangerous depression. In effect, this is a collusion with the depressed woman's withdrawal. Whether the husband feels he can "treat" her on his own or that she would not accept psychiatric help, or some other reason exists, we do not know the fictive premise. One day she ventures out into her kitchen and bakes some bread. Her husband and son mistakenly think she is recovering: "The force of the two joyful notes slipped under her door that evening pressed her into the corner of the little room." One day the inevitable happens: after a bout of domestic activities, she commits suicide. The innocent boy, continuing the fictions that have permeated the household for so long, says, "Look, Mommy is sleeping."

In contrast to the preceding story, a comic obsession takes

over a household in Steven Schrader's story titled "Hanging."
A man discovers the pleasures of being suspended from a bar
and takes this to an extreme. "Sometimes I would skip dinner
and my wife would bring her plate and sit on the mat beneath
me. My son would bring a book and I would read to him as
he drank his bottle. . . . One night I didn't go to bed. Instead
I hung on the bar." He is seen by his father, a doctor, a rabbi,
a welfare investigator, and a psychiatric case worker. For a time
his wife puts up with this. Then "One night she was so lonely
she invited everyone over" and the preceding group of people,
led by his father, joined him on the bar. The story concludes
with the narrator coming back down to earth. "They were all
pleased they had made it and they joked and shouted until the
wall cracked from the weight of their bodies and the bar came
loose and we toppled down." His family and community at first
refuse to accept the fiction but later on become part of it,
which ironically leads to his cure. (This gives a new twist to the
psychiatric advice to "meet the patient where he is at.")

Sometimes the fiction of obsession arises because of organic
causes, such as dementia. When an elderly physician becomes
demented in "Dr. Cahn's Visit" by Richard Stern, his confused mind searches for certainty in his favorite pastime:
bridge. "The vocabulary of the game deformed his speech. 'I
need some clubs' might mean 'I'm hungry.' 'My spades are
tired' meant he was. Or his eyes were." Meanwhile his wife is
suffering from a terminal illness and he is only making her
angry and irritated with his uninhibited comments on the
"game." Somehow, near the end of her illness, Dr. Cahn is
fairly appropriate during his last visit. But while riding home
in a taxi, although he responds correctly to his son's leading
question about being happy to see his wife, he also adds, "But
it's not a good day. It's a very poor day. Not a good bid at all."

Dr. Cahn is fortunately no longer a practicing physician. Of
course, there are instances when mistakes occur in the medical
setting, sometimes through incompetence, sometimes through
bizarre accidents beyond the physician's control. Fictions in
the medical setting can lead to disastrous complications. Like

any text, the medical record is vulnerable to misreadings. I once met a patient whom I questioned about his heart attack, which was listed in his medical history. He became quite irate and said he was tired of people asking him about his heart. It seemed that he had never had a heart attack, but somehow had been labeled as a cardiac patient. Ever since then, as consultants reviewed the chart and propagated this fiction in their own notes, his medical history had been transformed. Sometimes a misunderstanding on the patient's part can also lead to an incorrect medical history. One of my patients insisted that he did not have diabetes (even though he had hyperglycemia and was being treated with oral hypoglycemic medications), because "diabetics take insulin and I don't have to." Such misinterpretations are not rare in the medical setting, which is why clear communication is vital.

There may be instances when a physician is not using or is abusing his or her medical knowledge. When a physician ascribes behavioral eccentricities to a psychiatric problem instead of thoroughly ruling out organic causes, then the medical fiction of misdiagnosis has occurred. If in addition, as in "Tale of a Physician" by Robert Watson, the doctor gets emotionally and sexually involved with a patient, the malpractice is both medical and ethical. Because of a brain tumor's effects on her mental status, a woman has become estranged from her husband and seeks emotional and medical help from a physician who is having his own marital problems with a jealous and possessive wife. His patient is seductive, and he is unethical enough to allow a sexual liaison. Ironically, one day her visual problems open his eyes: "He had been careless, so careless, so certain that her aches and pains were psychosomatic, that she had lost her husband because of her neurosis and had trapped him."

In the preceding case, the physician violated not only sound clinical judgment but also a professional code of ethics to create a fiction. Sometimes the patient may be responsible. A variety of conditions predispose the patient to these fictions. For instance, patients with a systemic muscle disease called myotonic dystrophy have some curious behavioral features. Michael H. Brooke writes in his authoritative book, *A Clinician's View of Neuromuscular Diseases:* "there is an odd form of denial in these patients. This is frequently reflected in a suspicious and mildly hostile attitude toward the physician. Further, the multifarious symptoms which are presented by the myotonic patient during a succession of clinic visits can be so baffling and elusive that the physician may be tempted into a similar attitude on occasions." A related kind of fiction occurs when patients deliberately try to deceive a physician, like the one with endocarditis in John Stone's story "An Infected Heart." An arsonist in the Intensive Care Unit has severe burns all over his body and is in extreme pain. He deceives the cardiology team into thinking that he was actually burned while trying to save a child from a burning building. After his death, a sheriff guarding him reveals the truth. His "tale about his heroism, the young boy he'd saved, was a total lie, something he'd wanted us to believe and, in the haze of morphine, may have begun to believe himself." He might have thought that his fiction would affect the quality of his medical care. Or perhaps he desperately needed to die with the illusion of himself as a hero, which is why his story was so convincing.

The nature of illness is such that attempts to communicate the actual experience are often unsuccessful. Empathy for the patient and his or her condition is crucial. There are obvious examples of physical obstacles, such as a frustrated patient with aphasia who has trouble naming objects, and must resort to gestures and the written word to communicate. When asked to repeat numbers, he used "yes" for "eight" and "no" for "nine." One day I found him pointing to his paralyzed leg and crying; movement had started to come back and he could only tell me through his smiles and tears of happiness. Even when the patient is in full possession of the ability to communicate, the description of illness is nearly impossible. (Elaine Scarry has explored this quite thoroughly in her study titled *The Body in Pain.*) The story "Bringing the News" by Ellen Hunnicutt deals with the trauma of rape. Until fairly recently American culture has had a difficult time even acknowledging the extent of this societal problem. Women writers such as Adrienne Rich (in her poem titled "Rape") and Susan Estrich *(Real Rape)* have been among the first to explore the larger cultural and social meanings of this trauma. Ellen Hunnicutt's story begins with a woman's tender description of her husband and child, which is interrupted by the image of a female rabbit being set free from a cage: "Clutched by her belly, the rabbit thrashes frantically, flailing the air with helpless legs. Her ordeal is over in one swift moment as Mark sets her free for a romp on the grass, a lunch of carrot tops, but I look away, sickened. I have commanded my mind not to play these tricks, but I seem ruled by some fretful stranger who wills what I should think and feel." A long section of the story deals with her sister, who visited her in the hospital and shared her tears. The sister's response seems to the narrator to typify societal judgments: "But these tears were different, I could feel distance between us. My sister's voice became a gentle, comforting hum. I listened to the words, and then past them, with growing disbelief. Her voice carried a note of rebuke. Although she did not say it, she believed, and continues to believe, that in some way I am responsible for what has happened." Part of this response arises from fear and is the sister's defense mechanism, for she "believes that if she carries out certain precautions she will never be raped. It is easier for her to think I failed in some way than to believe she is vulnerable." Blaming the victim is a twisted defense mechanism for society, which prefers to take refuge in this fiction.

Another story about the medical issues of women also deals with the impossibility of communicating the harsh truths of medical dysfunction. The narrator of Kelly Cherry's story "What I Don't Tell People" describes the responses of people who "quiz" her about the details of her attempts at artificial insemination. First she feels obliged to explain herself: "Why am I, a single woman of an age that raises the risks entailed significantly and who does not earn enough to pay for day care, doing this? Because I want to hold a baby in my arms, which

I have never done in my life." In the brilliant ending, after all the clinical and legal and personal details, the narrator has described as much as one could expect, but admits: "What I don't tell people, what I never tell them, is that it feels like death."

Sometimes the explicit details of medicine are simply too much to inflict upon relatives. This is the reverse situation of the earlier two stories. The cliché "She (or he) went easily" is often a merciful varnishing of the truth. Who wants or needs to hear the full brutal description of cardiopulmonary resuscitation (a "code"), including the cattle-prod shocks to the heart, or the multiple attempts at intubating the trachea? During a code I once had to deliver a well-aimed fist over the chest wall of a patient with a serious cardiac dysrhythmia. He came back to sinus rhythm, but on the way down to the ICU, he began passing out and his monitor again showed ventricular tachycardia. After his fourth thump the medication (finally) took effect. He seemed to understand the need for this violent "treatment" after my explanation, but insisted that I spare his wife the details.

In a short, powerful vignette by Jeff Elzinga titled "Some Stories Should Have a Real Hero," a mother has brought her child, who has already succumbed to Sudden Infant Death Syndrome, to the emergency room. "The mother enters a step behind us and kneels beside her baby boy. She kisses his hands. She sucks on the little fingers. She begs us to warm him. . . . The mother begs the boy to forgive her." She is sent out and the team stops its ritual ministrations. Although one nurse suggests waiting because they "can't let the mother think it was her fault the baby died," another worker suggests she will realize it was an accident. A more callous sort says, "We have other work to do." At this, the "hero" of the story "suddenly announces—'If anyone moves another step closer to the door for any reason in the next five minutes, they will without a doubt get their face punched in." In a busy emergency room five minutes are precious. This span of time, creating a deliberately false impression, is the greatest gift that the team could have given the bereaved mother. In some instances the best possible therapy is a medical fiction. Of course, one has to walk the fine line between sparing a relative's feelings and being paternalistic.

Unfortunately, the therapeutic medical fiction is not very common. This may be due to the empiricism of the medical system, reflected in its insistence on verifiable data, precise case reports, and standardized procedures. An exception is the placebo, which is often used to determine if an experimental medication or procedure is in fact responsible for the therapeutic effect. I have found the placebo quite useful in the rehabilitation of patients with chronic pain, who are usually dependent on a pharmacopoeia. With an elixir instead of individual tablets, the patient can be gradually weaned off the narcotics and does not know when the medication is stopped. In many instances the use of a placebo raises questions of ethics. The possible therapeutic role of placebos in an ethical manner has been carefully discussed by Howard Spiro in *Doctors, Patients, and Placebos.*

When medical fictions arise, they are usually unintentional. A fiction often affecting my work in rehabilitation medicine is that patients with disabilities are to be pitied, to be treated with condescension, and to be given every possible assistance because they presumably cannot assist themselves. The disabled patient is not allowed to participate in the writing of his or her personal fiction. Given the chance, these people can be remarkably independent. Patients with spinal cord injury who have minimal movement below the neck often function very well, once their basic self-care has been managed. For instance, a patient with only movement at the shoulder and elbow can be quite independent in a wheelchair *and* a car with hand controls. These patients learn to deal with their *disabilities,* only to be stopped by *handicaps* imposed by society. Is it any wonder that some of these patients bitterly refer to so-called normal people as TABs (temporarily able-bodied)?

Modern medicine sometimes presumes that more technology is the answer to rehabilitation. This is yet another instance of an attempt to rewrite the patient's narrative, to create a dysfunctional fiction. During my residency at Boston University, I had the unforgettable experience of meeting a veteran of World War I whose leg had been amputated and who was using a *carved wooden* prosthesis. It fit perfectly, and, most important, he was able to get around in his house just fine. At the Amputee Clinic, the team of medical professionals marveled over this antique, changed only a few components, and saluted him as he strolled off with only a slight creaking from his prosthesis. Nobody had dared even mention the newest model with the foot made of the latest carbon/fiberglass material.

The patient in the story "Old Glasses" by M. Thorne Fadiman also believes in tried and true methods, however archaic they might seem to others. His congenital spastic paralysis resulted in a dislocated hip, and a physician friend advises him to try a new orthopedic operation that would allow him to walk with crutches for short distances. This recommendation is made in spite of his high level of function with a wheelchair. His wife is also quite enthusiastic. The turning point in the story occurs when he gets a new pair of glasses. "Everything is so bright—makes me dizzy. . . . I can't drive. The road is too close. Cars seem huge. Home, I sit on the porch and listen to the birds on the lawn, but the notes are sour, skewed, as if I'm wearing a kind of fuzzy hearing aid along with the glasses." This experience helps him make the decision to forgo the new surgical technique. The physician friend "can't believe it." After the phone call, he rolls out in his wheelchair to the porch and enjoys his previous, highly functional, vision. "I sit straight up, daring the moon to knock off my old pair of glasses. Some things you just don't want to change."

Vision is also the primary metaphor in Raymond Carver's story "Cathedral," which I had heard him read at Stanford about six years before his sad demise. While collecting stories for *Vital Lines*, I had sent out letters to writers whose work I enjoyed or that had been recommended to me. At the time, I was immersed in my clinical work and research as a resident, and had no idea that Raymond Carver was quite ill. He some-how managed to send me a cordial response in mid-July of 1988: "Please forgive the informality of this letter, but I'm away from my typewriter just now but wanted to get back to you with a response soon before we are overwhelmed with visitors and the like. You are most welcome to use 'Cathedral' in the section of the book 'Disability.' Good. I'm pleased. . . ." I imagine he had experienced all too intensely the fictions inherent in the medical setting and wanted to contribute to a better understanding of these therapeutic and patho-logic infusions of the imagination.

The medical fiction at work in "Cathedral" is that the reality of the blind and the sighted can never be the same, but this is rewritten by the end of the story. Although at first the narrator is quite blunt about his feelings ("A blind man in my house was not something I looked forward to."), during the story he struggles to understand the condition of blindness. At first this is quite crude, as when he imagines the blind man's late wife: "what a pitiful life this woman must have led. Imagine a woman who could never see herself 'reflected' in the eyes of her loved one. A woman who could go on day after day and never receive the smallest compliment from her beloved." When he arrives from the train station, the narrator exclaims, "This blind man, feature this, he was wearing a full beard!" Then there are the usual references to vision that sighted people make in the presence of the blind. Thinking of the scenic ride along the Hudson, he asks, "Which side of the train did you sit on, by the way?" The blind man takes this in stride and answers that he sat on the right side. Folklore about the blind appears later, as the two are smoking cigarettes. "I re-membered having read somewhere that the blind didn't smoke because, speculation had it, they couldn't see the smoke they exhaled." While his wife and the blind man reminisce, he comments with wry humor, "Robert had done a little of every-thing, it seemed, a regular blind jack-of-all-trades." Perhaps to relieve his unease, the narrator asks the blind man to share some marijuana. When they turn on a television program about cathedrals, the blind man asks him to describe one for him. The narrator does a poor job, at which the blind man suggests an "experiment." The narrator draws a cathedral on heavy paper with a ballpoint pen, with the blind man's hand resting on the narrator's moving hand. Then the blind man traces the shapes with his fingers, and asks the narrator to close his eyes. Now, from his tactile/spatial memory, he *guides* the "sightless" narrator's hand for some finishing touches on the cathedral. This control is suggested by "His fingers rode my fingers as my hand went over the paper." (I remember this part of the story quite well from the reading; my eyes were also closed and I was imagining my hand being guided over a cathedral.) Now the two men share the same reality. The separatist fiction that sighted and blind people have entirely different perceptions has been overturned. For the narrator, it is a tremendously liberating experience. "My eyes were still closed. I was in my house. I knew that. But I didn't feel like I was inside anything."

By reading these stories we can understand the quirks and subtleties of the many varieties of fiction in the medical world. As we have seen, these have many sources: patients, family and friends, medical personnel at all levels. On a larger scale, these fictions arise out of an entire profession or of certain segments of society, to be reinforced and encoded in our culture in a variety of ways. One of the most powerful is literature itself. This is why we can expect literature about medicine to reveal the fictions of medical practice. As in pharmacology, once we understand the mechanisms of action for these sometimes destructive and sometimes beneficial fictions, then we can try to find antidotes or improve the therapeutic ones. Just as our insight into texts and the resulting production of literary criticism improve with experience and study, so our reading of patients may lead to better medical care. Naturally, this applies to patients, family and friends, and medical workers, all of whom must learn to appreciate and work with the diversity of fictions in the medical setting. Ultimately the goal of medicine is to empower patients and their families: to encourage the writing of their own narratives by taking advantage of the fictions in medicine.

Everyone in this society has encountered the medical system in one form or another. That is why these stories about medical experiences speak to all of us. If we listen, all we have to do is close our eyes, expand the limits of the imagination's house until we don't "feel inside anything," and then, like the narrator in Raymond Carver's story, we may reach the epiphanic realization that "It's really something."

—JON MUKAND

THE MEDICAL ENVIRONMENT

· · · · · · · · · · · · · · · · · ·

THE WRATH-BEARING TREE

Lynne Sharon Schwartz

· · · · · · · · · · · · · · · · · ·

"Six-two-four Avenue D?" The old man asks me. He clutches at my wrist with knobby fingers. "Six-two-four Avenue D?"

"I'm very sorry. I can't help you."

"Come on, don't pay any attention," my father mutters impatiently, pulling at my other arm. We proceed. Behind my back the old man whimpers to a woman by his side, "No one wants to help me."

"That's the way it is with these young people. They won't give you the time of day."

Anger and guilt rise in me simultaneously like twin geysers. I hastily prepare two lines of defense, one to assuage the guilt, the other to justify the anger. Number one, he's already asked me three times today. Number two, I have enough troubles of my own.

I am taking my father for a stroll down the hospital corridor, our arms linked at the elbow like a happy couple on a date. An intrusive third wheel is the IV tube dangling from its chrome stand, a coatrack come to life. My father is here in order to die. Even now, terminally ill, he walks very fast, he runs.

The old man, the one searching for 624 Avenue D, is the spectacle of the floor. Ambulatory, he spends long hours in the waiting room, where he occasionally urinates on the floor. Also, from time to time he exposes himself, spreading wide the folds of his white cotton gown with a quick flapping like a gull's wings. This is disconcerting to new visitors, but my sister and I merely smile now, humoring him. We have found that a brief, friendly acknowledgment will satisfy him for the day. Between ourselves we call him the flasher, and giggle. "How's the flasher today?" "Not bad. He looked a little pale, though." Having seen his private parts so often, I feel on intimate terms with him, like family. He is not really annoying except when he gets on one of his 624 Avenue D jags, lasting for two or three days, after which he returns to simple urinating and self-exposure.

My father, thank God, would never expose himself. The humiliation. As a child I once accidentally glimpsed a patch of his pubic hair; he looked as though he might faint with shock when he saw me in the room. My father, thank God, is in full possession of his mental faculties. Just yesterday he gave a philosophical disquisition, shortly after taking a painkiller. "There are times," he said, "when the mere absence of pain is a positive pleasure." He paused, and swallowed with difficulty. We could see his throat muscles straining. "That is," he went on, "under certain extreme conditions a negative quality can become a positive one." My heart swelled with love and pride. Isn't he smart, my father? He cannot resist saying things twice, though, that is, paraphrasing himself, a trait I have inherited. I think it comes from a conviction of intellectual superiority, that is, an expectation of inferior intelligence in one's listeners.

"Six-two-four Avenue D?" The old man looms up, having padded in on soundless feet, before my sister and me in the waiting room.

"I think it's the other way," I say gently. "Try that way." He shuffles towards the door. My sister and I are chain-smoking and giggling, making up nasty surmises about the patients and their visitors.

"That one will probably put arsenic in her grandma's tea the day she gets home." She points to a young girl with long gold earrings and tattered jeans, who is speaking sternly about proper diet to an old woman in a wheelchair.

I nod and glance across the room at a fat, blue-haired woman wearing a flowered, wrinkled cotton housedress. "Couldn't she find anything better to visit the hospital in? He might drop dead just looking at her."

We giggle some more. "How did the Scottish woman's kidney operation go?"

"All right. They took it out. She'll need dialysis."

"At least she's okay." We lower our eyes gravely. We like the Scottish woman. There is a long silence.

"Norman died last night," she says at last.

"Oh, really. Well . . ." This is not a surprise. Norman was yellow-green for two weeks and wheeled about morosely, telling his visitors he was not long for this world. He convinced everyone and turned out to be right. "That's too bad. He was nice."

"Yes, he was," she agrees.

Suddenly we are convulsed with laughter. Just outside the waiting room the old man has flashed for an elegant slender woman in a gray silk suit and bouffant hairdo, and carrying a Gucci bag. It greeted her the instant she stepped off the elevator. The astonishment on her face is exquisite and will sustain our spirits for hours.

It occurs to me that my sister and I have not been so close since my childhood, when I used to hold the book for her as she memorized poems. I was eight when she began college. Her freshman English teacher made the class memorize reams of poetry; thanks to him my head is filled with long, luminous passages. I sat on her bed holding the book while she pranced around the room reciting with dramatic gestures:

> And this was the reason that, long ago,
>   In this kingdom by the sea,
> A wind blew out of a cloud, chilling
>   My beautiful Annabel Lee;
> So that her highborn kinsmen came
>   And bore her away from me,

To shut her up in a sepulchre
In this kingdom by the sea.

What are kinsmen, I wanted to know. And what is a sepulchre? I thought it terribly mean of her highborn kinsmen
to drag Annabel Lee away, even if she did have a cold.

" 'That is no country for old men,' " she intoned solemnly,
" 'The young / In one another's arms, birds in the trees . . .' "
When she came to "sick with desire / And fastened to a dying
animal," she grew melodramatic, clutching her heart and pretending to swoon. I was an appreciative audience. " 'Already
with thee! tender is the night.' " She would flutter her wings
like a bird, and if I giggled hard enough she would be inspired,
at "Now more than ever seems it rich to die," to stretch out
flat on the bedroom floor.

Eliot was her favorite. But even here, though reverent, she
could not resist camping. " 'I an old man, / A dull head among
windy spaces.' " She let her jaw drop and lolled her head about
like an imbecile. She sobered quickly, though, delivering the
philosophical section with an awesome dignity reaching its
peak at "These tears are shaken from the wrath-bearing tree."

"What does that mean?" I interrupted.

She could not tell me. She herself was only seventeen. But
she said it beautifully, standing still in the center of the room,
hand resting on her collarbone, head slightly cast down, long
smooth hair falling over her shoulders: " 'These tears are
shaken from the wrath-bearing tree.' "

Evenings, after I held the book and corrected her for about
an hour, she would get dressed to go out on dates. Indeed, my
memories of my sister at that period show her doing only those
two things—memorizing poetry and getting dressed for dates.
She let me watch her. She kept perfume in a crystal decanter
whose top squeaked agonizingly when it was opened or closed.
The squeak made me writhe on the bed in spasms of shivers.
She squeaked it over and over, to torment me, while I squealed,
"Stop, please, stop!" She laughed. "Come here," she said. "I'll
give you a dab." I went. But before she gave me a dab she

squeaked the top again. When she left home three years later to get married I inherited her large bedroom. She left the perfume decanter for me, and often, feeling lonely, I squeaked it for the thrill of the shivers and for the memories.

Now she is in her forties, the mother of two grown sons. "Do you still remember all the poetry?" I ask.

She smiles. She has an odd smile, withholding, shy, clever, and she says, " 'Shall I compare thee to a summer's day? Thou art more lovely and more temperate.' " When she gets to " 'Nor shall Death brag thou wand'rest in his shade,' " she stops, her voice choking. We light up more cigarettes. "Six-two-four Avenue D?" he asks us. "Oh, for Christ's sake," she says, stubs out the cigarette angrily, and stomps off to the ladies' room.

I sit at my father's bed, waiting for the night nurse to come. The man in the next bed and his wife are trying to make conversation with my father about an earthquake in China. My father, who in good health was gregarious and an avid follower of current events, has his lips sealed in wrath.

"Maybe he's not quite with it, huh?" the man's wife says.

I rise staunchly to his defense. "Oh, he's with it, all right."

She pulls the curtains around her husband's bed, as she does every evening for fifteen minutes. I envision them engaged in silent, deft manual sex.

"You don't have to stay here, you know," my father says.

"Why not? Don't you want me to stay?"

"Of course."

"So I'll stay then." This is the closest I have come to telling him I love him. Not very close. I long to tell him I love him and am sorry for his suffering, but am afraid he would consider that in bad taste. My father does not consider love or sorrow in bad taste, only, I imagine, talking about them. That he is dying is an evident obscenity that cannot be spoken. I do not want to say anything at this critical moment that he would consider in bad taste, or that might imperil his final judgment of me. My mouth waters with the sour bad taste of unspoken words. Reality, in fact, is in bad taste.

"Six-two-four Avenue D? Six-two-four Avenue D?" The flasher is at the bedside. I point towards the door and he moves off.

"What the hell does he want, anyway?" my father asks.

"Six-two-four Avenue D."

He shrugs and grins. I do the same, like a mirror. We understand each other.

The next day my mother and I stand at his stretcher in the corridor of the hospital basement after X-rays, waiting fifteen furious, endless minutes for an orderly to wheel him upstairs to his bed. He moans in pain on the hard pallet and wants my mother to wheel the stretcher upstairs herself. She says that is against hospital rules. Propping himself up on his elbows to glare at her, he shouts hoarsely: "Law and order! Law and order! That is the whole trouble with some people. Rules are made by petty minds, for petty minds to obey. Throughout history, the great achievements were made by those who broke the rules. Look at Galileo! Look at Lenin! Look at Lindbergh! Daring!" This speech has been too much for him. He falls back on the stretcher, his mouth wide open, panting. I grab the back of the stretcher with one hand, the IV pole with the other, and we dash on a madly veering course through the labyrinth of the basement towards the forbidden staff elevator. Our eyes meet in an ecstasy of glee and swift careening motion. I remember how he drove me anywhere I asked at seventy miles an hour, his arm out the window, fingers resting on the roof of the car, an arm sunburned from elbow to wrist. Oh Daddy, for you I am Galileo, I am Lenin, I am Lindbergh! Daring! We reach his bedside unstopped by any guardians of the law. He grips my hand in thanks, my life is fulfilled.

Actually, my mother is not at all a fanatical law-and-order person. Only right now she thinks, hopes, yearns to believe that if she obeys all the rules in life God will look down on her with favor and let my father live. I know that he cannot live, so I can afford to be lawless.

I carry his urine in a blue plastic jug given to me by an orderly like a sacred trust, to present to the proper nurse. I cannot find the right nurse, they all look alike. I have never looked at them, only stepped on the toe of one, in protest. As I search, a new patient approaches me, a small woman with straight white hair drifting about her cheeks in a girlish bob. "Have you seen my children?" She has a sweet face and a gentle, pleasing voice. "No? You haven't seen them? Two little children, a boy and a girl, curly hair?"

I shake my head again. "I'm awfully sorry, I haven't."

The next day I see them. They visit with her in the waiting room, large, weary, middle-aged, and kind. They treat her ever so kindly in the waiting room, and she treats them with aloof politeness. An hour after they leave she stops me in the corridor. "Have you seen my children? A boy and a girl, curly hair?"

The day before the operation, cousins whom I cannot bear arrive to pay their respects. I wish the flasher would come in and perform for them, but he stubbornly stays away. I even consider going to fetch him, but that would be exploitation. My sister is doing her duty entertaining the guests. Let her. She is the big sister.

"Take me out for a drink," I whisper to my nephew, her older son.

He is a smart boy, though only twenty-three. He understands that his mother and I are losing our father and must be treated like children. He rises promptly like a great blond hairy tree, six foot two, and steers me to the elevator.

"I bet I can drink you under the table," I say.

I order Johnnie Walker Red, he orders Johnnie Walker Black. I wonder what is the difference between the red and the black, but not wishing to appear so ignorant in front of a younger man, I don't ask. From the way he drinks I realize he is an adult, and feel almost resentful that he grew up secretly, behind my back. I imagine now that women look at him with lust. I try, merely for distraction, to look at him with lust but cannot manage it.

During the third double Scotch my nephew says, "Have you met the woman who's looking for her children?"

"Yes."

"You know, I thought if we could introduce her to Six-two-four Avenue D maybe we could make a match."

I choke with laughter, sputtering Scotch all over the table. What a brilliant sally, a pinnacle of wit. I wish I had thought of it. Yet inside I am thinking, That is really in bad taste. Such bad taste. Young people.

He drinks four, I drink only three. I feel old, middle-aged. What do the other drinkers think about us? I don't look old enough to be his mother, nor young enough to be his girlfriend. They think he is a young man doing a middle-aged woman a favor, which he is. I wonder if I am boring him with my gloom. The hours I spent holding the book for his mother long before he was born or even dreamed of come back to me.

> "Terence, this is stupid stuff:
> You eat your victuals fast enough;
> There can't be much amiss, 'tis clear,
> To see the rate you drink your beer.
> But oh, good Lord, the verse you make,
> It gives a chap the belly-ache."

That is unfair. He is a good boy and I love him dearly. I put my hand on his. "Thanks for getting me out of there." What I really want to say is this:

> 'Tis true, the stuff I bring for sale
> Is not so brisk a brew as ale:
> . . . .
> But take it: if the smack is sour,
> The better for the embittered hour;
> It should be good to heart and head
> When your soul is in my soul's stead;
> And I will friend you, if I may,
> In the dark and cloudy day.

But I don't think he cares for poetry. I doubt his mother ever told him how I held the book for her; she is not given to discussing the past, says she remembers very little.

The day of the crucial operation we crowd into the room to see my father wheeled out on the stretcher. There are too many of us for comfort, but what can we do? Everyone has a right to be there, everyone wants to say good-bye. Once again, his lips are sealed in wrath. You don't care about anyone but yourself, dying. Selfish. Brain. Heartless. I shout all this at him from behind closed, withering lips. What about us? What about me? Not one word for me? His eyes open. He looks around at us one by one, enumerating the members of his tribe. He is groggy from the shot, but he says mildly, "If you're all here, then who's home taking care of the little girls?"

Those are my little girls he's talking about. He has forgotten nothing and no one, keeps us arrayed in his eye like a family portrait, precious and indestructible. My heart leaps up, to a grief that cuts like a knife.

"Six-two-four Avenue D? Six-two-four Avenue D?" He edges up and appeals to the crowd of us around the stretcher. We ignore him. Go find the old woman with the children.

The odd thing is, I think, when it is over and we bid good-bye to the waiting room, that all along I knew exactly where 624 Avenue D was. It was near my high school. I had a friend who lived in 628, in a row of attached two-family houses on a modest, decent street. Had I met the flasher anywhere else but the terminal waiting room, I would gladly have given him directions to find his way home. There, I was powerless. I wish I could explain that to him.

GOING

Amy Hempel

· · · · · · · · · · · · · · · · · ·

There is a typo on the hospital menu this morning. They mean, I think, that the pot roast tonight will be served with buttered noodles. But what it says here on my breakfast tray is that the pot roast will be *severed* with buttered noodles.

This is not a word you want to see after flipping your car twice at sixty per and then landing side-up in a ditch.

I did not spin out on a stretch of highway called Blood Alley or Hospital Curve. I lost it on flat dry road—with no other car in sight. Here's why: In the desert I like to drive through binoculars. What I like about it is that things are two ways at once. Things are far away and close with you still in the same place.

In the ditch, things were also two ways at once. The air was unbelievably hot and my skin was unbelievably cold.

"Son," the doctor said, "you shouldn't be alive."

The impact knocked two days out of my head, but all you can see is the cut on my chin. I total a car and get twenty stitches that keep me from shaving.

It's a good thing, too, that that is all it was. This hospital place, this clinic—it is not your City of Hope. The instruments don't come from a first-aid kit, they come from a toolbox. It's the desert. The walls of this room are not rose-beige or sanitation-plant green. The walls are the color of old chocolate going chalky at the edges.

11

And there's a worm smell.

Though I could be mistaken about the smell.

I'm given to olfactory hallucinations. When my parents' house was burning to the ground, I smelled smoke three states away.

Now I smell worms.

The doctor wants to watch me because I knocked my head. So I get to miss a few days of school. It's okay with me. I believe that ninety-nine percent of what anyone does can effectively be postponed. Anyway, the accident was a learning experience.

You know—pain teaches?

One of the nurses picked it up from there. She was bending over my bed, snatching pebbles of safety glass out of my hair. "What do we learn from this?" she asked.

It was like that class at school where the teacher talks about Realization, about how you could realize something big in a commonplace thing. The example he gave—and the liar said it really happened—was that once while drinking orange juice, he'd realized he would be dead someday. He wondered if we, his students, had had similar "realizations."

Is he kidding? I thought.

Once I cashed a paycheck and I realized it wasn't enough.

Once I had food poisoning, and realized I was trapped inside my body.

What interests me now is this memory thing. Why two *days*? Why *two* days? The last I know is not getting carded in a two-shark bar near the Bonneville flats. The bartender served me tequila and he left the bottle out. He asked me where I was going, and I said I was just going. Then he brought out a jar with a scorpion in it. He showed me how a drop of tequila on its tail makes a scorpion sting itself to death.

What happened after that?

Maybe those days will come back and maybe they will not. In the meantime, how's this: I can't even remember all I've forgotten.

I do remember the accident, though. I remember it was like

the binoculars. You know—two ways? It was fast and it was slow. It was both.

The pot roast wasn't bad. I ate every bit of it. I finished the green vegetables and the citrus vegetables too.

Now I'm waiting for the night nurse. She takes a blood pressure about this time. You could call this the high point of my day. That's because this nurse makes every other woman look like a sex change. Unfortunately, she's in love with the Lord.

But she's a sport, this nurse. When I can't sleep she brings in the telephone book. She sits by my bed and we look up funny names. Calliope Ziss and Maurice Pancake live in this very community.

I like a woman in my room at night.

The night nurse smells like a Christmas candle.

After she leaves the room, for a short time the room is like when she was here. She is not here, but the idea of her is.

It's not the same—but it makes me think of the night my mother died. Three states away, the smell in my room was the smell of the powder on her face when she kissed me good-night—the night she wasn't there.

IN SEARCH OF THE RATTLESNAKE PLANTAIN

Margaret Atwood

. . . .

W e start in from the shore, through the place where there are a lot of birches. The woods are open, the ground covered with a mat of leaves, dry on the top, pressed down into a damp substratum beneath, threaded through (I know, though I don't look, I have looked before, I have a history of looking) with filaments, strands, roots, and skeins of leaf mould laid through it like fuses, branched like the spreading arteries of watercolour blue in certain kinds of cheese.

Against the dun colour of the fallen leaves, which recedes before us, the birches stand out, or lie. Birches have only a set time to live, and die while standing. Then the tops rot and fall down, or catch and dangle—widow-makers, the loggers used to call them—and the lopped trunks remain upright, hard fungi with undersides like dewed velvet sprouting from them. This patch of woods, with its long vistas and silent pillars, always gives me the same feeling: not fright, not sadness; a muted feeling. The light diffuses here, as through a window high up, in a vault.

"Should have brought a bag," says my mother, who is behind me. We go in single file, my father first, of course, though without his axe; Joanne second so he can explain things to her. I come next and my mother last. In this forest you have to be close to a person to hear what they say. The trees, or more probably the leaves, blot up sound.

14

"We can come back," I say. Both of us are referring to the birch bark, curls of which lie all around us. They ought to be gathered and used for starting the fire in the wood stove. With dead birches, the skin outlasts the centre, which is the opposite from the way we do it. There is no moment of death for anything, really; only a slow fade, like a candle or an icicle. With anything, the driest parts melt last.

"Should have used your brain," says my father, who has somehow heard her. They have the ability to hear one another, even at a distance, even through obstacles, even though they're in their seventies. My father raised his head without turning his voice, and continues to stomp forward, over the dun leaves and the pieces of Greek temple that litter the ground. I watch his feet, and Joanne's, ahead of me. Really I watch the ground: I'm looking for puffballs. I too have brought no bag, but I can take off my top shirt and make a bundle with it, if I find any.

"Never had one," says my mother cheerfully. "A ball of fluff. Just a little button at the top of my spine, to keep my head from falling off." She rustles along behind me. "Where's he going?" she says.

What we're doing is looking for a bog. Joanne, who writes nature articles, is doing a piece on bogs, and my father knows where there is one. A kettle bog: no way in for the water, and no way out. Joanne has her camera, around her neck on one of those wide embroidered straps like a yodeler's braces, and her binoculars, and her waterproof jacket that folds up into its own pocket and straps around the waist. She is always so well equipped.

She brought her portable one-person kayak up for this visit, assembled it, and whips around over the water in it like a Jesus bug, which is what they used to call those whirligig water beetles you find sheltering in the calm places behind logs, in bays, on stormy days, black and shiny like Joanne's curious eyes.

Yesterday Joanne stepped the wrong way into her kayak and rolled, binoculars and all. Luckily not the camera. We dried her out as well as we could; the binoculars are more or less all right. I knew then that this is the reason I am not as well equipped as Joanne: I am afraid of loss. You shouldn't have a kayak or binoculars or anything else, unless you're prepared to let it sink.

Joanne, who is bright and lives by herself and by her wits, is ready for anything despite her equipment. "They're only binoculars," she said, laughing, as she squelched ashore. She knew the address of the place where she would take them to get them dried out professionally, if all else failed. Also she had a spare pair of hiking boots. She's the kind of woman who can have conversations with strangers on trains, with impunity. They never turn out to be loonies, like the ones I pick, and if they were she would ditch them soon enough. "Shape up or ship out" is a phrase I learned from Joanne.

Up ahead my father stops, looks down, stoops, and pokes. Joanne stoops too, but she doesn't uncork the lens of her camera. My father scuffles impatiently among the dried leaves.

"What's he got there?" says my mother, who has caught up with me.

"Nothing," says my father, who has heard her. "No dice. I don't know what's happened to them. They must be disappearing."

My father has a list in his head of things that are disappearing: leopard frogs, certain species of wild orchid, loons, possibly. These are just the things around here. The list for the rest of the world is longer, and lengthening all the time. Tigers, for instance, and whooping cranes. Whales. Redwoods. Strains of wild maize. One species of plant a day. I have lived with this list all my life, and it makes me uncertain about the solidity of the universe. I clutch at things, to stop them, keep them here. If those had been my binoculars, there would have been a fuss.

But right now, right at this moment, I can't remember which thing it is that must be disappearing, or why we are looking for it in the first place.

We're looking for it because this isn't the whole story. The reason I can't remember isn't creeping senility: I could remember perfectly well at the time. But that was *at the time,* and this is a year later. In the meantime, the winter, which is always the meantime, the time during which things happen that you have to know about but would rather skip, my father had a stroke.

He was driving his car, heading north. The stroke happened as he turned from a feeder lane onto an eight-lane highway. The stroke paralyzed his left side, his left hand dragged the wheel over, and the car went across all four lanes of the west-bound half of the highway and slid into the guard rail on the other side. My mother was in the car with him.

"The death seat," she said. "It's a miracle we weren't mashed to a pulp."

"That's right," I say. My mother can't drive. "What did you do?"

This is all going on over long-distance telephone, across the Atlantic, the day after the stroke. I am in a phone booth in an English village, and it's drizzling. There's a sack of potatoes in the phone booth too. They don't belong to me. Someone must be storing them in here.

My mother's voice fades in and out, as mine must, for her. I have already said, "Why didn't you call me as soon as it happened?" and she has already said, "No point in upsetting you." I am still a child, from whom the serious, grown-up things must be concealed.

"I didn't want to get out of the car," my mother said. "I didn't want to leave him. He didn't know what had happened. Luckily a nice young man stopped and asked if we were having any trouble, and drove on and called the ambulance."

She was shaken up; how could she not be? But she didn't want me to fly back. Everything was under control, and if I were to fly back it would be a sign that everything was not under control. My father was in the hospital, under control too. The stroke was what they called a transient one. "He can talk again," said my mother. "They say he has a good chance of getting most of it back."

"Most of what?" I said.

"Most of what he lost," said my mother.

After a while I got a letter from my father. It was written

in the hospital, where they were doing tests on him. During the brain scan, he overheard one doctor say to another, "Well, there's nothing in there, anyway." My father reported this with some glee. He likes it when people say things they haven't intended to say.

We are past the stand of dying birch, heading inland, where the undergrowth is denser. The bog is somewhere back in there, says my father.

"He doesn't remember," says my mother in a low voice to me. "He's lost."

"I never get lost," says my father, charging ahead now through the saplings. We aren't on a path of any sort, and the trees close in and begin to resemble one another, as they have a habit of doing, away from human markings. But lost people go around in circles, and we are going in a straight line. I remember now what is disappearing, what it is we're supposed to be looking for. It's the rattlesnake plantain, which is a short plant with a bunch of leaves at the base and knobs up the stem. I think it's a variety of orchid. It used to be thick around here, my father has said. What could be causing it to disappear? He doesn't want one of these plants for anything; if he found a rattlesnake plantain, all he would do is look at it. But it would be reassuring, something else that is still with us. So I keep my eyes on the ground.

We find the bog, more or less where it was supposed to be, according to my father. But it's different; it's grown over. You can hardly tell it's a bog, apart from the water that oozes up through the sphagnum moss underfoot. A bog should have edges of moss and sedge that quake when you walk on them, and a dark pool in the centre, of water brown with peat juice. It should remind you of the word *tarn.* This bog has soaked up its water, covered it over and grown trees on it, balsam six feet high by now. We look for pitcher plants, in vain.

This bog is not photogenic. It is mature. Joanne takes a few pictures, with her top-of-the-line camera and never-fail close-up lens. She focusses on the ground, the moss; she takes a footprint filling with water. We stand around, slapping mosquitoes, while she does it. We all know that these aren't the pictures she'll end up using. But she is a good guest.

There are no rattlesnake plantains here. The rattlesnake plantain does not grow in bogs.

It's summer again and I'm back home. The Atlantic lies behind me, like a sheet of zinc, like a time warp. As usual in this house I get more tired than I should; or not tired, sleepy. I read murder mysteries I've read before and go to sleep early, never knowing what year I'll wake up in. Will it be twenty years ago, or twenty years from now? Is it before I got married, is my child—ten and visiting a friend—grown up and gone? There's a chip in the plaster of the room where I sleep, shaped like a pig's head in profile. It's always been there, and each time I come back here I look for it, to steady myself against the current of time that is flowing past and over me, faster and faster. These visits of mine blur together.

This one, though, is different. Something has been changed, something has stopped. My father, who recovered almost completely from the stroke, who takes five kinds of pills to keep from having another one, who squeezes a woollen ball in his left hand, who however is not paying as much attention to his garden as he used to—my father is ill. I've been here four days and he's been ill the whole time. He lies on the living room sofa in his dressing gown and does not eat or even drink. He sips water, but nothing more.

There have been whispered consultations with my mother, in the kitchen. Is it the pills, is it a virus of some kind? Has he had another stroke, a tiny one, when no one was looking? He's stopped talking much. There's something wrong with his voice; you have to listen very carefully or you can't catch what he's saying.

My mother, who has always handled things, doesn't seem to know what to do. I tell her I'm afraid he'll get dehydrated. I go down to the cellar, where the other phone is, and telephone the doctor, who is hard to reach. I don't want my father to hear me doing this: he will be annoyed, he'll say there's nothing wrong with him, he'll rebel.

I go back upstairs and take his temperature, using the thermometer I used to check my fertility when I was trying to get pregnant. He opens his mouth passively to let me do this; he seems uninterested in the results. His face, a little one-sided from the stroke, appears to have shrunk and fallen in upon itself. His eyes, under his white eyebrows, are almost invisible. The temperature is too high.

"You have a temperature," I tell him. He doesn't seem surprised. I bring a bowl of ice cubes to him, because he says he can't swallow. The ice cubes are something I remember from my childbirth classes, or could it be my husband's ulcer operation? All crisis is one crisis, an improvisation. You seize what is at hand.

"Did he eat the ice cubes?" says my mother, in the kitchen. He doesn't hear her, as he would have once. He doesn't say no.

Later, after dinner, when I am rereading a bad Agatha Christie dating from the war, my mother comes into my room.

"He says he's going to drive up north," she tells me. "He says there are some trees he has to finish cutting."

"It's the temperature," I say. "He's hallucinating."

"I hope so," says my mother. "He can't drive up there." Maybe she's afraid it isn't the temperature, that this is permanent.

I go with her to their bedroom, where my father is packing. He's put on his clothes, shorts and a white short-sleeved shirt, and shoes and socks. I can't imagine how he got all of this on, because he can hardly stand up. He's in the centre of the room, holding his folded pyjamas as if unsure what to do with them. On the chair is an open rucksack, beside it a package of flashlight batteries.

"You can't drive at night," I say. "It's dark out."

He turns his head from side to side, like a turtle, as if to hear me better. He looks baffled.

"I don't know what's holding you up," he says to my mother. "We have to get up there." Now that he has a temperature, his voice is stronger. I know what it is: he doesn't like the place he finds himself in, he wants to be somewhere else. He wants out, he wants to drive, away from all this illness.

"You should wait till tomorrow," I say.

He sets down the pyjamas and starts looking through his pockets.

"The car keys," he says to my mother.

"Did you give him an aspirin?" I ask her.

"He can't swallow," she says. Her face is white; suddenly she too looks old.

My father has found something in his pocket. It's a folded-up piece of paper. Laboriously he unfolds it, peers at it. It looks like an old grocery list. "The rattlesnake plantain is making a comeback," he says to me. I understand that, from somewhere in there, from underneath the fever, he's trying to send out some good news. He knows things have gone wrong, but it's only part of a cycle. This was a bad summer for wood mice, he told me earlier. He didn't mean that there were a lot of them, but that there were hardly any. The adjective was from the point of view of the mice.

"Don't worry," I say to my mother. "He won't go."

If the worse comes to the worst, I think, I can back my car across the bottom of the driveway. I remember myself, at the age of six, after I'd had my tonsils out. I heard soldiers, march-ing. My father is afraid.

"I'll help you take off your shoes," my mother says. My father sits down at the edge of the bed, as if tired, as if defeated. My mother kneels. Mutely he holds out a foot.

We're making our way back. My father and mother are off in the woods somewhere, trudging through the undergrowth, young balsam and hazelnut and moose maple, but Joanne and I (why? how did we get separated from them?) are going along the shore, on the theory that, if you're on an island, all you have to do is go along the shore and sooner or later you'll hit the point you started out from. Anyway, this is a shortcut, or so we have told each other.

Now there's a steep bank, and a shallow bay where a lot of driftwood has collected—old logs, big around as a hug, their ends sawn off clean. These logs are from the time when they used to do the logging in the winter, cross to the islands by the frozen lakes, cut the trees and drag them to the ice with a team of horses, and float them in the spring to the chute and the mill in log booms, the logs corralled in a floating fence of other logs chained together. The logs in this bay were once escapees. Now they lie like basking whales, lolling in the warmed inshore water, Jesus bugs sheltering behind them, as they turn gradually back to earth. Moss grows on them, and sundew, raising its round leaves like little greenish moons, the sticky hairs standing out from them in rays of light.

Along these sodden and sprouting logs Joanne and I walk, holding on to the shoreside branches for balance. They do the logging differently now; they use chain saws, and trucks to carry the logs out, over gravel roads bulldozed in a week. They don't touch the shoreline, though, they leave enough for the eye; but the forest up here is becoming more and more like a curtain, a backdrop behind which is emptiness, or a shambles. The landscape is being hollowed out. From this kind of logging, islands are safer.

Joanne steps on the next log, chocolate brown and hoary with lichen. It rolls in slow motion, and throws her. There goes her second pair of hiking boots, and her pants up to the knees, but luckily not the camera.

"You can't never trust nobody," says Joanne, who is laughing. She wades the rest of the way, to where the shore slopes down and she can squelch up onto dry land. I pick a different log, make a safe crossing, and follow. Despite our shortcut, my parents get back first.

In the morning the ambulance comes for my father. He's lucid again, that's the term. It makes me think of *lucent:* light comes out of him again, he is no longer opaque. In his husky, obscure voice he even jokes with the ambulance attendants, who are young and reassuring, as they strap him in.

"In case I get violent," he says.

The ambulance doesn't mean a turn for the worse. The doctor has said to take him to Emergency, because there are no beds available in the regular wards. It's summer, and the highway accidents are coming in, and one wing of the hospital is closed, incredibly, for the holidays. But whatever is or is not wrong with him, at least they'll give him an intravenous, to replace the lost fluids.

"He's turning into a raisin," says my mother. She has a list of everything he's failed to eat and drink over the past five days.

I drive my mother to the hospital in my car, and we are there in time to see my father arrive in the ambulance. They unload him, still on the wheeled stretcher, and he is made to disappear through swinging doors, into a space that excludes us.

My mother and I sit on the leatherette chairs, waiting for someone to tell us what is supposed to happen next. There's nothing to read except a couple of outdated copies of *Scottish Life*. I look at a picture of wool-dying. A policeman comes in, talks with a nurse, goes out again.

My mother does not read *Scottish Life*. She sits bolt upright, on the alert, her head swivelling like a periscope. "There don't seem to be any mashed-up people coming in," she says after a while.

"It's the daytime," I say. "I think they come in more at night." I can't tell whether she's disappointed or comforted by this absence. She watches the swinging doors, as if my father will come stomping out through them at any minute, cured and fully dressed, jingling his car keys in his hand and ready to go.

"What do you suppose he's up to in there?" she says.

A HOSPITAL FABLE

Diana Chang
· · · · · · · · · · · · · · · · ·

Ian C. Udell feared hospitals like the plague. Some people cross themselves when they pass churches, but Ian crossed his fingers when he passed hospitals. He could smell a hospital anywhere, even in foreign countries.

For instance, on his honeymoon in Paris, he and Julia, his bride, were strolling back to their hotel when he felt his hackles rising. Looking up, he saw looming ahead in large letters the word, *"L'Hôpital."* His fingers crossed instantly, and the bottle of perfume he'd insisted on carrying along with a copy of *Figaro* and a carton of Gitane Bleu cigarettes fell onto the cobblestone street. "White Shoulders" smashed into a smoking puddle that seemed to scent half of the Right Bank.

"How could you!" Julia exclaimed. "I told you to take these brioches instead. My perfume!" Julia flung the brioches into the gutter and ran ahead of him to their hotel.

In the hotel she pouted and lit one cigarette after another, puffing furiously, while he explained, "It's my initials . . . I.C.U. . . . you know what I.C.U. stands for: Intensive Care Unit." He shuddered convulsively.

Julia tried to give up smoking almost as often as Ian crossed his fingers. Fifteen years after their honeymoon, she was put into Eastside General Hospital by her internist, a man about her age. Terrified by her disease, Ian was even more in dread

24

of the hospital. Hating himself, he couldn't bring himself to visit her.

Day by day Julia grew thinner, until she was more a light in her eyes than a woman. After the first month she realized Ian would never overcome his fear of hospitals and come to see her. Her doctor, Ed Barnes, listened to her heart and, taking her pulse, got in the habit of holding her hand. He touched her forehead, stroked her white, parchmentlike shoulder. Their eyes locked, while she turned her wedding band around and around on her third finger. Neither of them pronounced Ian's name.

Julia was beautiful, and abandoned, and dying. Dr. Barnes regarded her as his one aesthetic experience. Before she breathed her last, she whispered to him, "You see, I deserted him by coming here. I deserted him, don't you agree?" It was then that he kissed her; he bent over her hands to hide his emotion and kissed them and kissed them.

Dr. Barnes attended her funeral, where he saw Ian C. Udell for the first time. Against a wall in the stuffy room of the funeral parlor, Ian wept stingily and steadily. Ed Barnes looked deep into an emptiness of his own. He shot angry glances at the widower from time to time. His Julia, he thought, married to that—that . . . He was a physical doctor and lacked the vocabulary to name Ian's behavior.

Ian was ten years older than Julia had been. Two years after her death, he remarried, but Sarah left him seven years later for another man. "I give you back to your hang-ups," she declared.

By this time he was almost fifty, a successful banker and given to dressing the part. He enjoyed chamber music, off-Broadway theater, books about Inca ruins, and aired his Weimaraner on Fifth Avenue twice a day. He was in no hurry to remarry. In fact, when he consulted his soul, he had to admit that he married the second time more to prove that he wasn't becoming ingrown than because he was in love with Sarah.

However, he was susceptible, and enjoyed the company of

many interesting women, to whom he was a highly eligible bachelor. In his way, he led a well-rounded life—deliberately. Julia's early death had affected him deeply, and he wanted his life, every day of it. He wanted to savor his work (his office was on the thirty-seventh floor overlooking lower Manhattan and the Statue of Liberty); he relished his enviable reputation in banking circles, and his cultivated pursuits. He was starting to grow several varieties of spiked and flamboyant orchids in his penthouse apartment. He was also beginning to limp a bit because gout afflicted one toe of his left foot. He bought himself a gold-headed walking stick, adding to his distinguished air.

One day, in a snowstorm, as he was leaving his club, a huge crab seemed to grab his chest. His hand went to his heart to pull off the crab. But it only gripped harder, would not let go. Twisting around, he staggered back into the club and ordered an attendant at the desk to phone Dr. Caruthers. It was while he was clutching the counter, breathing through his mouth, that what he had just done overcame him. He had arranged to be taken to a hospital! He broke out in a drenching sweat and did not come out of his faint until the ambulance reached the emergency entrance of Eastside General Hospital. There, the pain faded suddenly, his energy returned, and he tried to take command of the situation.

Two interns and a doctor rushed at him and seemed to him to want to tear off his clothes in order to examine him, to put him through the paces of a patient suffering an infarction or heart attack. He beat them off with his walking stick. They were caught off guard, one yelping with pain.

"Don't come closer! I'm leaving now. Now."

Fearing a malpractice suit if they didn't treat his case forcibly, but afraid to create a stressful scene, they hesitated. In that moment, confused, he walked toward the Cardiac Unit with the dignity of someone plowing his way through deep water. He was dressed in a custom-made coat, an English pin-striped suit, Italian shoes and gloves.

At the door of a private room, realizing he was disoriented, he braced himself, one hand on the jamb, the other flailing his cane.

They left him alone, though that doesn't describe their consternation, or the phone calls that went from unit to unit in search of a doctor with a solution. To force him into a straitjacket might, of course, have fatal results.

When his internist, Dr. Caruthers, who had another emergency that very hour, arrived, and when he returned the next morning, Ian was lying on top of his hospital bed fully clothed, his fur-collared coat buttoned up to his chin, his shoes on, his cane across his chest, his gloved fingers crossed.

To whoever came into the room Ian announced, "I am Ian C. Udell, and my initials are I.C.U.," as though that took care of the matter.

It must be said that the hospital hoped for a mild second heart attack that would make him lose consciousness, and after two days of refusing any food, he obliged them. They then went to work, doing everything they could, and since they were expert at it and employed the most sophisticated technology, they saved Ian's life.

He was in the hospital almost four weeks in a state of the most acute dread. Often his lips moved involuntarily, but he was not praying. "Poor Julia, poor, poor Julia," he uttered. He imagined sitting by her, holding her hand hour upon hour, her fingers growing thinner and thinner until they were ghost fingers, figments of dusk dissolving in his hand. It was then he fumbled for and touched the cane the nurses had orders to leave lying against his legs.

Although Ed Barnes was not Ian's internist, he noticed his name and stopped by his room unobtrusively to stare whenever Ian was dozing. No one is attractive sleeping with his mouth slack and open. Ed Barnes got some satisfaction from seeing Ian C. Udell off his guard and at his worst.

Ian's hand clenched and unclenched around his cane. He was married, in a sense, to the solidity of the curved and embossed gold handle that visited him with an image of a world and a life he clung to.

He said over and over, "She should not have died here. She should not have died here." If only he had it to do over. If only.

Three years after that, Ian experienced great pain again. He lay writhing on the floor, alone in his greenhouse. He pulled his cane closer, picked it up and with its curved head reached for something. It was not the telephone which, in fact, was on a low coffee table by his head. He yanked pots toward him, and was satisfied to go in the midst of orchids in bloom, and at home.

LOSSES

Layle Silbert

. . . .

My clothes are gone. I can keep my watch, glasses, and earrings. With my clothes has gone the right to go to the gift shop in the hospital lobby, to walk to the corner to buy a newspaper or pick up a nice take-out. The neighborhood is full of take-out places for the people who work here. Not for me.

Treatment for the disease they say I have is accompanied by successive stripping of more than clothes. As I sign in, a bracelet is put on my wrist for easy identification. Minutes later, still in the middle of the day, I undress and paradoxically lose my real identity. Loss extends to my feet on which—I am ambulatory—I wear only contrivances of spongy plastic pretending to be bedroom slippers.

Hospital gowns, like examining tables, are designed for convenience of doctors, easy access. I play the fighter and am allowed to wear tops and bottoms of men's pajamas with the name of the hospital in an allover pattern in Christmas colors. Not bad, but why no collar? The back of my neck is cold.

On the first morning my doctor has another means of deprivation for me. Naturally I sleep badly and only make it by early morning. Right after, a light goes on and there he stands, the dear man, all six feet two of him in his white coat, who seems not to sleep or rest. It's six o'clock and he wants to examine me and ask questions.

Lost in the fog in my head, I can't remember any answers. Later that day, cunningly, I wrote down answers. But the next morning Dr. Fox doesn't give me time to put on my glasses to read them. So I use the answers later that day when a group of residents and interns troop in to continue their education.

One magical night my losses are made up to me. The nurse who starts work at midnight comes in to tuck me in. She kisses me good night on the forehead, something nobody has done for a couple of decades. But after that lovely moment the stripping goes on.

Next are diagnostic tests. I am in a technologically advanced hospital. Tests therefore consist largely of insertion of my person into enormous machines each costing enough to pay for a bomber. Thus enclosed, I fight claustrophobia and draft through my outsized pajamas. I make feeble jokes to keep up my spirits. Nobody understands my jokes.

My doctor draws up a plan of treatment.

"No, no," I say to Dr. Fox. "I don't want it." Who wants this barbaric treatment? Who wants to lose her hair? "Leave me alone," I say and argue on, knowing I have no choice.

It's the only way they know to treat my disease, he explains. To me the proposed treatment is only aimed at my skull to depilate it.

"Why? Why not?" says another doctor, visiting as a friend. "It will grow back. I guarantee it."

He means my hair. To me it's the final loss. Nobody will recognize me or know who I am. What is he guaranteeing? That my hair will spring back all at once, all twenty-one inches of it? Not on your life.

The treatment begins. It doesn't take long before it does take away my hair. Back at home now, I cover all the mirrors as in a family in mourning to spare myself the terrible sight. When I do catch a glimpse, I am reminded of pictures of the Holocaust. Even the shadow of my head like a shot in a spooky movie is painful. For a while I save every hair as it frees itself. I measure. Yes, twenty-one inches. My sweaters and scarves are covered with loose hairs.

I take to wearing a large kerchief on my head as in those pictures in the news of women in Russia. The cold winter wind goes through. Hair has a purpose; it keeps the skull warm. I fiddle with kerchiefs, scarves, match them to my clothes. Nothing helps. It's still a head covering. My hair is gone.

Nobody I meet says a word, as though my kerchiefs were invisible. Why doesn't somebody ask? I want to explain. No, I don't. Finally one man says, "Why are you wearing a scarf on your head like a Yemeni woman?"

I don't explain. I say, "Oh for a change," very airily, at the same time liking the idea of being a Yemeni woman. I remember this is all temporary. Isn't that what I was promised?

I am getting better even as I undergo bizarre, unthinkable side effects: bellyaches, earaches, jaw aches, and plenty of heartaches. The big expensive machines in the hospital say I am better. More claustrophobia.

My cousin Ardyth in Chicago, who is undergoing the same, calls me. Never have I felt closer to her. "Is your hair gone too?"

"It's growing back," she says.

"How long is it?"

"Oh, an eighth of an inch."

I go to look, unveil a mirror. Is it growing back even before the treatment is over? I look hard. I see my beautiful naked skull, the skin whiter than any other place on my body. In new ease I turn around, look over my shoulder, hold a hand mirror so I can see the back. Not bad. I can see the shape of my head, which had been hidden from me all my life. How pure and real. It feels honest.

Look at me, the real me, I address my mirrored image. Months before, I saw a fellow patient come into the doctor's waiting room, her naked head uncovered and her face with no expression whatsoever. I felt shock, then admiration. "She should wear a wig," my best friend, Estelle, said when I told her.

Should I wear a wig? I can't explain why I won't. Not that I dread skulking into a salon on Fifty-seventh Street to order one. It would be like wearing falsies. Insurance companies pay for a wig, calling it a prosthesis. A wig wouldn't be part of me any more than a wooden leg is part of anybody. The one-legged person needs the wooden leg. I can live without a prosthesis.

Not long after—it's early spring—I take a deep breath and walk out into the world, my scalp fuzzy. I am wearing my biggest earrings. In the doorway of my apartment house I hesitate. Should I turn back? No, I brazen it out. I remember the famous indifference of New Yorkers to anomalies and eccentricities. People who step over a dead body on the sidewalk aren't likely to stone me off the street. A half block from home I make it, even forget for a while.

Somebody I run into weeks later says, "What made you decide to cut your hair? It looks good."

THE OPERATION

Scott Russell Sanders

. . . .

R euben woke again with his hand between his legs. All
night the hospital room was still and dark. A pointed
snake of light cut through the dark, across the linoleum, over
the brass railings of the bed, across the stiff sheets. It lay like
a finger on his belly, on the hump his hand made in the sheets.
He could hear others breathing down the line of beds. He
swatted the light, but it gathered again like a snake on the
wrinkled sheets. Awake in the hollow hospital room, he lay
back, and his heart beat against the stiff linen.

A man in a stained coat, an intern, with long frail hands,
crept through the slant of light toward Reuben's bed. With
one hand resting on the brass railing, he said:

"Wake up. Hey, wake up."

His fingers were narrow and pointed in their curl around the
railing.

"I am awake," Reuben said. "Whatcha want?"

"Time for a shave," the intern said. "Let's go for a little
ride."

He pushed a chrome table covered with sheets and a pillow
into the dark room, down the slant of light. Reuben rolled onto
the table and said nothing. His head lay against the pillow,
which smelled of soap, and he watched the ceiling lights pass
like grinning teeth as the intern wheeled the table down the
hall.

In a room somewhere they stopped. The light hurt Reuben's eyes. He rolled onto another table, with another pillow. He could smell alcohol.

"Pull your gown up to your chest," the intern said. "You don't want cut, do ya?"

Reuben shook his head. The intern was young and he smiled like a razor. The cotton dipped in alcohol, and then the glassy metal blade was cold against Reuben's belly. From his navel over his belly, and below, the intern shaved the blond fuzz. His hands were thin; they brushed Reuben's skin as he shaved. The touch felt funny. He did not think he liked it, but he was not sure. The intern's fingers were narrow and moved softly over his skin.

"That's it. That'll do it," the intern said. "Time for some sleep."

Reuben watched the ceiling lights pass, and he was back again in the first bed. As the hall door closed the light narrowed again to a finger on his stomach. His belly felt smooth. *Sleep,* he thought. *Should sleep because operation in morning. Lots of rest, says Doc Pickens. His hands wet on me in his new office and his nurse standing there. Can I die? Nonsense, says Mom. Home in two weeks. Come to see me every day. Too ornery, says Dad. Docs'll boot me out in a week for being ornery. And don't talk about dying. Don't talk about dying.*

A very young, dark nurse with a bright yellow badge on her chest came in. Reuben put his hands behind his head.

"Anything the matter?" she asked.

"Nope."

Her uniform was blue. When she walked she sounded like starched curtains. Reuben turned over on his side towards her and started crying.

"It's late," she said. "Try to sleep. Mustn't wake the other children."

Her hand was warm on his face. Reuben watched the yellow badge on her chest move under the finger of light from the door. There was a buzzer in the hall, and the dark nurse left. She did not come back.

He could not remember having slept when he saw the window shades yellow with the morning. Other children began to rustle the brittle sheets and some started crying. A girl with burns over her mouth was trying not to smile. Her hair was black and very long and messy. Reuben wondered if she would ever smile. In the next bed on the other side was a skinny boy who talked all the time with an accent and wore orange dotted pajamas. He had something wrong with his chest, and he did not know what, and Reuben did not know what. Reuben could listen to the skinny boy breathe and tell his sound from everyone else's in the room. A sound like when you turn the prop on a model airplane. Nurses were giving pills and shots and baths and taking temperatures.

Dr. Pickens was tall with white hair and so barrel-chested that he looked top-heavy. When he sat on the edge of Reuben's bed, it sagged. His voice sounded like an echo, and when he talked close, Reuben could smell something like when you mow the grass.

"How's the slugger this morning?"

"Okay," Reuben answered. "Last night was awful long. Is't about time?"

"Just about. Someone will come for you in a few minutes."

"Doc."

"Yes?"

"Will it hurt? When you cut, I mean, will it hurt then?"

"No, not a bit, like cutting hair. You'll sleep right through it and wake up a new man." His eyes were grey and hard to see into. "See you in a little while. Nothing to it."

"Will it make any difference, when you cut, you know, will it make any . . ."

But the doctor was leaving and did not hear. He had five pencils and pens in his pocket, two of them silver, and he leaned forward when he walked.

All the room was yellow sunshine and smelled like someone's gardenias when the man pushed in the chrome table-cart. It looked like glass in the daytime. One of the children was laughing, but the skinny boy was silent in his orange pajamas, and Reuben could hear him breathing. The man who pushed the cart looked tired. He had a red moustache that hung from his nose like a caterpillar. Reuben smelled soap on the pillow as he was wheeled out into the corridor. He watched the naked lights, like a row of grinning teeth, like white bones, as he passed beneath them on his back. People went by on both sides but no one looked at him as the cart went into an elevator and up to another floor. The man with the red caterpillar moustache said nothing.

They rolled past a room with silver machines and white lights and dials, then stopped. The cart man disappeared. The cart was over against one wall of the tile corridor, and Reuben could only see the lights in the ceiling. A nurse came up and said, "Good morning, Prince Charming." She didn't have a yellow badge on her chest. She didn't wear lipstick and was very pale. She walked across the hall and came back wearing a white cloth mask.

Someone pushed the table into the operating room among the silver machines and bright lights. The nurse with the pale face held a sheet over Reuben and he took off his gown. Then he was lying on smooth cloth on top of the chrome operating table. Dr. Pickens looked down at him from very high up. Reuben could not see into his grey eyes. Was he smiling behind the mask? Reuben wondered. All the nurses were looking at where his belly was under the sheets.

He lay watching white lights and was not going to cry when someone said, "Relax, now, and when I tell you, count to ten." Suddenly inside Reuben's right arm there was a quick burning. Then he could not feel anything.

"Now count," someone said.

Reuben was not going to cry . . . one, he said, two . . . *and he felt warm like when the nurse put her hand on his forehead* . . . three . . . *the white light was moving why was it moving* . . . four . . . *he could not cry the cold metal intern's hands* . . . five . . . *finger on his stomach cutting don't talk about it.* . . .

Reuben could not feel below his waist, and then he could.

It felt far away, as though someone else were hurting. His belly ached, and between his legs. His mother was there.

A nurse with a wrinkled face brought something sour in a cup. Reuben could feel her breath when she bent down to make him drink. She smelled like the medicine cabinet at home.

"Where's the other nurse?" he asked.

"Which one?" She took his pulse and her hands were cold.

"She wore a yellow badge—there—" and he pointed at her chest—"but . . . nothing."

Reuben listened for the skinny boy's breathing.

"And the kid with the orange peejays—where's he? The one who breathes funny."

"Oh, they took him away this morning."

"Where to?"

"Away, away," the nurse answered, "he's gone away now," and she waved her hand.

"Don't worry about it now, Reuben," his mother said.

*Don't talk about—*Reuben thought.

"Am I gonna be all right?"

"Just fine, just fine," his mother answered. "Try to get some sleep."

But Reuben was not sure. With sunlight yellow in the room he started to think at least he didn't die. He knew there were bandages over his belly and between his legs where it hurt. Something was different beneath the bandages, beneath the sheets, and he wondered what.

PATIENTS LOOK AT ILLNESS

. . . .

ONLY THE LITTLE BONE

David Huddle

· · · · · · · · · · · · · · · · · ·

This summer our county has more cases of polio than any
county in the nation. You catch polio from other people.
Our parents decree that my brother and cousin and I must stay
inside our yard. Until further notice we can't go out, and our
friends can't come to see us.

Ours is an interesting yard, maybe an acre of mowed grass,
an old tennis court gone to honeysuckle, and a bushy patch of
woods far below the house that we call the jungle. If you had
to spend a whole summer inside a yard, this one is better than
most.

On the very day of the decree, we boys become bored and
restless. Theoreticians of the small group advise that three is
a lousy number, two against one the given dynamic. Duncan
and I pick on Ralph, or Duncan and Ralph pick on me. Ralph
is our cousin from Kingsport. Duncan doesn't get picked on,
but he's the one who has to answer to our mother when she
gets fed up with the whining.

Which is frequently. But since she interferes with our natural method of entertainment, she's the one we look to to
provide us with peaceful activities. So she buys us comic books
downtown, sometimes half a dozen a day. She hates it. She was
raised to think of comic books as something that trashy people
buy and read. I can't go with her to see her doing it, but I can

imagine her standing down there at Mrs. Elkins's store in front of the comic-book rack trying to pick out ones we haven't read yet. She has to ask for the new Batman, the new Monty Hale. She's embarrassed and a little mad about it, but what can she do? She selects carefully, because if she brings us one we've already read, we howl and mope around the house for hours.

But she has to bake them before she gives them to us. The baking removes the germs. It also stiffens them, gives them an odd smell, makes them wear out quickly. Now she has acquired some skill at it, but she burned a few in the early weeks, charred a Sears & Roebuck catalogue pretty thoroughly by giving it extra minutes in the oven for its size. The baked comic books go along with the boiled water and the almost-boiled milk that tastes like liquid aluminum.

I commence a study of June bugs, those hefty green beetles. I tie threads around their legs and let them fly in circles around me. June bugs have shiny gold bellies and a sweet, oily smell. June bugs are uncommonly healthy, stupid, hard to kill, more or less blind, harmless. If you yank the thread too hard, though, you can jerk their legs off pretty easily.

This summer we are more than usually aware of our father's working too hard, always coming home tired. After supper maybe he'll toss the baseball with us or play a couple of games of croquet. But mostly what he wants to do is sit and rest. When he is home, though, we look to him to relieve us of our circumstance, all four of us hanging around him like hungry dogs. Our mother needs him to distract Duncan and Ralph and me, to give her a little rest, to let her go upstairs and take a nap. During certain late-afternoon and early-evening hours there is the radio: the Lone Ranger, Sky King, Jack Benny, Amos and Andy.

When we catch lightning bugs and when our parents aren't looking, we crush them and smear them on our hands, then make weird gestures at each other. More fun than lightning bugs is throwing brooms up in the air trying to hit bats. There are lots of bats swooping all around our yard of an evening, and Duncan claims to have hit one once with a broom. I doubt he did, but I have to admit it is deeply pleasurable to pitch brooms up into the air with the hope of knocking down a bat. Ah Lord, one can collapse with such laughing and fall down in the cool grass and gaze up at the first stars of the night sky.

Our mother is frazzled. Our grandmother comes to visit, to help. The situation is charged. Our grandmother is a small woman, mild-mannered for the most part, but a formidable Methodist. Our mother is also uncompromising in her Methodism. These two, mother and daughter, are temperamental and likely to fall out with each other. Anger and righteousness are directly linked in Methodist ladies of my mother's and grandmother's sort. If they become angry, it is because someone else has done wrong, and they relent only if the other admits the wrong and swears to change. On other occasions of my grandmother's visiting us, she and my mother have quarreled and taken to not speaking to each other. Nights, after we boys were supposed to be asleep, we have heard the two of them carrying on their argument by speaking through my father: "If she thinks she can come into my house and tell me . . ." and "If she thinks that's the way a daughter can speak to her own . . ."

Our grandmother is good for canasta, the one card game, apparently, the god of Methodists must figure is O.K. Duncan and Ralph and I adore canasta, the huge hands, the double deck, the "melding" all over the table, the frequent occasions for clowning around, trying to get a laugh out of our stone-faced grandmother. Our grandmother is also good for Cokes. She drinks two a day, one at ten-thirty and another at a little after three in the afternoon. We boys usually don't get Cokes, but when our grandmother is there we get two a day. In the afternoon, we use our Cokes to make what in our family we call "foolishness," ice cream in a big glass with Coke poured over it.

But our grandmother is not accustomed to such intense exposure to my brother and cousin and me. On her other visits, our presence has been balanced by our absence: we go down the hill to Gilmer Hyatt's house to seine in the Rosemary branch for crawfish and minnows, or out to our grandfather's (our father's father's) farm to pester the men who work for him. This summer we are around her all the time, and our grandmother is more and more reluctant to accept our invitations to play canasta. She is more and more often in the guest room upstairs with the door closed.

Ralph and I sometimes sense Duncan sliding away from us. Sometimes he isn't laughing when we are. Sometimes we'll head outdoors, to the jungle, the trapeze, or somewhere, and Duncan won't be with us. He takes to spending time alone in his laboratory, the old back room upstairs where he put his chemistry set and a lot of junk that he said he didn't want Ralph and me getting into and ruining. Our mother tells Ralph and me that when Duncan is back there and doesn't want to be bothered, we are to leave him alone.

Ralph is homesick for Kingsport, but he can't go home because his mother is sick. He begins a series of temper tantrums, one a day, sometimes two. He blows himself up, gets red in the face, screams, breaks something that's handy if he's serious. I notice, though, that he chooses pretty carefully what he breaks.

I go into my pious phase. When Ralph does a tantrum, I counter with a lengthy speech about how they put people like him in reform schools and as soon as they get old enough they transfer them to prison. People who act like that. I tell him God's bad opinion of people who bust up their cousin's Army Command Post that he worked so hard to make out of glued-together used popsickle sticks from the trash can at school. When grownups are around, I try to carry myself with dignity, to speak with unusual wisdom for somebody my age.

I have noticed qualities of my voice that are remarkably similar to certain qualities of the voice of Roy Rogers, namely a certain tenor, lyrical sweetness and also the ring of rectitude. In seeing the films of Roy and in reading his comic books, I have sensed a special link between him and me. We share the same taste in holsters, saddles, hats, boots, and shirts. For

Christmas I received an orange and white Roy Rogers neckerchief that I cherish as the outward and visible sign of my
kinship with Roy. Wearing the scarf is what I do when I have
other things on my mind, but my preferred use of it is to run
with it in my hand, trailing it in the wind behind me. I wish
only that I could see it better. When the wind catches that
scarf, I know that I am in the presence of beauty.

In mid-August Mother hears that no new cases of polio have
been reported for the month. She tells each one of us when we
come downstairs for breakfast. She keeps explaining to us until
we demonstrate to her that we are happy. Even our grandmother is cheerful. We decide to take a ride to Elmo's Creek
to celebrate the end of the polio epidemic.

What should be very familiar landscape for my brother and
cousin and me today is so new and vivid in the warm August
sunlight that we are more or less quiet going out of our driveway and down the hill to the highway and then turning toward
town. My mother drives slowly, chatting with my grandmother
in the front seat. She asks my grandmother to keep an eye on
Duncan and Ralph and me in the back seat because she can't
really turn around, she has a crick in her neck. The slowness
with which we travel on the highway out of town seems to be
appropriate for the occasion, a decorous speed for three boys
who haven't been out of their yard all summer and their
mother and grandmother. Cars pass us honking their horns,
but not one of us finds that trashy behavior worth remarking.

At the creek itself of course we boys must ask my mother if
we can't go swimming. We whine just enough to let her know
that we would in fact go into the water if she agreed to let us,
but of course we all know she won't since we brought no
bathing suits and since we all know how Elmo's Creek, with
its bottom full of rusted beer cans, must be swarming with
polio germs. Her denial is full of good cheer. We turn around
and head back home.

Vanity is not the moving force behind all that follows. On
the contrary, I am wholly without awareness of self, am without
sorrow or desire, nostalgia or greed, am in that state of pure,
thoughtless spirit that I later come to understand as aesthetic

experience, as I hold my Roy Rogers neckerchief out the car window and watch it fly gorgeously in the wind. I have had to bargain with Ralph for the place beside the door, and I have had to exercise considerable discretion in sticking my hand and arm out the window. My mother's stiff neck prevents her from turning to see what I am doing, and I am sitting behind my grandmother, whose sense of well-being is directly proportional to the stillness of her grandsons. Even Duncan and Ralph, who are inclined to sabotage any pleasure I might be taking by myself, sit quietly regarding me and the neckerchief; I think of them, too, as being under the powerful influence of art.

Then the scarf slips loose from my fingers and flies back behind the car, curling in the wind, lightly coiling down to the gray asphalt. I am too stunned to speak, and anyway I have my whole head out the window now, looking back at what I have lost, but Duncan and Ralph speak up for me, cry out for my mother to stop the car, explaining to her what has happened. She does stop. She isn't able to turn completely around in the seat, but she sits and listens to my brother and my cousin and agrees that I can get out of the car to run back along the road and retrieve my neckerchief.

In the gravel and stubble I run along beside the highway, thinking that my neckerchief is much farther away than I would have imagined it and is strangely still there in the road after having been so lively when I held it in my hand. The day is hot and bright. The fields of Mr. John Watts's farm stretch out on both sides of the highway; even though Mr. Watts hung himself in his bedroom several years ago, the land is still farmed by his kinspeople. When I reach the scarf and hold it again in my hand, I am not comforted, as I had imagined I would be. I stand on a curving slope, a gentle slope but one that seems to be pulling me away back toward the creek, away from my parents' car that has begun slowly backing down the incline toward me but that seems such a distance from me that it will be long minutes before I can climb into the back seat with Duncan and Ralph and we can resume our stately homeward ride.

At the top of the hill another car appears, the sun flashing on its chrome grille and bumper. At a fair speed it heads down toward my family's car, which my mother has maneuvered into the middle of the highway in her effort to back up to me. I am concerned that there will be a collision, and I sense myself standing on the roadside, first on one foot and then the other. The strange car, a black sedan, doesn't slow down as it approaches our car. I can see the dilemma the driver faces, which way around my mother's middle-of-the-road-backing-up-vehicle he should take. He chooses the side that sends him directly toward me, not slowing and, once he has aimed himself toward me, not veering to left or right. Wanting to move but not being able to make my feet step in any direction, I stand on the side of the road, aware of raising my hands as if to ward off a pillow thrown by Duncan or Ralph. I catch a glimpse through the car's windshield of a Negro woman's face, looking directly at me, her mouth open and shouting something I can't hear. Then the car brushes me, I spin and fall and see the car sail over the fence into Mr. John Watts's alfalfa field.

I am surprised at what has transpired, intensely interested in the car in the field, all the doors of which are now opening, with Negro men and women climbing out and looking back at me on the roadside. Then my mother is there, so grimly calm that I barely recognize her. She wants to know if I am all right, and I tell her that I am. She tries to help me up, but I find that one of my legs won't hold me. It doesn't hurt—I tell her that, too—but I prefer sitting down in the road. She gathers me into her arms.

A Negro man with a kind face helps Mother carry me to the front seat of our car. He winces whenever he looks into my face, and so I tell him that I am all right, I just can't stand up. Someone brings me my neckerchief. My mother and the Negro man speak to each other with enormous civility. His name is Charlie Sales. He is from Slabtown. He will stay there with his car until the police come. My mother will take me to Dr. Pope's office back in town. The car door shuts. She holds me. People look in at us through the windows. My grandmother, in the driver's seat, says she can't drive our car, then puts it into low gear and drives it all the way to Dr. Pope's office.

The small bone of my left leg is cracked. At the Pulaski Hospital they pull a stretch-sock over my whole leg, then they wrap that with wet plaster-of-Paris bandages; the bandages are warm, and the hands wrapping them around my leg and smoothing out the plaster of Paris are comforting to me. My toes stick out, and a nurse holds them while the others work. I don't sleep well in the hospital that night, but my mother is there in the room with me to murmur to me in the dark, bring me water, put her cool hand on my forehead.

Charlie Sales had no brakes in that car. He feels terrible about what happened. My parents take no action against him; our families have known vaguely of each other for years. My mother takes her share of the blame for the accident because of her car being in the middle of the road because she was backing up, but she had that crick in her neck so that she couldn't really see straight. When people ask her about the nigger that was driving the car that hit me, she says it wasn't Mr. Sales's fault. When they see my mother's attitude, they don't call Mr. Sales a nigger anymore. In the family, though, my mother wants it understood that it is her magnanimity that is saving Charlie Sales from being put in jail and losing every cent he has. Our family generally tries to do good in the world, but among ourselves we want credit for our excellence. Whenever anybody says that name, Charlie Sales, I see not him but that woman's face looking at me through the windshield, her mouth open, saying or shouting something I can't hear. Maybe she is Mrs. Sales. I don't know. When I imagine the accident again, it is graceful. The car brushes me, almost gently, and I spin a turn or a half a turn and fall. The car breaks the top strand of barbed wire on the fence when it sails into the field.

When I go home I have to stay in bed a week or two, and then I can ride in a wheelchair with a contraption that sticks out for me to rest my leg on. The cast is heavy for me, and someone must help me lift it when I move. The wheelchair is an old-fashioned wood-and-metal apparatus that is unwieldy in our house. I am always knocking into furniture or walls or something. I quickly learn that I won't be disciplined by my parents and that Duncan or Ralph are reluctant to do anything to me in my wounded state. I continue to think of myself as benign and heroical, in the mode of Roy Rogers during the few days he sometimes spends with his arm in a sling. But when Duncan and Ralph are home I follow them in my wheelchair from one room to another, insisting that they play with me.

One day I throw my cap pistol at Duncan. I miss him, but our grandmother sees me do it. She wants me to be spanked. I can see her point, but I'm glad my mother won't do it and won't let her do it. The righteous anger of the Methodists sets in on both sides. They don't speak. The grandmother demands to be taken home. My father agrees to take her after the air show we've planned to attend in Pulaski on Saturday.

My mother and grandmother don't want us boys to know they are quarreling, and so they try to act as if the condition of their not speaking to each other and the grandmother's barely speaking to me while being warmly solicitous of Duncan and Ralph is the normal condition for us all to be in. We three boys pretend we know nothing, but we eavesdrop on all their conversations, which can take place only when my father is there. Our spirits can't help but be dampened in the presence of the adults, who sigh and gaze out the windows at mealtime. Ralph, trying to relieve the social anguish of one suppertime, slouches down in his chair to allow his mouth to come to plate level; and he scrapes the food in. Duncan and I find that pretty funny and register our amusement with sly grins. Our mother, however, sees the grins and sees the source of them, reaches over and whacks Ralph lightly on top of the head so that his face plops into his plate. Ralph looks up with bits of corn sticking to his face. All of us laugh, and for a moment the old family pleasure is there among us. Then our grandmother excuses herself but goes to sit only as far away as the living room. Solemnity comes quickly down again.

It rains at the air show. Many of the acts are canceled, others are invisible, though an announcer describes them to us through a static-crackling P.A. system. There is a parachutist who comes down close enough to our car to make us boys not want to leave the show. But mostly we sit in the car in a field full of other cars, and our grandmother and mother both cry, sitting beside each other in the front seat while my father tries to make himself invisible with his hat down over his eyes. We boys whine to get out of the car into the rain and whine for refreshments and whack and pinch each other, writhing in our state of misery and hilarity. Duncan and Ralph must be wary of my leg in the cast. I have the advantage over them.

You'd think things would improve immediately with the grandmother gone, but they don't. For one thing, Duncan has taken to exercising what he sees as his "adult privileges." Eating breakfast one morning, he calls our mother by her first name, and she throws the empty dish-drainer at him. For another thing, I become so impossible in my behavior and demands that it does become necessary for my mother to spank me. This is very hard on her. And finally, I become much more mobile. My cast has gradually lightened its pull on my leg. Sitting on my butt, I can scoot up and down the steps without assistance. And my grandfather has made crutches for me. These are sturdy crutches, just the right size, probably made with the help of three or four of his men. I am delighted with them and launch myself around the house on them.

And take a fall immediately. And continue falling several times a day, great splatting, knocking-into-furniture-and-breaking-things falls that cause everyone in the family to come running to me, my mother frequently in tears. My grandfather has forgotten to put rubber tips on the ends of my crutches. When we figure this out and buy the rubber tips and put them on the crutches, I stop falling. But by then the bone-set that was coming along nicely has slipped, and the doctor has ordered me back to the wheelchair for another several weeks, has ordered the cast kept on for an additional month or five weeks.

The missing crutch-tips are the first clue I have to this peculiar family trait, one that for lack of any better term I must call "flawed competence." We Bryants are a family of able and clever people, industrious, intelligent, determined, and of good will. We are careful in our work. Remember, my grandfather measured me on two occasions before he made the crutches. But we usually do something wrong.

Four years later I become increasingly aware of "flawed competence" when I develop a plan for converting our old grown-over tennis court into a basketball court. My grandfather is always interested in plans, and in this planning session, we decide that he will make the hoops, and he will help me make the backboards. Clearing the ground and smoothing the surface will be my tasks. So I rip out honeysuckle and hatchet down a few little scrub cedars, working a couple of hours a day after school for a week. It becomes clear to me that there is at least ten times more work to be done here than I had in mind originally, but I hold fast to my plan and continue the work. We Bryants are known for setting our minds to things.

Then my grandfather delivers the hoops. They are beautifully designed and constructed, metalwork of a high order for such amateurs as my grandfather and his men, who are mostly talkers, cursers, storytellers, spitters, and braggers. But the hoops are twice as big around as ordinary basketball hoops.

I say, simply, that they are too big. I am not ungrateful, not trying to be hateful, not in my opinion being overly fastidious. I am simply describing a characteristic of the hoops. But my grandfather's feelings are damaged. No, they can't be made smaller, and no, he's not interested in helping me with the backboards now or with any other part of my plan. He's sorry he got involved in the first place. This, too, is a corollary of "flawed competence." We are sensitive, especially about our work, especially about the flawed part of our work.

At the place where I work twenty-eight years after the basketball hoops, I am given a new office, a corner one with two large windows and a view of the lake. There's a string attached, though, and that is that I have to build my own bookcases. I commence planning with enthusiasm. That's another, less harmful family trait, that attraction to making plans. I measure, I look at other people's shelves, I get a guy to help me attach brackets to my office walls.

It is while I am cutting a notch in one of the uprights to allow access to the light-switch by the door that I suddenly think of my grandfather and those basketball hoops. I feel a light sweat break out on my forehead. A pattern of genetic fate reveals itself to me: I'm going to gum up these bookshelves just as my grandfather before me would have gummed them up. This very idea I'm working on, the notch in the upright for the light-switch, is a Granddaddy Bryant kind of idea. No doubt I'm sawing the notch in the wrong place. This epiphany comes to me at night in my new office with a fluorescent ceiling light shining down on me and my reflections from both windows mocking me full-length while I stand there with the saw in my hand.

The whole time I work I wait to see where the screw-up is going to come. I imagine what my colleagues will be saying about me in the hallways. Did you know that Bryant built his shelves so they tilt? Did you know that Bryant's books rejected the color he painted his shelves? But the screw-up doesn't appear. I paint the shelves red, and they look O.K. (Granddaddy Bryant once painted yellow a whole row of company houses he built.) I paint a rocking chair blue and red, and it's a little silly-looking, but it picks up the blue of the carpet and the red of the shelves. The vision isn't nearly as impressive as I thought it would be, but then what vision ever is? We plan-makers are accustomed to things turning out not-quite-as-good-as-what-we-had-in-mind. Our *Weltanschauung* includes the "diminished excellence" component. Diminished excellence is a condition of the world and therefore never an occasion for sorrow, whereas flawed competence comes out of character and therefore is frequently the reason for the bowed head, the furrowed brow. Three months later, when I try to turn the heat off in my office, I discover that I have placed one of the shelf uprights too close to the radiator to be able to work the valve. The screw-up was there all along, but in this case I am relieved to find it. I am my grandfather's grandson after all.

In the spring, on a visit to my parents' home, I am out in the toolshop behind the garage. Up in the rafters I find those old basketball hoops. Since I have so recently thought about them, I take them down and stand for a moment weighing them, one in each hand. My grandfather has been dead for twelve years now, and I have this moment of perfect empathy with the old man: the thing he worked on so as to be part of my life was no good; when I told him, "They're too big," I pushed him that much further away from me and that much closer to his own death. Those old hoops are monuments to something. They're indestructible, and perfectly useless. God knows what some archaeologists of the future will make of them when they dig them up out of the rubble.

Stashing the hoops back up in the rafters, I find this other thing, too, the cast from my broken leg. When the doctor sawed it off, somebody taped together the two parts and gave the thing to us to take home. It is a child's leg, slightly bent at the knee, grayish-white, not much larger than my arm. It is at one and the same time utterly strange and utterly familiar. The little bone of my leg was broken one day because I'd dropped my Roy Rogers scarf out the car window when we were taking a ride to Elmo's Creek to celebrate the end of the polio epidemic the summer we had to stay inside the yard and my mother couldn't back up straight because she had a crick in her neck, and so Charlie Sales, whose car had no brakes, had to swerve and miss her and therefore hit me. Holding that cast in my hands, I can almost understand the wacky logic of that accident.

That light, hollow little leg that is somehow my own calls up layer after layer of memory in me. Both my mother and my grandmother have softened their tempers, have taken on that Methodist sweetness that you feel in hymns like "Bringing in the Sheaves" and "A Walk in the Garden." Whatever wrongs that grandmother might have committed, she has been harshly dealt with, first with glaucoma and then with a skin cancer that works on her slowly. I doubt she even remembers the day of the rained-out air show when she and my mother wept in the front seat while my father pulled his hat down over his eyes and Duncan and Ralph and I writhed in the back seat.

My mother still remembers when Charlie Sales hit me, still holds herself responsible, still takes on a sober expression and a sad voice when she speaks of that day. And once at a party in New York, I met a black woman who spoke to me of people she was related to, Saleses from Madison County, Virginia. That seemed so significant to me. I told her the story about Charlie Sales hitting me with his car and breaking my leg. I told the story in such a way as to make it seem all my fault and my mother's, Charlie having to choose which one of us to hit. I thought the story would make an incredible impression on this dignified black woman. I thought she would acknowledge our deep and lasting kinship. I still remember her face—serene, interested, kind, polite. Yes, she said, it was probably her kin-people who came piling out of that car, she said, she didn't know for sure, she hadn't been back there since she was a child. And she turned away from me to talk with someone else. But, in my memory, her face became the face of the woman I saw in the front seat of Charlie Sales's car, just before it touched the little bone in my leg. Memory and fact are old cousins yammering away about whether or not there even was a strand of barbed wire on that fence for the car to snap when it flew into the field and how could I have seen it anyway, having just been knocked and spun around by the car.

I stand there holding that cast in my hands, reading something somebody in my third-grade class wrote on the side of the knee, and I know that everything that happens is connected to everything else and nothing that happens is without consequence. I am washed by one memory after another like ripples moving backward to their source. All of a sudden I am no one. Or I am this stranger standing in an old toolshop with memory trying in its quirky way to instruct him. A man came home to visit his parents, a man who got an office and built bookshelves, a man whose grandfather died and who was a soldier for a little while, a boy whose leg was broken by a car and who did not become a basketball or a football player, a boy who stayed a summer with his brother and his cousin inside his family's yard. The moment of my disappearance passes, and I come back to myself. Now, holding this cast in my hand, standing just in this one place, I feel like I could remember all of human history. If I put my mind to it.

THIS YEAR'S VENISON

Pamela Ditchoff

. . . .

He removes his gloves and lights the hand warmer. The kerosene heater would have been warmer, but then the deer might smell it, and this is the last chance. The sun will be up in about twenty minutes. He pushes the orange crate through the few inches of snow, rubbing it into the semifrozen ground. His mother-in-law had been right about the deer. She'd called him at the hospital and said while she and her friend were talking in the car in her driveway, they saw a deer come down the hill. She said it ate the crabapples on the ground, and wasn't it funny that all the men had gone up north to hunt and here was a deer right in her own backyard. He saw the tracks this morning when he came up the hill and got down real close to the ground to see if there were tracks under the tree.

He put the red plastic hot seat on the crate and settled in, Styrofoam squishing under his weight. There is some light now coming through the naked treetops. Enough to see a cardinal in the bush a few yards away. He knows it's a male; his red is brilliant against the snow.

He pulls his stocking hat a bit farther down over his ear-muffs. His head gets so cold outdoors. Inside the hospital room it doesn't matter. Ted Brooks had used an ice cap when he had the chemo and it had saved his hair. But it doesn't really matter; it's all a matter of time anyway.

He raises his Winchester 32 Special to his shoulder, sighting. Then lowers it across his knees, running his hand down the custom-made mahogany stock. This is a fine gun. This gun has brought down four buck. He remembers each one well.

The sun is beginning to swell pale yellows. He notices the breeze is slight, just teasing the few clinging, shaky leaves. His position is good, he is downwind from the crest of the hill.

He begins to shudder, then thinks of the words to a song. This technique works, a practiced technique, mind over matter; he gets cold so quickly, so easily now. His wife gave him hell for coming out, but not too much. She knows this is the last deer. And it feels so good to be outside. It's clean and crisp and open, far away from transfusions and needles and uncomfortable friends shifting in bedside chairs with empty faces.

It's quiet too, except for some traffic noise from the highway down in front of the house. This is a hell of a place to hunt, but then it's the last chance and he wants to taste venison this year. Not someone else's venison—his, from the deer *he* brings down. When his father-in-law called yesterday, he said Bob had got an eight-point, but none of the other guys had any luck. They were all up there. That's where he'd gotten his four. He hopes they'll call tonight. After they eat dinner at the camp, they all go into town and have beers and retell hunting stories of today and the seasons before. He'll tell them tonight about the buck, twelve or fourteen points, how it was bending its neck to munch crabapples when he fired the shot.

The sun's up now. The birds are calling. They'll settle in the crabapples to feed, and he'll watch for them. For them all to rise at once in a wave when the buck comes. He releases the safety and gets set, still. What is that call—a mourning dove—no, it's an owl, an owl on the hunt for rabbits or field mice. It's closer now. That story, they made it into a song a few years ago, the story from Boy Scouts, Indian folklore. The owl has called my name. He'll tell his son tonight that when he was out hunting he heard an owl and it called out his name and when he's old enough to be a Scout, he'll hear that story about the Indian who heard the owl call his name, and then he'll remember the night his dad brought home a buck and promised him the antlers and told him the story about the owl calling his dad's name, before he went back to the hospital, and he hopes his son doesn't cry, and he can't cry now; the buck is approaching.

WOUNDED SOLDIER
(Cartoon Strip)

George Garrett

· · · · · · · · · · · · · · · · · · ·

When the time came at last and they removed the wealth of bandages from his head and face, all with the greatest of care as if they were unwinding a precious mummy, the Doctor—he of the waxed, theatrical, upswept mustache and the wet sad eyes of a beagle hound—turned away. Orderlies and aides coughed, looked at floor and ceiling, busied themselves with other tasks. Only the Head Nurse, a fury stiff with starch and smelling of strong soap, looked, pink-cheeked and pale white as fresh flour, over the Veteran's shoulders. She stared back at him, unflinching and expressionless, from the swimming light of the mirror.

No question. It was a terrible wound.

—I am so sorry, the Doctor said.—It's the best we can do for you.

But the Veteran barely heard his words. The Veteran looked deeply into the mirror and stared at the stranger, who was now to be himself, with an inward wincing that was nearer to the sudden gnawing of love at first sight than of self-pity. It was like being born again. He had, after all, not seen himself since the blinding, burning instant when he was wounded. Ever since then he had been a mystery to himself. How many times he had stared into the mirror through the neat little slits left for his eyes and seen only a snowy skull of gauze and bandages!

He imagined himself as a statue waiting to be unveiled. And now he regretted that there was no real audience for the occasion except for the Doctor, who would not look, and the Head Nurse—she for whom no truth could be veiled anyway and hence for whom there could never be any system or subtle aesthetic of exposure or disclosure by any clever series of gradual deceptions. She carried the heavy burden of one who was familiar with every imaginable kind of wound and deformity.

—You're lucky to be alive, she said.—Really lucky.

—I don't know what you will want to do with yourself, the Doctor said.—Of course, you understand that you are welcome to remain here.

—That might be the best thing for any number of good reasons, the Head Nurse said. Then to the Doctor:—Ordinarily cases like this one elect to remain in the hospital.

—Are there others? the Veteran asked.

—Well . . . the Head Nurse admitted, there are none quite like you.

—I should hope not, the Veteran said, suddenly laughing at himself in the mirror.—Under the circumstances it's only fair that I should be able to feel unique.

—I am so sorry, the Doctor said.

Over the Veteran's shoulder in the mirror the Head Nurse smiled back at him.

That same afternoon a High-ranking Officer came to call on him. The Officer kept his eyes fixed on the glossy shine of his boots. After mumbled amenities he explained to the Veteran that while the law certainly allowed him to be a free man, free to come and go as he might choose, he ought to give consideration to the idea that his patriotic duty had not ended with the misfortune of his being stricken in combat. There were, the Officer explained, certain abstract obligations that clearly transcended those written down as statute law and explicitly demanded by the State.

—There are duties, he continued, waxing briefly poetic, which like certain of the cardinal virtues, are deeply disguised. Some of these are truly sublime. Some are rare and splendid like the aroma of a dying arrangement of flowers or the persistent haunting of half-remembered melodies.

The Veteran, who knew something about the music of groans and howls, and something about odors, including, quite recently, the stink of festering and healing, was not to be deceived by this sleight of hand.

—Get to the point, he said.

The High-ranking Officer was flustered, for he was not often addressed by anyone in this fashion. He stammered, spluttered as he offered the Veteran a bonus to his regular pension, a large sum of money, should he freely choose to remain here in the hospital. After all, his care and maintenance would be excellent and he would be free of many commonplace anxieties. Moreover, he need never feel that his situation was anything like being a prisoner. The basic truth about any prisoner is—is it not?—that he is to be deliberately deprived, insofar as possible, of all the usual objects of desire. The large bonus would enable the Veteran to live well, even lavishly in the hospital if he wanted to.

—Why?

Patiently the Officer pointed out that his appearance in public, in the city or the country, would probably serve to arouse the anguish of the civilian population. So many among the military personnel had been killed or wounded in this most recent war. Wasn't it better for everyone concerned, especially the dependents, the friends and relatives of these unfortunate men, that they be permitted to keep their innocent delusions of swirling battle flags and dimly echoing bugle calls, rather than being forced to confront in fact and flesh the elemental brute ugliness of modern warfare? As an old soldier, or as one old soldier to another, surely the Veteran must and would acknowledge the validity of this argument.

The Veteran nodded and replied that he guessed the Officer also hadn't overlooked the effect his appearance might have on the young men of the nation. Most likely a considerable cooling of patriotic ardor. Probably a noticeable, indeed a measurable, decline in the number of enlistments.

—Just imagine for a moment, the Veteran said, what it would be like if I went out there and stood right next to the recruiting poster at the Post Office. Sort of like a "before and after" advertisement.

At this point the Officer stiffened, scolded, and threatened. He ended by reminding the Veteran that no man, save the One, had ever been perfect and blameless. He suggested to him that, under the strictest scrutiny, his service record would no doubt reveal some error or other, perhaps some offense committed while he was a soldier on active duty, which would still render him liable to a court-martial prosecution.

Safe for the time being with his terrible wound, the Veteran laughed out loud and told the Officer that nothing they could do or think of doing to him could ever equal this. That he might as well waste his time trying to frighten a dead man or violate a corpse.

Then the Officer pleaded with the Veteran. He explained that his professional career as a leader of men might be ruined if he failed in the fairly simple assignment of convincing one ordinary common soldier to do as he was told to.

The Veteran, pitying this display of naked weakness, said that he would think about it very seriously. With that much accomplished, the Officer brightened and recovered his official demeanor.

—I imagine it would have been so much more convenient for everyone if I had simply been killed, wouldn't it? the Veteran asked as the Officer was leaving.

Still bowed, still unable to look at him directly, the Officer shrugged his epauleted shoulders and closed the door very quietly behind him.

Nevertheless the Veteran had made up his mind to leave the sanctuary of the hospital. Despite his wound and appearance, he was in excellent health, young still and full of energy. And the tiptoeing routine of this place was ineffably depressing. Yet even though he had decided to leave, even though he was certain he was going soon, he lingered, he delayed, he hesitated. Days went by quietly and calmly, and in the evening when she was off duty, the Head Nurse often came to his room to talk to him about things. Often they played cards. A curious and easy intimacy developed. It seemed almost as if they were husband and wife. On one occasion he spoke to her candidly about this.

—You better be careful, he said.—I'm not sexless.

—No, I guess not, she said.—But I am.

She told him that she thought his plan of going out into the world again was dangerous and foolish.

—Go ahead. Try it and you'll be back here in no time at all, beating on the door with bloody knuckles and begging to be readmitted, to get back in. You are too young and inexperienced to understand anything about people. Human beings are the foulest things in all creation. They will smell your blood and go mad like sharks. They will kill you if they can. They can't allow you to be out there among them. They will tear you limb from limb. They will strip the meat off your bones and trample your bones to dust. They will turn you into dust and a fine powder and scatter you to the four winds!

—I can see you have been deeply wounded, too, the Veteran said.

At that the Head Nurse laughed out loud. Her whole white mountainous body shook with laughter.

When the Veteran left the hospital, he wore a mask. He wanted to find a job, and wearing the mask seemed to him to be an act of discretion that would be appreciated. But this, as he soon discovered, was not the case at all. A mask is somehow intolerable. A mask becomes an unbearable challenge. When he became aware of this, when he had considered it, only the greatest exercise of self-discipline checked within him the impulse to gratify their curiosity. It would have been so easy. He could so easily have peeled off his protective mask and thereby given to the ignorant and innocent a new creature for their bad dreams.

One day he came upon a small traveling circus and applied for a job with them.

—What can you do? the Manager asked.

This Manager was a man so bowed down by the weight of weariness and boredom that he seemed at first glance to be a hunchback. He had lived so long and so closely with the oddly gifted and with natural freaks that his lips were pursed as if to spit in contempt at everything under the sun.

—I can be a clown, the Veteran said.

—I have enough clowns, the Manager said. Frankly, I am sick to death of clowns.

—I'll be different from any other clown you have ever seen, the Veteran said.

And then and there he took off his mask.

—Well, this is highly original, the Manager said, studying the crude configuration of the wound with a careful, pitiless interest. This has some definite possibilities.

—I suppose the real question is, will the people laugh?

—Without a doubt. Believe me. Remember this—a man is just as apt to giggle when he is introduced to his executioner as he is to melt into a mess of piss and fear. The real and true talent, the exquisite thing, is of course to be able to raise tears to the throat and to the rims of the eyes, and then suddenly to convert those tears into laughter.

—I could play "The Wounded Soldier."

—Well, we'll try it, the Manager said. I think it's worth a try.

And so that same night he first appeared in his new role. He entered with all the other clowns. The other clowns were conventional. They wore masks and elaborate makeup, sported baggy trousers and long, upturned shoes. They smoked exploding cigars. They flashed red electric noses on and off. They gamboled like a blithe flock of stray lambs, unshepherded. The Veteran, however, merely entered with them and then walked slowly around the ring. He wore a battered tin helmet and a uniform a generation out-of-date with its old-fashioned, badly wrapped puttees and a high, choker collar. He carried a broken stub of a rifle, hanging in two pieces like an open shotgun. A touch of genius, the Manager had attached a large clump of barbed wire to the seat of his pants.

The Veteran was seriously worried that people would not laugh at him and that he wouldn't be able to keep his job. Slowly, apprehensively, he strolled around the enormous circle and turned his wound toward them. He could see nothing at all outside of the zone of light surrounding him. But it was not long before he heard a great gasp from the outer darkness, a shocked intaking of breath so palpable that it was like a sudden breeze. And then he heard the single, high-pitched, hysterical giggle of a woman. And next came all that indrawn air returning, rich and warm. The whole crowd laughed at once. The crowd laughed loudly and the tent seemed to swell like a full sail from their laughter. He could see the circus bandsmen puffing like bullfrogs as they played their instruments and could see the sweat-stained leader waving his baton in a quick, strict, martial time. But he could not hear the least sound of their music. It was engulfed, drowned out, swallowed up by the raging storm of laughter.

Soon afterwards the Veteran signed a contract with the circus. His name was placed prominently on all the advertising posters and materials together with such luminaries as the Highwire Walker, the Trapeze Artists, the Lion Tamer, and the Bareback Riders. He worked only at night. For he soon discovered that by daylight he could see his audience, and they knew that and either refused to laugh or were unable to do so under the circumstances. He concluded that only when they were in the relative safety of the dark would they give themselves over to the impulse of laughter.

His fellow clowns, far from being envious of him, treated him with the greatest respect and admiration. And before much time had passed, he had received the highest compliment from a colleague in that vocation. A clown in a rival circus attempted an imitation of his art. But this clown was not well received. In fact, he was pelted with peanuts and hot dogs, with vegetables and fruit and rotten eggs and bottles. He was jeered at and catcalled out of the ring. Because no amount of clever makeup could rival or compete with the Veteran's unfortunate appearance.

Once a beautiful young woman came to the trailer where he lived and prepared for his performance. She told him that she loved him.

—I have seen every single performance since the first night, she said. I want to be with you always.

The Veteran was not unmoved by her beauty and her naïveté. Besides, he had been alone for quite a long time.

—I'm afraid you don't realize what you are saying, he told her.

—If you won't let me be your mistress, I am going to kill myself, she said.

—That would be a pity.

She told him that more than anything else she wanted to have a child by him.

—If we have a child, then I'll have to marry you.

—Do you think, she asked, that our child would look like you?

—I don't believe that is scientifically possible, he said.

Later when she bore his child, it was a fine healthy baby, handsome and glowing. And then, as inexplicably as she had first come to him, the young woman left him.

After a few successful seasons, the Veteran began to lose some of his ability to arouse laughter from the public. By that time almost all of them had seen him at least once already, and the shock had numbed their responses. Perhaps some of them had begun to pity him.

The Manager was concerned about his future.

—Maybe you should take a rest, go into a temporary retirement, he said. People forget everything very quickly nowadays. You could come back to clowning in no time.

—But what would I ever do with myself?

The Manager shrugged.

—You could live comfortably on your savings and your pension, he said. Don't you have any hobbies or outside interests?

—But I really like it here, the Veteran said. Couldn't I wear a disguise and be one of the regular clowns?

—It would take much too long to learn the tricks of the

trade, the Manager said. Besides which your real clowns are truly in hiding. Their whole skill lies in the concealment of anguish. And your talent is all a matter of revelation.

It was not long after this conversation that the Veteran received a letter from the Doctor.

—Your case has haunted me and troubled me, night and day, the Doctor wrote. I have been studying the problem incessantly. And now I think I may be able to do something for you. I make no promises, but I think I can help you. Could you return to the hospital for a thorough examination?

While he waited for the results of all the tests, the Veteran lived in his old room. It was clean and bright and quiet as before. Daily the Head Nurse put a bouquet of fresh flowers in a vase by his bed.

—You may be making a big mistake, she told him. You have lived too long with your wound. Even if the Doctor is successful—and he may be, for he is extremely skillful—you'll never be happy with yourself again.

—Do you know? he began. I was very happy being a clown. For the first and only time in my life all that I had to do was to be myself. But, of course, like everything else, it couldn't last for long.

—You can always come back here. You can stay just as you are now.

—Would you be happy, he asked her, if I came back to the hospital for good just as I am now?

—Oh yes, she said. I believe I would be very happy.

Nevertheless the Veteran submitted to the Doctor's treatment. Once again he became a creature to be wheeled into the glaring of harsh lights, to be surrounded and hovered over by intense masked figures. Once again he was swathed in white bandages and had to suffer through a long time of healing, waiting for the day when he would see himself again. Once again the momentous day arrived, and he stood staring into a mirror as they unwound his bandages.

This time, when the ceremony was completed, he looked into the eyes of a handsome stranger.

—You cannot possibly imagine, the Doctor said, what this moment means to me.

The Head Nurse turned away and could not speak to him.

When he was finally ready to leave the hospital, the Veteran found the High-ranking Officer waiting for him. A gleaming staff car was parked at the curb, and the Veteran noticed by his insignia that the Officer had been promoted.

—We all hope, the Officer said, that you will seriously consider returning to active duty. We need experienced men more than ever now.

—That's a very kind offer, the Veteran said. And I'll certainly consider it in all seriousness.

HOW TO GET HOME

Bret Lott

. . . .

Paul had been in the hospital for four days now, on I.V. the entire time. They had moved to this city only five days before, and his doctor, a man he had never seen before his wife had brought him to the emergency room, had told him he would be in for two, possibly three days more. There was no way to tell, the doctor had said; the virus was just there in him and would run its course.

The symptoms continued: his stomach would cramp up suddenly, and he would have to make his way to the bathroom, pushing along the I.V. on its stand, then pulling open the thick wooden door of the bathroom, pushing it closed behind him. In the five days he had lived in this new city—four of them spent here in the hospital—he had lost nine pounds, and he could feel that loss when he stood or sat up in bed too quickly, could feel the whirl and pop of the room around him, could hear the wash of gray sound in his ears.

And so he lay there in bed each day, the television on, programs on that he had never seen before: soap operas with stories so intricate he could piece together little; on one program, a woman was going to have an abortion that neither she, her husband, nor the father of the child wanted her to have; on another, a man had killed a woman whose restaurant had mysteriously burned years before. He noticed that in these programs there seemed to be no time frame; people lived lives, worked, made love, killed one another all simultaneously. One scene switched to the next to the next, so much drama in so many lives in such a small space of time.

He also watched the morning repeats of old prime-time programs, programs he had already seen while in the living room of his old home, the house he and his wife and his two children had moved from only last week, five days that seemed to him months. There was *Love Boat, Facts of Life, Dynasty,* and he was amazed while watching these programs: episodes it seemed had been on only last season—perhaps not even that long ago—were peopled now by stars with darker hair, slimmer figures, fewer wrinkles than he remembered, and the programs made him wonder at himself, at his growing older, at his being here in the hospital for some sickness no one could name, and at the doctor's reticence at giving him an exact time for release. Sometimes during the nights he had been here he would wake up sweating, disoriented, this room not his own, his wife not in bed next to him. Then he would wonder whether or not he would make it out alive, or if he would die here, in a hospital room; die in the night away from his wife, his children, his family.

But then in the morning, just as had happened this the morning of the fourth day, he would awaken, and the room would be filled with light, and his wife would be there next to the bed, sitting in a chair, waiting for him to look at her, recognize her, tell her how he had slept.

Kate would tell him how things were going at home: the unpacking, the telephone being installed, the exterminator's visit, enrolling the kids at the elementary school, more unpacking. He would look at her, his wife, her face unchanged to him but nevertheless changed, older, and he would feel sorry for her having to set up their house without him. She knew no one, and this made him feel even worse. At least he knew a few people at his office.

Yet she smiled telling him all this; smiled while talking of the three pieces of china she had discovered broken only minutes after signing the moving company's release form; smiled telling him of Jill's first day at school, and how she got lost walking the five blocks home; smiled while telling him of the wasp nest David had discovered in the eaves just above the back door.

All these things happening, he thought, things going on without me, and he felt even more deeply that his life would stop soon, that he would be finished, because the world had already continued on without him.

Later Kate smiled, kissed his forehead, and left for the day. There were things that needed to be done, she said, and he nodded, watched her leave the room. She peeked back into the room, told him she would try to make it back in the afternoon if she could find a baby-sitter. Then she was gone.

For the second time since he had been in the hospital the nurse had to change the I.V. from one arm to the other. He had known this was coming; within the last half hour his right arm, the plastic catheter there in the back of his hand, had begun to turn red and puffy, the arm itself feeling thick and tingling and dead all at once.

The first time the catheter had been moved was late the second night, when he had been rousted from sleep by a face-less nurse, the harsh new light from the bulb directly above his bed clicking on and blinding him so that he kept his eyes closed the entire time, through first the dull pull of the catheter out of the left hand, then the cold swipe across the right, the drawing taut of the tourniquet, the hard thump of the nurse's finger on a vein. Then came the quick prick of pain, almost an electrical shock, he had thought as he lay there, silence around him, the entire floor quiet. After that had come the insertion of the catheter, and the cold liquid draining into his hand, arm, and on into his shoulder before he could no longer trace its cool path in his body.

But now it was midmorning, and he was wide awake, an old episode of *Dallas* playing on the set, and a certain fear took into him: he wondered if this would be the last time he would have to have the I.V. changed from one location to the next, or if he would be changing locations again and again and again until he died. Already the I.V. had destroyed veins in the backs of both hands; the nurse was now searching the top and sides of his right forearm.

She was softly rubbing his arm, her hand almost a caress. He looked at her. She had blond hair in what he thought must have been a new perm, the curls just too tight and wet-looking. She had on a white pantsuit, over her shoulders a blue cardigan. She wore plenty of makeup, too, and he thought he could distinguish on her eyelids four different shades of eye shadow.

He let his head fall back to the pillow and looked away from her. He tried to make small talk then, asked her which schools around were any good, which were bad. She gave him the name of the school her children were in, and though the name had meant nothing to him, he had nodded. He mentioned looking for a good church to start up at, but she said she didn't attend anywhere. Then he commented on the weather, and on how fine it had been since they had moved here.

Still her hand was moving over his arm, but then it stopped, and he felt his muscles tighten everywhere, felt his palms and feet begin to sweat.

She said, "You're not fooling me, you know," and turned his arm so that his hand lay flat on the bed. "Nobody likes this to happen to them. But what you're going to have to do is relax, or else it's not going to work."

"Fine," he said, and he did his best to take a deep breath. His other hand, now free of the tube, felt heavy and stiff. He wanted to do something with it, to bring it up and lay it above his head on the pillow, or to hold onto the railing of the bed. Instead, he did not move it, the hand aching where the catheter had been.

"Think of anything," she said. "Think of your kids," she said, and with a single-edged razor blade she dry-shaved an area a few inches above his wrist on the back of his forearm.

He thought of them, needing only that suggestion; pictured his son, now nine—*nine*, he thought—and, his eyes closed, conjured up his face and listened for him to say something. But he heard nothing, and he had before him only that face, his brown hair thick and wavy and unruly, his smile a concocted one, one he had developed before he was even two: teeth clenched, lips open wide to show almost every tooth. Then he saw his daughter, six now, her black hair and pale skin, and thought for some reason of when she had been born, the heart rate on the fetal monitor dipping too low for too long, the quiet apprehension on the doctor's face as he sat on the stool there between his wife's legs, and then the birth, and the baby's cries, faint but sharp enough to cut through him even today. Six years ago, he thought, six years.

He opened his eyes, and the nurse was finished, was packing things into the white plastic toolbox she had brought in with her. She was smiling at him.

He looked at his arm. The catheter was in place, and he looked at the I.V. bag. The liquid was falling in steady drops at a juncture of tubes, and already he could feel the cool seeping into his arm.

"Finished," she said, and left the room.

He thought of the few moments again, tried to remember something, some pain that would make him see that he had been aware of the needle going in, but he could not.

That afternoon his new boss, the regional sales manager, came into his room. Paul had one of the soap operas on, this one revolving somehow around an impossible wedding that, as far as he could tell, had been put off, postponed, or canceled any number of times.

His boss stood in the doorway holding a large, lush plant, something of a miniature rubber tree, he thought, the pot wrapped in green foil and tied off with a golden bow, and for a moment Paul did not know this man in his room, did not recognize the black horn-rimmed glasses, the flushed face, the crisp brown suit and white shirt and red tie as belonging to anyone he knew, but then the man smiled, said, "Paulie," and made his way across the room to set the plant on the sill below the window.

The instant gone—this was the man who had promoted him

from branch to regional, the man who had given him this new position—Paul reached with his free hand to the console on the railing, and turned off the TV. "Mr. Sumner," he said, and was surprised at how small his voice seemed, how inconsequential. He cleared his throat. "You didn't have to—"

"No," Mr. Sumner said, and raised a hand to wave off his words. "No, no, the truth is I should have come sooner. I should have been here earlier than this, and I feel as bad as all hell about it." He centered the plant on the sill and turned around.

Afternoon light sliced through the open blinds and the room to form white lines across his bed, and Paul thought he could see motes of dust on the air between him and Mr. Sumner, motes lifting and falling, rising and shooting, circling.

He realized he had on only his old blue short-sleeved pajamas, years old, and immediately he was embarrassed, his boss here to visit him, him lying here in a bed, a tube into his arm, his head almost too heavy to lift from the pillow. He looked away from Mr. Sumner and, again with his free hand, began to straighten out the bunched blanket and sheet, lifting a corner and pulling it toward him, reaching across to pull up the other corner. Paul said, "I'm sorry about all this. This is one hell of a way to start out a new position." He glanced up at Mr. Sumner.

Mr. Sumner hadn't moved from the window and had his hands in front of him. He said, "Don't worry about it. You're feeling sorry when *you're* the one in the hospital. These things can't be helped, so you just relax and take it easy." He looked down, his face serious, his eyebrows together, his mouth closed. Quickly, smoothly, he unbuttoned the suit coat, moved his hands to his back pockets so that his coat flared out at either side. He took a step, then another and another, crossing the room, and then he turned around, moved back to the window.

He was pacing, Paul saw, and he wondered if this was it, if, perhaps, he really was going to lose his job over his being sick. Or if, he thought, Mr. Sumner knew something about the sickness that Paul did not, knew some final diagnosis and hadn't the guts to look him in the face, see this man who was going to die sometime soon.

Mr. Sumner, still pacing, still looking at the floor, said, "Your wife—God, she's been a trooper through all this—she told me the doctors don't have any idea."

"They said maybe two or three days before I'm out," Paul said. He could feel the force of gravity on his body, his head slowly moving, despite all his efforts, back to the pillow.

"No, no," Mr. Sumner said, again waving him off with one hand. He still hadn't looked up. "I don't give a damn when you get back in. I don't give a damn about time out. No." He was quiet a moment, then said, "I'll bet you if it's just some virus, that stress is in there, too. That stress is the culprit, the real culprit."

Mr. Sumner kept walking, and suddenly—it was always suddenly, always out of the blue, though once it started it was as familiar and expected by this time as taking the next breath—the cramps began again. He felt the chill and twist in his lower abdomen, felt the muscles everywhere tighten up, felt the immediate beads of sweat on his forehead and neck and upper lip.

"I've read somewhere," Mr. Sumner went on, and Paul wondered how he could do that, simply talk and walk when the room seemed to be collapsing down on the two of them. "I can't remember exactly where," he said, "but I read that moving, just moving yourself and your family and all your belongings, is the second most stressful thing that will happen in your life. Number one, I think, is when one of your parents dies. I think that's it." Mr. Sumner stopped and turned to Paul. He said, "Can I get the nurse for you? Are you okay?"

"Don't worry," Paul heard himself say, unaware he had spoken. The room changed perspective then, and he realized he was sitting up, that now he was moving himself and the I.V. stand toward the thick wooden door, and that he was giving a smile of some sort to Mr. Sumner, a smile he thought might have shown how embarrassed he was, not just at going off to the bathroom, but for having been sick in the first place, his body overwhelming his intentions: to start big at regional, to hit all four states in two weeks, to increase sales for the quarter by 15 percent—all goals he had gone over with, *sold* to Mr. Sumner when he had interviewed for the position less than a month ago. He was embarrassed at his inability even to make it to the office the first day he had intended, that day now two days gone, and so Paul pulled open the door, that door seeming to weigh tons now, and then, almost in relief of this display of helplessness, pushed the door to, and sat on the toilet, the I.V. stand beside him, always beside him.

He took a deep breath and heard movement outside, more steps back and forth. Mr. Sumner said, "So. You know my daughter, Sylvia? Well, you'll meet her. She's going to baby-sit your kids tonight so your wife can come over and stay with you. She called up the office today trying to find somebody who knew a good baby-sitter. You didn't tell me you needed a baby-sitter."

Mr. Sumner was silent, waiting, Paul knew, for some word from him. Finally, after what seemed to him minutes, Paul said, "Sorry," the word echoing off the tile, the linoleum, the buffed stainless-steel rails around the bathroom, and he wondered if the word had even escaped the confines of this small space, if it had slipped under the door to reach Mr. Sumner, or if it had ricocheted from surface to surface in here until it had dissolved into only his own ears.

Mr. Sumner said, "Don't be sorry. Don't. You just get better. It's stress. Got to go. Got a three-thirty with Pacernak. You take care, and don't worry about work."

He heard Mr. Sumner's steps out of the room. Later a nurse knocked on the bathroom door, asked if he was all right. "Yes," he had managed to say. Still later, when he finally came out, the room had gone near dark, the lines of light across his bed gone, the plant on the sill black against the orange and violet sky outside his window.

That night, after a dinner of apple juice and crackers and Jell-O, he watched more television, a spinoff of one of the morning reruns he had watched earlier that same day. The star of this show had been only a regular on the morning program, but now here he was, the man with the nicest clothes, the sharpest wit, the most beautiful women.

But this star, like everyone else, had aged; though he hadn't put on any more weight, his hair was shorter, parted on the side now, not in the middle, and gave off the slightest hint of gray. There were lines beside his eyes, lines unimaginable earlier in the day, lines that no amount of makeup could hide, and Paul imagined the star's aging occurring in only the real time of this day, the tint and hue of hair changing in minutes, the wear and crease of skin in a matter of hours.

Kate came into the room, smiled at him and kissed him, taking his free hand and squeezing it. He looked at her. He looked at her and looked at her, and thought for a moment that she too had aged since that morning, the lines beside *her* eyes, those eyes smiling at him, had appeared only since he had seen her earlier. Her lips had gone a little dry, her hair somehow different, and he wondered what he must have looked like to her, how much older, how much closer to his death he must have come.

The cramps came again, and the sweat, and the constricting of muscles, it seemed, everywhere. He felt Kate look at him, and then she helped him up, knowing already, he knew, that the change in his face—in the set of his jaw, the glaze of his eyes—signaled his sickness, and he was glad for her being there, gladder than he could remember being, thankful for her hand at his elbow, for her gentle steering, for her pushing the I.V. stand herself, for opening the door for him.

When he came out, he felt, of course, even weaker, and she again helped him along to the bed, the sheets there new and clean and warm, and as he lay down he looked at his wife again, convinced that yes, there had been a change in her face, but not a change to which he could object. Just the inevitability of time passing before him, before her, before them all, and the changes it wreaked, changes he could do nothing about.

Then, after they watched three more sitcoms and after an

orderly had brought them each a ginger ale, he began to feel something different happening in him, and he knew, after only the faintest tilt of the room, the slowest creep of cold into his feet, that he would indeed die. The cold went into his legs, then his arms, the catheter still in him, the I.V. bag still dripping away. Next it went into his abdomen and chest, and he began to shiver, the sheet and blanket no longer keeping in any warmth, the thin pajamas useless. He rolled onto his side, felt himself curl up and into himself.

Kate stood, leaned over him, and he closed his eyes. She said, "Paul. Paul, honey."

He looked up at her, whispered, "Kate," her face no different now, no less beautiful than when he had married her, than when they had first made love, than in that delivery room, than yesterday, this morning, his love for her and for his children as large as he had ever known it to be. He closed his eyes again, and let the shivering take him over. And there was a certain calm in that, in letting something else take over, in surrendering intent to time and what it would do, and then, he believed, gently and easily, he died.

When he awoke it was still dark, the only light in the room that from the fluorescent bulbs of the hallway outside, his door open halfway. There stood a nurse, not the blonde who had put in the I.V., but another one, one he didn't recognize, her face lost in the dark.

His eyes had opened without any hesitancy; he had been asleep, then he had woken up. Vague images came to him: coming awake in darkness, being too hot, the sheets around him soaked, three or four blankets heaped over him, and the comfort he had felt.

He blinked, swallowed, his throat and mouth dry.

The nurse said, "You've slept a whole day away. A whole day. What a luxury," and he could make out in the darkness a smile on her face.

He heard movement to his right, below the window, and then Kate stood up, came to him. In the light from the hallway he could see her, her face puffy with sleep and no sleep, her hair tangled and flat on one side, her blouse wrinkled. She smiled at him, and the nurse left.

"I've been here," she said. "You slept all day and night." she put her hand to his face. "The doctor said it's what your body needed to do, to tough it out. He said he knew it was going to happen. How do you feel?" She took her hand from his face and touched his shoulder, squeezed it.

"Okay," he said. "Hungry. Sleepy."

She said, "You sleep. You just keep sleeping," and she kissed him. Though he felt as if he should be up, felt as though he'd had enough rest, he closed his eyes. A moment later he was asleep again.

Two days later the doctor let him go, the I.V. having been taken out the day before, his visits to the bathroom now merely once every few hours. Certainly there was medication he would have to take, foods to avoid, rest to be had, and he assured the doctor—this same doctor now like some old friend, like some fellow veteran of a foreign conflict—that he would do as instructed, Kate standing next to the doctor and nodding her head, looking first at Paul, then the doctor, and then Paul, who sat on the edge of the bed, his clothes on now, a different set from what he had worn in a week ago. Though the clothes were his own, an old sports shirt and Levis and tennis shoes, they felt strange on him, somehow coarser, or maybe it was just how they fit him now that he had lost, altogether, twelve pounds. He shook hands with the doctor, said good-bye, and he and Kate waited for the orderly to come with the wheelchair.

Paul couldn't remember the last time he had ridden as a passenger in their car, and the inside seemed huge, the blue sky through the giant windshield even bluer, brighter than he remembered, and he watched as she drove through the streets of this brand-new city, a city that hadn't existed before they had moved there. On the way home he pointed things out to her, too: a Shell station where they could gas up, an Alpha Beta

Market he hadn't known was so close to their house, a $1.50 theater, a Mexican restaurant not a mile from home.

Kate only nodded, he saw, as if she knew all these things already, though he had been the one who had flown out to search for a place to live, and though he had been the one to find the house they had finally decided upon.

She turned left at a light, descended a hill that seemed steeper than it had before, and then they were approaching what he knew to be the entrance to their tract, the first right past the second light from the bottom of the hill.

But when they neared the street and he saw that his wife was not slowing down, he nearly shouted, "Here, turn here!" his words taking most of his energy, most of his air, and he felt momentarily dizzy. He pointed to the street, watched as they passed it, the houses in there what had been his new landmarks, houses he'd seen the first time the realtor had shown him their house.

Kate momentarily took her foot off the gas pedal. "Oh," she said, surprised. "No," she smiled, "this way's quicker," and she drove on to the next right into the tract, turned, and moved the car along houses that were alien to him, ones he had never seen.

They turned at one street, then another, then another. He was confused, disoriented and still a little dizzy, and yet his wife took still another turn, and he saw in her movement, in her turning of the wheel the same resolve as in the first turn she had made, her eyes on the street, the houses, these foreign places.

He looked at her, felt for a moment he didn't know this woman behind the wheel, wondered how long he really had been gone. He looked out the windshield and tried to remember what color their house was, how many bedrooms, what furniture they had and how the woman next to him might have placed it through the house, and he wondered, too, what his children looked like now, how much they had grown.

He was lost now, and with yet another turn onto yet another

alien street, he realized he could only do what was necessary:
sit back in the seat and wait, wait for his wife to show him how
to get to where their things were, how to get to his children,
how to get home.

AN INFECTED HEART

John Stone

. . . .

I saw him first in April on cardiology consultation rounds. I was working with two emergency medicine residents and two cardiology fellows that month, swooping all over the hospital to see patients with suspected or clear-cut heart disease. The call over the beeper was from the burn unit.

We entered the sanctum of the unit through the swinging doors. Signs on the wall confronted us: Did you wash your hands? We did. And donned the gowns, masks, and puffy surgeons' caps that were required for the unit. We began to review the chart.

The man was young—maybe twenty-five years old—and had been burned—widely, severely. The surgeons had struggled for weeks to try to cover the burned areas with skin grafts before his wounds could become irreversibly infected. He'd been in the hospital since January—almost four months now. I thought of how much it hurts to burn a finger on a hot stove, then tried to mentally magnify it.

We listened as one of the fellows took the history: How had he been burned? The patient told us he'd been walking late one night in January when he spotted the distinctive orange glow and thick smoke of a major fire in a building he passed. He knocked loudly on the door and yelled for help. A young boy appeared at an upstairs window. The patient told us he broke in the door, roused the family out, then went back in for the boy. He'd saved the boy, but had been badly burned in the process.

The man—his name was Robert—was sitting upright in a high-backed wheelchair. His limbs, abdomen, and back were swathed in bandages; he sat propped up on foam so as to put as little pressure as possible on the tender skin underneath. From a distance, his face reminded me of one painted by Rouault: dark, broad brush strokes outlining it, another dark stroke lending prominence to the nose, and lighter tones for the rest of the face. Up close, the landscape of his face was made up of glistening caramel-colored islands of partially melted tissue; they were separated by—and seemed to be eroded by—the angry channeling red pigment of his blood that looked ready to well up at any moment from beneath the burned skin. The effect was that of a variably cooling recent lava flow. But that was not the most striking aspect of his countenance: his eyes had the look of pure terror, pupils dilated, lids widely separated—the eyes that everyone in medicine sees sooner or later. They lent to his face the unmistakable appearance of someone who's seen death and been changed by it.

We examined Robert's heart. It was racing: 160 beats a minute. There was a soft heart murmur: PfffFF . . TT, PfffFF . . TT, PfffFF . . TT. Not loud, but not normal either, we decided among ourselves.

Robert had done surprisingly well for several weeks as his own good skin was grafted over the burned areas. But then infection had set in. Antibiotics were started—first one, then two, then another set, as the bacteria became resistant to the drugs. The spiking daily fevers began—and drenching sweats. Cardiology was called to see him after bacteria were cultured from his blood. Does he have endocarditis? asked the consultation note.

We decided to do an echocardiogram. The machine was trundled up from the sixth floor of the hospital and set up in the room. An echocardiogram harks back to the sonar units used by submarines—the ones we all saw at the movies on Saturday afternoons while we were growing up, blithely unaware of any hearts but our own. The echo machine uses ultrasound waves, as does sonar, bouncing the waves off the interior anatomy of the body. Using the echo, one can visualize the heart's perpetual energy and, within it, in the swirling sea of blood, the graceful heart valves keeping the blood flowing straight and full speed ahead.

Robert's valves all looked normal, thin but with great tensile strength, smoothly opening and closing, all except the mitral valve. Instead of smoothly dancing in place, the mitral valve's motions were weighed down by a mass of heavy echos that could mean only one thing: the blood and bacteria-laden abnormal appendages of endocarditis. His heart was infected all right, seeded from his infected burns and then itself constantly reseeding all parts of the body in its natural centrifugal energy. We were trapped and so was Robert. We might have had a better chance to cure the endocarditis had we not had the infected burns to contend with. As it was, the situation was a desperate one. We wrote out our orders and tried to explain the dilemma to Robert, being as optimistic as possible.

We saw Robert daily over the next two weeks. At first, by switching to yet another, more toxic, set of antibiotics, we seemed to be making some progress. His temperature came down—for four days it was almost normal. All the while, the surgeons worked to cover his burns with grafts. They didn't take. Robert was given several transfusions of blood. But his kidneys were beginning to fail. We adjusted medications, meeting incessantly to decide how to approach each new crisis. I could tell we were losing ground. Robert looked weaker and more resigned on each of our successive visits. The raging fever returned. He was going out in a blaze, an inferno of infection.

Several days ago, as the group of us approached the door of Robert's room, we saw that he had a visitor. The visitor's back was toward us, but his gown was open. His suit was black and, above the tie-strings of the gown around his neck, we could see the white collar of the priesthood. We backed quietly out of the room and waited. In a few minutes the priest came out, closing his Bible as he approached us, a silver cross dangling from a broad white ribbon folded over his forearm. We nodded to his nod. We examined Robert. He looked exhausted. There was a rosary in his hand. He barely noticed that we were in the room.

That afternoon the cardiology team got an emergency call to the unit. As we arrived, donning our apparel quickly, we found the entire surgical team gathered around Robert's bed, always a bad sign. Robert had had a seizure, then his heart had skipped, shuddered, and stopped. Despite our efforts, there was no way to save him. For my part, I wasn't at all sure that Robert *wanted* to be saved any longer. I thought about our sessions in ethics class on "quality of life." Robert had had little of that in the last few months.

As we left the room, a deputy sheriff was outside. He asked about Robert. We told him what had happened, that we'd lost the battle. It was only then that we learned the truth about Robert. Robert, said the deputy, was an arsonist. He had set blazes in two parts of a building back in January. But he'd gotten trapped between the two fires, was badly burned, and had barely escaped with his life by jumping from a second-story window. Robert's tale about his heroism, the young boy he'd saved, was a total lie, something he'd wanted us to believe and, in the haze of morphine, may have begun to believe himself. Ordinarily, he would have been placed under an around-the-clock guard, said the deputy; but, as he told us, "In his condition, he wasn't goin' no place."

We shrugged out of our gowns, shaking our heads in disbelief. We'd been had, all right. Robert must have figured that things would go better for him medically if his doctors thought he was a hero and not an arsonist. I like to think that knowing the truth about Robert wouldn't have affected our efforts to save him. But who can be sure of that? Robert couldn't.

HE READ TO HER

Anne Brashler

. . . .

She locked the bathroom door, sprayed the small closed room with lemon odor, then removed her robe. The colostomy bag was full and leaking; brown stains seeped down her belly and across old scars, new scars, old stretch marks. Her stomach looked like a map of dirt roads. "Crap," she said. She cupped her hand under the bag, holding it like a third breast, then held her breath long enough to break the seal, remove the bag, and quickly tie its contents into a white plastic container. Her colostomy resembled a brown puckered rose.

The bathroom filled with billowy steam as she stayed under the shower. When her husband rapped on the door, she said, "I'm fine. Leave me alone." As she stepped from the tub, refreshed and clean, the puckered rose exploded with bile, shooting brown stinking liquid over the sink, the mirror, the toilet bowl. Doubling up her right hand, she smashed the mirror to smithereens. Her husband removed the bathroom door and, gagging from the odor, placed her on the sofa bed on the porch, cleaned her off, then dressed her open wound, positioning a clean bag over the plastic rim that held it in place. "There," he said. "Everything's going to be all right. You're going to be just fine."

"I was brushing my hair," she said. "My hand slipped." He pulled mirror slivers out of her fist with tweezers, swabbed the cuts in her hand with witch hazel, saying, "There. That's better."

"Nothing you say or do will make me feel better," she said. She smelled the bile; tasted it at the back of her mouth. She ran her tongue along her teeth, convinced they had turned green. "I want my red bed jacket," she said. "Not this raggedy thing. Why didn't you bring me the red one?"

"I'm fixing tea," he said, running from the room. She heard him gag in the kitchen.

"I don't want tea!" she shouted. "Just leave me alone." The kettle whistled, playing an organ strain from Bach, sounding nervous. She knew he'd bring the tea, the double-crostics book, the reference books. She'd looked up the Down answers of the puzzle he'd been working on so that when he got stuck, she'd be able to provide the correct solution, shorten the game. He'd made a cherry wood bed tray, carved flowers around its edges, and was carrying it in, its legs splayed like a little dog flying. "Tea," he said. "Lemon slices, sugar; a rose for my beautiful wife."

"You creep," she said. "That's not going to do any good." She watched his face pale, contort, then smooth out like a person beatified. "I have something different today," he said. He held a book behind him like a surprise.

"Oh yeah?" she said. "It's a quote by Thomas Wolfe from *Look Homeward, Angel.* The definition for Number One Down is 'geometric progression.'" She wished she could hurt him but didn't know how; double-crostics was the best she could do.

"You looked," he said. "But that isn't it. I did that puzzle after you went to bed last night." He puffed pillows into shape, then tucked them under her head, ignoring her when she made her body stiffen. The bag gurgled as liquid hit the plastic.

"Why don't you just leave me alone?" she said and was instantly sorry. Lord knows it wasn't his fault. Lord knows. A joke. Lord, Lord, have mercy. Outside a squirrel chased a blue jay up a willow tree; blue and gray among silvery leaves. Their porch was over the garage, so in summer, with trees filled out, it felt as though they were in the branches of a forest. Their daughter had insisted she recuperate here, in this room, her favorite.

He sat down, ignoring her, then opened the book and began to read in a soft clear voice: *"Call me Ishmael. Some years ago—never mind how long precisely—having little or no money in my purse, and nothing particular to interest me on shore, I thought I would sail about a little and see the watery part of the world . . . ."* His face was intense, as if he'd turned into a priest since she'd been away.

"Are you going to read the whole damn book out loud?" she asked. She wondered if she'd be angry for the rest of her life. She'd hoped she'd be able to laugh again, say something nice once in a while.

"I thought I might," he said.

A breeze picked up leaves, turned them over, making different shades of green. The children had guests; they were racing with inner tubes in the pool. Her son had found huge truck tires at a flea market, hosed them off, patched the inner tubes with colored swatches. Her daughter had taken over the household chores while she'd been in the hospital. They'd kept the family running, shipshape. Her husband, too; he'd had a shock, nearly losing her, going out of his mind with guilt, with self-loathing, the worst kind of pain. "I'd like that, Darly," she finally said. The tea was cold but she drank it anyway.

"Say that again."

"Say what?"

"What you just said."

"Darly? I stole it from some story," she said. Her bag filled suddenly and she thought how convenient it all was.

"I like that. Call me that. Will you call me that?" he asked. He leaned forward, his gray head nestling in the hollow of her shoulder.

"But it's not mine," she said.

"I don't care. I like it."

"Some man said it to his wife. He called her that before they divorced." Was she threatening? Lord knows.

"I don't care," he said.

"Darly," she said, sighing. "Read to me." They'll sort it out later. When cheers for the winner of the inner tube race rose from the pool, she pretended the cheers were for her; she pretended she was a star.

"*. . . Whenever I find myself growing grim about the mouth; whenever it is a damp, drizzly November in my soul . . .*" She lay back and closed her eyes. His voice was music; he became Ishmael, telling her a story.

SOLO DANCE

Jayne Anne Phillips

. . . .

She hadn't been home in a long time. Her father had a cancer operation, she went home. She went to the hospital every other day, sitting for hours beside his bed. She could see him flickering. He was very thin, and the skin on his legs was soft and pure like fine paper. She remembered him saying, "I give up" when he was angry or exasperated. Sometimes he said it as a joke, "Jesus Christ, I give up." She kept hearing his voice in the words now even though he wasn't saying them. She read his get-well cards aloud to him. One was from her mother's relatives. "Well," he said, "I don't think they had anything to do with it." He was speaking of his divorce two years before.

She put lather in a hospital cup and he got up to shave in the mirror. He had to lean on the sink. She combed the back of his head with water and her fingers. His hair was long after six weeks in the hospital, a gray silver full of shadow and smudge. She helped him get slowly into bed, and he lay against the pillows breathing heavily. She sat down again. "I can't wait till I get some weight on me," he said. "So I can knock down that son-of-a-bitch lawyer right in front of the courthouse."

She sat watching her father. His robe was patterned with tiny horses, sorrels in arabesques. When she was very young, she had started ballet lessons. At the first class her teacher raised her leg until her foot was flat against the wall beside her head. He held it there and looked at her. She looked back at him, thinking to herself it didn't hurt and willing her eyes dry.

Her father was twisting his hands. "How's your mother? She must be half crazy by now. She wanted to be by herself and brother that's what she got."

LOOKING AT DOCTORS

· · · · · · · · · · · · · · · · · · ·

ANNIVERSARY

Elaine Marcus Starkman

· · · · · · · · · · · · · · · · · ·

W e've grown so alike standing before our bedroom mirror this morning. Today, our fifteenth wedding anniversary. Even our reflections look alike. Two full faces, steady hazel eyes hidden beneath silver-rimmed glasses, sensitive lips, he, balding, I with the color of my hair gone drab.

Wordless he shaves, black stubble from his electric razor falling into our double-bowl vanity, onto our white carpet. Hum of his razor and my toothbrush droning under harsh fluorescent light.

He pulls out the plug, stuffs razor into our toothpaste-smudged drawer, that drawer like all our dresser drawers. Cluttered with indispensable litter that ties us together. Inside: notes, change, mismatched socks, graying underwear. Outside: surgical journals, poems, math tests, tennis shoes.

He throws his pajamas into the old straw laundry basket and dresses, clothes unstylish and conservative as the day we met. Dark suit, narrow lapels. Reluctantly pulls on the blue-flowered shirt I gave him for his birthday.

Banging of bathroom door, burnt toast, bitter coffee, frantic search for jackets and lunch money fade into morning routine. House silent. Only whirring of washer and dryer. When did I start them?

An ordinary morning. Hair unclipped, terry-cloth robe

stained. Yet different. Fifteenth anniversary, and I find his face among towels. How he rushed in late last night, high beneficent forehead pink with chill, glasses steamy.

"Sorry, got stuck again. Just a standard procedure. Nothing interesting. Maybe we could go to a movie tomorrow. The one by that woman film director is playing in Berkeley."

"*Swept Away?* I thought you said it was too violent."

"It's the old taming of the shrew updated, isn't it?"

"Yes. You won't like it."

"Probably not, but you said it was important to see. Ingmar Bergman's got a new film out. Maybe I'll come home early. We can go to either one."

What sudden extravagance, when has he ever cared about films? Has he remembered our anniversary this year? The year of my migraines, his weight gain, our son's running away, our daughter's school failure? The summer we fought on the Santa Cruz beach in front of a crowd of strangers, I screaming, "Doctor, doctor, doctor," he slapping me across the cheek, voice seething, "Shut up; I'm sick of you. From now on I'll do what *I* want." We drove home from his day off, the children shocked into silence. Those endless hot months, no classes, no poems to sustain me, only family responsibility. I hated what I'd once loved. Maury, a doctor before he was born. He *had* to be. And I his wife.

Throw wet towels into the dryer. What would I do in my spare time without laundry? Golf, shop, drive to the city, join the hospital auxiliary?

Brush my hair and dress. Our wedding portrait. How voguish I look. Blond teased pageboy. Squinting through my contact lenses. A tiny pearl crown on my head. My mother sighing with relief: *A doctor she's marrying, thank God; she's nearly twenty-three.* Except for his baldness, he hasn't changed a bit. Same soft eyes, same earnest smile, same uncompromising values, same rabbinical look. In those days I'd look away modestly and say, "I love you." Even when he cut short our three-day honeymoon to return to his residency. How understanding I was.

How quickly we fell into routine. The long weekends of his

final year, endless hours in the emergency room, his exhaustion, my posing with a huge belly in the St. Louis snow. After lovemaking he'd stand awkwardly in the hall in his white gown almost afraid to say those words: "I have to go now, Nina. I'll be back tomorrow night."

"All right," I lied.

"Maybe you should phone your mother so you won't be lonely."

"No, no, everything's fine. I'd rather be alone."

"Then why are you crying? You knew it would be this way."

"It's okay. Go on." Listen to footsteps resound in the dark hallway of our apartment building.

Five years and we never quarreled. *Nina, my friend needs a loan. But, Maury, we haven't gone anywhere for so long. I've got to lend him some money. All right, Maury. Time to visit my family. Can't we skip this Friday night? You don't have to say anything. Just sit with them. Listen, let's invite them here next week. Maury, you know I can't cook anything your mother does. Make something simple; it doesn't matter.*

How grateful I was. His family called me lucky. What could I do to please such a giving man? Only conceive and that I managed despite our obstetrician-friend's prognosis: *her pelvis is small.* But they came anyway, three births in five years, the miracle of our children's lives escaping us, distracting us from our own goals. They ran through the town house shrieking, crying, tumbling down the stairs, biting each other, demanding love and attention. He loved them; they bewildered him. "Why are they so wild?" He scratched his head.

"Because they're spoiled. Didn't your mother spoil you?"

"She didn't have time. She always worked in the grocery to save money for our schooling."

"Why don't you humor them? Why are you so strict?"

"Because I love them, because I want them to know right from wrong."

How problematic they were—Joey repeating first grade, Amy moody and withdrawn, Rachel with her temper tantrums. Every year we were unprepared for their growing pains. And our own as well. Every year he said, *The medical profession's got to change. No, Maury, you've got to adapt to it. What you want is impossible.* Six times we moved chasing impossibilities. All the time our parents hovering in the background: *Tell him medicine is a business; his income depends on that.*

Our final move to the West Coast nearly destroyed us. Here, away from friends and family, among capricious San Francisco temperaments, Rachel crawls out of diapers and into kindergarten. "I'm sick of your ideals. Sick of being called 'doctor's wife.' I'm going after mine now," I rant.

"What are you going to do?"

"I don't know, but I'll find out."

"Do what you want. Have I ever stopped you from doing what you want?"

"Your very presence stops me. Your—"

"That's your fault, not mine. I could never please you anyway. Just don't ask *me* to change; just leave me alone."

I don't ask. I sit in the kitchen of our new California-style house late at night writing poems. For the first time in years. Those poems, that passion, born of my guts, my joy alone, not his, *mine.* Published in an obscure feminist university journal. I'm a feminist, liberated. Suburban mother of three, I howl with delight. Dance with the children, drive to the top of Mount Diablo, shout from its peaks: *Mamma's gone mad.*

With that madness 1970 breaks, and I'm transformed. Nina the Iconoclast. Chipping away at his pedestal. He's rigid, unathletic, boring, *too moral.* I'll leave. Go to live in a women's commune in Berkeley, fly to Israel and build the desert, make up for lost time. Drown myself in Bergman, look for the young Chicano I met in the poetry stacks. But I watch him say *Kaddish* for the death of his patient, listen to the sound of his Danish rocker and favorite Oistrakh, look into his deep hazel eyes that refuse to see the senselessness of our lives, and bound off to the laundry room like a hurt puppy. There in that familiar maze of underwear, old texts, and paperbacks, I announce, "I'm starting school again."

"Good idea, but don't become too compulsive about it."

How well he knows my compulsiveness. School's not so easy now. My forehead tingles, my stomach cramps. Rachel asks why I'm not room-mother. "Because I have to study," I snap, a dragon at dinner hour. Course after course. Women and Madness, La Raza Studies, Seminar in Faulkner, Tai Chi, the Yiddish Novel.

The children's diapers are replaced by braces, lessons, tutors, car pools, conferences, puberty. They alone grow. We merely age, I studying at night toward some unknown pursuit, Maury reading journals and Middle East news reports.

"Ten o'clock. I'm on call. I've got to get some rest."

"Go ahead. I'm studying."

"Why do you play this game every night?"

"What game?"

"All right, study. Study until you beg me to touch you. I'm fed up. You and your games."

"I'm not playing games. I just have no desire."

"Then why don't you leave? It's fashionable for women to leave men these days. I'll give you anything you want. Just go so I can have some peace."

"Don't be ridiculous; you think I'd leave you and the children?"

"Why not? You probably have a lover anyway."

"Are you mad? Are you *absolutely* mad?"

"Then why do you act like this?"

"Like what?"

"Your lack of desire, your inability to manage the kids. Why don't you go for help?"

"Because I'm trying to change? Because I'm trying to do something for myself? You're the one who should go. You've lost touch with reality."

"Go in the kitchen and study. You don't respect anything I believe in. You want something I can't give you. I'm just a small man."

The yellow wallpaper rages in silence. All these years— wasted. He with his kindness has made me afraid of the world, he with his selflessness has made me nothing, and I've let it happen. What am I next to him?

The phone rings. He dresses and leaves. I close my text and creep into our bedroom, lie by the telephone on his side of the bed. Browse in a new novel. What reckless heroines, what cads the men are. Why can't we be like that?

He's gone an hour now. The rage dissolves into a whimper. The wind bangs at the patio windows, dogs bark, children moan, the faucet drips. What if Maury dies? Would I mourn him for years? Would I ever take a lover?

Phone again. A woman I met at school.

"One partner in fourteen years? This is the Age of Aquarius."

"For him it isn't."

"And for you?"

"Me? I don't know."

"You're still hung up because he's a doctor."

"It's not that. It's the kind of person he is."

"You mean *you* are. You'll change, you'll see. By the end of the year you'll change."

"Not in *that* way. You know I still have some traditional values."

"You and he are just alike, killing yourselves with an out-moded moral code. You have to move with the times."

"I know, I know."

"No, you don't. Otherwise you'd forget your fantasies or admit you still care for him."

"I can't."

At 2:00 A.M. he comes in, face sallow, tired, blood on his undershorts. "A terrible case, Nina, a young man. Motorcycle accident. He'll be dead by morning. Let me hold you. I can't do my work without you."

A winter moon floods our bedroom. Succumb but don't surrender. Don't share his act of love. Separate mind, nourish it with illusions of young men in my classes. He falls asleep immediately, not waking to wash. Listen to his snoring. Anesthetic on his fingers, spittle on his lip. How could I ever leave? He'd work himself to death. I'm the small one, not he. If only I'd let go of my anger, if only I'd stop blaming him for my failures. Sleep, morning, obligation, make lunch, the children—

We wake, shut off from one another, two strangers. Wordless, he shaves, runs off to the hospital. Phones me at ten. A sudden joy in his voice. "Nina, he's going to *live*. There *must* be a God, do you hear? When I told that to the men, they laughed. Nina, say something."

I can't. He waits for my silence to end. "Listen, I know this has been a hard month. One of the men told me about a place in Mexico. Maybe we could drive down with the kids when they're on spring vacation."

"I don't think they'll want to go. Last time we took them with us it was a disaster. You hollered at Joey the whole time, and Amy's complaints drove me crazy."

"We could leave them with Mrs. Larsen."

"Rachel hates Mrs. Larsen."

"How about Mrs. Bertoli?"

"Too expensive."

"Well, I just wanted to check before I take extra call this month. This malpractice insurance will either kill me or make me retire."

"Take the call, Maury; we'll stay at home."

"You're sure?"

"I'm sure; you're not ready to retire. Maury—I'm glad about your patient."

"Don't be glad for me, be glad for him."

He didn't even mention our anniversary; he didn't remember. Every year he forgets. Yes, we'll stay home this time as we have all the other times. And yet there's something different this year as I sort the towels. His key in the door, breakfast dishes unwashed. He's home so soon flipping on the news.

"It's too early for lunch."

"I know." Hands me a single rose, kisses my neck. "Happy anniversary." Looks so helpless I want to reach out but don't. My eyes wet. "Come on. I'll make you lunch. What time do you have to be back?"

"I don't; the anesthesiologist is on strike. No work."

He changes into his gardening pants. When did he let his sideburns grow? They're nearly gray. How he loves watering the garden. Always has been more nurturing than I. Awkward eating without the children. What to say to each other—just two of us alone. A new phase we're entering this fifteenth year.

"The salad's great. You know, we should become vegetarians." He suddenly laughs.

"Can you see Joey existing without his sloppy joes and hot dogs?"

"Give him five more years, he will. He get off okay this morning? He was mumbling about some science project."

"Fine, he's even turning into a decent kid. Decent but different from us."

"He's growing up in such different times; it's hard on him. Good to be home. After seeing that patient this morning I promised myself not to worry about anything. Are you angry at me?"

"Why do you ask?"

"You seemed upset this morning."

"I was angry at myself."

"What for?"

"Because I've let myself become too much like you."

"Why do you say that? We have our separate friends, interests—"

"Even Bob Stoller said we're getting to look alike."

He grins. "Only our noses. Did you know that Stoller and his wife broke up last week?"

"Nothing surprises me these days. How come you didn't tell me?"

"What's the use of telling bad news? Nina, let's sell the house; let's go live in the country. I'm sick and tired of everything. I'm going to look at a place this weekend."

"Are you kidding?"

"I'm not. Let's finish lunch and talk about it in bed."

"But Rachel comes home at two, and I've got to finish a poem."

"Forget the poem. If you work too hard, you'll become a poet. Then what would I do?"

"Maury, you're a chauvinist!"

"No, I'm not, just jealous."

"You're jealous of *me?"*

"You've more time to think, to be yourself."

"I suppose I do."

"More time to do what you want."

"Oh, come on now."

"Well, I can't do what I want either. People like us have too many responsibilities. We live limited lives."

He stands there in his underwear, his pale skin covered with black down. The veins in his neck pulsate like the days in our old St. Louis apartment when we were first married. March twenty-first, 1960. First day of spring. *I still care, I still care.* I didn't know that I did, but I do.

THREE DOCTORS

Jim Heynen

. . . .

Three doctors were sailing in the bay. The winds were strong, but no match for their skill as sailors.

The surgeon was tending the sheets. Let me take that, said the general practitioner. If you get a finger caught in the winch, you're out of business.

All right, said the surgeon, taking the tiller.

Keep an eye on the jib, said the GP. If it jibes, the main's next.

No sweat, said the surgeon.

Everything seems to be under control, said the psychiatrist and went below for the bourbon.

They sat back to relax. They sipped their bourbon. They started to chat.

How have things been at the office? the surgeon asked the GP.

Oh, all right, but we are having a harder time collecting than ever before.

Same problem, said the surgeon.

Same here, said the psychiatrist. I wonder how people imagine the world can continue to function when they can't take care of the simple matter of paying their bills.

I don't know. I don't know either, said the other two.

I had one woman said that having therapy taught her not

to worry about money, said the psychiatrist. She said the money was my worry and maybe I should see a psychiatrist.

My god, said the general practitioner. Though I had a case that was just as bad. This woman called me on the phone so she wouldn't have the expense of an office call. She said she was into preventative medicine. Wanted me to recommend ways to care for her children so they wouldn't get sick. I suggested a balanced diet, lots of sleep, and instilling a positive outlook on life. I figured this is what she wanted to hear. Next week all three of her kids had the flu. She came in with them and not only expected a free office call but free drugs. She said that was the least I could do for the bad advice.

My god, said the psychiatrist.

Listen to this one, said the surgeon. I had one welfare mother wanted to barter me some painted gourds for her back surgery. She said she spent twelve hours painting them—that she wouldn't charge me for the seeds and the planting and the rest of the gardening. She figured we were even. She said, I put in four hours for you for every one you put in for me, and that should be fair!

Something is going to have to change, that's for sure, said the psychiatrist.

You can say that again, said the GP.

Sooner or later, said the psychiatrist. The world can't go on like this forever, that's for sure.

The blocks creaked as the doctors brought the stern into the eye of the wind and hauled in the mainsheet.

Ready? said the surgeon.

Ready, said the GP.

Jibe-o, said the surgeon.

The mainsail snapped over and the boat shivered slightly as it crossed the wind.

Okay. Main out, said the GP.

Piece of cake, said the surgeon.

Piece of cake, said the psychiatrist, setting up another round.

DR. CAHN'S VISIT

Richard Stern

· · · · · · · · · · · · · · · · ·

"How far is it now, George?"

The old man was riding next to his son, Will. George was his brother, dead the day after Franklin Roosevelt.

"Almost there, Dad."

"What does 'almost' mean?"

"It's Eighty-sixth and Park. The hospital's at Ninety-ninth and Fifth. Mother's in the Klingenstein Pavilion."

"Mother's not well?"

"No, she's not well. Liss and I took her to the hospital a couple of weeks ago."

"It must have slipped my mind." The green eyes darkened with sympathy. "I'm sure you did the right thing. Is it a good hospital?"

"Very good. You were on staff there half a century."

"Of course I was. For many years, I believe."

"Fifty."

"Many as that?"

"A little slower, pal. These jolts are hard on the old man." The cabbie was no chicken himself. "It's your ride."

"Are we nearly there, George?"

"Two minutes more."

"The day isn't friendly," said Dr. Cahn. "I don't remember such—such—"

"Heat."

"Heat in New York." He took off his gray fedora and scratched at the hairless, liver-spotted skin. Circulatory difficulty left it dry, itchy. Scratching had shredded and inflamed its soft center.

"It's damn hot. In the nineties. Like you."

"What's that?"

"It's as hot as you are old. Ninety-one."

"Ninety-one. That's not good."

"It's a grand age."

"That's your view."

"And Mother's eighty. You've lived good, long lives."

"Mother's not well, son?"

"Not too well. That's why Liss and I thought you ought to see her. Mother's looking forward to seeing you."

"Of course. I should be with her. Is this the first time I've come to visit?"

"Yes."

"I should be with her."

The last weeks at home had been difficult. Dr. Cahn had been the center of the household. Suddenly his wife was. The nurses looked after her. And when he talked, she didn't answer. He grew angry, sullen. When her ulcerous mouth improved, her voice was rough and her thought harsh. "I wish you'd stop smoking for five minutes. Look at the ashes on your coat. Please stop smoking."

"Of course, dear. I didn't know I was annoying you." The ash tumbled like a suicide from thirty stories, the butt was crushed into its dead brothers. "I'll smoke inside." And he was off, but, in two minutes, back. Lighting up. Sometimes he lit two cigarettes at once. Or lit the filtered end. The odor was foul, and sometimes his wife was too weak to register her disgust.

They sat and lay within silent yards of each other. Dr. Cahn was in his favorite armchair, the *Times* bridge column inches from his cigarette. He read it all day long. The vocabulary of the game deformed his speech. "I need some clubs" might mean "I'm hungry." "My spades are tired" meant he was. Or his eyes were. Praise of someone might come out "He laid his hand out clearly." In the bedridden weeks, such mistakes intensified his wife's exasperation. "He's become such a penny-pincher," she said to Liss when Dr. Cahn refused to pay her for the carton of cigarettes she brought, saying, "They can't charge so much. You've been cheated."

"Liss has paid. Give her the money."

"Are you telling me what's trump? I've played this game all my life."

"You certainly have. And I can't bear it."

In sixty marital years there had never been such anger. When Will came from Chicago to persuade his mother into the hospital, the bitterness dismayed him.

It was, therefore, not so clear that Dr. Cahn should visit his wife. Why disturb her last days? Besides, Dr. Cahn seldom went out anywhere. He wouldn't walk with the black nurses (women whom he loved, teased, and was teased by). It wasn't done. "I'll go out later. My feet aren't friendly today."

Or, lowering the paper, "My legs can't trump."

Liss opposed his visit. "Mother's afraid he'll make a scene."

"It doesn't matter," said Will. "He has to have some sense of what's happening. They've been the center of each other's lives. It wouldn't be right."

The hope had been that Dr. Cahn would die first. He was eleven years older, his mind had slipped its moorings years ago. Mrs. Cahn was clearheaded, and, except near the end, energetic. She loved to travel, wanted especially to visit Will in Chicago—she had not seen his new apartment—but she wouldn't leave her husband even for a day. "Suppose something happened." "Bring him along." "He can't travel. He'd make an awful scene."

Only old friends tolerated him, played bridge with him, forgiving his lapses and muddled critiques of their play. "If you don't understand a two bid now, you never will." Dr. Cahn was the most gentlemanly of men, but his tongue roughened with his memory. It was as if a lifetime of restraint were only the rind of a wicked impatience.

"He's so spoiled," said Mrs. Cahn, the spoiler.

"Here we are, Dad."

They parked under the blue awning. Dr. Cahn got out his wallet—he always paid for taxis, meals, shows—looked at the few bills, then handed it to his son. Will took a dollar, added two of his own, and thanked his father.

"This is a weak elevator," he said of one of the monsters made to drift the ill from floor to floor. A nurse wheeled in a stretcher and Dr. Cahn removed his fedora.

"Mother's on eight."

"Minnie is here?"

"Yes. She's ill. Step out now."

"I don't need your hand."

Each day his mother filled less of the bed. Her face, unsupported by dentures, seemed shot away. Asleep, it looked to Will as if the universe leaned on the crumpled cheeks. When he kissed them, he feared they'd turn to dust, so astonishingly delicate was the flesh. The only vanity left was love of attention, and that was part of the only thing that counted, the thought of those who cared for her. How she appreciated the good nurses, and her children. They—who'd never before seen their mother's naked body—would change her nightgown if the nurse was gone. They brought her the bedpan and, though she usually suggested they leave the room, sat beside her while, under the sheets, her weak body emptied its small waste.

For the first time in his adult life, Will found her beautiful. Her flesh was mottled like a Pollock canvas, the facial skin trenched with the awful last ditches of self-defense; but her look melted him. It was human beauty.

Day by day, manners that seemed as much a part of her as her eyes—fussiness, bossiness, nagging inquisitiveness—dropped away. She was down to what she was.

Not since childhood had she held him so closely, kissed his cheek with such force. "This is mine. This is what lasts," said the force.

What was she to him? Sometimes little more than the old organic scenery of his life. Sometimes she was the meaning of it. "Hello, darling," she'd say. "I'm so glad to see you." The voice, never melodious, was rusty, avian. Beautiful. No actress could match it. "How are you? What's happening?"

"Very little. How are you today?"

She told her news. "Dr. Vacarian was in, he wanted to give me another treatment. I told him, 'No more.' And no more medicine." Each day she had renounced more therapy. An unspoken decision had been made after a five-hour barium treatment that usurped the last of her strength. (Will thought that might have been its point.) It had given her her last moments of eloquence, a frightening jeremiad about life dark beyond belief, nothing left, nothing right. It was the last complaint of an old champion of complaint, and after it, she had made up her mind to go. There was no more talk of going home.

"Hello, darling. How are you today?"

Will bent over, was kissed and held against her cheek. "Mother, Dad's here."

To his delight, she showed hers. "Where is he?" Dr. Cahn had waited at the door. Now he came in, looked at the bed, realized where he was and who was there.

"Dolph, dear. How are you, my darling? I'm so happy you came to see me."

The old man stooped over and took her face in his hand. For seconds there was silence. "My dearest," he said; then, "I didn't know. I had no idea. I've been so worried about you. But don't worry now. You look wonderful. A little thin, perhaps. We'll fix that. We'll have you out in no time."

The old man's pounding heart must have driven blood through the clogged vessels. There was no talk of trumps.

"You can kiss me, dear." Dr. Cahn put his lips on hers.

He sat next to the bed and held his wife's hand through the low rail. Over and over he told her she'd be well. She asked about home and the nurses. He answered well for a while. Then they both saw him grow vague and tired. To Will he said, "I don't like the way she's looking. Are you sure she has a good doctor?"

Of course Mrs. Cahn heard. Her happiness watered a bit,

not at the facts but at his inattention. Still, she held on. She knew he could not sit so long in a strange room. "I'm so glad you came, darling."

Dr. Cahn heard his cue and rose. "We mustn't tire you, Minnie dear. We'll come back soon."

She held out her small arms, he managed to lean over, and they kissed again.

In the taxi he was very tired. "Are we home?"

"Almost, Dad. You're happy you saw Mother, aren't you?"

"Of course I'm happy. But it's not a good day. It's a very poor day. Not a good bid at all."

OUTPATIENT

Rosalind Warren

. . . .

T he waiting room is crowded. Mothers watch fidgety children, couples sit together on drab sofas, adult children
talk in soothing voices to elderly parents. Everyone in the
waiting room has someone with them. Luisa has come alone.

"New patient?" the receptionist asks. Luisa nods.

The receptionist hands her a clipboard that holds a form.
"You'll have to fill this out," she says. When Luisa returns it
a few moments later, the receptionist looks it over. "You
haven't filled in your occupation," she says.

"Hypnotist," says Luisa.

"Oh?" The receptionist meets Luisa's eyes. They're unusual
eyes. Clear blue, almost violet. They often remind people of
deep bodies of water.

"It's the family business," says Luisa. "Both my parents were
hypnotists. As were two of my grandparents."

"How lovely," says the receptionist.

"The doctor will see me right away," says Luisa, still looking
into the receptionist's eyes. She enunciates each word slowly
and carefully.

"But we call people in the order they arrive."

"I arrived first," says Luisa.

"You arrived first," agrees the receptionist.

Luisa has barely glanced at *Life* magazine's special Winter

Olympics issue when a nurse calls her name. She follows the nurse down a corridor to a small examining room. The nurse hands her the usual skimpy garment, telling Luisa to remove her clothes and put it on. When the nurse leaves, Luisa strips, puts the thing on, and sits down on the edge of the examination table. It's cool. Almost immediately she has goose bumps.

Luisa doesn't look great in the drab shapeless garment, but she looks better than most. She is of an indeterminate age. Certainly past forty. She would probably be described as "well preserved." She is tall and strong-looking and has longish red hair. Not beautiful but striking. The nurse comes back in and smiles when she notices that Luisa's fingernails and toenails are painted cherry-blossom pink.

"Stand on the scale," she instructs. Luisa gets on the scale, and the nurse adjusts the indicator back and forth, minutely, until it finally rests on 130.

"One hundred thirty," she says.

Luisa turns to look at her. "What about my eyes?" she asks.

"Hmmm?" the nurse says, writing. She looks up and meets Luisa's eyes. "Oh!" she says. She gazes at Luisa for a moment. "They're such a nice color," she says.

"Really?" asks Luisa. "Tell the truth."

"They're a little weird."

"Scary?" asks Luisa.

"Nope." The nurse smiles. "I like them."

Luisa smiles. "I weigh one fifty-seven," she says. The nurse glances down at her clipboard and frowns. She erases the 130 and writes 157.

"But I carry it well," says Luisa. "Don't I?"

"You certainly do," says the nurse. "Now I have to take your blood pressure." She straps the arm band on, pumps it up, and looks at it. "One hundred ten over sixty," she says.

"One twenty over seventy," Luisa says. The nurse gazes at her blankly. "I'm sorry," says Luisa. "But these silly games are quite harmless, and they're crucial if I'm to stay in practice. I'll stop if it disturbs you."

The nurse smiles. "It doesn't disturb me." She writes 120 over 70 on Luisa's chart. "I think it's interesting."

"What happens now?" Luisa asks.

"You wait for Dr. Heller."

"I probably don't even need Dr. Heller," says Luisa. "I'm ninety percent sure I've got bronchitis. Everyone in my family has bronchitis. Everyone on my *block* has bronchitis. But I can't just write myself out a prescription for antibiotics, can I?"

"No," says the nurse. "You can't."

"What's Dr. Heller like?" Luisa asks.

"He's very nice."

"Tell the truth."

"He's a complete jerk," says the nurse. Then she looks startled, and they both burst out laughing.

"But he's a very competent doctor," the nurse says. "He can diagnose your bronchitis as well as the next doc."

"Thanks for putting up with me," says Luisa. "You will feel happy for the rest of the day. You will walk around thinking life is a piece of cake."

"I certainly look forward to that," says the nurse.

Luisa snaps her fingers. The nurse blinks, then moves quickly to the door. "Dr. Heller will be right with you," she says as she leaves. She has left the clipboard with Luisa's chart on the table, and Luisa quickly changes her weight and blood pressure to the correct numbers.

Time passes. Ten minutes. Twenty minutes. Nothing happens. The nurse had left her with the impression that the doctor would be right in. Clearly, he won't be. There is nothing to distract her. She should have brought her magazine with her. She imagines parading out into the waiting room dressed as she is to retrieve her copy of *Life*. She decides against it.

She looks around the room. It's a generic examination room. No windows. No pictures or photos. Nothing interesting or unusual to hold her attention. Luisa hasn't much interest in things, anyway. Things rarely hold surprises; people do.

Another twenty minutes pass. Luisa is beginning to think they've forgotten all about her. She's starting to feel woozy. It angers her. Sitting here half dressed is the last thing she needs. She knows that in examining rooms up and down this hallway sick people sit in skimpy hospital garments waiting for the doctor. It's more convenient for him this way. She tries to calm herself. This treatment isn't life-threatening, she tells herself. It may be dehumanizing and demoralizing, but it won't kill you. They only do it this way because they can get away with it.

Finally the door opens and a big man in a white coat breezes in. He's in his mid-thirties, large and bearded. He looks like a lumberjack. His blue eyes are intelligent but not particularly kind. He moves in a rush.

"Well, Luisa," he says loudly, glancing down at the clipboard, "I'm Dr. Heller. What's the trouble?"

"Sorry to keep you waiting," says Luisa.

"Hmmm?" he says, scanning her chart.

"I said I was sorry to keep you waiting."

He looks up at her. "Symptoms?" he asks.

"Fever," she says. "Sore throat. Bad cough. I think I have bronchitis."

"*I'm* the doctor," he says, making notations on her chart. He places his stethoscope on her back. "Cough!" he barks.

Luisa coughs as he moves his stethoscope about on her back and then her chest. His movements are all precise and quick, and his touch is firm and cold. He looks into the distance, concentrating. He doesn't look at her.

"It began two weeks ago," Luisa says. "I woke up with a bad sore throat. Three days later I began running a slight fever." She stops. He isn't listening.

"How much pain have you caused your patients by not listening to them?" she asks quietly.

"Hmmm?" He takes a thermometer from a drawer. "Open," he says, angling the thermometer toward her mouth. Luisa pushes it away.

"Listen to me!" she says.

He stops and looks at her, his eyes dark and angry. Their eyes meet. It's a struggle. But Luisa is angry.

"You will slow down and give me a good, thorough examination," she says finally. "You will take your time, pay attention, and explain the reason for each procedure. You will listen to me when I speak. Not only am I older than you and deserving of your respect for no other reason, but I live in this body. I may know something about it that can help you."

The doctor gazes at her, unblinking.

"I'm not just a body with an illness," says Luisa. "I'm a person. You care about my feelings."

"I care about your feelings," he says. He sounds doubtful.

But he continues the examination at a much slower, kinder pace, and Luisa is surprised at how good he is. His cold hands even seem to warm up slightly. But it's clear that he's fighting the impulse to race through the exam and get on to the next patient.

"Why are you in such a hurry?" she asks.

"I have so many patients. I hate to keep them waiting."

"You don't care about that. Tell the truth."

"You've got a fabulous body," he says. "I love older women with big breasts."

"Not about that," she laughs. "Why are you in such a hurry?"

"This way I stay in control."

"What if you aren't in control?"

"I have to be in control."

"Why?"

"I'm the doctor."

"And you're the doctor because you have to stay in control," says Luisa. "Right?"

"Yes," he says. "I do like your eyes. They're . . ."

"What?"

"Calming."

He finishes the examination. "You have bronchitis," he says. "I'm writing you a prescription for 500mg of ampicillin."

"What would make you listen to your patients?" she asks. "What would make you care?"

"Nothing," he says. He is writing the prescription. "Take this four times daily with plenty of water." He hands it to her and turns toward the door.

"Wait," she says.

He stops. "Take your clothes off," she says. He turns around and stares into her eyes. He begins to unbutton his shirt.

As he removes his clothing, Luisa puts hers back on. By the time he's naked, she's fully clothed. He stands there looking very pale. He has goose bumps. She hands him the hospital garment. He puts it on.

"You will sit here and wait," she says, "until the nurse comes looking for you. You'll see what it's like."

He sits down on the edge of the examination table and sighs.

She pauses at the door. "When the nurse comes, you'll forget about me."

"I'll forget about you." He sounds happy about that.

"But you'll never forget the next half hour."

As Luisa leaves the room, she sees the nurse heading toward her with a clipboard. "Dr. Heller is in the examining room," she tells the nurse. "He asked not to be disturbed for at least a half hour. But he wanted you to explain to the patients who are waiting that there'll be a delay. And to apologize."

"That's new," says the nurse.

"That's right," says Luisa. She meets the nurse's eyes. "Have an interesting day," she says.

THE DISCUS THROWER

Richard Selzer

. . . .

I spy on my patients. Ought not a doctor to observe his patients by any means and from any stance, that he might the more fully assemble evidence? So I stand in the doorways of hospital rooms and gaze. Oh, it is not all that furtive an act. Those in bed need only look up to discover me. But they never do.

From the doorway of Room 542 the man in the bed seems deeply tanned. Blue eyes and close-cropped white hair give him the appearance of vigor and good health. But I know that his skin is not brown from the sun. It is rusted, rather, in the last stage of containing the vile repose within. And the blue eyes are frosted, looking inward like the windows of a snowbound cottage. This man is blind. This man is also legless—the right leg missing from mid-thigh down, the left from just below the knee. It gives him the look of a bonsai, roots and branches pruned into the dwarfed facsimile of a great tree.

Propped on pillows, he cups his right thigh in both hands. Now and then he shakes his head as though acknowledging the intensity of his suffering. In all of this he makes no sound. Is he mute as well as blind?

The room in which he dwells is empty of all possessions—no get-well cards, small, private caches of food, day-old flowers, slippers, all the usual kickshaws of the sickroom. There is only

115

the bed, a chair, a nightstand, and a tray on wheels that can be swung across his lap for meals.

"What time is it?" he asks.

"Three o'clock."

"Morning or afternoon?"

"Afternoon."

He is silent. There is nothing else he wants to know.

"How are you?" I say.

"Who is it?" he asks.

"It's the doctor. How do you feel?"

He does not answer right away.

"Feel?" he says.

"I hope you feel better," I say.

I press the button at the side of the bed.

"Down you go," I say.

"Yes, down," he says.

He falls back upon the bed awkwardly.

His stumps, unweighted by legs and feet, rise in the air, presenting themselves. I unwrap the bandages from the stumps and begin to cut away the black scabs and the dead, glazed fat with scissors and forceps. A shard of white bone comes loose. I pick it away. I wash the wounds with disinfectant and redress the stumps. All this while he does not speak. What is he thinking behind those lids that do not blink? Is he remembering a time when he was whole? Does he dream of feet? Of when his body was not a rotting log?

He lies solid and inert. In spite of everything, he remains impressive, as though he were a sailor standing athwart a slanting deck.

"Anything more I can do for you?" I ask.

For a long moment he is silent.

"Yes," he says at last and without the least irony. "You can bring me a pair of shoes."

In the corridor, the head nurse is waiting for me.

"We have to do something about him," she says. "Every morning he orders scrambled eggs for breakfast, and, instead of eating them, he picks up the plate and throws it against the wall."

"Throws his plate."

"Nasty. That's what he is. No wonder his family doesn't come to visit. They probably can't stand him any more than we can."

She is waiting for me to do something.

"Well?"

"We'll see," I say.

The next morning I am waiting in the corridor when the kitchen delivers his breakfast. I watch the aide place the tray on the stand and swing it across his lap. She presses the button to raise the head of the bed. Then she leaves.

In time the man reaches to find the rim of the tray, then on to find the dome of the covered dish. He lifts off the cover and places it on the stand. He fingers across the plate until he probes the eggs. He lifts the plate in both hands, sets it on the palm of his right hand, centers it, balances it. He hefts it up and down slightly, getting the feel of it. Abruptly, he draws back his right arm as far as he can.

There is the crack of the plate breaking against the wall at the foot of his bed and the small wet sound of the scrambled eggs dropping to the floor.

And then he laughs. It is a sound you have never heard. It is something new under the sun. It could cure cancer.

Out in the corridor, the eyes of the head nurse narrow.

"Laughed, did he?"

She writes something down on her clipboard.

A second aide arrives, brings a second breakfast tray, puts it on the nightstand, out of his reach. She looks over at me, shaking her head and making her mouth go. I see that we are to be accomplices.

"I've got to feed you," she says to the man.

"Oh, no you don't," the man says.

"Oh, yes I do," the aide says, "after the way you just did. Nurse says so."

"Get me my shoes," the man says.

"Here's oatmeal," the aide says. "Open." And she touches the spoon to his lower lip.

"I ordered scrambled eggs," says the man.

"That's right," the aide says.

I step forward.

"Is there anything I can do?" I say.

"Who are you?" the man asks.

In the evening I go once more to that ward to make my rounds. The head nurse reports to me that Room 542 is deceased. She has discovered this quite by accident, she says. No, there had been no sound. Nothing. It's a blessing, she says.

I go into his room, a spy looking for secrets. He is still there in his bed. His face is relaxed, grave, dignified. After a while I turn to leave. My gaze sweeps the wall at the foot of the bed, and I see the place where it has been repeatedly washed, where the wall looks very clean and very white.

DOCTOR

Tema Nason

. . . .

Dear Doctor,
How can you calmly light a cigarette when my insides
are retching? How can you calmly cross your legs when I want
to fall to my knees in front of you and beg you to take back
those words, "seriously crippled . . . had hoped for better
results." What am I supposed to do with those words, that's
the trouble, Doctor, you have such a neat way of tying up my
feelings in words . . . KNOTS . . . and put into words it doesn't
sound too bad . . . crippled. A word. A word is not serious. Look
at all the words we have. Does crime sound any worse than
Crimea? But a leg that doesn't work, dammit, is . . . so keep
your damn words. Because to you, words are words . . . but to
me it's my son and his deformed leg and the rest of our lives
. . . all spelled out in that lousy single word, *crippled.*

If I were Mama, I'd burst out crying, I'd cry and cry and cry
until all the water in my body drained up and out of me into
a wet, scaly puddle on the floor as I sit here in this stupid red
plastic chair. Along with the sick feeling inside. How do you
feel, you ask. Sick, I answer. Another word and who the hell
knows what sick stands for. A little under the weather? . . . a
little sniffle? . . . or your whole insides gutted up and stuck
together like rotting slimy oilcloth. If it were Mama, she would
cry and cry and cry and then she'd accept *her tears,* not your

words, her tears are real to her, not your lousy cool English words. . . . *Narren! Fools!* she'd say, reaching into her bag of Old World wisdom. *What do they know? . . .* and from her old bag she'd pull out what she knew she needed to survive . . . and go about doing what she had to . . . . I remember the story she told long ago . . . about Hersch and how when he was an infant, maybe less than a year, how sick he was . . . how his little chest was filled with fluid and he'd cough night and day . . . he was burning up with fever and his eyes dried up into the bony sockets and they were losing him, minute by minute, and the village doctor said, "Mother, let him die in peace. That's the least you can do for the child. It's God's will, Mother," and he reached for the cross he always wore around his neck, for he was a religious man, the kind doctor, and he hated to see the relatives of his patients suffer needlessly. If only they would turn to God! Just so nowadays we turn to our secular gods, our psychiatrists, and they, too, console us with empty words . . . reality, adjustment, face into . . . just recite daily like a litany . . . it'll work. . . .

But Mama didn't listen to the village doctor in Zelve, and she grabbed her black shawl and the baby and wrapped him carefully in many blankets, for it was still winter, and said, "I'm going to Warsaw . . . there must be better doctors there who won't let my baby die."

And I remember her telling us how on that old rattling train to Warsaw, this young woman, my mother, who had never been on a train before or left her tiny village; the baby never stopped crying though he had no strength left and his fever rose higher and the other passengers took pity and pleaded with her. "Take him home," pleaded an old grandmother. "Mother, let him at least die in his own crib," but my mother said, *nyet*, no, no, no, no, no, no, no no no, I'm taking my baby to Warsaw and I will find a doctor who will save my baby's life. Pity, pity, that's what she didn't want, couldn't use. Worthless! Just like this doctor's I'm so sorry. Mrs. Lowenthal, I know how you feel. Empty . . . empty words. Stop it! *You don't know how I feel.*

And when Mama came to the doctor with the crying infant, now so shrunken and almost gone, in her arms, he was a good man, a really good man, and he said to her. "Mother, you were right to bring him here . . . we will try to do all we can for him . . . it's pleurisy . . . Maybe, maybe . . . " And in those long-ago days with no penicillin and no sulfa, they operated . . . and removed a section of his shoulder blade and drained all the blue-white sick fluid in his chest . . . and they carefully sewed him up . . . and Mama stood guard right by his crib . . . she never left him, even though the nurses were gentle and understanding and promised they would take good care of him. "Get some rest, Mother," they urged, but she shook her head . . . "*nyet*, no, no, I must stay. . . . " And the doctor said, "Now it *is* up to God. Pray, Mother."

Six weeks went by . . . and the health flowed back into his body, nourished by Mama's sheer will, and he got well. And at the end of the six weeks the doctor said, "Now you can take him home, Mother. He will be all right. The scar will heal, probably fade . . . but he will always have a scar."

"That's not important," Mama said, "he is living."

And she told us how the trip home was so beautiful. Hersch rested comfortably in her arms and slept, and she looked out the streaked dirty windows, and tiny green buds were showing on the trees, and the long-frozen ground was coming alive with green tips and the green roll of skunk cabbage.

But I sit here saying nothing, struggling to control myself because to cry in this land is unseemly. Not done. Why? Why do I have to play it cool as though I were an American when I'm a Jewish girl who saw my mother cry?

TALE OF A PHYSICIAN

Robert Watson

. . . .

T he young doctor helped his old nurse on with her overcoat and held open the door to the flagstone path that
led to his office. It was winter and Alpine Village was covered
with a foot of fresh glistening snow, glistening now under the
few streetlights on Main Street. The doctor said, "Take care,
Miss Plumb, don't slip on any of the icy patches."

"Good night, Dr. Herndon. It's only half a block."

Dr. Herndon washed his hands, took off his white jacket, and
opened the door to the hall that led past the kitchen, where
he could smell a meat loaf roasting, and into the living room
with its yellow wallpaper and early American maple furniture.

"Hello, there," he said to the baby, who was pushing a toy
car around the playpen.

Then he kissed his buxom wife, more buxom than normal
for she was expecting a second child. She was folding diapers
on the sofa. Mrs. Herndon had been a nurse in the hospital
where he had served his residency. All the young nurses were
wild about Dr. Herndon, his tall, dark good looks marred only
by his thick glasses, but Mary Ann, whose feminine instincts
and timing surpassed the other nurses, landed the doctor. In
short order little Bobby arrived, and the doctor was established
as the only physician in Alpine Village, which, despite its
name, was a lakeside summer resort. Though the doctor would

be especially busy in the summer, Mary Ann would find it enjoyable. She would simply sit all day on the beach with her babies playing in the sand.

The phone rang only once during supper. "A Billy Craddock. Funny voice for a man. Too ill to come to the office. I said you'll stop by after your hospital calls. Twenty-one Lakeside Drive."

"Good meat loaf," said the doctor.

A light snow was beginning to fall when the doctor backed his car out of the driveway. Thank goodness, he thought, I left the chains on. The nearest hospital was ten miles away in Newton, the county seat, and that night the doctor had only one patient to visit, the local plumber, who was recovering from a case of lobar pneumonia. The snow had stopped when he returned to his secondhand black Plymouth, but it still swirled across the roads, covering and uncovering dangerous patches of ice. The doctor drove very slowly.

Twenty-one Lakeside Drive had a Swiss-chalet look about it. The doctor took off his galoshes on the porch, and while he was knocking the snow off them, he saw by the porch light a note protruding from the mailbox. "Please come right in. I am in the bedroom at the top of the stairs."

"Billy Craddock?" He stared down at the mass of long coffee-colored hair and the pale young face.

"Yes, Wilhelmina. Isn't that a disaster of a name. So I'm Billy."

"What's the trouble?" he asked, setting his bag on the dresser and opening it.

"I've been getting these terrible pains in my head. They come in waves so bad I feel sick to my stomach and so dizzy I can hardly stand up. They get so bad that my neck hurts, my shoulders, sides, and chest. The pain moves, but mostly my head."

He popped a thermometer into her mouth and turned on the reading lamp on the table next to her bed. But she didn't stop talking.

"And in between I get these pains down here," she said,

pointing over the blankets in the direction of her lower abdomen. "They started this morning. At first I just thought it was . . . you know what."

"Premenstrual pains?"

"Yes," and she was quiet.

He took her pulse. Both her pulse and her temperature were normal. He looked down her throat, felt the glands in her neck, looked in her ears and up her nose. With his stethoscope he listened first to her back and then to her chest.

"I feel dizzy," she said. She was sitting on the bed with her bare feet on the floor and her white nightgown lowered to her waist. She placed her hand on his shoulder and leaned forward against him to steady herself. She had told him she was alone in the house, but he would have felt more comfortable if a husband or mother had been present.

"You can lie down now. Just pull up your nightgown. I want to examine your stomach. Relax now. Relax your muscles. All right. You can get back under the covers."

He could find nothing wrong. She was tense during the examination, and he could see the muscles in her jaw working as she kept grinding her teeth. "Any gas? How are the bowels?" No, nothing. She was beautiful.

"Where is the bathroom?"

He came back with a glass of water and fetched a bottle of pills from his bag. "Here, take these," he said, handing her two white pills and the glass of water. "Have you been under any great strain lately?" He had noticed black circles under her large brown eyes that never left his.

"No."

"Do you sleep well?"

"Oh, I have a terrible time sleeping," she said, placing the glass of water back on the bedside table. He reached for her hand and turned it over.

"What's this? What's this scar on your wrist?"

Tears filled her eyes. "My husband left me in August. I made it with a razor. Not serious. I guess I just wanted him to feel sorry for me." Her body shook with tears, and she covered her eyes with her arm. The doctor patted her gently twice on the shoulder.

"I'm sorry," he said. "I think you have a migraine headache. Anyway tension. I'll leave you enough pills for a day. You can take two every four hours. I'll call in a prescription for you first thing in the morning."

He stood up, but she reached over and with surprising strength pulled his shoulders down over her with both hands until his face was only a few inches from hers. "I saw you at the gas station once. I don't think you saw me. I'm lonely here and I'm frightened." She leaned forward until their lips were no more than an inch apart. He tried to pull back, but her grip was too strong.

"I'm a doctor," he said. "I'm happily married and have a child and another one on the way."

"I don't want you," she said. "I don't want you that way. I just want you to kiss me. Kiss me."

He kissed her tenderly on the forehead and stood up to go. She reached for his hand and brought it up to her lips and kissed it. Then he felt her teeth—short and somewhat pointed—go through his skin. She held his hand up to her eyes, looked at the blood, and for the first time smiled, a funny odd smile. He raised his bleeding hand about to strike her when with a quick gesture she threw all the covers over the end of the bed. The doctor turned, snapped his bag shut, and said, "Good night, Mrs. Craddock. Don't catch cold."

A small disaster struck in the morning. The old nurse slipped on the ice getting in her milk and broke her hip. His wife was sullen all day. She couldn't help him out, what with the baby and with her own unpredictable morning sickness. As luck would have it, the plumber's niece—he was a widower—had come to Alpine Village to help him out until he got back on his feet. She was twenty years old, a registered nurse, a striking blonde, and a notorious flirt on the beach, as Mrs. Herndon had noticed. She was a knockout in a two-piece bathing suit.

"Viola," said Mrs. Herndon, "is utterly irresponsible. You wouldn't hire her, would you? She would be worse than no one."

In the end the plumber settled it. He didn't have enough money to pay his hospital or the doctor's bills and wouldn't until he got back on his feet. Viola would work for the doctor part-time for nothing. Later on he would pay back Viola. Since the plumber got Mrs. Herndon on the phone and made all the arrangements through her—where would her husband get a nurse in Alpine Village in the dead of winter?—Mrs. Herndon bitterly agreed. Her husband, she believed, had had many affairs with the nurses during his residency. She didn't trust men. But in two months the old nurse would be back on the job. Maybe that wouldn't be too bad, Mrs. Herndon thought as she took a call at supper that night and wrote down, without paying attention to what she was doing, a message for the doctor to stop at Billy Craddock's. The pains were worse. That damned flirt Viola, she thought.

"Have you lost any weight lately?" inquired the doctor. He looked down into Billy's red-rimmed eyes. She's a neurotic, he thought. Having a breakdown? Billy kept rubbing his side with her hand.

"Doctor," she said, "I don't have cancer, do I? I felt better when you kissed me on the forehead."

"I think you had better get another physician," he said.

"No, please, please. You must stop again tomorrow night. I'll go out of my mind if you don't." She lay back on the pillows and closed her eyes. "Just—just tell me I'm beautiful."

"You're beautiful," he said.

For the next two days he was tense and nervous, his wife was grim, and Viola talked without stopping. On his fourth visit to Billy Craddock, he told her to remove her nightgown. He shed his own clothes and took her standing up next to the bed. There were no more phone calls from Billy, and very little chance that the doctor's car would be seen on the two or three evenings a week he would call. The houses near Billy's were all closed up for the winter. Besides, Billy's driveway circled the house so that he would park in the darkness near the back door.

In her loud raucous voice Viola would call the female patients "honey" and the male patients "handsome." "All right now, handsome, strip to the waist," her voice would ring through the walls of the examination room. She was forever patting the doctor on his back and on his hand and forever patting the patients. Viola looked tired. The patients loved her because her chatter took their minds off their troubles. The doctor's wife hated her, and her jealousy expanded with the size of her stomach. And Mary Ann knew women too. They couldn't keep their hands off him. Wedding rings? Children? For a woman after a man they simply didn't exist. And the hypocrisy! Viola always cooing after the baby. And asking how she felt. And offering to cook dinner on the nights she didn't feel up to it. That bitch. That no good . . . cunt. That's what she is. She talks about that boyfriend of hers in Newton. The football coach. But who would have a football coach when a physician could be had? She could hear them joking now, jokes about her probably. Then she heard doors close and the doctor come in for his dinner.

By the end of February, after practicing in Alpine Village for only seven months, the doctor found himself very busy. A flu epidemic had swept the state, leaving many of his patients with secondary infections—earaches, respiratory troubles, and general exhaustion. And also the doctor carried around with him a feeling of inexperience, a fear of making mistakes, and above all a distaste for his affair with Billy. What he feared most of all was Billy. What was she up to? What would she do? When he would tell her he could only stay a minute or two because of the pressure of calls or claim that he was dead tired and had to get sleep, she would frown, purse her lips, and say nothing until he left—or stayed, which was more often the case. No longer did she thrust her body at him and cry out in pleasure. "I think," he said, "we should break it off. It's not healthy for you to live here alone in winter. You've got nothing to do. I'm very fond of you, but I don't think it's good for me either."

"Nonsense. Men have mistresses. What you are saying is that you don't like me. I have no place to go and no money. My husband has given me this house. I'm not trained for anything. Besides, I don't feel up to it. If you leave me, I'd just as soon die. You understand me. You're all I have."

In March the baby came—a healthy girl they named Matilda. Miss Plumb, whose hip was mending more slowly than expected, sent word that she planned to retire. His wife fell into the deep depressions of postpartum, fell into a complete negligence, a hopelessness.

Mary Ann went down on her knees to him. "I can't stand it. You've got to get rid of Viola. For my sake. If you love me at all, get rid of Viola."

"Of course I love you. Don't be foolish. But how can we manage without her? Not just me, but you." The doctor was alluding to the house, which Mary Ann had abandoned. Dishes were piled in the sink, the bathroom smelled of unwashed diapers, dust rolls were everywhere. Two or three times a week Viola would put the wash in the machine, wash the dishes, and vacuum the house. "I'll put another ad in the paper. But then, of course, I have hired a nurse, but she doesn't graduate until June. Can't you wait until June?"

"Another young one. Another young one," was all Mary Ann would say.

"Doctor," said Viola the next morning with no preliminary pats or flattering phrases, "I want to give my notice today."

"What? Why?"

"Mrs. Herndon called up both my uncle and my fiancé and said that you and I were having an affair. Uncle and Fred are furious."

"Didn't you tell them the truth?"

"Of course I did. They're worried what other people might say. I know your wife is sick, but she had no right doing that."

"I know. I know," said the doctor. "But what can I do?" He was pointing to the telephone that had been ringing throughout their conversation. I can't get another nurse. Miss Plumb is spending the rest of the winter with her sister in Georgia."

"I'm sorry," said Viola. "I can't get mixed up in a mess like this. If it weren't for Fred, I'd stick by you. I'm real sorry for you. I'm sure you can find someone, somewhere."

The rumor must somehow have leaked out in Alpine Village. Perhaps Viola's sudden departure from the doctor's office with no explanation, no reason given, gave rise to the rumor. The doctor thought he could hire a high-school girl or a housewife to answer the phone, keep the records, and help his wife. No luck. But for an exorbitant wage, he finally hired a fat, sullen woman to drive over from Newton. She acted as if every patient in the waiting room or over the telephone was an imposition. She was better than no one, he supposed.

Dr. Herndon had noticed on his last visit to Billy that she kept bumping into things. A lamp. The bathroom door. The dresser. "How do you feel?"

"It's probably nothing," she said. "I really don't feel well at all. Continuous headache and dizziness. And my left eye feels funny, as if I weren't seeing out of it. I keep dropping things. But I keep telling myself it's all my imagination. Tell me I'm beautiful and that you love me."

"You're beautiful and I love you, but let me see that eye."

He had been careless, so careless, so certain that her aches and pains were psychosomatic, that she had lost her husband because of her neurosis and had trapped him. He had felt in her dimly lit bedroom, where he always saw her either in a nightgown or nude, that she was acting out sexual fantasies, that her bedroom and himself in the bedroom were merely an extension of the fantasizing side of her mind. He said nothing until he had buttoned up his topcoat.

"At eight o'clock tomorrow morning I am driving you to Newton Hospital to make some tests I can't do here. Don't worry. I think we may really be able to do something about your headaches and that eye."

"It's cancer. I've got cancer."

"Don't be ridiculous," he said. Yet as he drove home in the brisk air of early spring, he felt both relief and more apprehension. He felt relief that he would be rid of her, apprehension over the state of her health.

Her parents drove up from Newark—he didn't see them—

and took her from the Newton Hospital to the Medical Center in New York, where she was successfully operated on for a brain tumor—benign. Then silence, thank heavens, he thought. The fruit trees were blooming, and if only Mary Ann would improve, his life might be not only tolerable but pleasant.

Mary Ann did not improve; if anything she grew worse. She would have fits of crying over her "uselessness" and being a "burden" to him. She would have fits of crying because she didn't love her children. She would have fits of both crying and rage because of his infidelity to her. Maybe she had been wrong about Viola, though most likely not, but there was someone, maybe several she knew. In late April, to help set Mary Ann's mind at rest, the doctor took her in the car with him on his evening calls, which in this season were mercifully few. It did no good. Mary Ann said it was a trick and that he could be unfaithful in the daytime as well as at night. She would sit blubbering in the car. Her appetite, though, never failed her, and she grew heavy and hardly bothered with her clothes. They grew tight and the skirts were too short with very uneven hems.

Surprisingly Miss Plumb appeared in his office one day in early May. She couldn't bear sitting around in her sister's house in Georgia all day with nothing to do. Could she have her job back, if only on a part-time basis? He fired the fat bitch from Newton that very day.

"Doctor," said Miss Plumb a week later, "you'll think I'm an awful old busybody. I'm seventy-eight years old, and though I may not look it I never led a sheltered life. I'll put it bluntly: you had better do something about your wife. It's none of my business, but you are so tired from tending to her—well, it can't keep up. You'll burst at the seams."

"What can I do," said the doctor in annoyance.

"I've had a lot of professional experience in these cases. You had better send her to a sanatorium where she can get good psychiatric treatment."

He looked at her with some relief. "You really think so?"

"Yes, you can't treat her. If something isn't done, you'll both be dragged down. One of you has to stay afloat.

"Don't you worry, Mary Ann, the only other woman will be me," she told her. "You can rest assured of that. Your trouble is that you are worn out having two babies so soon. Just think of the sanatorium as a good vacation. Get all your strength back."

"Thank Heaven for Miss Plumb," said the doctor to himself during Mary Anna's first week in the sanatorium. At last he felt rested, free from strain, and had regained some confidence in his abilities. His last patient had just left, and Miss Plumb was putting away medical histories in the file.

Mary Ann returned home cured. In short order she had both children in her complete charge, did the housework and laundry meticulously, and renewed her own wardrobe with purchases and alterations at her own sewing machine. Though still on the buxom side, she could no longer be called fat. Every week she went to the beauty parlor in Newton to have her hair done, and every other week she played bridge with the Episcopal Women's Auxiliary. Every Wednesday evening Mary Ann and the doctor had dinner together at the Alpine Inn. On Saturday evenings, they either accepted invitations, entertained themselves, or went to a movie.

In mid-June Barbara, who had just finished her nurses' training, joined Miss Plumb in the office. Barbara was just as pretty as Viola, though more intelligent and serious-minded—she had a lonely look about her, as if she was waiting for someone to come to her rescue.

Mary Ann since her return from the sanatorium had never once alluded to the doctor in connection with another woman. In fact, though only the doctor knew, Mary Ann had closed and locked a steel door between them. She never complained, seemed very happy, but would never discuss anything with him but the children, her plans for a garden, her bridge club. The only time she ever seemed annoyed with him was when he brought up his medical practice, his patients, Miss Plumb, or Barbara. She would hear nothing about his professional life, which occupied eighty-five percent of his time. Mary Ann was interested, or appeared interested, only in herself and her own sphere. She was cured, but he was living with a stranger.

The doctor felt very much alone. He didn't mingle easily with the men in Alpine Village, either the natives or summer visitors. For one thing, he didn't play golf, and for another he didn't play poker. After his second year of practice in Alpine Village, an older doctor—in his late fifties—who owned a summer cottage there gave up his city practice for the slow pace of a country one. Dr. Herndon's practice then dwindled during the winter months, not enough so that he couldn't pay his bills but enough so that he had time on his hands. Mary Ann, though, kept very busy. She joined the Red Cross and took a course in pastel drawing, for which she had a knack. Half the day, it seemed to him, she was chatting on the telephone with her friends.

In the evenings either after his calls or more usually just to get out of the house, the doctor would drive out past Lakeside Drive and turn left up High Peak Road, a steep and twisty road, to the very top of High Peak. From there he could look down on moonlit nights and see all of Alpine Village and Alpine Lake. On all but cloudy nights he could look down and see the lights of the village and the cottages around the lake that were occupied. Over the months the doctor's thoughts kept turning back to Billy, her long coffee-colored hair, her look of pain as she kept saying, "Tell me I am beautiful. Tell me you love me." She was so beautiful. He could see the rise and fall of her breasts under the white nightgown as she sobbed. "You are beautiful and I love you," he had said. "I love you."

On a hot July afternoon, a Wednesday and the doctor's afternoon off, he decided to spend a few minutes on the beach, just to sit there, not to swim. The doctor didn't know how to swim. Mary Ann and some of her friends from the church had taken their children on a picnic lunch and from there were going to the horse show.

He recognized Billy from the back. She was sitting on the little sandy beach that was surrounded by lawn and willow trees. It was early and she was the only one on the beach, though he could make out someone sunning on the raft about a hundred yards from the shore. The doctor thought of turning around, but she had already seen him. A quick turn of her head, and then she looked back down at the book she was reading. She was wearing a white one-piece bathing suit and large sunglasses. It was more than three years now since he had seen her. The house on Lakeside Drive had been empty all this time. When he sat down in the sand about ten feet from her, she looked at him but said nothing.

"You certainly look well," he said. "How are you?"

"I've been fine," she said in a flat voice. Then after a long pause, "How have you been?"

"Fine. Up for the summer?"

"No. Just a few days. Jim and I—he's out on the raft—are getting the cottage ready. We're selling it."

"Oh, I see. Jim?"

"Yes. Jim's my husband. You see after my operation he came back. As you know I had been acting irrationally, and once he learned that I wasn't really such a bitch, that there was a physical cause, he came back and we resumed our regular life."

Although the doctor kept speaking, he had sunk back into himself. "Too bad you have to sell the cottage. Nice place here in the summer."

"We don't have to sell it. I want to sell it. It holds bad memories for me."

"Oh, yes. Being so ill and alone there."

"No, Doctor. I'm selling it because of you."

"Of me? I don't really understand." But he did.

"Doctor, you took advantage of me when I was very sick. I feel guilty with my husband and I can never tell him."

"I thought your husband had run away with another woman. That's what you told me. And really you were the one who made the advances. You persisted."

"Doctor, Doctor. My husband had good reason to run off with another woman, the way I behaved. He didn't know I was really sick. You're a doctor. You knew I was sick and irresponsible. No matter what I said or how I acted, you as a physician should have controlled the situation. How many sick women, Doctor, hysterical and frightened and lonely women, have you slept with?"

"None. Though you probably won't believe it. Don't you

remember saying over and over again, 'Tell me I'm beautiful, tell me you love me'?"

"Yes. I do. I feel nauseated every time I remember. I feel nauseated now. I love my husband."

"I'm sorry," said the doctor, who wanted nothing more than to say then and there that he loved her. He stood up and brushed the sand from his pants.

She looked down at her book. Without another word between them, he walked off the beach, under the willow trees, up the grassy slope to the small parking lot where his car stood. The metal was so hot he could have fried eggs on the hood. "You're beautiful. I love you," he said to himself. He drove back to his office, where perhaps someone would phone in an emergency call.

FATHERING

Bharati Mukherjee

. . . .

Eng stands just inside our bedroom door, her fidgety fist on the doorknob, which Sharon, in a sulk, polished to a gleam yesterday afternoon.

"I'm starved," she says.

I know a sick little girl when I see one. I brought the twins up without much help ten years ago. Eng's got a high fever. Brownish stains stiffen the nap of her terry robe. Sour smells fill the bedroom.

"For God's sake leave us alone," Sharon mutters under the quilt. She turns away from me. We bought the quilt at a garage sale in Rock Springs the Sunday two years ago when she moved in. "Talk to her."

Sharon works on this near-marriage of ours. I'll hand it to her, she really does. I knead her shoulders, and I say, "Easy, easy," though I really hate it when she treats Eng like a deaf-mute. "My girl speaks English, remember?"

Eng can outcuss any freckle-faced kid on the block. Someone in the killing fields must have taught her. Maybe her mama, the honeyest-skinned bar girl with the tiniest feet in Saigon. I was an errand boy with the Combined Military Intelligence. I did the whole war on Dexedrine. Vietnam didn't happen, and I'd put it behind me in marriage and fatherhood and teaching high school. Ten years later came the screw-ups

135

with the marriage, the job, women, the works. Until Eng popped up in my life, I really believed it didn't happen.

"Come here, sweetheart," I beg my daughter. I sidle closer to Sharon, so there'll be room under the quilt for Eng.

"I'm starved," she complains from the doorway. She doesn't budge. The robe and hair are smelling something fierce. She doesn't show any desire to cuddle. She must be sick. She must have thrown up all night. Sharon throws the quilt back. "Then go raid the refrigerator like a normal kid," she snaps.

Once upon a time Sharon used to be a cheerful, accommodating woman. It isn't as if Eng was dumped on us out of the blue. She knew I was tracking my kid. Coming to terms with the past was Sharon's idea. I don't know what happened to *that* Sharon. "For all you know, Jason," she'd said, "the baby died of malaria or something." She said, "Go on, find out and deal with it." She said she could handle being a stepmother— better a fresh chance with some orphan off the streets of Saigon than with my twins from Rochester. My twins are being raised in some organic-farming lesbo commune. Their mother breeds Nubian goats for a living. "Come get in bed with us, baby. Let Dad feel your forehead. You burning up with fever?"

"She isn't hungry, I think she's sick," I tell Sharon, but she's already tugging her sleeping mask back on. "I think she's just letting us know she hurts."

I hold my arms out wide for Eng to run into. If I could, I'd suck the virus right out of her. In the jungle, VC mamas used to do that. Some nights we'd steal right up to a hootch—just a few of us intense sons of bitches on some special mission— and the women would be at their mumbo jumbo. They'd be sticking coins and amulets into napalm burns.

"I'm hungry, Dad." It comes out as a moan. Okay, she doesn't run into my arms, but at least she's come as far in as the foot of our bed. "Dad, let's go down to the kitchen. Just you and me."

I am about to let that pass, though I can feel Sharon's body go into weird little jerks and twitches when my baby adds with emphatic viciousness, "Not her, Dad. We don't want her with us in the kitchen."

"She loves you," I protest. Love—not spite—makes Eng so territorial; that's what I want to explain to Sharon. She's a sick, frightened, foreign kid, for Chrissake. "Don't you, Sharon? Sharon's concerned about you."

But Sharon turns over on her stomach. "You know what's wrong with you, Jase? You can't admit you're being manipulated. You can't cut through the 'frightened-foreign-kid' shit."

Eng moves closer. She comes up to the side of my bed, but doesn't touch the hand I'm holding out. She's a fighter.

"I feel fire-hot, Dad. My bones feel pain."

"Sharon?" I want to deserve this woman. "Sharon, I'm so sorry." It isn't anybody's fault. You need uppers to get through peacetimes, too.

"Dad. Let's go. Chop-chop."

"You're too sick to keep food down, baby. Curl up in here. Just for a bit?"

"I'd throw up, Dad."

"I'll carry you back to your room. I'll read you a story, okay?"

Eng watches me real close as I pull the quilt off. "You got any scars you haven't shown me yet? My mom had a big scar on one leg. Shrapnel. Boom boom. I got scars. See? I got lots of bruises."

I scoop up my poor girl and rush her, terry robe flapping, to her room which Sharon fixed up with white girlish furniture in less complicated days. Waiting for Eng was good. Sharon herself said it was good for our relationship. "Could you bring us some juice and aspirin?" I shout from the hallway.

"Aspirin isn't going to cure Eng," I hear Sharon yell. "I'm going to call Dr. Kearns."

Downstairs I hear Sharon on the phone. She isn't talking flu viruses. She's talking social workers and shrinks. My girl isn't crazy; she's picked up a bug in school as might anyone else.

"The child's arms are covered with bruises," Sharon is saying. "Nothing major. They look like . . . well, they're sort of tiny circles and welts." There's nothing for a while. Then she says, "Christ! No, Jason can't do enough for her! That's not what I'm saying! What's happening to this country? You think we're perverts? What I'm saying is the girl's doing it to herself."

"Who are you talking to?" I ask from the top of the stairs. "What happened to the aspirin?"

I lean as far forward over the railing as I dare so I can see what Sharon's up to. She's getting into her coat and boots. She's having trouble with buttons and snaps. In the bluish light of the foyer's broken chandelier, she looks old, harrowed, depressed. What have I done to her?

"What's going on?" I plead. "You deserting me?"

"Don't be so fucking melodramatic. I'm going to the mall to buy some aspirin."

"How come we don't have any in the house?"

"Why are you always picking on me?"

"Who was that on the phone?"

"So now you want me to account for every call and every trip?" She ties an angry knot into her scarf. But she tells me. "I was talking to Meg Kearns. She says Dr. Kearns has gone hunting for the day."

"Great!"

"She says he has his beeper on him."

I hear the back door stick and Sharon swear. She's having trouble with the latch. "Jiggle it gently," I shout, taking the stairs two at a time. But before I can come down, her Nissan backs out of the parking apron.

Back upstairs I catch Eng in the middle of a dream or delirium. "They got Grandma!" she screams. She goes very rigid in bed. It's a four-poster with canopy and ruffles and stuff that Sharon put on her MasterCard. The twins slept on bunk beds. With the twins it was different, totally different. Dr. Spock can't be point man for Eng, for us.

"She bring me food," Eng's screaming. "She bring me food from the forest. They shoot Grandma! Bastards!"

"Eng?" I don't dare touch her. I don't know how.

"You shoot my grandmother?" She whacks the air with her bony arms. Now I see the bruises, the small welts all along the insides of her arms. Some have to be weeks old, they're that yellow. The twins' scrapes and cuts never turned that ochre. I can't help wondering if maybe Asian skin bruises differently from ours, even though I want to say skin is skin; especially hers is skin like mine.

"I want to be with Grandma. Grandma loves me. I want to be ghost. I don't want to get better."

I read to her. I read to her because good parents are supposed to read to their kids laid up sick in bed. I want to do it right. I want to be a good father. I read from a sci-fi novel that Sharon must have picked up. She works in a camera store in the mall, right next to a B. Dalton. I read three pages out loud, then I read four chapters to myself because Eng's stopped up her ears. Aliens have taken over small towns all over the country. Idaho, Nebraska: no state is safe from aliens.

Some time after two, the phone rings. Since Sharon doesn't answer it on the second ring, I know she isn't back. She carries a cordless phone everywhere around the house. In the movies, when cops have bad news to deliver, they lean on your doorbell; they don't call. Sharon will come back when she's ready. We'll make up. Things will get back to normal.

"Jason?"

I know Dr. Kearns's voice. He saw the twins through the usual immunizations.

"I have Sharon here. She'll need a ride home. Can you drive over?"

"God! What's happened?"

"Nothing to panic about. Nothing physical. She came for a consultation."

"Give me a half-hour. I have to wrap Eng real warm so I can drag her out in this miserable weather."

"Take your time. This way I can take a look at Eng, too."

"What's wrong with Sharon?"

"She's a little exercised about a situation. I gave her a sedative. See you in a half-hour."

I ease delirious Eng out of the overdecorated four-poster,

prop her against my body while I wrap a blanket around her. She's a tiny thing, but she feels stiff and heavy, a sleepwalking mummy. Her eyes are dry-bright, strange.

It's a sunny winter day, and the evergreens in the front yard are glossy with frost. I press Eng against my chest as I negotiate the front steps. Where the gutter leaks, the steps feel spongy. The shrubs and bushes my ex-wife planted clog the front path. I've put twenty years into this house. The steps, the path, the house all have a right to fall apart.

I'm thirty-eight. I've let a lot of people down already.

The inside of the van is deadly cold. Mid-January ice mottles the windshield. I lay the bundled-up child on the long seat behind me and wait for the engine to warm up. It feels good with the radio going and the heat coming on. I don't want the ice on the windshield to melt. Eng and I are safest in the van.

In the rear-view mirror, Eng's wrinkled lips begin to move. "Dad, can I have a quarter?"

"May I, kiddo," I joke.

There's all sorts of junk in the pockets of my parka. Buckshot, dimes and quarters for the vending machine, a Blistex.

"What do you need it for, sweetheart?"

Eng's quick. Like the street kids in Saigon who dove for cigarettes and sticks of gum. She's loosened the blanket folds around her. I watch her tuck the quarter inside her wool mitt. She grins. "Thanks, soldier."

At Dr. Kearns's, Sharon is lying unnaturally slack-bodied on the lone vinyl sofa. Her coat's neatly balled up under her neck, like a bolster. Right now she looks amiable, docile. I don't think she exactly recognizes me, although later she'll say she did. All that stuff about Kearns going hunting must have been a lie. Even the stuff about having to buy aspirin in the mall. She was planning all along to get here.

"What's wrong?"

"It's none of my business, Jason, but you and Sharon might try an honest-to-goodness heart-to-heart." Then he makes a sign to me to lay Eng on the examining table. "We don't look so bad," he says to my daughter. Then he excuses himself and goes into a glass-walled cubicle.

Sharon heaves herself into a sitting position of sorts on the sofa. "Everything was fine until she got here. Send her back, Jase. If you love me, send her back." She's slouched so far forward, her pointed, sweatered breasts nearly touch her corduroy pants. She looks helpless, pathetic. I've brought her to this state. Guilt, not love, is what I feel.

I want to comfort Sharon, but my daughter with the wild, grieving pygmy face won't let go of my hand. "She's bad, Dad. Send *her* back."

Dr. Kearns comes out of the cubicle balancing a sample bottle of pills or caplets on a flattened palm. He has a boxer's tough, squarish hands. "Miraculous stuff, this," he laughs. "But first we'll stick our tongue out and say *ahh.* Come on, open wide."

Eng opens her mouth real wide, then brings her teeth together, hard, on Dr. Kearns's hand. She leaps erect on the examining table, tearing the disposable paper sheet with her toes. Her tiny, funny toes are doing a frantic dance. "Don't let him touch me, Grandma!"

"He's going to make you all better, baby." I can't pull my alien child down, I can't comfort her. The twins had diseases with easy names, diseases we knew what to do with. The thing is, I never felt for them what I feel for her.

"Don't let him touch me, Grandma!" Eng's screaming now. She's hopping on the table and screaming. "Kill him, Grandma! Get me out of here, Grandma!"

"Baby, it's all right."

But she looks through me and the country doctor as though we aren't here, as though we aren't pulling at her to make her lie down.

"Lie back like a good girl," Dr. Kearns commands.

But Eng is listening to other voices. She pulls her mitts off with her teeth, chucks the blanket, the robe, the pajamas to the floor; then, naked, hysterical, she presses the quarter I gave her deep into the soft flesh of her arm. She presses and presses that coin, turning it in nasty half-circles until blood starts to pool under the skin.

"Jason, grab her at the knees. Get her back down on the table."

From the sofa, Sharon moans. "See, I told you the child was crazy. She hates me. She's possessive about Jason."

The doctor comes at us with his syringe. He's sedated Sharon; now he wants to knock out my kid with his cures.

"Get the hell out, you bastard!" Eng yells. *"Vamos!* Bang bang!" She's pointing her arm like a semiautomatic, taking out Sharon, then the doctor. My Rambo. "Old way is good way. Money cure is good cure. When they shoot my grandma, you think pills do her any good? You Yankees, please go home." She looks straight at me. "Scram, Yankee bastard!"

Dr. Kearns has Eng by the wrist now. He has flung the quarter I gave her on the floor. Something incurable is happening to my women.

Then, as in fairy tales, I know what has to be done. "Coming, pardner!" I whisper. "I got no end of coins." I jiggle the change in my pocket. I jerk her away from our enemies. My Saigon kid and me: we're a team. In five minutes we'll be safely away in the cold chariot of our van.

FAMILY AND FRIENDS

. . . .

ROTH'S DEADMAN

Joe David Bellamy

· · · · · · · · · · · · · · · · · ·

The deadman's head was rotated slightly toward the window, and the desultory afternoon, the sun hard on the trees beside the parking lot and the sprinklers working in the grass, encroached upon the room in unbroken vividness and multiformity. The plastic intravenous tube was still taped at the ankle, the swollen yellow ankle, yellow and swollen as the face and neck of the man, fifty-four years old according to his wrist band, now dead, admitted three days previously, alive upon arrival, two days in a coma, and gone now ten minutes before Roth could get there to see it happen.

The chart in the nurse's station said the deadman in 117 was: J. B. Houk; business executive; L. R. Downing, Inc.; divorced, two children; possibly alcoholic.

Roth, the new orderly, had often come to stand quietly behind the curtain and watch the phenomenon of J. B. Houk before he died. Roth would stand over the bed and wonder what kind of man J. B. Houk was. The barrel chest of the man heaved irregularly, and his body always appeared to be sucking dextrose from the intravenous tube, drawing in the liquid with ruthless energy. There was something vaguely brutal or unscrupulous in the face, lines about the mouth fixed through time into an automatic hypocritical grimace of benevolence displayed for some selfish end. The hair was pure white above the jaundiced face—some might have called him a distinguished-looking man—and the eyes had been blue, very light blue and surprisingly transparent when Roth first saw them, before J. B. Houk closed his eyes that second day and allowed his body to labor on unburdened by consciousness.

Ray was already stripping clothes out of the closet and folding them up at the foot of the bed. "What should I do?" Roth said.

"I was waiting till you got here to do the body," Ray said. He brought a small suitcase out of the closet and a scarlet-patterned bathrobe on a hanger and placed the clothes he had finished folding into the suitcase, then the bathrobe, exposing the baldspot in his flattop as he bent down. "We'll have to take care of all these belongings," Ray said, pointing to the night-stand. "I'm supposed to show you how to finish him up so you can do it yourself next time."

"Will we have to take him downstairs?"

"No, Scobie's will be here in a few minutes. They'll take care of him. We don't usually store them here at the hospital." Roth visualized the door to the morgue, identical to the other doors he passed every afternoon on the basement floor after punching his time card except for the black lettering on it (he might have expected that kind of door to be made of stone or heavy metal).

Ray handed him a paper bag, and Roth went to the night-stand and opened the drawer. Inside was a pair of glasses without a case, a gold wristwatch, wallet, set of car keys, ball-point pen, four or five packs of matches from a cocktail joint, two large twenty-five-cent cigars, and a circular indexed marker for locating appropriate Biblical passages "when in doubt," "when laden with temptation," "when suffering ill health," etc. Roth placed the articles carefully in the open bag like packed groceries. In the cabinet section of the nightstand was a Gideon Bible and a dog-eared pile of magazines, a blur of red-margined covers with words like "consumer" and "world" on them—graphs, statistics, and pictures of other businessmen. Roth scooped them up and laid them in the open suitcase with the folded paper bag.

"Miss Trigg said to be sure not to disturb Mr. Tilney," Ray whispered. "He's liable to have another cardiac." Roth reached back and pulled the curtain taut that separated the two beds in the room, wondering for a moment what the frightened unknown little man who lay two yards away might be thinking.

"He's been playing possum, I think," Ray whispered. The bedsprings squeaked at this, and Ray chuckled nervously.

"Thinks it might be a bad omen. They're likely to start going three at a time, you know." Roth shrugged.

"Now," Ray said, "the first thing you do is remove any dentures he might have, close his mouth so his jaw won't freeze open, and get his head straight on the pillow, nose up—otherwise you might get a blue cheek."

"Right."

"You can imagine how a blue cheek would go over with the funeral home." Ray quickly inserted his fingers in the half-opened mouth, pushed the tongue back, brought his hands out again almost immediately, and closed the jaw with his palm. Then he gripped the head above the hairline and turned it counterclockwise away from the window. The head stayed where he put it.

"He hasn't got any false teeth."

"Good."

"Notice how I was careful not to touch the skin except where I had to. Wherever you touch him, that part's going to turn color, so you've got to be careful."

"How will they get this yellow out of him? He seems pretty discolored already."

"They have ways. Yellow's easier than blue, and yellow's not our fault. They'll have him laid out looking like the picture of health. Don't worry. He'll be the healthiest-looking man at the funeral."

"Shouldn't we get this intravenous out?" Ray nodded.

"It doesn't matter much if you touch him there because nobody sees that." Ray quickly unraveled the bandage at the ankle and was extracting the needle. Roth unhooked the dextrose bottle to give him slack, scrutinizing the greenish underwater effigy of his face reflected from the glass container, his head weirdly suspended above the starched hospital shirt.

Just then Roth heard a sound of rubber-soled shoes shrieking on the vinyl of the outer hall. The door of the room across the hall was slightly ajar, but nothing was visible but the door itself, surrounded by the immaculate tile walls of the corridor. Then Miss Trigg, the head nurse, came shrieking through the door frame. Roth and Ray started like grave robbers.

"The family's here to visit," she said. "Have you got him ready? Dr. Shantril hasn't told them yet. He's on his way down."

A brown-haired woman appeared in the hallway, and Miss Trigg blushed and turned to look at the body. The suitcase was still lying open next to it on the bed, and the bony feet and ankles, bruised and purple from the intravenous, were sticking out where the sheet was pulled up. The body was uncovered above the waist.

"He's not quite ready yet," Ray said.

Roth's hand was gripping the iron barrel of the intravenous rack. He could see the woman pause in the doorway and speak to someone out of sight. Miss Trigg yanked the sheet, covering the toes, and quickly tucked it in across the bottom. Ray was reaching toward the suitcase, still clutching the ankle bandage, when Roth saw the woman start to move.

"She's coming in," Roth said.

"I'm sorry," Miss Trigg said, partially blocking the woman at the foot of Mr. Tilney's bed, "you'll have to wait until the doctor arrives." Two girls, one about twelve, one about sixteen, had come in behind the woman. They looked at Miss Trigg expectantly.

"Has there been any change?" the woman said. The sixteen-year-old girl was watching Roth as he wheeled the intravenous rack against the wall. She had brown fluffy hair down to her shoulders. Ray brought out the closed suitcase and crossed behind Miss Trigg and laid it on the chair. Miss Trigg seemed to be at a loss for words. The older girl gave her a frightened look and suddenly stepped around her and planted herself beside the deadman's bed. She seemed to rise up on the balls of her feet.

"The doctor should be here any minute, Mrs. Houk," Miss Trigg said. "I'm sorry." They were all looking at the body now.

The woman's expression was haggard, resigned, immediately resigned, faintly disgusted. "I'll be all right," she said. Then the older girl threw herself upon the swollen, yellow man and desperately kissed the rigid face. Her back heaved up and down.

"Oh, Daddy," she sobbed. "Oh, Daddy, Daddy."

BY THAT I MEAN ANGINA PECTORIS

Gregory Burnham

. . . .

I braced myself. By that I mean I expected the worst. I opened the big front door. By that I mean nothing would ever be the same. Nurses flitted about peripherally. By that I mean I didn't care about them. I felt as if I had no body. By that I mean I was preoccupied with the reason I was there. I asked a green wall for directions. By that I mean I was so disoriented I didn't know what I was doing. Doors opened and closed both ways. By that I mean I was unable to determine if I was coming or going. The hour was white. By that I mean time was especially relative in that building. I understood the way. By that I mean I tracked down the right room with a sense I didn't know I had. Nurses smoked and their smoke seeped through the crack of the lounge door into the corridor. By that I mean they were relaxing between patients. I stepped in and said the name of my father. By that I mean I inquired as to his current condition. Smoke paused. By that I mean no answer was immediately forthcoming, even though they all knew the answer. Our family doctor rose from his chair and glided over to me in his white coat like an angel. By that I mean I suddenly knew the plaid bow tie he always wore was no joke. He quietly offered some probable cause, and some medication to calm my mother. By that I mean there was nothing he could do.

HOW TO WIN

Rosellen Brown

· · · · · · · · · · · · · · · · · ·

All they need at school is permission on a little green card that says, *Keep this child at bay. Muffle him, tie his hands, his arms to his ankles, anything at all. Distance, distance. Dose him.* And they gave themselves permission. They never even mentioned a doctor, and their own certified bureaucrat in tweed (does he keep a badge in his pocket like the cops?) drops by the school twice a year for half a day. But I insisted on a doctor. And did and did, had to, because Howard keeps repeating vaguely that he is "within the normal range of boyish activity."

"But I live with it, all day every day."

"It? Live with *it?*"

Well, Howard can be as holy as he likes, I am his mother and I will not say "him." Him is the part I know, Christopher my first child and first son, the boy who was a helpless warm mound once in a blue nightie tied at the bottom to keep his toes in. ("God, Margaret, you are dramatic and sentimental and sloppy. How about being realistic for a change?") "It" is what races around my room at night, a bat, pulling down the curtain cornice, knocking over the lamps, tearing the petals off the flowers and stomping them, real or fake, to a powder.

Watch Christopher take a room sometime; that's the word for it, like an army subduing a deserted plain. He stands in the doorway always for one extra split-split second, straining his shoulders down as though he's hitching himself to some machine, getting into harness. He has no hips, and round little six-year-old shoulders that look frail but are made of welded steel that has no give when you grab them. Then what does he see ahead of him? I'm no good at guessing. The room is an animal asleep, trusting the air, its last mistake. (See, I am sympathetic to the animal.) He leaps on it and leaves it disemboweled, then turns his dark eyes to me where I stand—when I stand, usually I'm dervishing around trying to stop the bloodshed—and they ask me, Where did it go? What happened? Who killed this thing, it was just breathing, I wanted to *play* with it. Christopher. When you're not here to look at me I have to laugh at your absurd powers. You are incontinent, you leak energy. As for me, I gave birth to someone else's child.

There is a brochure inside the brown bottle that the doctor assigned us, very gay, full-color, busy with children riding their bicycles right through patches of daffodils, sleeping square in the middle of their pillows, doing their homework with a hazy expression to be attributed to concentration, not medication. NONADDICTIVE! NO SIGNIFICANT SIDE EFFECTS! Dosage should decrease by or around puberty. Counterindications epilepsy, heart and circulatory complications, severe myopia and related eye problems. See *Journal of Pediatric Medicine,* III 136, F'71; *Pharmacology Bulletin,* v. 798, 18, pp. 19–26, D'72. CAUTION: DO NOT ALLOW CHILDREN ACCESS TO PILLS! SPECIAL FEATURE: U-LOK-IT CAP! REMEMBER, TEACH YOUR CHILD THE ETIQUETTE OF THE MEDICINE CABINET!

I know how he dreams me. I know because I dream his dreams. He runs to hide in me. Battered by the stick of the old dark, he comes fast, hiccoughing terror. By the time I am up, holding him, it has hobbled off, it must be, into his memory. I've pulled on a robe, I spread my arms—do they look winged or webbed?—to pull him out of himself, hide him, swear the witch is nowhere near. He doesn't go to his father. But he won't look at my face.

It was you! He looks up at me finally and says nothing, but I see him thinking. So: *I* was the witch, with a club behind my bent back. I the hundred-stalked flower with webbed branches. I with the flayed face held in my two hands like a bloody towel. Then how can I help him?

I whisper to him, wordless; just a music. He answers, "Mama." It is a faint knocking, through layers of dirt, through flowers.

His sister Jody will dream those dreams, and all the children who will follow her. I suppose she will, like chicken pox every child can expect them: there's a three o'clock in the dark night of children's souls too, let's not be too arrogant taking our prerogatives. But if she does, she'll dream them alone, no accomplices. I won't meet her halfway, give her my own last fillip, myself in shreds.

I've been keeping a sort of log: a day in the life. For no purpose, since my sense of futility runs deeper than any data can testify to. Still it cools me off.

He is playing with Jacqueline. They are in the Rosenbergs' yard. C. is on his way to the sandbox, which belongs to Jackie's baby brother, Brian, so I see trouble ahead. I will not interfere. No, *intervene* is the word they use. Interfere is not as objective, it's the mess that parents make, as opposed to the one the doctors make. As he goes down the long narrow yard at a good clip, C. pulls up two peonies, knocks over Brian's big blond blocky wooden horse (for which he has to stop and plant his feet very deliberately, it's that well-balanced, i.e., expensive). Kicks over short picket fence around tulips, finally gets to sandbox, walks up to Jackie, whose back is to him, and pushes her hard. She falls against fence and goes crying to her mother with a splinter. She doesn't even bother to retaliate, knowing him too well? Then he leans down into the sand. Turns to me again, that innocent face. It is not conniving or falsely naive, I swear it's not. He isn't that kind of clever. Nor is he a gruff bully boy who likes to fly from trees and conquer turf; he has a small peaked face, a little French, I think, in need of one of those common Gallic caps with the peak on the front; a narrow forehead on which his dark hair lies flat like a salon haircut. Anything but a bully, this helpless child of mine—he has a weird natural elegance that terrifies me, as though it is true, what I feel, that he was intended to be someone else. . . . Now he seems to be saying, Well, take all this stuff away if you don't want me to touch it. Get me out of this goddamn museum. Who says I'm not provoked? *That's what you say to each other.*

Why is *he* not glass? He will break us all without so much as chipping.

The worst thing I can think. I am dozing in the sun, Christopher is in kindergarten, Jody is napping, and I am guiltily trying to coax a little color into my late-fall pallor. It's a depressing bleary sun up there. But I sleep a little, waking in fits and snatches when Migdalia next door lets her kid have it and his whine sails across the yards, and when the bus shakes the earth all the way under the gas mains and water pipes to China. The worst thing is crawling through my head like a stream of red ants: What if he and I, Howie and I, had been somewhere else way back that night we smiled and nodded and made Christopher? If the night had been bone-cracking cold? If we were courting some aloneness, back to back? But it was summer, we'd been married three months, and the bottom sheet was spread like a picnic cloth. If there is an astrologer's clock, that's what we heard announcing to us the time was propitious; but I rehearse the time again. We lived off Riverside Drive that year and the next, I will float a thundercloud across the river from the Palisades and just as Howie turns to me I will have the most extraordinary burst of rain, sludgy and cold, explode through the open windows everywhere and finish us for the evening. The rugs are soaked, our books on the desk are corrugated with dampness, we snap at each other, Howie breaks a beer glass and blames me. We unmake him. . . . Another night we will make a different child. Don't the genes shift daily in their milky medium like lottery tickets in their fishbowl? I unmake Christopher's skin and bone: egg in the water, blind;

a single sperm thrusts out of its soft side, retreating. Arrow swimming backwards, tail drags the heavy head away from life. All the probability in the universe cheers. He is unjoined. I wake in a clammy sweat. The sun, such as it was, is caught behind the smokestacks at the far end of Pacific Street. I feel dirty, as though I've sinned in my sleep, and there's that fine perpetual silt on my arms and legs and face, the Con Ed sunburn. I go in and start making lunch for Christopher, who will survive me.

Log: He is sitting at the kitchen table trying to string kidney beans on a needle and thread. They do it in kindergarten. I forgot to ask why. Jody wakes upstairs, way at the back of the house with her door closed, and C. says quietly, without looking up from his string, "Ma, she's up." It's like hearing something happening, I don't know, a mile away. He has the instincts of an Indian guide, except when I stand right next to him to talk. Then it blows right by.

And when she's up. He seems to make a very special effort to be gentle with his little sister. I can see him forcibly subdue himself, tuck his hands inside his pockets or push them into the loops of his pants so that he loses no honor in restraint. But every now and then it gets the better of him. He walked by her just a minute ago and did just what he does to anything that's not nailed down or bigger than he is: gave her a casual but precise push. The way the bathmat slips into the tub without protest, the glass bowl gets smashed, its pieces settling with a resigned tinkle. I am, of course, the one who's resigned: I hear them ring against each other before they hit the ground, in the silence that envelops the shove.

This time Jody chose to lie back on the rug—fortunately it wasn't cement, I am grateful for small favors—and watch him. An amazing, endearing thing for a two-year-old. I think she has all the control that was meant for the two of them, and this is fair to neither. Eyes wide open, untearful, Jody, the antidote, was thinking something about her brother. She cannot say what.

When his dosage has been up a while, he begins to cringe before her. It is unpredictable and unimaginable but true, and I bear witness to it here. As I was writing the above he ran in and hid behind my chair. Along came J., who had just righted herself after the attack on her; she was pulling her corn popper, vaguely humming. For C., an imagined assault? Provoked? Real? Wished for?

Howard, on his way out of the breakfast chaos, bears his brief-case like a shield, holds it in front of him for lack of space while he winds his way around the table in our little alcove, planting firm kisses on our foreheads. On his way out the door he can be expected to say something cheerful and blind to encourage me through the next unpredictable half hour before I walk Christopher up the block to school. This morning, unlocking the front gate, I caught him pondering. "Well, what are other kids like? I mean we've never had any others so how do we know where they fall on the spectrum?"

"We know," I said. "What about Jody?"

"Oh," he said, waving her away like a fly. "I mean boys."

"We also know because we're not knots on logs, some of us, that's how we know. What was it he did to your shaver this morning?"

Smashed it to smithereens is what he did, and left cobweb cracks in the mirror he threw it at.

To which his father shrugged and turned to pull the gate shut fast.

Why did we have Jody? People dare to ask, astonished, though it's none of their business. They mean, and expect us to forgive them, how could we take such a martyr's chance? I tell them that when C. was born I was ready for a large family. You can't be a secretary forever, no matter how many smash titles your boss edits. Nor an administrative assistant, nor an indispens-able right hand. I've got my own arms, for which I need all the hands I've got. I like to be boss, thank you, in my own house. It's a routine by now, canned as an Alka-Seltzer ad.

But I'll tell you. For a long time I guarded very tensely against having another baby. C. was hurting me too much, already he was. Howard would rap with his fist on my night-gowned side, demanding admission. For a while I played virgin. I mean, I didn't try, I wasn't playing. He just couldn't make any headway. I've heard it called dys-something; also cross-bones, to get right down to what it's like. (Dys-something puts me right in there with my son, doesn't it? I'll bet there's some drug, some muscle relaxant that bones you and just lays you out on the knife like a chicken to be stuffed and trussed. . . .) Even though it wasn't his fault I'll never forgive Howard for using his fists on me, even as gently and facetiously as he did. Finally I guess he got tired of trying to disarm me one night at a time, of bringing wine to bed or dancing with me obscenely like a kid at a petting party or otherwise trying to distract me while he stole up on me. So that's when he convinced me to have another baby. I guess it seemed easier. "We'll make Christopher our one exceptional child while we surround him with ordinary ones. We'll grow a goddamn garden around him, he'll be outnumbered."

Well—I bought it. We could make this child matter less. It was an old and extravagant solution. Black flowers in his brain, what blight would the next one have, I insisted he *promise* me. He lied, ah, he lied with his hand between my legs, he swore the next would be just as beautiful but timid—"Downright phlegmatic, how's that?"—and would teach Christopher to be human. So I sighed, desperate to believe, and unlocked my thighs, gone rusty and stiff. But I'll tell you, right as he turned out, by luck, to be, I think I never trusted him again, one of my two deceitful boys, because whatever abandon I once had is gone, sure as my waist is gone. I feel it now and Howard is punished for it. Starting right then, making Jody, I have dealt myself out in careful proportions, like an unreliable cook bent only on her batter.

Meanwhile I lose one lamp, half the ivory on the piano keys, and all my sewing patterns to my son in a single day. On the same day I lose my temper, lose it so irretrievably that I am

tempted to pop one of Christopher's little red pills myself and
go quietly. Who's the most frightening, the skimpy six-year-old
flying around on the tail of his bird of prey, or his indispensable
right-hand mama smashing the canned goods into the closet
with a sound generally reserved for the shooting range? All the
worse, off his habit for a few days, his eyes clear, his own, he
is trying to be sweet, he smiles wanly whenever some catastro-
phe overtakes him, like an actor with no conviction. But someone else controls his muscles. He is not riding it now but lives
in the beak of something huge and dark that dangles him just
out of my reach.

Our brains are all circuitry; not very imaginative, I tend to
see it blue and red and yellow like the wires in phones, easier
to sort impulses that way. I want to see inside Christopher's
head, I stare viciously though I try to do it when he's involved
with something else. (He never is, he would feel me a hundred
light years behind him.) I vow never to *study* him again, it's
futile anyway, his forehead's not a one-way mirror. Promises,
always my promises: they are glass. I know when they shatter—
no, when he shatters them, throwing something of value—
there will be edges to draw blood, edges everywhere. He says,
"What are you *looking* at all the time? Bad Christopher the
dragon?" He looks wilted, pathetic, seen-through. But I
haven't seen a thing.

"Chrissie." I put my arms around him. He doesn't want to
bruise the air he breathes, maybe we're all jumbled in his sight.
He doesn't read yet, I know that's why. It's all upside down or
somehow mixed together—cubist sight, is there such a thing?
He sees my face and the top of my head, say, at the same time.
Or everything looms at him, quivering like a fun-house mirror,
swollen, then slowly disappears down to a point. He has to
subdue it before it overtakes him? How would we ever know?
Why, if he saw just what we see—the cool and calm of all the
things of the world all sorted out like laundry ("Oh, Margaret,
come off it!")—why would he look so bewildered most of the
time, like a terrier being dragged around by his collar, his small
face thrust forward into his own perpetual messes?

He comes to me just for a second, pulling on his tan windbreaker, already breathing fast to run away somewhere, and while I hold him tight a minute, therapeutic hug for both of us, he pinches my arm until the purple capillaries dance with pain.

"Let me take him with me when I go to D.C. next week." Howard.

I stare at him. "You've got to be kidding."

"No, why would I kid about it? We'll manage, we can go see some buildings after my conference is out, go to the Smithsonian. He'd love the giant pendulum." His eyes are already there in the cool of the great vaulted room where everything echoes and everything can break. I am fascinated by his casualness. "What would he do all day while you're in your meeting? Friend. My intrepid friend."

"Oh, we'd manage something. He'd keep busy. Paper and pencil . . ."

"Howie." Am I crazy? Is he? Do we live in the same house?

He comes and takes both my hands. There is that slightly conniving look my husband gets that makes me forget, goddammit, why I married him. He is all too reasonable and gentle a man most of the time, but this look is way in the back of his eyes behind a pillar, peeking out. I feel surrounded. "You can't take him." I wrench my hands away.

"Maggie—" and he tries to take them again, bungler, as though they're contested property.

"I forbid it. Insanity. You'll end up crushing him to death to get a little peace! I know."

He smiles with unbearable patience. "I know how to handle my son."

But I walk out of the room, thin-lipped, taking a bowl of fruit to the children who are raging around, both of them, in front of the grade-A educational television that's raging back.

The next week Howie goes to Washington and we all go to the airport to see him off. I don't know what Howard told him, but while Jody sleeps Christopher cries noisily in the back of the car and flings himself around so wildly, like a caged bear, that I have to stop the car on the highway shoulder and buckle him into his seat belt. "You will walk home," I threaten, calm because I can see the battle plan. He's got a little of his father in him; that should make me feel better.

He hisses at me and goes on crying, forcing the tears and walloping the back of my seat with his feet the whole way home.

Log: The long long walk to school. A block and a half. Most of the kids in kindergarten with Christopher walk past our house alone, solidly bearing straight west with the bland eight o'clock sun at their backs. They concentrate, they have been told not to cross heavy traffic alone, not to speak to strangers, not to dawdle. All the major wisdom of motherhood pinned to their jackets like a permission slip. Little orders turning into habits and hardening slowly to superego: an amber that holds commands forever. Christopher lacks it the way some children are born without a crucial body chemical. Therefore, I walk him to school every day, rain or shine, awake or asleep.

Jody's in her stroller, slouching. She'd rather be home. So would I. It's beginning to get chilly out, edgy, and that means the neighborhood's been stripped of summer and fall, as surely as if a man came by one day confiscating color. What little there is, you wouldn't think it could matter. Blame the mayor. The window boxes are crowded with brown stringy corpses, like tall crabgrass. Our noble pint-sized trees have shrunk back into themselves; they lose five years in winter. Fontaine, always improving his property, has painted his new brick wall *silver* over the weekend—it has a sepulchral gleam in the vague sunlight, twinkling as placidly as a woman who's come in sequins to a business meeting, *believing* in herself. Bless him. Next door to him the Rosenbergs have bought subtle aged wood shutters—they look like some dissected Vermont barn door—and a big rustic barrel that will stand achingly empty all winter, weighted with a hundred pounds of dirt to exhaust the barrel burglars. I wonder what my illusions look like through the front window.

Christopher's off and running. "Not in the street!" I get so tired of my voice, especially because I know he doesn't hear it. "Stay on the curb, Christopher." There's enough damage to be done there. He is swinging on that new couple's gate, straining the hinges, trying to fan up a good wind; then, when I look up from attending to Jody's dropped and splintered Ritz cracker, he's gone—clapping together two garbage can lids across the street. Always under an old lady's window, though with no particular joy—his job, it's there to be done. Jody is left with her stroller braked against a tree for safekeeping while I retrieve him. No one ever told me I'd grow up to be a shepherdess; and bad at it too—undone by a single sheep.

We are somehow at the corner, at least I can demand he hold my hand and drag us across the street where the crossing guard stands and winks at me daily, as dependably as a blinking light. She is a good lady, Mrs. Cortes, from a couple of blocks down in the projects, with many matching daughters, one son, Anibal, on the sixth-grade honor roll, and another on Riker's Island, a junkie. She is waving cars and people forward in waves, demonstrating "community involvement" to placate the gods who are seeing to Anibal's future, I know it. I recognize something deep behind her lively eyes, sunk there: a certain desperate casualness while the world has its way with her children. Another shepherdess without a chance. I give her my little salute.

By now, my feet heavy with the monotony of this trip, we are on the long school block. The barbed wire of the playground breaks for the entrance halfway down. This street, unlived on, is an unrelenting tangle—no one ever sees the generous souls who bequeath their dead cars to the children, but there are dozens, in various stages of decay; they must make regular deliveries. Christopher's castles; creative playthings, and broken already so he never gets blamed. For some reason he picks the third one. He's already in there, across a moat of broken windshield glass, reaching for the steering wheel. The back seat's burned out, the better to jump on. All the chrome has been cannibalized by the adults—everything that twists or lifts off, leaving a carcass of flung bones, its tin flesh dangling.

"Christopher, you are late and I. Am. Not. Waiting." But he will not come that way. My son demands the laying-on of hands. Before I can maneuver my way in, feeling middle-aged and worrying about my skirt, hiked up over my rear, he is tussling not with one boy but with two. They fight over nothing—just lock hands and wrestle as a kind of greeting. "I break the muh-fuh's head," one announces matter-of-factly—second grader maybe. Christopher doesn't fight for stakes like that, though. Whoever wants his head can have it, he's fighting to get his hands on something, keep them warm. I am reaching over the jagged door, which is split in two and full of rainwater. The school bell rings, that raspy grinding, and the two boys, with a whoop, leap over the downed windshield and are gone. Christopher is grater-scraped along one cheek, but we have arrived more or less in one piece.

I decide I'd better come in with him and see to it his cheek is washed off. He is, of course, long gone by the time I park the stroller and take the baby out. He never bothers to say good-bye. Maybe six-year-olds don't.

I pull open the heavy door to P.S. 193. It comes reluctantly, like it's in many parts. These doors are not for children. But then, neither is the school. . . . It's a fairly new building, but the 1939 World's Fair architecture has just about caught up with the lobby—those heavy streamlined effects. A ship, that's what it looks like; a dated ocean liner, or the lobby of Rockefeller Center, one humble corner of it. What do the kids see, I wonder? Not grandeur.

There's a big lit-up case to the left that shows off sparse student pieties, untouchable as seven-layer cakes at the bakery. THIS LAND IS *Your* LAND, THIS LAND IS *My* LAND. Every figure in the pictures, brown, black, dead-white (blank), mustard yellow, tulip red and olive green (who's that?) is connected more or less at the wrist, like uncut paper dolls (HANDS ACROSS THE SEA). The whole world's afraid to drop hands, the hell with summit talks, SALT talks, we're on the buddy system. Well, *they* go up and down the halls irrevocably linked so, their lips sealed, the key thrown over their endless shoulder, only the teacher nattering on and on about discipline and respect, wearing heels that must sound like SS boots, though they are intended merely to mean business. Christopher tells me only that his teachers are noisy and hurt his ears; he does not bother to specify how.

And what he sees when he puts his thin shoulder to the door at 8:30 and heaves? He probably catches that glaring unnecessary shine on the floor, an invitation, and takes it. That worried crease between big eyes, his face looks back at him out of deep water. Deeper when he's drugged. So he careens around without ice skates, knocks against other kids hard, thumps into closed doors, nearly cracks open THIS LAND IS YOUR LAND. He is the wiseacre who dances to hold the door for his class, then when the last dark pigtail is through skips off in the wrong direction, leaps the steps to the gym or the auditorium or whatever lives down there in deserted silence most of the morning, the galley of this ship. I don't blame him, of course I don't, but that isn't the point, is it? I am deprived of these fashionable rebellious points. We only, madam, allow those in control to be out of control. As it were. If you follow. Your son, madam, is not rebelling. He is unable. Is beyond. Is utterly. Is unthinkable. Catch him before we do.

We are certainly late, the lines are all gone, the kids settling into their rooms, their noise dwindling like a cut-back motor. Jody and I just stand for a minute or two tuning in. Her head is heavy on my shoulder. Already there's a steady monitor traffic, the officious kids scurrying to do their teachers' bidding like tailless mice. I was one of them for years and years, God, faceless and obliging: official blackboard eraser (which meant a few cool solitary minutes just before three each day, down in the basement storeroom clapping two erasers together, hard, till they smoked with the day's vanished lessons). I would hardly have stopped my frantic do-gooding to give the time of day (off the clocks that jerked forward with a click every new minute) to the likes of Christopher. I'd have given him a wide berth, I can see myself going the other way if I saw him coming toward me in the narrow hall.

This hall, just like the ones I grew up in except for the "modernistic" shower tile that reaches halfway up, has a muted darkened feeling, an underwater thrum. Even the tile is like the Queens Midtown Tunnel, deserted. I will not be particularly welcome in Christopher's kindergarten room; there is that beleaguered proprietary feeling that any parent is a spy or come to complain. (I, in my own category, have been forbidden to complain, at least tacitly, having been told that my son really needs one whole teacher to himself, if not for his sake, then for the safety of the equipment and "the consumables," of which he is not one.)

Christopher has disappeared into his class which—I see it through the little porthole—is neat and earnest and not so terribly different from a third-grade room, say, with its alphabets and exhortations to patriotism and virtue above eye level. They are allowed to paint in one color at a time. A few, I see, have graduated to two; they must be disciplined, promising children in their securely tied smocks. One spring they will hatch into monitors. Christopher is undoubtedly banned from the painting corner. (Classroom economy? Margaret, your kitchen, your bedroom, your bathroom this morning. Searching for the glass mines hidden between the tiles.) Mrs. Seabury is inspecting hands. The children turn them, patty-cake, and step back when she finishes her scrutiny, which is as grave as a doctor's. Oh Christopher! She has sent him and another little boy to the sink to scrub; to throw water, that is, and stick their fingers in the spout in order to shower the children in the back of the room. I am not going in there to identify myself.

Mrs. Seabury is the kind of teacher who, with all her brown and black kids on one side of the room (this morning in the back, getting showered), talks about discrimination and means big from little, forward from backward, ass from elbow. Now I see she has made Christopher an honorary Black child, or maybe one of your more rambunctious Puerto Ricans. They are all massed back there for the special inattention of the aide, who is one of my least favorite people: she is very young and wears a maxi skirt that the kids keep stepping on when she bends down. (Therefore she bends down as little as possible.) The Future Felons of America and their den mother. I'm caught somewhere between my first flash of anger and then shame at what I suppose, wearily, is arrogance. What am I angry at? That he has attained pariah-hood with them, overcoming his impeccable WASP heritage in a single leap of adrenaline? Jesus. They are the "unruly characters" he's supposed to be afraid of: latchkey babies, battered boys and abused girls, or loved but hungry, scouted by rats while they sleep. Products of this-and-that converging, social, political, economic, each little head impaled on a point of the grid. Christopher? My warm, healthy, nursed and coddled, vitamin-enriched boy, born on Blue Cross, swaddled in his grandparents' gifts from Lord & Taylor? What in the hell is our excuse? My pill-popping baby, so sad, so reduced and taken from himself when he's on, so indescribable, airborne, when he's off. This week he is off; I am sneaking him a favor.

I see him now flapping around in a sort of ragged circle with the other unimaginables, under the passive eye of that aide. Crows? Buzzards? Not pigeons, anyway. They make their own rowdy music. Then Christopher clenches his whole body—I see it coming—and stops short, slamming half a dozen kids together, solid rear-end collisions. It looks like the New Jersey Turnpike, everybody whiplashed, tumbling down. No reason, no whys, there is never anything to explain. Was the room taking off, spinning him dizzy? Was he fending something off, or trying to catch hold? The others turn to him, shout so loud I can hear them out here where I'm locked, underwater—and they all pile on. Oh, can they pile! It's a sport in itself. Feet and hands and dark faces deepening a shade. The aide gets out of the way, picking her skirt out of the rubble of children at her feet.

One heavy dark boy with no wrists finally breaks through the victor: his foot is on Christopher's neck. The little pale face jerks up stiffly, like an executed man's. I turn away. When I make myself turn back the crowd is unraveling as Mrs. Seabury approaches. Faces all around are taking on that half-stricken, half-delighted "uh-oh" look. I was always good at that, one of the leaders of censure and shock. It felt good.

But Christopher sinks down, quiet. She reaches down roughly and yanks his fresh white collar. Good boy, he doesn't look up at her. But something is broken. The mainspring, the defiant arch of his back that I would recognize, his, mine, I find I am weeping, soundless as everything around me, I feel it suddenly like blood on my cheeks. This teacher, this stranger and her cohorts have him by his pale limp neck. They are teaching him how to lose; or me how to win. My son is down for the count, breathing comfortably, accommodating, only his fingers twitching fiercely at his sides like gill slits puffing, while I stand outside, a baby asleep on my shoulder. I am the traitor, he sees me through my one-way mirror, and he is right. I am the witch. Every day they walk on his neck, I see that now, but he will never tell me about it. I weep but cannot move.

SOME STORIES SHOULD HAVE A REAL HERO

Jeff Elzinga

. . . .

There's a woman at our window. Rain is running from her chin. She steps to the glass and holds a bundle in her arms for us to have.

I run into the treatment room and lay the bundle on the table. Our nurse with the red hair quickly breathes into the empty lungs. Her fingertips massage the silent heart.

The mother enters a step behind us and kneels beside her baby boy. She kisses his hands. She sucks on the little fingers. She begs us to warm him.

Our surgeon readies a feeding tube. I quickly move stimulants into a syringe. A crowd gathers around the table to push and pull. The mother begs the boy to forgive her.

Lights flash in the tiny dry eyes. Needles prick the swollen gray skin. But we are practicing on a stiff pillow.

The mother is crying now. She confesses how she found him in his little crib beneath a blanket. It's where he would hide, she says, whenever I got angry with him. And tonight—she tells us—he fell asleep with the blanket in his mouth.

The boy's face is puffed and marble blue. The mother wholly kisses the little feet. Her red lips float on the wetness of her tongue and move up the tiny gray legs like a snail.

"Get her out of here."

Two student nurses finally remove the woman from our room. The door swishes shut. We stop our work.

166

The surgeon closes the little eyes.

The skin I touch is cold, like fresh fish. I wrap the baby boy in a clean bath towel. He becomes a tiny white package on a large green table in a crowded room.

Our nurse then says we all have to wait awhile before going back out, that we can't let the mother think it was her fault the baby died.

"Don't worry," someone says. "She didn't do it. It's an accident."

"But she won't believe that," the nurse says. "The longer we wait the more it'll look like her baby was alive when she came in, and then we lost him here. We can't let her feel guilty. It's our job to wait."

Some of us still disagree and move to the door, saying we should stop acting ridiculous. She'll understand if we break it to her right. We have to tell the truth. We have other work to do.

A new voice from the crowd suddenly announces—"if any-one moves another step closer to the door for any reason in the next five minutes they will without a doubt get their face punched in."

Later I watch the mother in the waiting room sitting on a long orange couch. Her nightgown is watery and pasted to naked pink skin. Her two lifeless breasts hang like sausages in a butcher's window.

She has pressed her hands between bare knees and now slowly she works the fingers up into a knot in her crotch. She prays out loud to our ceiling and walls as leftover rain slips in perfect drops from her head to her shoulders.

Our nurse with the red hair covers these shoulders with a small blanket. Then sitting beside the mother she begins to tell the story of what happened.

STUNG

By E. S. Creamer

. . . .

We threw pebbles down through the grate until I believed my own lie: there was no sewer below. It was a bottomless pit. Day after day we threw pebbles from our yard, the yard next door, the yard across the street, the yard next door to that, until there were no more pebbles in our neighborhood, or so it seemed to us. Then we settled for rocks, rocks we then could barely get our fingers around. Rocks that now might seem like pebbles. And still we heard no splash, no rock hitting pebble or rock hitting rock. The stones never piled up, never overflowed through the grate. The pit was bottomless. What other explanation could there be? He couldn't think of one, and even if I could, do you think I'd tell?

I remember one day, a day like any other, and we were throwing pebbles down the grate, my brother and I. Suddenly there was a bumblebee fizzing through the air around us. I don't know what was scarier about the bee: its sound or size. It was as big as our fists, as big as the rocks we threw down the grate—this was past the time we'd given up on pebbles—and had a hum as loud as my dad's electric razor only not as steady. A razor on the fritz.

"Freeze," I said, and we froze like statues.

The bee buzzed around us, between us. My heart beat strong in my ears, warm ears. My brother's beat in his. I could tell.

That's when the bee stung him, on his pinkie. My mom found the stinger and pinched it out. She said that meant the bee wouldn't sting anyone else. Couldn't. Not me, not my mom, not anyone in our family. Not anyone in the world. The bee had only one sting in him.

We played games then, and not just Tag and Hide-and-Seek. We played our own games—Dance-Till-the-Music-Stops and Invisible—and when there were other people, Capture the Flag, Murder in the Dark, and Levitation. And we caught lightning bugs. At night right after dinner but before Mr. Softee drove down our street, we caught lightning bugs and stowed them in cleaned-out peanut butter jars. My mom stabbed holes in the lids with the can opener so the lightning bugs could breathe and live at least until morning. But by bedtime they were usually still.

Of the games we played with others, my favorite was Murder in the Dark. My brother's was Levitation. For Murder in the Dark there'd be one murderer and one detective; the rest were plain people—victims to be protected or killed. We used cards to choose who was who: Ace of Spades—murderer, Jack of Diamonds—dick. No face cards or aces otherwise. If there were, the littler kids would get confused and then you'd have more than one murderer walking around. More people would die sooner and the game would be over in half the time.

The detective called out who he was right away so from the start you knew the one person you were safe with. You couldn't be killed as long as the detective had you in sight.

When I visit him in that room, its walls as white as the backs of cards well-wishers send, I wonder if his skin is milky from being so long indoors or if that, too, comes from his bones. I think of asking a doctor, but reasons don't change anything. What is, is.

They tell me my own marrow isn't good enough. It cannot make him safe. The doctors scratch their heads. Blink.

I wish I had been more careful the other times. Taken the bee sting at least if not this. I didn't have to lay my hands on

his neck first time, every time I was the Murderer in the Dark.
I didn't have to, but I did. I'd murder him first, put him out
of the game, though I could have saved him for later. I could
have done him in last.

Now here: my little brother, who has long been bigger than
I, whom I loved but did not cherish, like my old thermos I did
not think to cry over until I opened it one recess to find
splintered, silvery innards floating in milk. I'd fallen on the way
to school. Dropped it.

My brother grows nostalgic. He likes to reminisce. I say I
remember even when I don't.

"Remember?" he'll ask, eyes as urgent as that time we froze
like statues, his body just as still.

"Well," I say.

He doesn't recall the time about the bee. But he remembers
the stones.

For old times' sake I would offer to play his favorite again,
only I think we already are. We have been for some time.

First: the how it happened, the how this came about.

Next: words once said in play left now unspoken—"He looks
dead."

Then, but not finally, he is as he looks: still—still as the
lightning bugs my brother and I meant no harm.

After: the body has no weight—"He looks as light as a
feather."

My brother's skin is translucent, pale. I shall soon look upon
his feather bones.

Last: eyes down, no-smiles solemn—"On the count of three,
we will lift him." My brother lies in this bed that is not his and
asks if I remember things I do not know.

"One, two . . . ."

In the end my brother will be pitched down, like the pebbles.

Some things stay. The jacks I scattered, then snatched up while
the red ball bounced down-up are somewhere. There is the
yellow Frisbee lost at sea our dog was not moved to fetch. That

is somewhere, too. Even my old thermos is somewhere. And there is a Great Wall of China down that sewer, stone upon stone. Solid, safe, thanks to my brother and me. It is there still, will be. I know. I can tell. What is, is.

THE SIGNING

Stephen Dixon

. . . .

My wife dies. Now I'm alone. I kiss her hands and leave the hospital room. A nurse runs after me as I walk down the hall.

"Are you going to make arrangements now for the deceased?" he says.

"No."

"Then what do you want us to do with the body?"

"Burn it."

"That's not our job."

"Give it to science."

"You'll have to sign the proper legal papers."

"Give me them."

"They take a while to draw up. Why don't you wait in the guest lounge?"

"I haven't time."

"And her toilet things and radio and clothes." .

"I have to go." I ring for the elevator.

"You can't do that."

"I am."

The elevator comes.

"Doctor, doctor," he yells to a doctor going through some files at the nurses' station. She stands up. "What is it, nurse?" she says. The elevator door closes. It opens on several floors before it reaches the lobby. I head for the outside. There's a security guard sitting beside the revolving door. He looks like a regular city policeman other than for his hair, which hangs down past his shoulders, and he also has a beard. Most city policemen don't; maybe all. He gets a call on his portable two-way set as I step into one of the quarters of the revolving door. "Laslo," he says into it. I'm outside. "Hey, you," he says. I turn around. He's nodding and pointing to me and waves for me to come back. I cross the avenue to get to the bus stop. He comes outside and slips the two-way into his back pocket and walks up to me as I wait for the bus.

"They want you back upstairs to sign some papers," he says.

"Too late. She's dead. I'm alone. I kissed her hands. You can have the body. I just want to be far away from here and as soon as I can."

"They asked me to bring you back."

"You can't. This is a public street. You need a city policeman to take me back, and even then I don't think he or she would be in their rights."

"I'm going to get one."

The bus comes. Its door opens. I have the required exact fare. I step up and put my change in the coin box.

"Don't take this man," the guard says to the bus driver. "They want him back at the hospital there. Something about his wife who was or is a patient, though I don't know the actual reason they want him for."

"I've done nothing," I tell the driver and take a seat in the rear of the bus. A woman sitting in front of me says, "What's holding him up? This isn't a red light."

"Listen," the driver says to the guard, "if you have no specific charge or warrant against this guy, I think I better go."

"Will you please get this bus rolling again?" a passenger says.

"Yes," I say, disguising my voice so they won't think it's me but some other passenger, "I've an important appointment and your slowpokey driving and intermittent dawdling has already made me ten minutes late."

The driver shrugs at the guard. "In or out, friend, but unless you can come up with some official authority to stop this bus, I got to finish my run."

The guard steps into the bus, pays his fare, and sits beside me as the bus pulls out.

"I'll have to stick with you and check in if you don't mind," he says to me. He pushes a button in his two-way set and says "Laslo here."

"Laslo," a voice says. "Where the hell are you?"

"On a bus."

"What are you doing there? You're not through yet."

"I'm with the man you told me to grab at the door. Well, he got past the door. I tried to stop him outside, but he said I needed a city patrolman for that because it was a public street."

"You could've gotten him on the sidewalk in front."

"This was at the bus stop across the street."

"Then he's right. We don't want a suit."

"That's what I thought. So I tried to convince him to come back. He wouldn't. He said he'd kissed some woman's hands and we can have the body. I don't know what that means but want to get it all in before I get too far away from you and lose radio contact. He got on this bus. The driver was sympathetic to my argument about the bus not leaving, but said it would be illegal his helping to restrain the man and that he also had to complete his run. So I got on the bus and am now sitting beside the man and will get off at the next stop if that's what you want me to do. I just didn't know what was the correct way to carry out my orders in this situation, so I thought I'd stick with him till I found out from you."

"You did the right thing. Let me speak to him now."

Laslo holds the two-way in front of my mouth. "Hello," I say.

"The papers to donate your wife's body to the hospital for research and possible transplants are ready now, sir, so could you return with Officer Laslo?"

"No."

"If you think it'll be too trying an emotional experience to return here, could we meet someplace else where you could sign?"

"Do what you want with her body. There's nothing I ever want to have to do with her again. I'll never speak her name. Never go back to our apartment. Our car I'm going to let rot in the street till it's towed away. This wristwatch. She bought it for me and wore it a few times herself." I throw it out the window.

"Why didn't you just pass it on back here?" the man behind me says.

"These clothes. She bought some of them, mended them all." I take off my jacket, tie, shirt and pants and toss them out the window.

"Lookit," Laslo says, "I'm just a hospital security guard with a pair of handcuffs I'm not going to use on you because we're in a public bus and all you've just gone through, but please calm down."

"This underwear I bought myself yesterday," I say to him. "I needed a new pair. She never touched or saw them, so I don't mind still wearing them. The shoes go, though. She even put on these heels with a shoe-repair kit she bought at the five-and-dime." I take off my shoes and drop them out the window.

The bus has stopped. All the other passengers have left except Laslo. The driver is on the street looking for what I'm sure is a patrolman or police car.

I look at my socks. "I'm not sure about the socks."

"Leave them on," Laslo says. "They look good, and I like brown."

"But did she buy them? I think they were a gift from her two birthdays ago when she gave me a cane picnic basket with a dozen-and-a-half pairs of different-colored socks inside. Yes, this is one of them," and I take them off and throw them out the window. "That's why I tried and still have to get out of this city fast as I can."

"You hear that?" Laslo says into the two-way radio, and the man on the other end says, "I still don't understand."

"You see," I say into it, "we spent too many years here together, my beloved and I—all our adult lives. These streets. That bridge. Those buildings." I spit out the window. "Perhaps even this bus. We took so many rides up and down this line." I try to uproot the seat in front of me but it won't budge. Laslo claps the cuffs on my wrists. "This life," I say and I smash my head through the window.

An ambulance comes and takes me back to the same hospital. I'm brought to Emergency and put on a cot in the same examining room she was taken to this last time before they moved her to a semiprivate room. A hospital official comes in while the doctors and nurses are tweezing the remaining glass splinters out of my head and stitching me up. "If you're still interested in donating your wife's body," he says, "then we'd like to get the matter out of the way while some of her organs can still be reused by several of the patients upstairs."

I say, "No, I don't want anyone walking around with my wife's parts where I can bump into him and maybe recognize them any day of the year," but he takes my writing hand and guides it till I've signed.

DYING WITH WORDS

Reginald Gibbons

· · · · · · · · · · · · · · · · · ·

The dirt was bare and the funeral flowers lay twisted and shrunken in the red mud, the gold foil-wrapped cans knocked over, the blossoms all brown. The very day before she died, this woman and her husband had had a fight because she had been worsening fatally for months and he still hadn't bought a plot and she was angry at him for not having bought it. He'd stopped doing anything at all, she'd said. But now she was buried, although there was no stone, only the raw mound that had slightly sunk already because it had rained, and the little two-year-old boy started suddenly to dig into it to help her get out.

Someone had told the father that his children must face the reality of death, but no one could explain to the boy where his mother had gone. No more than she had been able to explain, when she was alive, where he had been before he was born. So perhaps he couldn't not think that she was under the heap of mud, perhaps he couldn't think that she was, but he began to dig.

No more, for that matter, had she been able to explain to herself how she had "conceived a child," for it had seemed to her that she had thought him into existence, lying in bed every night and wishing for him, praying for him, after she had raised his sister for a few years and wanted, needed, a son as well. No more than she could conceive that she was going to die soon.

Lying in her hospital bed between visits from her husband and two children, she had begun to distract herself with looking up words in a dictionary, till it was no longer a distraction but a string of hints to the mystery, although the answer wouldn't come clear.

She learned to go back further, she asked her husband for more dictionaries, bigger ones, and he brought them to her with a resignation that could make her furious. She tried to hide her anger from him, just as she tried to hide her panic and fear, always to spare him, although he could have borne much more; after all it wasn't he who was dying. At the same time, she could tell that he thought—because he was not capable of taking the measure of her helplessness and despair, and did not realize that he could not—he thought his own feelings of bereft loneliness and irritation were stronger, deeper, somehow more important, than her feelings.

She looked up "female," which was what she still was. Her quiet hands were more beautiful than they had ever been; the radiation had killed almost all her hair, and even her pubic hair had mostly gone, leaving her looking like a girl. (Yet later, after the dictionaries had grown too heavy for her to hold, she wanted to shave her legs one day, and she had to ask a nurse to do it, and it was the nurse who cried, bending over the straight, still, silken limbs.) But maybe "female" had nothing to do with beauty anymore. "Female" comes from a Latin word, and the Latin word came from other words, older ones, further back from the Romans than the Romans were from her, and it meant "she who suckles," and that is also where the Latin word for daughter, that she liked the lacy sound of, "filia," came from. Or else that oldest word meant simply "to be, to exist, to grow." First we suck, then we grow. Her boy had sucked and grown; she had given suck and was dying. The word didn't apply to her, after all.

Then she looked at the "being" and "existing," and she found that in the dark and cold of Norway, whence the word had come to her through ages for her to use without thinking, "to live" meant "to prepare," and it also meant bondage. To live is to be in bondage—she knew someone had said, "Free at last, free at last, thank God Almighty I'm free at last." She had not listened to him, had not needed to. Had not wanted to.

So before she died she thought that after her death she would no longer be female, because she could not suckle her son, and she would be released from the bondage of her illness. There was another word back in that remote aeon that made the Romans seem modern, that meant "to retreat with awe," and she began to do this, backing into her own death, awed not by the death that was coming but by the life she was losing. "Don't leave," she said to the three of them one afternoon, by which she meant that she was leaving.

Her husband, to whom she had been bound, and her daughter, whom she had raised for a few years, and her son, whom only months ago she had fed at her full, unaccountably painful breast, went to the grave. (It had been dug by discreet laborers who had stayed away, behind large headstones, till the funeral was over, and then, keeping their distance, had approached at the backs of the mourners as these were returning to their cars.) Carrying in his mind an idea, some bad advice, a witlessness, her husband brought the children back to see the grave the next week. He was not wondering where "she" was; he was putting all that out of his mind so that he could live through this day, even if his living was then and afterward would be a kind of bondage that *she* would not have been able to bear; he had so wrapped himself in his own arms, for comfort, that he was excusably, perhaps, far from his children and the things, every little one of them, that had excited or pleased or pained *her*, all the daily sensation and stuff she had clung to more tightly as she had sickened. They were different persons, he and she; they had been.

The little girl felt that her mother would hide from her forever and never explain herself; although she felt that what the grave held might not be a person, she was angry. The boy put his hands in the mud and started to dig, getting filthy, thinking maybe of her beautiful breast, the one that had been left, and wanting a voice, a warmth, and some unnameable third thing that was gone.

Her husband had wanted sex with her in the hospital. That came at a "female" different from the one she had tried to understand. She hadn't let him do it. He had chafed at his own grief and new responsibilities; another sort of man, in his place, might have cried and kissed her. But she lay dying and turned her head away from him to spare him the judgment she knew was in her own eyes, and to take her eyes off the further injury he had become to her, in his simple ordinary failure. She was sorry she had had to reach the end of her life to learn that a terrible trial or terrible need would not bring, as a right, some saving presence, a rescue, a mothering.

One particular case, one man and woman. It doesn't stand for all or anyone. This was just a way of making an approximate statement of the test to which they were put. But words, like men, keep failing.

Among all unnamed and unnameable things there is not only what the little boy wanted, for which no one word is large enough, and the brute, inappropriate, undeniable longing his father felt in the white hospital room that had none of the noise of life in it, but also the sort of kindness, finally, that the wife gave her unwitting husband when she turned her face away from him so he would not see what she felt, when she let it go, let it all go. You can dig through all the dictionaries there are, you can muddy your arms to the elbows with words, and you won't find the word for that.

GIRLS

Tess Gallagher

· · · · · · · · · · · · · · · · · ·

Ada had invited herself along on the four-hour drive to Corvallis with her daughter, Billie, for one reason: she intended to see if her girlhood friend, Esther Cox, was still living. When Billie had let drop she was going to Corvallis, Ada had decided. "I'm coming too," she said. Billie frowned, but she didn't say no.

"Should I wear my red coat or my black coat?" she'd asked Billie. "Why don't I pack a few sandwiches." Billie had told her to wear the red coat and said not to bother about sandwiches; she didn't like to eat and drive. Ada packed sandwiches anyway.

Billie had on the leather gloves she used when she drove her Mercedes. When she wasn't smoking cigarettes, she was fiddling with the radio, trying to find a station. Finally she settled on some flute music. This sounded fine to Ada. "Keep it there, honey," she said.

"Esther was like a sister to me, an older sister," Ada said. "I don't know anyone I was closer to. We did the cooking and housekeeping for two cousins who owned mansions next door to one another—the Conants was their name. Esther and I saw each other every day. We even spent our evenings together. It was like that for nearly four years." Ada leaned back in her seat and stole a look at the speedometer: seventy-five miles an hour.

"It's like a soap opera," Billie said. "I can't keep the names straight or who did what when." She brought her eyes up to the rearview mirror as if she were afraid someone was going to overtake her.

Ada wished she could make her stories interesting for Billie and make it clear who the people were and how they had fit into her life. But it was a big effort, and sometimes it drove her to silence. "Never mind," she'd say. "Those people are dead and gone. I don't know why I brought them up." But Esther was different. Esther was important.

Billie pushed in the lighter and took a cigarette from the pack on the dash. "What are you going to talk to this person about after all these years?" she said.

Ada considered this for a minute. "One thing I want to know is what happened to Florita White and Georgie Ganz," Ada said. "They worked up the street from us and they were from Mansfield, where Esther and I were from. We were all farm girls trying to make a go of it in the city." Ada remembered a story about Florita. Florita, who was unmarried, had been living with a man, something just not done in those days. When she washed and dried her panties she said she always put a towel over them on the line so Basil, her man, couldn't see them. But that was all Ada could remember Florita saying. There had to be more to the story, but Ada couldn't remember. She was glad she hadn't said anything to Billie.

"You might just end up staring at each other," Billie said.

"Don't you worry," Ada said. "We'll have plenty to say." That was the trouble with Billie, Ada thought. Since she'd gone into business, if you weren't *talking* business you weren't talking. Billie owned thirty llamas—ugly creatures, Ada thought. She could smell the llama wool Billie had brought along in the back seat for the demonstration she planned to give. Ada had already heard Billie's spiel on llamas. There were a lot of advantages to llamas, according to Billie. For one thing, llamas always did their job in the same place. For another, someone wanting to go into the back country could break a llama in two hours to lead and carry a load. Ada was half inclined to think Billie cared more about llamas than she did about people. But then Billie had never gotten much out of people, and she *had* made it on llamas.

"Esther worked like a mule to raise three children," Ada said.

"Why are you telling me about this woman?" Billie said, as if she'd suddenly been accused of something. She lit another cigarette and turned on her signal light. Then she moved over into the passing lane. The car sped effortlessly down the freeway.

Ada straightened herself in the seat and took out a handkerchief to fan the smoke away from her face. What could she say? That she had never had a friend like Esther in all the years since? Billie would say something like: *If she was so important, then why haven't you seen her in forty-three years?* That was true enough, too; Ada couldn't explain it. She tried to stop the conversation right where it was.

"Anyway, I doubt if she's still living," Ada said, trying to sound unconcerned. But even as she said this Ada wanted more than ever to find Esther Cox alive. How had they lost track? She'd last heard from Esther after Ada's youngest son had been killed in a car crash, twenty years ago. Twenty years. Then she thought of one more thing about Esther, and she said it.

"The last time I saw Esther she made fudge for me," Ada said. "You'll see, Billie. She'll whip up a batch this time too. She always made good fudge." She caught Billie looking at her, maybe wondering for a moment who her mother had been and what fudge had to do with anything. But Ada didn't care. She was remembering how she and Esther had bobbed each other's hair one night, and then gone to the town square to stroll and admire themselves in the store windows.

In the hotel room Ada hunted up the phone book.

"Mother, take off your coat and stay awhile," Billie said as she sat down in a chair and put her feet up on the bed.

Ada was going through the C's, her heart rushing with hope

and dread as she skimmed the columns of names. "She's here! My God, Esther's in the book." She got up and then sat back down on the bed. "Esther. She's in the book!"

"Why don't you call her and get it over with," Billie said. She was flossing her teeth, still wearing her gloves.

"You dial it," Ada said, "I'm shaking too much."

Billie dropped the floss into a wastebasket and pulled off her gloves. Then she took Ada's place on the bed next to the phone and dialed the number her mother read to her. Someone answered and Billie asked to speak to Esther Cox. Ada braced herself. Maybe Esther was dead, after all. She kept her eyes on Billie's face, looking for signs. Finally Billie began to speak into the phone. "Esther? Esther Cox?" she said. "There's someone here who wants to talk to you." Billie handed Ada the phone, and Ada sat on the bed next to her daughter.

"Honey?" Ada said. "Esther? This is Ada Gilman."

"Do I know you?" said the voice on the other end of the line.

Ada was stunned for a moment. It *had* been a very long time, yes. Ada's children were grown. Her husband was dead. Her hair had turned white. "We used to work in Springfield, Missouri, when we were girls," Ada said. "I came to see you after my first baby was born, in 1943." She waited a moment and when Esther still did not say anything, Ada felt a stab of panic. "Is this Esther Cox?" she asked.

"Yes, it is," the voice said. Then it said, "Why don't you come over, why don't you? I'm sorry I can't remember you right off. Maybe if I saw you."

"I'll be right over, honey," Ada said. But as she gave the phone to Billie she felt her excitement swerving toward disappointment. There had been no warm welcome—no recognition, really, at all. Ada felt as if something had been stolen from her. She listened dully as Billie took down directions to Esther's house. When Billie hung up, Ada made a show of good spirits.

"I'll help you carry things in from the car," she said. She could see Billie wasn't happy about having to drive her anywhere just yet. After all, they'd just gotten out of the car.

Billie shook her head. She was checking her schedule with

one hand and reaching for her cigarettes with the other. "We don't have much time. We'll have to go right now."

The street they turned onto had campers parked in the front yards, and boats on trailers were drawn up beside the carports. Dogs began to bark and pull on their chains as they drove down the street.

"Chartreuse. What kind of a color is that to paint a house?" Billie said. They pulled up in front of the house and she turned off the ignition. They didn't say anything for a minute. Then Billie said, "Maybe I should wait in the car."

The house had a dirty canvas over the garage opening, and an accumulation of junk reached from the porch onto the lawn. There were sheets instead of curtains hung across some of the windows. A pickup truck sat in the driveway with its rear axles on blocks. Esther's picture window looked out onto this. Ada stared at the house, wondering what had brought her friend to such a desperate-looking place.

"She'll want to see how you turned out," Ada told Billie. "You can't stay in the car." She was nearly floored by Billie's suggestion. She was trying to keep up her good spirits, but she was shocked and afraid of what she might find inside.

They walked up to the front door. Ada rang the bell and, in a minute, when no one answered, she rang the bell again. Then the door opened and an old, small woman wearing pink slacks and a green sweater looked out.

"I was lying down, girls. Come in, come in," the woman said. Despite the woman's age and appearance, Ada knew it was Esther. She wanted to hug her, but she didn't know if she should. Esther had barely looked at her when she let them in. This was an awful situation, Ada thought. To have come this far and then to be greeted as if she were just anyone. As if she were a stranger.

A rust-colored couch faced the picture window. Esther sat down on it and patted the place beside her. "Sit down here and tell me where I knew you," she said. "Who did you say you were again?"

"God, woman, don't you know me?" Ada said, bending down and taking Esther's hand in hers. She was standing in front of the couch. "I can't believe it. Esther, it's me. It's Ada." She held her face before the woman and waited. Why wouldn't Esther embrace her? Why was she just sitting there? Esther simply stared at her.

"Kid, I wished I did, but I just don't remember you," Esther said. "I don't have a glimmer." She looked down, seemingly ashamed and bewildered by some failure she couldn't account for.

Billie hovered near the door as if she might have to leave for the car at any moment. Ada dropped the woman's hand and sat down next to her on the couch. She felt as if she had tumbled over a cliff and there was nothing left now but to fall. How could she have been so insignificant as to have been forgotten? she wondered. She was angry and hurt, and she wished Billie *had* stayed in the car and not been witness to this humiliation.

"I had a stroke," Esther said and looked at Ada. There was such apology in her voice that Ada immediately felt ashamed of herself for her thoughts. "It happened better than a year ago," she said. Then she said, "I don't know everything, but I still know a lot." She laughed, as if she'd had to laugh at herself often lately. There was an awkward silence as Ada tried to take this in. Strokes happened often enough at their age so she shouldn't be surprised at this turn of events. Still, it was something she hadn't considered; she felt better and worse at the same time.

"Is this your girl? Sit down, honey," Esther said and indicated a chair by the window stacked with magazines and newspapers. "Push that stuff onto the floor and sit down."

"This is my baby," Ada said, trying to show some enthusiasm. "This is Billie."

Billie let loose a tight smile in Esther's direction and cleared a place to sit. Then she took off her gloves and put them on the windowsill next to a candle holder. She crossed her legs, lit a cigarette and gazed out the window in the direction of her Mercedes. "We can't stay too long," she said.

"Billie's giving a talk on business," Ada explained, leaving out just what kind of business it was. "She was coming to Corvallis, so I rode along. I wanted to see you."

"I raise llamas," Billie said, and turned back into the room to see what effect this would have.

"That's nice. That's real nice," Esther said. But Ada doubted she knew a llama from a goat.

"Now don't tell me you can't remember the Conants— those cousins in Springfield we worked for," Ada said.

"Oh, I surely do remember them," Esther said. She was wearing glasses that she held to her face by tilting her head up. From time to time she pushed the bridge of the glasses with her finger. "I've still got a letter in my scrapbook. A recommendation from Mrs. Conant."

"Then you must remember Coley Starber and how we loaned him Mrs. Leslie Conant's sterling silver," Ada said, her hopes rising, as if she'd located the scent and now meant to follow it until she discovered herself lodged in Esther's mind. Billie had picked up a magazine and was leafing through it. From time to time she pursed her lips and let out a stream of smoke.

"Coley," Esther said and stared a moment. "Oh, yes, I remember when he gave the silver back. I counted it to see if it was all there. But, honey, I don't remember you." She shook her head helplessly. "I'm sorry. No telling what else I've forgot."

Ada wondered how it could be that she was missing in Esther's memory when Coley Starber, someone incidental to their lives, had been remembered. It didn't seem fair.

"Mom said you were going to make some fudge," Billie said, holding the magazine under the long ash of her cigarette. "Mom's got a sweet tooth."

"Use that candle holder," Esther told Billie, and Billie flicked the ash into the frosted candle holder.

Ada glared at Billie. She shouldn't have mentioned the fudge. Esther was looking at Ada with a bemused, interested air. "I told Billie how we used to make fudge every chance we got," Ada said.

"And what did we do with all this fudge?" Esther asked.

"We ate it," Ada said.

"We ate it!" Esther said and clapped her hands together. "We *ate* all the fudge." Esther repeated the words to Billie as if she were letting her in on a secret. But Billie was staring at Esther's ankles. Ada looked down and saw that Esther was in her stocking feet, and that the legs themselves were swollen and painful-looking where the pantleg had worked up while Esther sat on the couch.

"What's making you swell up like that?" Billie said. Ada knew Billie was capable of saying anything, but she never thought she'd hear her say a thing like this. Such behavior was the result of business, she felt sure.

"I had an operation," Esther said, as if Billie hadn't said anything at all out of line. Esther glanced toward a doorway that led to the back of the house. Then she raised up her sweater and pulled down the waistband of her slacks to show a long violet-looking scar that ran vertically up her abdomen. "I healed good, though, didn't I?" she said. Esther lowered her sweater, then clasped her hands in her lap.

Before Ada had time to take this in, she heard a thumping sound from the hallway. A man appeared in the doorway of the living room. His legs bowed at an odd angle, and he used a cane. The longer Ada looked at him, the more things she found wrong. One of his eyes seemed fixed on something not in this room, or in any other for that matter. He took a few more steps and extended his hand. Ada reached out to him. The man's hand didn't have much squeeze to it. Billie stood up and inclined her head. She was holding her cigarette in front of her with one hand and had picked up her purse with the other so as not to have to shake hands. Ada didn't blame her. The man was a fright.

"I'm Jason," the man said. "I've had two operations on my legs, so I'm not able to get around very easy. Sit down," he said to Billie. Jason leaned forward against his cane and braced himself. She saw that Jason's interest had settled on Billie. Good, Ada thought. Billie considered herself a woman of the world. Surely she could handle this.

Ada turned to Esther and began to inquire after each of her other children, while she searched for a way to bring things back to that time in Springfield. Esther asked Ada to hand down a photograph album from a shelf behind the couch, and they began to go over the pictures.

"This arthritis hit me when I was forty," Jason said to Billie.

"I guess you take drugs for the pain," Billie said. "I hear they've got some good drugs now."

Ada looked down at the album in her lap. In the album there were children and babies and couples. Some of the couples had children next to them. Ada stared at the photos. Many of the faces were young, then you turned a page and the same faces were old. Esther seemed to remember everyone in the album. But she still didn't remember Ada. She was talking to Ada as to a friend, but Ada felt as if the ghost of her old self hovered in her mind waiting for a sign from Esther so that she could step forward again and be recognized.

"But that wouldn't interest you," Esther was saying as she flipped a page. Suddenly she shut the book and gazed intently at Ada.

"I don't know who you are," Esther said. "But I like you. Why don't you stay the night?" Ada looked over at Billie, who'd heard the invitation.

"Go ahead, Mother," Billie said, a little too eagerly. "I can come for you tomorrow around two o'clock, after the luncheon."

Ada looked at Jason, who was staring out the picture window toward the Mercedes. Maybe she should just give up on getting Esther to remember her and go back to the hotel and watch TV. But the moment she thought this, something unyielding rose up in her. She was determined to discover some moment when her image would suddenly appear before Esther from that lost time. Only then could they be together again as the friends they had once been, and that was what she had come for.

"You'll have to bring my things in from the car," Ada said at last.

"I wish I could help," Jason said to Billie, "but I can't. Fact is, I got to go and lay down again," he said to the room at large. Then he turned and moved slowly down the hallway. Billie opened the door and went out to the car. In a minute she came back with Ada's overnight bag.

"Have a nice time, Mom," she said. "I mean that." She set the bag inside the door. "I'll see you tomorrow." Ada knew she was glad to be heading back to the world of buying and selling, of tax shelters and the multiple uses of the llama. In a minute she heard Billie start up the Mercedes and heard it leave the drive.

The room seemed sparsely furnished now that she and Esther were alone. She could see a table leg just inside the door of a room that was probably the dining room. On the far wall was a large picture of an autumn landscape done in gold and brown.

"Look around, why don't you," Esther said, and raised herself off the couch. "It's a miracle, but I own this house."

They walked into the kitchen. The counter space was taken up with canned goods, stacks of dishes of every kind, and things Ada wouldn't expect to find in a kitchen—things like gallon cans of paint. It was as if someone were afraid they wouldn't be able to get to a store and had laid in extra supplies of everything.

"I do the cooking," Esther said. "Everything's frozen but some wieners. Are wieners okay?"

"Oh, yes," Ada said. "But I'm not hungry just yet."

"I'm not either," Esther said. "I was just thinking ahead because I've got to put these feet up. Come back to the bedroom with me."

Ada thought this an odd suggestion, but she followed Esther down the hallway to a room with a rumpled bed and a chrome kitchen chair near the foot of the bed. There was a dresser with some medicine containers on it. Ada helped Esther get settled on the bed. She took one of the pillows and placed it under Esther's legs at the ankles. She was glad she could do this for her. But then she didn't know what to do next, or what to say. She wanted the past and not this person for whom she was just an interesting stranger. Ada sat down in the chair and looked at Esther.

"What ever became of Georgie Ganz and Florita White?" she asked Esther, because she had to say something.

"Ada—that's your name, isn't it? Ada, I don't know who you're talking about," Esther said. "I wish I did, but I don't."

"That's all right," Ada said. She brightened a little. It made her feel better that Georgie and Florita had also been forgotten. A shadow cast by the house next door had fallen into the room. Ada thought the sun must be going down. She felt she ought to be doing something, changing the course of events for her friend in some small but important way.

"Let me rub your feet," Ada said suddenly and raised herself from the chair. "Okay?" She moved over to the bed and began to massage Esther's feet.

"That feels good, honey," Esther said. "I haven't had anybody do that for me in years."

"Reminds me of that almond cream we used to rub on each other's feet after we'd served at a party all night," Ada said. The feet seemed feverish to her fingers. She saw that the veins were enlarged and angry-looking as she eased her hands over an ankle and up onto the leg.

After a little while Esther said, "Honey, why don't you lie down with me on the bed. That way we can really talk."

At first Ada couldn't comprehend what Esther had said to her. She said she didn't mind rubbing Esther's feet. She said she wasn't tired enough to lie down. But Esther insisted.

"We can talk better that way," Esther said. "Come lay down beside me."

Ada realized she still had on her coat. She took it off and put it over the back of the chair. Then she took off her shoes and went to lie down next to Esther.

"Now this is better, isn't it?" Esther said, when Ada was settled. She patted Ada's hand. "I can close my eyes now and rest." In a minute she closed her eyes. And then they began to talk.

"Do you know about that preacher who was sweet on me

back in Mansfield?" Esther asked. Ada thought for a minute and then remembered and said she did. "I didn't tell that to too many, I feel sure," Esther said. This admission caused Ada to feel for a moment that her friend knew she was someone special. There was that, at least. Ada realized she'd been holding her breath. She relaxed a little and felt a current of satisfaction, something just short of recognition, pass between them.

"I must have told you all my secrets," Esther said quietly, her eyes still closed.

"You did!" Ada said, rising up a little. "We used to tell each other everything."

"Everything," Esther said, as if she were sinking into a place of agreement where remembering and forgetting didn't matter. Then there was a loud noise from the hall, and the sound of male voices at the door. Finally the front door closed, and Esther put her arm across Ada's arm and sighed.

"Good. He's gone," Esther said. "I wait all day for them to come and take him away. His friends, so called. He'll come home drunk, and he won't have a dime. They've all got nothing better to do."

"That must be an awful worry," Ada said. "It must be a heartache."

"Heartache?" Esther said, and then she made a weary sound. "You don't know the start of it, honey. 'You need me, Mom,' he says to me, 'and I need you.' I told him if he stopped drinking I'd will him my house so he'd always have a place to live. But he won't stop. I know he won't. He can't.

"You know what he did?" Esther asked and raised up a little on her pillow. "He just looked at me when I said that about willing him the house. I don't think he'd realized until then that I wasn't always going to be here," Esther said. "Poor fellow, he can't help himself. But girl, he'd drink it up if I left it to him."

Ada felt that the past had drifted away, and she couldn't think how to get back to that carefree time in Springfield. "It's a shame," she murmured. And then she thought of something to tell Esther that she hadn't admitted to anyone. "My husband nearly drank us out of house and home, too. He would have if I hadn't fought him tooth and nail. It's been five years since he died. Five peaceful years." She was relieved to hear herself admit this, but somehow ashamed too.

"Well, I haven't made it to the peaceful part yet," Esther said. "Jason has always lived with me. He'll never leave me. Where could he go?"

"He doesn't abuse you, does he?" Ada said. *Abuse* was a word she'd heard on the television and radio a lot these days, and it seemed all-purpose enough not to offend Esther.

"If you mean does he hit me, no, he doesn't," Esther said. "But I sorrow over him. I do."

Ada had done her share of sorrowing too. She closed her eyes and let her hand rest on Esther's arm. Neither of them said anything for a while. The house was still. She caught the faint medicinal smell of ointment and rubbing alcohol. She wished she could say something to ease what Esther had to bear, but she couldn't think of anything that didn't sound like what Billie might call "sappy."

"What's going to become of Jason?" Ada said finally. But when she asked this she was really thinking of herself and of her friend.

"I'm not going to know," Esther said. "Memory's going to fall entirely away from me when I die, and I'm going to be spared that." She seemed, Ada thought, to be actually looking forward to death and the shutting down of all memory. Ada was startled by this admission.

Esther got up from the bed. "Don't mind me, honey. You stay comfortable. I have to go to the bathroom. It's these water pills."

After Esther left the room Ada raised up in bed as if she had awakened from the labyrinth of a strange dream. What was she doing here, she wondered, on this woman's bed in a city far from her own home? What business of hers was this woman's troubles? In Springfield Esther had always told Ada how pretty she was and what beautiful hair she had, how nicely it took a wave. They had tried on each other's clothes and shared letters from home. But this was something else. This was the future, and she had come here alone. There was no one to whom she could turn and say without the least vanity, "I was pretty, wasn't I?" She sat on the side of the bed and waited for the moment to pass. But it was like an echo that wouldn't stop calling her. Then she heard from outside the house the merry, untroubled laughter of some girls. It must be dark out by now, she thought. It must be night. She got up from the bed, went to the window and pulled back the sheet that served as a curtain. A car was pulling away from the house next door. The lights brushed the room as it moved past. In a moment she went back to the bed and lay down again.

For supper Esther gave her wieners, and green beans fixed the way they'd had them back home, with bacon drippings. Then she took her to the spare room, which was next to Jason's room. They had to move some boxes off the bed. Esther fluffed up the pillows and put down an extra blanket. Then she moved over to the doorway.

"If you need anything, if you have any bad dreams, you just call me, honey," she said. "Sometimes I dream I'm wearing a dress but it's on backwards and I'm coming downstairs, and there's a whole room full of people looking up at me," she said. "I'm glad you're here. I am. Good night. Good night, Ada."

"Good night, Esther," Ada said. But Esther went on standing there in the doorway.

Ada looked at her and wished she could dream them both back to a calm summer night in Springfield. She would open her window and call across the alley to her friend, "You awake?" and Esther would hear her and come to the screen and they would say wild and hopeless things like, Why don't we go to California and try out for the movies? Crazy things like that. But Ada didn't remind Esther of this. She lay there alone in their past and looked at Esther, at her old face and her old hands coming out of the sleeves of her robe, and she wanted to yell at her to get out, shut the door, don't come back! She hadn't come here to strike up a friendship with this old scarecrow of a woman. But then Esther did something. She came over to the bed and pulled the covers over Ada's shoulders and patted her cheek.

"There now, dear," she said. "I'm just down the hall if you need me." And then she turned and went out of the room.

Sometime before daylight Esther heard a scraping sound in the hall. Then something fell loudly to the floor. But in a while the scraping sound started again and someone entered the room next to hers and shut the door. It was Jason, she supposed. Jason had come home, and he was drunk and only a few feet away. She had seen her own husband like this plenty of times, had felt herself forgotten, obliterated, time after time. She lay there rigid and felt the weight of the covers against her throat. Suddenly it was as if she were suffocating. She felt her mouth open and a name came out of it. "Esther! Esther!" she cried. And in a few moments her door opened and her friend came in and leaned over her.

"What is it, honey?" Esther said, and turned the lamp on next to the bed.

"I'm afraid," Ada said, and she put out her hand and took hold of Esther's sleeve. "Don't leave," she said. Esther waited a minute. Then she turned off the light and got into bed beside Ada. Ada turned on her side, facing the wall, and Esther's arm went around her shoulder.

The next day Billie came to the house a little early. Ada had just finished helping Esther wash her hair.

"I want you to take some pictures of us," Ada said to Billie. "Esther and me." She dug into her purse and took out the Kodak she'd carried for just this purpose. Billie seemed in a hurry to get on the road now that the conference was over.

"I was a real hit last night," Billie said to Ada as if she'd missed seeing her daughter at her best. Little tufts of llama wool clung to Billie's suit jacket as she took the camera from Ada and tried to figure out where the lens was and how to snap the picture. Ada felt sure she hadn't missed anything, but she understood Billie's wanting her to know she'd done well at something. That made sense to her now.

"Let's go out in the yard," Billie said.

"My hair's still wet," Esther said. She was standing in front of a mirror near the kitchen rubbing her hair with a towel, but the hair sprang out in tight spirals all over her head.

"You look all right," Ada said. "You look fine, honey."

"You'd say anything to make a girl feel good," Esther said.

"No, I wouldn't," Ada said. She stood behind Esther and, looking in the mirror, dabbed her own nose with powder. They could be two young women readying themselves to go out, Ada thought. They might meet some young men while they were out, and they might not. In any case, they'd take each other's arm and stroll until dusk. Someone—Ada didn't know who— might pass and admire them.

Billie had them stand in front of the picture window. They put their arms around each other. Esther was shorter and leaned her head onto Ada's shoulder. She even smiled. Ada had the sensation that the picture had already been taken somewhere in her past. She was sure it had.

"Did you get it?" Ada said as Billie advanced the film and moved closer for another shot.

"I'm just covering myself," Billie said, squatting down on the lawn and aiming the camera like a professional. "You'll kill me if these don't turn out." She snapped a few more shots from the driveway, then handed the camera back to her mother.

Ada followed her friend into the house to collect her belongings and say good-bye. Esther wrapped a towel around her head while Ada gathered her coat, purse, and overnight bag.

"Honey, I'm so sorry I never remembered you," Esther said.

Ada believed Esther when she said this. *Sorry* was the word a person had to use when there was no way to change a situation. Still, she wished they could have changed it.

"I remembered *you,* that's the main thing," Ada said. But a miserable feeling came over her, and it was all she could do to speak. Somehow the kindness and intimacy they'd shared as girls had lived on in them. But Esther, no matter how much she might want to, couldn't remember Ada, and give it back to her, except as a stranger.

"God, kid, I hate to see you go," Esther said. Her eyes filled. It seemed to Ada that they might both be wiped from the face of the earth by this parting. They embraced and clung to each other a moment. Ada patted Esther's thin back, and then moved hurriedly toward the door.

"Tell me all about your night," Billie said, as Ada slid into the passenger's seat. But Ada knew this was really the last thing on Billie's mind. And anyhow, it all seemed so far from anything Ada had ever experienced that she didn't know where to begin.

"Honey, I just want to be still for a while," Ada said. She didn't care whether Billie smoked or how fast she drove. She knew that eventually she would tell Billie how she had tried to make Esther remember her, and how she had failed. But the important things—the way Esther had come to her when she'd called out, and how, earlier, they'd lain side by side—this would be hers. She wouldn't say anything to Billie about these things. She couldn't. She doubted she ever would. She looked out at the countryside that flew past the window in a green blur. It went on and on, a wall of forest that crowded the edge of the roadway. Then there was a gap in the color and she found herself looking at downed trees and stumps where an entire hillside of forest had been cut away. Her hand went to her face as if she had been slapped. But then she saw it was green again, and she let her hand drop to her lap.

WOMEN

. . . .

WHAT I DON'T TELL PEOPLE

Kelly Cherry

· ·

People quiz me for details, and this is what I tell them: We eat breakfast and then he goes upstairs to the bathroom to jack off into the little plastic vial I have given him. I settle myself in the reading chair in my living room and open my book to a story by Grace Paley. And now, this is what life and literature conspire to teach me: My last lover, who, I begin to suspect, may prove to be the last I will ever have, and who has already receded one entire agonizing year into the past, covered me with indulgences. Oh, god, yes, he touched my cheek, the back of my neck, he held my hand, I walked around in a space that was warmed by the knowledge that he shared it. He sweetened my mouth with his tongue, he was passionate and gentle. These are the virtues of a man past forty. The Paley story is a short one, I have no doubt I will finish it, but I have not even turned the page when my twenty-one-year-old donor reappears on the staircase. He has put the vial into the discreet brown-paper lunch bag I thought to provide. "One baby boy, ready to roll," he says, holding it out to me.

The nurse has told me to be sure to keep it warm. Warm? In a Wisconsin winter? With ice on the windshield and a windchill factor that hit fifty below last night?

I put on my parka and he tucks the lunch bag into my inside pocket, where my body heat can make its contribution. We

200

knock the snow off the roof of the car and drive down Regent. The nurse has also said we have to do all this within a half hour of my appointment. She doesn't know that my donor is only twenty-one, up from Memphis, and accustomed to a Porsche. He's speeding, feeling she has given him license to. A cop makes us pull over. Angus rolls the window down and cold air sweeps in like it is the caboose from the Siberian Express the weatherman is always talking about on TV. The cop asks Angus what the hurry is. "Young man," the cop says.

Angus says with a straight face, "I have to get this woman to the hospital right away, Officer. She's trying to get pregnant."

I am afraid we're going to be made to pay for this wisecrack, but the cop doesn't register it. He hears something like "She's pregnant," and my parka obligingly makes me look fat and he lets us go.

In the examining room I lie on the table with my feet in stirrups, waiting for the doctor. The vial is sitting on the supply table. Minutes march by—*hup, hup, hup* on the clock on the wall. An army of minutes. A goddamn *Chinese* army of minutes—they seem innumerable. I look at the vial. Angus's youthful sperm are aging rapidly. I imagine a war going on between the spermatozoa and the militarily disciplined minutes. The sperm are disorganized, headlong, brave, and not too smart. They joke a lot in the trenches. They get hysterical when frustrated or frightened. In forty-eight hours they will keel over from battle fatigue. Time is winning. At last the doctor comes in. "How are you today, Nina?" he says. I want to tell him I have just witnessed scenes of carnage, that I'm drained, but I say, "Fine."

He takes the lid off the vial and draws the specimen up into a syringe and sits on a stool between my legs. If you don't provide your own donor, you bring twenty dollars in cash to slip him while you're still in this position, reaching into your purse, which he hands you. Insurance does not cover the cost of the semen. The procedure is billed as a pelvic exam. The doctor drafts one of the donors from his list and asks him to come into the office thirty minutes before you do—so you never see who it is—and pays him out of his own pocket, and then you pay the doctor. You do this two or three times per month, depending on your basal body temperature and your mucus. You sign a piece of paper that says that you are a happily married couple but that the husband-half of you, "while not impotent," is "seemingly" infertile—someone thought carefully about those words, preserving the male ego—and you feel your marriage would be so enriched by a child that you will not hold the doctor responsible for any genetic or congenital defects or, since the semen is fresh and therefore untested, any disease you may contract. Why am I, a single woman of an age that raises the risks entailed significantly and who does not earn enough to pay for day care, doing this? Because I want to hold a baby in my arms, which I have never done in my life. I want to create a life that is independent of mine. I have a hunger for obligations, responsibilities. I have a hunger to set someone free of me purposely instead of just always watching as a man I like, or in the most recent instance, deeply love, pulls away from me, when I'm willing him, with all the emotional force I can command, to stay. I always wanted children. Nobody ever proposed, except for a man I'm sorry to say I did marry, and he said I wasn't mentally healthy enough to have a child. He thought a child would be like a little neurosis that had been converted to a material form. But that's a story so old I almost never tell it anymore. Things are more exciting now. When you shake off someone who's been telling you how to view yourself, your horizons expand. The world opens up like a flower through the agency of time-lapse photography. I have just learned to drive so that I can chauffeur the kid to slumber parties and swimming lessons. Of course, no one ever asks a married woman to justify why she wants a baby.

The doctor squirts me with the syringe, says, "Lift up your bottom," and pulls a platform out that raises the lower half of my body an inch or two, and leaves the room. Thinking quickly, I have asked him to turn down the Muzak, but if my ears get a rest, my eyes don't: I'm staring straight up at a high-wattage fluorescent light. I've still got my sweater and thermal undershirt on, but I'm naked from the waist down, under a single, thin, cotton sheet, and my legs are cold. I have to keep my feet in the stirrups. I have to stay like this for fifteen minutes. To my right is a magazine rack with pamphlets about herpes and how to check your breasts. I have brought a book of poems to read. The author of this book dedicated it to the memory of a mutual friend, a man I spent a weekend with a decade ago. A man who used to call me up long-distance just to talk and laugh. I thought I might be pregnant from that weekend but I wasn't. A few years later my friend killed himself. He swallowed a host of sleeping pills, dozens of them, red and white and yellow like the races of the world, and wrote a note apologizing for his action. All that grace and beauty—emptied of air like a flat tire. All his joyful high jinks—kaput. I wasn't in love with him, but he had a sweetness of spirit I would like for my child, so I read the poems dedicated to his memory and think about him. I read some other poems set behind the Iron Curtain, where another man I cared about lives. This brings me almost to the end of my list of men whose children I might have had. The only one left is the man I loved so much, Cliff. For Clifford, not, thank you, Heathcliff. I actually was pregnant by him. A year ago—almost to the day. Dark anniversary: I had a miscarriage. Relief for him, sorrow for me—but happiness too, because it meant I could get pregnant, something that for years I'd been told would never happen.

I am staring at the light, my legs mottling in the cold glare, and I realize: This baby is going to be born with a broken heart. Cliff, damn you, where are you?

This is not a productive line of thought, and I abandon it. I read more poems and check my watch and then I get up and pull on my jeans and go downstairs, where Angus has been patiently waiting for over an hour.

Angus is the friend of a young friend of mine. When my young friend heard I was determined to have a baby, now that I knew I could get pregnant, she said, "Wait a minute! We'll have to make sure you get some good chromosomes!" I said I couldn't wait, I was running out of time. Cliff had left me for another woman—a married woman, for crying out loud—and there wasn't another boyfriend on the horizon. "No sweat," she said. "I know just the person."

She said he would look on this as an adventure, a kind of lark—how could he not, at twenty-one? He would see himself striding into my life, virile and good-natured and subservient to nothing except maybe Kryptonite, ready to rescue me from what the doctors call nulliparity, the condition of having no children. Even so, what a generous person he is, I think, to have traveled so far and taken a week out of his life to help me have a baby. I say this to him. He is six-five in his boots, and whenever I want to make eye contact with him while he's standing up I have to bend over backwards. He has a square face with a strong chin. He is handsome but not prettyish, and he looks ten years older than he is and owns his own company. He has dated movie stars. How does he feel about his sperm milling around in my vagina? This is not a party that they are going to in my uterus, a convention; this is a serious business. How does he feel about it?

The next morning we go to see my lawyer. On the way to the car, in front of my house, he lets out a rebel yell. He is, after all, despite everything, twenty-one. I cringe, wondering if we've disturbed my neighbors. He sees me hurriedly folding into myself like a collapsible plastic traveling cup and laughs. He yells again: "HOO-HA." The Confederacy is alive and well. The South has risen, and it's not yet nine.

What can I do? I grin back.

The lawyer is the opposite of a wheeler-dealer legalist. He is an attractive, understanding man my own age, the adoptive father of multiracial children. He makes me feel not-crazy. Kindness emanates from him.

I barely know him, but he knows weird things about me: He knows I haven't had a date in a year. He knows I haven't got the courage to sleep with Angus.

"This is going to be a tall kid," he says softly, shaking Angus's hand. And he is no midget. "Hello, Nina," he says.

We sit in captain's chairs facing his reassuringly solid desk. The office is in one of the old houses downtown, just off the Square. This area is inundated with lawyers. In the middle of the Square stands the state capitol, a building that is like a *frisson* made visible, a delicate shiver of white stone. At night, lights on the capitol make it a compass point. Through the clear night the capitol glows like a beacon, a silvery haze haloing the sweet dome.

Angus is wearing a black-and-white houndstooth coat, which he leaves on. It makes him look dominant. The lawyer is in a three-piece suit. I am wearing a gray wool skirt, light gray silk blouse, gray knit vest, gray boots, and my good black coat with the low-slung back belt. This elegance is atypical. This is long-john country. We are dressed for the occasion.

Angus wants to know if we are setting a precedent. The lawyer thinks we may be, at least for Wisconsin, which is, despite rumors to the contrary, primarily a conservative, Republican state.

The lawyer has researched the situation. There is indeed a law that covers us, although as recently as a year ago it wouldn't have. Wis. Stats. S891.40(2) states:

> The donor of semen provided to a licensed physician for use in artificial insemination of a woman other than the donor's wife is not the natural father of a child conceived, bears no liability for the support of the child and has no parental rights with regard to the child.

A year ago someone "quietly removed," he says, the word "married," which previously had modified "woman."

I express my admiration for anyone in Wisconsin who can accomplish such a change "quietly." The political system in our state is generally exceptionally noisy, punctuated with loud lobbyists. The background for all this is populism, a philosophy that says that for every taxpayer there should be two legislators, preferably in conflict with each other.

Angus says he wants the kid's middle name to be Precedent.

"In this Agreement," the lawyer says, sliding two copies of it across the great desk, one to Angus and one to me, "you are affectionately known as Donor and Recipient." He smiles at me.

What the Agreement says is simply that Angus and I are both aware of the law and agree to be bound by it. It takes four pages to say this, but since Angus is not a resident of Wisconsin, it seems like a good idea, insurance for both of us, to do this. I assume all risks posed by the insemination and indemnify Donor. He will have no parental rights or responsibility and shall furnish Recipient with any and all information required by Recipient pertaining to his genetic or medical characteristics. The child will have no claim of inheritance against Donor's estate and all of the provisions of this Agreement and of S891.40(2), Wis. Stats. shall be binding upon the respective heirs, next of kin, executors and administrator of the parties. IN WITNESS WHEREOF, Angus and I take turns signing the original.

The lawyer carries the original out to the Xerox machine and returns with two more copies, one for each of us to keep. I ask him if he feels like a midwife.

From a frame on his desk, the light brown faces of two young boys in striped T-shirts who feel self-conscious but pleased about their father's photographing them laugh as they look out at us. I imagine them pushing against each other while their father tells them to hold still. Such energy contained within the boundaries of that frame! Such happiness!

Now Angus and I are outside again. Snow creaks and crunches under my fashionable gray boots.

In the car we tease each other about the lawyer. At long last we have something to talk about—something in common that is not too embarrassing to discuss. (We have almost nothing in common.) We say all the funny lines we can think of. When we park the car in the lot under my office building, he bounds out and races around to my side to open the door for me. He is Southern through and through, a gentleman.

We stand in the cold, hollow basement called Lower Parking. I feel the concrete floor pressing up against my boot soles. The walls come closer, crowding me. The dampness has fingers that invade us, wriggling their way between our buttons, under our coats.

Angus is still excited about our Agreement. He is going to walk up State Street, buying red Badger sweatshirts and souvenirs and picking up girls. In his enthusiasm, he tries to kiss me good-bye—only a peck, but I pull away. "At least let me give you a hug," he says, baffled, and again moves toward me.

I am looking around wildly, terrified that someone may be taking all this in. "No!" I say, much too adamantly, as if he were presuming upon our relationship when all he is doing is being friendly. "No!" I am ashamed of myself but scared, so scared I can feel my heart trying to run away, but it's trapped in my body, nowhere to go.

Am I angry with him for not being Cliff? Do I feel I'm at his mercy, unable to interest a man my own age long enough to entice him to deposit some semen? I try to recover; I give him my office number and tell him he can stop in later. When he does, I introduce him to a young woman with lovely black brows that fly above her face like black swans above a pale wintry marsh. Later he asks if she wants to make a baby too.

At the restaurant where we go for lunch I see Cliff but he doesn't see me. He is in corduroy, wearing his contacts. From this far away I can nevertheless see his right hand, on which he is resting the side of his head, in detail. It is like a detail from a painting by Rembrandt. The unusually long, well-defined fingers remind me how it felt to be touched by him. With that hand he altered my life. I tell Angus he has to swap seats with me. I want Cliff to see me sitting there with Angus when he comes over to pay the cashier. I want this even though I know Cliff prides himself on never feeling jealous. A year has gone by, Cliff has replaced me so completely that I am to him a distant event he only vaguely recalls, a phone number he could get right because it sticks in the way phone numbers do but which he never thinks to dial, and yet I am being hit by a tidal wave of anxiety, I am drowning, I am going under right here in the Ovens of Brittany, amid hanging ferns, also hanging Persian carpets, the muted strains of the Pachabel canon (what else?), and spinach gâteau. I want to go over and tell him that when I look at him the Reptilian part of my brain responds like a lizard to light, turning to him as a source of warmth. But when he gets up, he leaves money on the table and goes out the back way instead of coming up to the cash register. He never finds out I'm here. I have been erased. He would be offended if anyone said that to him, but it's true—whole days we were together have already fallen into obscurity and no-time, eliminated from his personal history.

When I come home from work, Angus is wearing the running pants he bought on State Street. They are skintight, Lycra, I think, the kind of pants cross-country bicyclists wear. He's got thighs like Eric Heiden (a Wisconsin boy). In these pants he would make Mikhail Baryshnikov look like a rube in baggy trousers. These pants are so tight they must serve some mathematically precise engineering function with respect to the wind, as he cleaves the blue air like a Delta wingtip.

He stands in my living room with his legs spread wide, bending his torso forward from the waist, shifting his weight back and forth, left leg to right and back again, to, he says, stretch his muscles. I try to look anywhere except at what is right in front of me. What am I doing with this monumentally male figure, masculine youth in oh, my god, full bloom, here before me in innocent self-delight? He overpowers my modest living room. The pants are silver; he is a walking cannon. He makes Superman look underdeveloped—and his face bears a strong resemblance to Christopher Reeve's, at that.

I catch my breath after he closes the door behind him and takes off down the street. I sit in the reading chair, trying not to think about his genetic endowment.

I have asked some friends to come by for drinks after dinner. If they look out their windows before then, before dark, they may see Angus flying by, a bullet, and ask themselves, startled,

Who was that? The father of my future child, I will mumble casually. A mere wonder of the world.

I want my friends to see what good taste I have, to understand that I have not gone bananas and hauled a weirdo in off the streets to impregnate me. It is important to me that they realize that the father of my child is decent and admirable, not to say a hunk.

Is there a child already in me, is there life igniting, a little blaze that will burn brighter and brighter, melting all the snow?

It is important to me that Angus see me in context. I want him to understand that I have a nexus, I am part of a community, I may be single but I am not without social meaning, I have ramifications, my days overlap with the days of my friends like a chain of links. I cannot be intimidated. I am not desperate.

We are drinking Mumm's from Styrofoam cups, a note of celebration sounded by my friends from across the street, Sam and Mary Clementi. We are toasting my other friends from across the street on the other side of my house, Ian and Shelley Wallace, who were married, a second marriage for both, a couple of weeks ago. My friend Sarah is also here. The subtext is a toast to the baby, but no one wants to embarrass Angus by actually mentioning it. I like candles and have lit several, on the marble-top telephone table, the small teak table next to the reading chair, and the fireplace mantel. The candlelight blues the green on the houseplant leaves. My dog is in the kitchen, behind the baby gate, because if I let him out he would leap from lap to lap, so overwhelmed by a plethora of human companions that he would not be able to choose among the riches. He sits politely and eagerly, wagging his tail whenever anyone goes to the gate to pet him; he is on his best behavior, so full of contentment I want to cry when I look at him, but then, I am unregenerately mushy about my dog. He is my family— except, of course, for the baby I hope is writing itself into existence right now, a character sketch polishing itself in my body.

I pass around plates of cheese, bowls of peanuts and raisins, chocolate mints. Angus has built a fire, and it draws us close to one another, gives us a center; firelight flickers over my friends' dear faces—they, too, are my family. Angus and Sam and Mary are discussing computers. Sarah and Ian and Shelley are talking about the advantages of front-wheel drive. Last week Sarah skidded off the road on the way to Chicago but managed to turn the car in the direction of the skid and so regained control of it. As she was continuing on, trying to calm her nerves, she saw beside her a car full of returning hunters, a deer strapped to the hood, blood still running down the front windshield. The men in the front seat were eating fast-food burgers. In a voice made mysterious by the fire and the candles she explains how this image affected her. Our voices, which had swollen in volume with the champagne, drop to a sympathetic murmur. In our minds the image grows—a deer so big its antlers are branching trees, blood as red as paint, men with fangs, and the unemotional snow falling past the headlights as if nothing could ever be any different from the way it is.

I think: Nature is autistic.

Mary asks me if my dog can join us. He careens into the living room, his little claws ticking on the hardwood floor like a clock.

It's late, and home they go. Holding Sarah's coat for her while she slips her arms into the sleeves, I hear her ask me why I don't just do it the natural way, he's so good-looking. Have some fun, she whispers—it won't be much fun later. She takes a dim view of my intent but is in favor of sex.

He sleeps in the small bedroom on a cot that is too short for his long legs.

I am in my bedroom, under the electric blanket, with my dog curled next to me at my hipbone.

He knocks on my door, advances into my room. My dog doesn't stir; he's exhausted from the evening's excitement.

It's a big room, running from the front to the back of the house. Someone once turned up at my front door to announce that he had lived here when he was a child. He had four sisters, he said, and they slept in a row in this long room. I imagine them in their single beds, girls in white flannel nightgowns with dots of creamy moisturizer on their faces. I can hear them giggling. I wonder what their grown-up lives are like.

At least this room can contain him. I sit up in bed, propping myself on my pillow, trying not to jump to conclusions but jumping to them all the same.

And he says, "I'm sorry you're having such a hard time. I wish I could do something to help. I could go to a motel."

I am appalled. I didn't mean to make him feel like an intruder. I have tried not to look sad or stressed. It is not his fault that Cliff didn't love me. It is certainly not his fault that I am childless. I try to tell him this—without revealing the extent to which I feel I've failed at life. I don't want to burden him with that—but how did he know I was sad? How did he know that I have escaped into this room, pressured by our immediate intimacy until I must flee, lose myself in solitude and sitcoms?

I am amazed by how perceptive men can be, even young boys. I never knew such men until I met Cliff or my friend Rajan, and Sam and Ian. I grew up thinking men had no inner life that defied their will—they were creatures of cool. This was, indeed, my brother's reality, which, however, I misapplied to all men.

He is so considerate, Angus is. I thank him for his thought-fulness. I tell him I'm sorry I haven't been better company but that I've enjoyed doing things with him. (We have been to movies, a play, dinner.) I think of making love with him, but I no longer have the body of a coed. And it will be better for my child if I don't. He doesn't suggest it, anyway. He says good night and vanishes into the other room.

That handsome high-tech whiz-kid sleeps behind a door a few feet away. I chastise myself for not responding to him more openly or readily. I am so greedy: I wanted a man in my own peer group who would love and honor me, return cherishing for cherishing, and not get going when the going got tough. I thought Cliff was the one. Walking through the woods one day, Cliff had said it worried him that I was so eager to go ahead with something he might want to do with me in a couple of years. A baby. I thought his statement implied a future. I erected a city of children on that sentence, begat generations.

Drifting to sleep, I remind myself that although the way I am doing this may not be the right way, or the best way, you can only play the hand you're dealt. This is the only game in town.

Angus and I go to dinner at L'Etoile, a fine restaurant on the second story of a building on the Square. There is a red rose in a delicate vase on the white tablecloth. One end of the room is all window, and we look out over the Square to the capitol, a golden-lighted Christmas tree of a building, a cold breath caught in air and carved. Night is a mystery, a time when we regress to our earlier selves, when we stayed awake listening to our parents rehearse: The Razoumovskys spilled beauty on our lids like sand, and we were borne into the world of an ambition that reaches beyond the nameable world. This is our hope: to create, to create, to create, to caress the eye and the ear, to love. Children are the fulfillment of that drive.

The phone rings the day after he's gone, and it's Angus, laughing into my pleased ear. "It feels good to have the house to yourself again, doesn't it?" he says, and again I want to ask him how he *knows*.

"Did you have a good flight?" I ask. "Is it cold down there?"

"Hey," he says, "I've been lying in the sun."

He tells me again that where he lives people don't think you're strange if you say hello when you pass them on the sidewalk. Though he doesn't say it, I can hear he's glad to be back home.

I hear scraping sounds from my front stoop. My favorite teenager has come to shovel the new snow that fell last night. (My favorite teenager is the son of friends who live on Regent. I leave the shovel by the stoop. Sometimes when he finishes he comes inside and we chat about his English teacher, who is giving him a hard time unnecessarily.)

"Call me as soon as you know something, okay?" Angus's voice is a unilateral nonaggression pact, a careful drawl that feints as it approaches. "Nina?" he adds.

"I will," I promise. "I will."

And so I begin to wait. I continue to take my basal body temperature, reaching for the thermometer on my nightstand every morning before I get out of bed. My sleep is always so broken that I never completely believe in the readings, but I record them regularly on my chart. I steer clear of alcohol, substitute Sanka for caffeine, cut down on sugar, take calcium supplements—all just in case.

I scrutinize the bookstore for books on pregnancy and childbirth. In the Women's Health section I run into Carolyn Gilbert. Carolyn's face is still red from the drug she took for six months to tame her endometriosis. She and her husband have been trying to have a baby for two years. Last week she had another miscarriage—her third. As she tells me this, she looks as though she is going to cry. She has fibroid tumors, she tells me, and doesn't know whether or not to have an operation, which is long and involved and offers only a limited chance of success anyway.

I wonder what is wrong with us, two women who have "made it" in a man's world but who cannot seem to accomplish the most elementary of female roles.

Carolyn is rattling on, not quite looking at me. I sense hidden hysteria and touch her hand, which she is nervously running over the spines of books as if they were a xylophone, as if they could play a tune. "I know how you feel," I say. "Even if you get pregnant again, you can't replace the one you lost. Each miscarriage is a lost possibility. You have a right to grieve."

She looks grateful, relieved. I don't know her well, and it's only a moment—but it has a penumbra that stays with me, a space I walk in, feeling I have made a connection. All that week and from time to time during the following week, I think about Carolyn, her pain and her courage. And when I start to bleed, I tell her. I call Angus and tell him. I tell the doctor, the lawyer. One by one, I inform my friends. People are kind—they can't help being curious. They ask me, now that it seems to be something that is safely in the past, what it feels like to be artificially inseminated. It feels just like what it sounds like, I say: fake fucking. They quiz me for details, which I'm glad to tell them. What I don't tell people, what I never tell them, is that it feels like death.

SUNDAY MORNING

Pat Carr

. . . .

"Just take it easy. It doesn't hurt that much."

His voice was suave, calm, practiced.

The pain welled out, radiating, cutting her in half so sharply, so abruptly that her breath stopped. There was nothing but the white pain filling her, consuming her. Then it started receding, drawing back into itself somewhere inside that was not a part of her, and she remembered that she wasn't supposed to hold her breath, that she was supposed to pant like a dog instead.

"Now see."

He put his hand heavily on the white swathed mound and she felt it and knew it was a part of her he was touching, something that had belonged to her but somehow didn't anymore.

She moved her ankles against the straps, the metal against her heels, but she couldn't see them over the mound.

It started again.

She knew she could stand it, she was prepared for it, and she remembered to open her mouth and take in the short choppy bits of air. But it was worse than she'd thought as it swelled, carrying her with it behind her closed eyelids and passed what she could stand.

"Just relax," the nurse said from somewhere outside the pain. "They're coming along nicely now, Doctor."

It went down again, lowering her with it onto a glass shelf. But she'd tensed against it and she was stiff.

"Breathe, breathe. That's the girl."

She should concentrate on relaxing the next time it came, telling herself it couldn't win, but a woman was screaming through a wall in the next cubicle, and she couldn't close out the sound enough to think herself calm.

"Listen to the one Dr. Davis got," the nurse said.

As it started, a hand pressed down on the mound and it fought against the hand, sharpening itself, breaking her in two. She wanted to push the hand away, but both of hers were strapped down and she could only move her head from side to side.

Breathe, breathe, pant like a dog next time.

She didn't know if it was actually worse or if she was merely giving in to it a little more each time, letting it swallow her, melt away a little more of her, feed on her from inside, grow each time.

When it recoiled, she wouldn't be blind and could focus, hear their voices.

She didn't know how long it had been coming, receding, its swells of brilliant pain sweeping her up, out, faster, the lowerings shorter, almost without a chance to pause. She lost contact with time and her arms and legs knotted into clenched muscles.

Then, "I see the head coming," he said.

But somehow that didn't mean anything in the grip of the terrible grinding pain. She tried to rise above it, to breathe, but she couldn't find the rim of it and her lungs wouldn't work around it.

"Push now."

Again and again, faster, one swell coming before the last had quite gone down. Moans were close around her, and she felt the clamminess of her forehead like blood.

"Push!"

She had to defecate but the pain clamped around her and it was as if her insides were crashing through the partition of her bowels.

"There!"

A great rushing, bursting shattered the glass shelf.

"There," one of them said again.

It receded again and a hand touched her. It had gone down enough for her to open her eyelids.

He was holding up a baby. A slick blue yellow body, long and lifeless, a narrow and hairless animal.

Then he slapped his hand against it and the body quivered, took a breath that washed through it in a pink flood and changed the yellow. It let the breath out again in a fierce cry.

He gave it to the nurse who began busily wiping it at another table as the pain started again.

She gasped and was betrayed. It hadn't ended. She moaned.

"That's the afterbirth coming now," he said complacently and put his hand on the white mound again.

She looked at it startled even over the pain. It hadn't gone down, hadn't changed at all, and yet the baby was already out. But then she could see it ripple, looser than it had been, sway as the pain came and went, lessening, lessening.

"Do you feel that?"

He was sitting at the foot of the table below the mound, and she couldn't see him.

She waited to see if there was anything to feel. "No."

"I'm sewing you up now, but I didn't think you'd feel anything. Usually the pressure of the head has deadened everything."

He went on talking, and she could see the long rough strand pull up in a hemming motion as he sewed.

Her muscles ached with excruciating stiffness, and the waves of pain were still coming, going. But it had weakened, it was over and she knew it.

The woman next door was still moaning.

They had taken the baby away, and she realized she hadn't asked what it was. That didn't seem to matter somehow.

Without interest she let them do whatever they were doing. She lay racked, waiting.

Finally they released her ankles and wrists, but the cramps didn't go away immediately as she'd thought they would. The nurse brought another stiff new sheet and recovered, rearranged her. They put a needle in her arm and hooked it to colorless tubes that ran to a colorless liquid in a bottle above her head.

"There we are."

In a bright glare of lights two white-suited men wheeled her out into the hallway.

Whitney was there and pressed her hand with his until her bones hurt. He was smiling, patting her hand all the way down the hall to the room.

The baby was already there in a white bassinet laced with a blue ribbon over the top, and she wondered if that meant it was a boy.

They wheeled her next to it, rolled her and the colorless tubes onto the hospital bed there beside the bassinet, covered her with the stiff sheet and a white cotton spread.

"Is this ours?" He was peering down into the curve of the bassinet.

It wasn't, it was hers, but she looked over, not to have to say it, looking toward but not really seeing the baby, and nodded.

FERTILITY ZONE

Patricia Eakins

. . . .

"**H**arley," I said when I'd crawled home through the dewy petunias, "Harley, you know that dead woman?"

"Mmmmmm," says Harley, who stuffs the covers in his mouth.

"That dead woman went and had her baby."

"Is it all right?" asks Harley, sitting right up.

"Born with everything where it should be! Dr. Conroy says it's the easiest birth ever, even if it was a Caesarian. Says he wished they were all like her—never a groan. 'Course they had her under drugs; I don't know why, if her brain was dead."

"How could the baby be all right if the mother was dead?"

"Well, her chest was going up and down, and they were feeding her through that I.V., all what the baby needed. That baby got better nourishment than she would have at home. You know what people eat—tortilla chips and beer."

"I don't like it," Harley says.

"You don't have to," I say.

But there's that motherless child, born from a brain-dead anonymous, they're going to shove in an orphanage; here's me and Harley sticking teddy-bear decals on a brand-new crib. Makes me spit. But no use arguing once Harley gets that tone to his voice.

"I'm going to fix my breakfast and turn in," I say, and I go about getting my rice puffs and raisins—you can see I eat like an elf on a mushroom. It's my glands pump me up to two-twenty-five. Harley reads the scale because I can't see past my stomach. I *look* pregnant, but I been trying for seven years.

First thing you wake, before you even tinkle, you take your temperature. And you better have remembered to shake that mercury down when you put out the light. You can't shake it down just before you jab the thermometer under your tongue, because shaking drives your heat up. You're trying to record it unaffected, at waking's first calm, before the hot presence of mind moves you to rub the hard sleep from the corners of your eyes. You're trying to find your true underlying temper, so you'll notice one day when your degrees drop. That's when your egg is falling through your tubes, falling and falling, like an astronaut, falling toward what he doesn't know. After, your temperature leaps, and then you conceive.

So Harley and I keep track of tenths of degrees, and make a graph, connecting dots. I let Harley do that part.

The night the dead woman gave birth, we were in my fertility zone, so I gulped my cereal, 'cause if I don't crawl in with Harley right off the bus, nothing's going to happen. Harley ambles off to work when he's sober—an outdoor job at Robbins's Nursery—lots of shoveling. I always say we got something in common, him spreading manure and me collecting bedpans. I've got a hoister's biceps from lifting and turning the patients, washing them, changing their bedclothes—I don't mind. Because you're helping out, as I see it, helping the needy. Not like working in the five-and-dime. There you say, "Can I help you?" But what do you have that anyone needs?

Anyway. Running home to Harley from work, I'm still painted up, my eyelashes curled, my lips bee-stung. I'm not trying to woo with my hair in rollers, lure with a hairnet over the lumps.

"Harley," I coo, and I can pout so's you'd think of a doll. "Harley," I drawl, "how you feeling, honey, can I get you something?"

"Just knead this pain in my shoulder," he says. Or his foot

or his stomach. He's been home in bed all night, and I've been hefting trays and cranking beds, but I don't mind. I rub him where it hurts and hope. He talks to me, and if he's been drinking he cries a flood. Sooner or later he passes out, snores like a giant lizard stalking his dinner on the late-late show, but I let it be. I don't question. Oh, I might hint now and then. "Harley, those names you call me when you're tight . . ." And he feels so bad to hear he crowned me Miss Dual-Wheel-Stomach. He swears he loves me; just the liquor talked. I pray he don't drink around our little girl.

It's going to be a little girl, I know, just like I knew the dead woman's baby would be a girl. I could see it in the air around the mother, a soft shine like the glow of a new spring leaf.

It was just a girl-glad luster she had, though her face, it's still, without expression. Like nothing affects her, sorrow or joy, except way far in where her soul shines, that one little candle in the dark of the song, beyond caring. But who am I to say she doesn't care? Maybe she does. I'm sure she does! But her feelings aren't connected to facial expressions. Her face and all you can see is so tired, so tired from the shock and the stress of the accident, tired to dying and death.

That's how her brain died, an accident. Hit-and-run in the rain on the freeway. What was she doing jerking her thumb on that access ramp, pregnant? Trying to get somewhere good from somewhere bad? Well, aren't we all?

I hear they brung her in in thrift-shop clothes—nothing matching, all outmoded, smelling like inside abandoned cars, all wet and mousy and old—she was too young to smell so old. The rain soaking her hair down over her eyes, she may not have seen the car that would hit her. Maybe among the patter-splatting raindrops she couldn't hear the car's purr, couldn't even hear her own heart beat.

Last night her heart was beating still. They talked of disconnecting her—the baby was safe by then, you know—but they left her till the committee meets, tomorrow. Oxygen tubes jammed up her nose, the I.V. tube needled into her veins, a suction tube poked down her throat. That one's connected to a mopping machine goes *Zub! Zub! Zub!* just like a washer. Anyone would be depressed to wake up tumbled and spun to the sound of washing. Brain-washing—before you know it, you're clean of thoughts, words, and deeds, your life is bleached and plain. I wish I'd brought that woman some of those sweet peas I've been growing near the birdbath, just brought them in an old jelly glass, plunked it near her call button, case she did have some little shred of who she is left.

"Harley," I say, "you watch any good shows last night?"

"The ball game," he says, "but I slept right through."

Sometimes me and Harley, I feel we're in the two worlds, the matter and the antimatter, you read about in his comics. And I wonder where our little girl would live—in the cracks between?

I used to think, I'll quit work and take care of her, long as Harley's at the nursery. But now I think different, 'cause he's been laid off from two nurseries. And the *Nurseries* in the Yellow Pages isn't that long. For a while I thought he could sit with her nights while I was at work. But what if she choked, and he'd passed out? Now I think our little girl, Mary Ellen, she'd have to stay with Alma Parker, the widow who drives me to the Laundromat so I can flip through her photos and coo. Those little shifty-eyed gap-toothed grand-kids visit, so Mary Ellen could have slumber parties. Oh, how I like to think of them all in pajamas with feet!

In the Sears catalog's a little pink suitcase with doggies dancing I want her to have. And a little pink phone! Harley says my gears are stripped, buying so much in advance, but I want the girl to know, her mother didn't just make do at tag sales, Second Time Around. Oh, I'll take hand-me-downs, but I've knit seven pair of booties, three receiving blankets, a play-suit, a bunting, a snowsuit, and four kimono sweaters, two with matching hats, all pink, though I did knit one blue sweater set in case.

Harley laughs, but who do you think put that swing out back and damn near fell out of the tree doing it? It was Harley built that little table and chairs and painted them white, but I found the tea set. Aren't those the cutest little tiny flowered cups? When Harley's figuring out what lumber he needs for Mary Ellen's sandbox, he doesn't drink; it's only when he's watching TV and reading comics. Well, I'd drink too if I read G.I. Joe meets the insects from Mars. G.I. Joe, always escaping from trapped cars underwater, he's hardly human. And those ball-players, in helmets, pads, gloves, and masks, tiny and faraway on TV, their humanity is suspect too.

"It's time to build a dollhouse," I say as I cuddle on Harley's back. "Mary Ellen will cry for it soon."

"Mary Ellen Pig Flap," he says.

Harley, Harley. If I didn't have him, I'd be burning in a narrow bed, twitching to amble over to Bea's, drape myself around a bar stool, pretend to listen while Bea rambles on about Ed. As long as I can remember, Ed's been lying in the back near the radio tuned to the country and western station. He breathes like the dead woman, no expression even when it's all static, but Bea says the love is still in their marriage, thank God. Now Bea's is where I met Harley. Oh, I was never one of those waiting for her to open at ten A.M., never one to stretch the happy hour till closing, not even on vacation days. I only started dropping by when the bowling lanes asked me to hang up my shoes. Said the leagues complained about my bulk shaking alleys, knocking over pins, and changing the path of balls. *Anyway.*

"Harley," I say, cute as a buttercup, "Harley, honey."

"We've got all day. I'm not going in."

He pulls the covers over his head.

"What'd you do, Harley?"

"What do you mean, what'd I do?"

"To lose it."

"Lose what?"

"Harley, don't be cute."

"I didn't do a goddamn thing. That Robbins never liked me. Well, I'm as strong as I ever was. I'm going to try for the roads next spring."

"What are we going to do till spring?"

"I'll get odd jobs."

"There might be something steady at the school—"

"Oh, cootie catchers."

I used to cut the Jell-O cubes and smear the baloney with mayo for the kids' free lunch, but Harley said I smelled like government cheese and teacher perfume.

"We can build a henhouse, you can have chickens in back."

"Neighbors too close."

"We could move."

"Moving costs."

"As much as loafing?"

"My neck is stiff. I need my sleep."

"You watch the late, late show, that golden oldies special offer one too many times?"

"Mind your mouth or I swear, I'll smack it."

"What's come over you?"

"You, waking me up to yap about a dead baby."

"Nobody—"

"I know you. I know you. I know how your pea-brain flashes signals through your fat!"

"Harley, I'm a woman with human desires, and when you're not drunk, you're human too."

"One hundred and ten percent, drunk or sober," he says. "Now quit mouthing off. Get some sleep, or you'll lose your job."

And he turns over. And that's that. I'm staring at his spine, which is stiff and still. *We're together,* I want to say. *Remember that comic "Grunts on the Moon?" We're wearing our life suits, walking on the bottom of the Sea of Fertility, marooned in a cold, dead place, beaming S.O.S., S.O.S., Mayday! Mayday! Help!* But I don't say it. I don't say a thing. I don't even tell him what I did on my break.

I started off to see Mary Ellen—that's what everyone else was doing on their break. The miracle baby, born from the dead. But something just drew me to the mother, her mouth so dumb around the suction tube, the breath rattling in her chest. I sat by her bed and I picked up her hand, her pale, freckled hand, so limp.

"Honey," I said, "I know you've had a hard life, else you wouldn't have been out on the highway so far along. You'd have waited close to home, to the little pink room with the little pink bed. Not that you're to blame.

"Now you're dead, and tomorrow you'll be deader. I'm worried no one told you right out, you gave birth to a fine girl. I know you'd like to hold her, your good red kid bawling for life. I'd like to hold her myself. To tell you the truth, I was headed that way, but then I saw the nurses huddled around her, even those starchy R.N.'s. And I had to admit she was cared for. She was set. You were the one alone.

"So here I am, a walking, talking, jumbo-sized greeting card. If you want, pretend I'm someone else. But, honey, I'm here for all my break. Yes," I said, "for now I'll stay."

And I swear she was listening, her breathing so quiet. I edged her suction tube aside and kissed her on the mouth.

THE BABY IN MID-AIR

Sandra Thompson

· · · · · · · · · · · · · · · · · · ·

As she sees the baby in mid-air, her brown head falling toward the floor, her legs and red shoes above it, the mother—too far out of reach to catch her or even to break the impact of her fall—feels the moment at the base of her womb, its sides contracting with a sharp pain as though the child were being born again. There is a light thud as the small body hits the floor. There is a cry, a deepening in the color of the baby's face from ivory to red, the baby's placid face scrunched into a tight mask. The mother scoops up the baby as though she is weightless, presses her to her breast, presses her small shaking body into her own where it had once been safe, yet unborn.

The baby dances on tables. She cries out in a deep, lusty voice that is unchildlike. She howls in delight at the sound her soles make on the tabletop, at her great height, at her power to yell and dance at the top of the world. The mother holds her breath as the child dances, fearing the fall from this bravado of innocence. (She imagines her own birth, emerging from her mother's womb, cautious, scanning the faces around her before she lets out her first cry.)

While she was pregnant, she dreamed she left the baby sleeping in a bar, on the seat of a booth like a pocketbook.

*　　　*　　　*

She dreamed she gave birth to a baby who looked like a flipper, and she embraced it, not anyway, but on its own terms.

She was told not to expect much: that her newborn child would look like a veal roast.

Her belly grew larger and she felt inside it little kicks like tap dancing, and, later, somersaults, as though she housed some sort of circus or zoo. Still, she didn't believe it was a baby who caused the movement. She dreamed she sat in the delivery room, on top of the cold steel table, and while she waited to give birth, watched her belly become smaller, then smaller and smaller until it was flat. The intern, in the voice of a department store salesman, explained, "There must have been some mistake."

In the delivery room she struggles to keep her eyes open against their impulse to close as she pushes down. She must see the baby as it emerges, before it becomes air in the doctor's gloved hands.

The baby doesn't wait to be slapped, but cries at once. The baby is complete; the mother will have to do nothing more, nothing. Already, without her knowledge or planning, there are eyes, and hands and feet with toes like pebbles, black wet strands of hair against the scalp.

The sky has darkened outside the hospital window. The baby is two hours old. The mother wakes from a Demerol sleep, holds onto the edge of the bed as she lowers herself, tests the cold tile floor with her bare feet. She walks out into the hallway and follows the distant wail to the nursery. But a white curtain has been pulled across the nursery window. (Three years later the baby flies down the sidewalk on a red motorcycle, professionally dragging one tiny foot as she disappears around a corner.)

The nurse wheels the baby into the mother's room in a colorless, transparent plexiglass tray, closer and closer to the mother, who sees the white of the nurse's uniform, the gleaming cold white tile floor—the baby in mid-air, the white tiles, red blood spreading out around the tiny body like ripples in a pond, the nurse holding the baby out to her like an offering, the tiles, the red blood whelming over the body, a squashed fruit.

"Don't leave me!" the mother cries.

The baby is a neat, tightly wrapped bundle in a white blanket, like a small mummy; only her face is not wrapped. Her face is a small moon, a pale light in the mother's arms, in the darkening room. The mother holds the baby lightly, like a girl carrying a bough of flowering branches across her arms.

The baby's face is calm, her eyes open, waiting for the discovery. (It is the same look the baby will have two years later when she hides by turning her back to her mother and being still.) And the mother begins to cry because the baby is not a stranger to her and her feeling for her is overwhelming and unmistakable, is what she had imagined falling in love might be like. As she looks at her child, the names she'd considered—Vanessa, Zoë, Claire—shift in her mind, boy or girl shifts in her mind, distinctions that no longer matter.

Peripherally, she notices the flowers that arrive in high waxed paper wrapping like a bishop's hat. She sees her baby's face in the opening roses, hears her cry when the room is still. At night she lies awake and, in the light from the streetlamps, looks at the face of her watch. At six in the morning the baby will be brought to her to be fed. Her breasts burn and throb, leaking milk into small pools on the sheets.

She sees the faces of her husband and friends as though underwater; she hears their voices as echoes from a deep tunnel.

The baby in mid-air falling

She dreamed she left the baby in a booth

*   *   *

At home the baby sleeps small in the vast expanse of crib, her head a small moon on the sheet. The mother lies awake, listening: a pause in the rhythm of breath, as a yawn or cough is forming, and the mother stops breathing, suspended midair until the rhythm begins again.

In the daytime, when the baby is sleeping, the mother peeks over the edge of the crib, waiting until she sees the baby's lips flutter ever so slightly as breath passes. Doing the dishes, she hears the baby's cry in the whine of the hot-water faucet; outside, she hears the baby's cry as a bus rounds the corner. The cries bleed into the quiet, and the mother lives within the cry.

The baby in mid-air

The baby is two-and-a-half, still small, with delicate bones like her mother's. She stands alone outside a barbed-wire fence, her hands cupped on either side of her mouth. She is calling the horses. "Pu-oy!" she calls her favorite horse, Pie, in her Brooklyn accent, and the horse, grazing out in the field, turns. "Hor-ses!" The baby's deep alto lifts a note on the second syllable, holds onto the "s" in an echo of the voice of the stablehand. The horses thunder toward her, stop short at the fence, and snort. The baby stands with her hands clasped behind her back, rocks back on her heels, and grins.

The mother, who is afraid of horses, shivers around the corner of the barn.

The baby in mid-air

The sturdy baby, in red boots, talks to the horses, a spirited gibberish with emphasis on the word "hay." The mother turns and walks from the barn toward the house, conscious of each foot as it passes the other, hears the neighs and the stomping and the baby's throaty squeals, and she feels a coolness on the palms of her hands like raindrops.

A STORY ABOUT THE BODY

Robert Hass

· · · · · · · · · · · · · · · · · · ·

The young composer, working that summer at an artist's colony, had watched her for a week. She was Japanese, a painter, almost sixty, and he thought he was in love with her. He loved her work, and her work was like the way she moved her body, used her hands, looked at him directly when she made amused and considered answers to his questions. One night, walking back from a concert, they came to her door and she turned to him and said, "I think you would like to have me. I would like that too, but I must tell you that I have had a double mastectomy," and when he didn't understand, "I've lost both my breasts." The radiance that he had carried around in his belly and his chest cavity—like music—withered, very quickly, and he made himself look at her when he said, "I'm sorry. I don't think I could." He walked back to his own cabin through the pines, and in the morning he found a small blue bowl on the porch outside his door. It looked to be full of rose petals, but he found when he picked it up that the rose petals were on top; the rest of the bowl—she must have swept them from the corners of her studio—was full of dead bees.

MOTHER

Hilma Wolitzer

. . . .

Despite what everyone said, Helen wasn't sure that she'd seen the baby. Maybe the ether had taken her memory of recent events, or maybe she simply couldn't believe that anything this important had really happened to her. Ten years before, she'd been a spinster, working in a typing pool at a textile company, and still living at home in Brooklyn with her father. How he must have pitied and despised her for having his broad, ruddy face, and such a sorry awkwardness in the world of men and women. It was to escape his sympathy that she'd gone to the dance that night and met Jon. Her father had come to the doorway of her room and caught her posing in the mirror, trying on her mother's crystal beads. When she saw him standing there, stout and pink in his uniform, she felt her face and throat blotch in that awful way. He smiled and said, "Going out tonight, Helen?" She'd had no intention of going anywhere. Nellie, another typist in the pool, had told her about a get-acquainted dance a single women's club was holding, to celebrate Harding's election. Helen wasn't interested—she knew the political event was only an excuse for the social one, and she hated standing on the sidelines, wearing a frozen smile of expectation when she expected nothing. But she told her father that she was going out. "Just to a dance," she muttered.

"Well, that's nice, dear, that sounds like fun," he said. He touched his forehead, his breast, and his holster in a kind of nervous genuflection and pushed their hopeless conversation further. "Mother loved to dance in her heyday, you know," he said. He indicated the box of her mother's jewelry on the dresser. "Maybe you ought to wear some of that stuff . . . gussy up a little."

She pitied and hated him then, too, for pretending that twenty-eight was not a desperate age for a woman, that "gussying up" was the secret of fatal attraction, that he believed her capable of abandoned fun. Her mother had probably never danced. Maybe she'd never made love, either, with that great, aching hulk in the doorway. Maybe Helen had been born of some chaste, clothed act that produced only lesser beings. Her face blazed up again. Maybe she was going crazy at last, the way they said all lustful virgins eventually did. Her father continued to stand there, smiling.

The very worst thing, she was certain, was not human misery, but its nakedness, and the naked witness of others. And as her father knew her secret heart, so she knew his. She'd seen him standing for minutes in front of the open, smoking icebox, staring inside as if he expected something beyond butter or milk to be revealed. Then, with a heaving sigh, he always settled for butter and milk. His whole life had whizzed by like a bullet from the gun he'd never fired off the firing range, and here he was: long-widowed, still a foot patrolman, and with a sullen old-maid daughter on his hands. She'd inherited his homely looks, and out of spite she'd deny him his immortality. Her mother had died of pneumonia when Helen was two years old, and all she could recall were a few real or imagined impressions—breast, hair, shadow.

Lying now in the maternity ward at Bellevue Hospital, she couldn't conjure up even the vaguest image of the living child they'd said she'd delivered. All the other women in her ward, but one, had infants at their breasts at regular intervals. The nurses wheeled them in in a common cart; like the vegetables sold by street peddlers. The woman in the bed opposite Helen's had given birth to a stillborn son. Before the wailing babies were distributed among the new mothers, a three-sided screen was arranged discreetly around her bed, and she could be heard weeping behind it.

Helen felt remote from the celebration around her, as she had felt remote from the festive possibilities of the dance the night she'd met Jon. The ballroom had been romantically lit for the occasion, and adorned with political banners and posters. As soon as she walked in, she knew that her dress was wrong—she would disappear in the shadows. It was November and cold, and everyone, all the magazines, said that simple black was always smart and always right. Yet even Nellie and Irene, who lived by the dictates of fashion, wore gaily colored dresses and matching headbands. Oh, what difference did it make? There were so many women, in bright noisy clusters, and only a few men, aside from the band that was just warming up.

Irene glanced around and said, "Boy, I bet we'd find more fellas at a convent." She and Nellie leaned together, giggling. Helen didn't see what was so funny. They weren't beautiful or in such hot demand, either, and the Great War had diminished all their chances even further. But she was rallying to laugh along with them, to be a good sport, when the huge mirrored ball suspended from the center of the ceiling began to slowly revolve. Facets of light ricocheted off every surface and struck her painlessly on her arms, her dress, her shoes. The band started to play the lively melody of some popular song she couldn't name but that she found herself humming. Everyone was wearing the same restless pattern of light. In that way they were all united, like jungle beasts marked by the spots or stripes of their species. Helen felt that something was about to happen. It was in the very air. President Harding gazed down at her from the enormous posters like a stern but benevolent chaperon. And look, the ballroom was filling up—so many men were coming in! Irene said it was because *they* only had to pay half price, but who cared? Couples went whirling by in one another's arms. Before long, Nellie was pulled into the maelstrom, and a few minutes later Irene was gone, too. Soon someone would come for her, would know intuitively her concealed qualities: that she'd been golden blond as a child, and her body skin attested to it; that she had lovely breasts; that she could type sixty flawless words a minute.

A man seemed to be coming purposefully in her direction. She felt an immediate affinity with the gawkiness of his stride, the way his cowlick had resisted combing. He appeared hellbent in his mission, and a quivery thrill traveled through her body. Then she saw that he'd meant someone else, the gyrating flapper in fringed pink standing next to her, who shook her head no at him and turned to another man. Helen drew her breath in deeply and put up her arms, as if he'd meant her all along. He hesitated for the barest moment before he held out his own arms. She was careful not to lead.

They were married on Inauguration Day, and Jon moved in with Helen and her father. He was a typesetter for *The Sun*, with a modest salary. Their living arrangement enabled them to save money for the house they'd buy after they'd begun their own family. Helen stored their wedding gifts neatly in the walk-in cedar closet, so that everything would still be new no matter when they moved. The closet's cool, scented interior was like a little forest glade, and she often just stood there and daydreamed, surrounded by the artifacts of her future.

Helen didn't become pregnant, though not for want of trying. Each disappointing month she wept in the privacy of the cedar closet, wiping her eyes carefully on a corner of one of the monogrammed wedding sheets. Old Dr. Kelly insisted she was fine, that nature would take its course, wait and see. When Helen asked if she should see a specialist, he laughed and shook his head. "Isn't the family doctor best when you want to start a family?" he said. "Didn't I deliver herself in my little black bag?"

Oh, yes, she thought, and took my mother away in it. He was like a gentle, cheerful priest, his undaunted cheer shaking her faith, but she gave him the tremulous smile he wanted. Finally, though, they did consult a specialist, in his Gramercy Park offices. She gasped during his examination and fainted during the first treatment to expand her Fallopian tubes. He prescribed a nerve powder and told Jon that it was inadvisable for Helen to continue working in her condition.

She stayed home for two years, prowling the house like a high-strung watchdog. She'd left her job, but her fingers refused to give up typing. They tapped out imaginary letters about late shipments and damaged goods, on the tabletops and the walls. She played game after game of Patience, telling herself that if the next hand worked out she would become pregnant that month. It was a relief to go back to work at last, to give up hope, if not the longing that had impelled it.

Helen and Jon developed the peculiar exclusive closeness of childless couples. After Helen's father died, walking the orbit of his beat, they became even closer, and insulated from the world of real families. Jon's parents and sisters were far away, on a farm in Minnesota he'd left years before. He and Helen had friends, of course, but their only important connection was to one another, a wondrous and scary thing. Once they'd stopped trying so hard to conceive, though, they made love less often, and it became more a matter of mutual comfort than a passionate pursuit.

When the Depression began, Jon's salary was cut in half and Helen lost her job, but they told themselves how lucky they were not to have to worry about anyone else during such difficult times. Helen took inordinate pride in her resourcefulness and her capacity for thrift. She made filling soups out of battered produce and scraps of meat, and screwed low-wattage light bulbs into all the lamps and fixtures. Going from door to door, she found various kinds of piecework they could do at home. She typed envelopes and stuffed them with fliers, and they both pasted glitter onto celluloid Kewpie dolls. The stuff got into everything; it stuck to their fingers and was scattered in the carpets and on their clothing. At night Helen saw a trace of phosphorescent glitter on the pillows, like a sprinkling of celestial dust. It reminded her of the fairy tales her father had read to her years ago, in which worthy wishes were granted and deprivation was ultimately rewarded. The story she'd loved best was *The Goose Girl,* about an orphan who carried around a cambric stained with three drops of her mother's blood. Helen had always favored the most morbid stories: *The Goose Girl* with her bloody cambric and decapitated talking horse; *The Hardy Tin Soldier* melting away for love and heroism; and, of course, *Sleeping Beauty.* But even happy endings couldn't dispel the essential melancholy of Grimm and Anderson. The Goose girl would lament, "Alas, dear Falada, there thou hangest," and the horse's head would answer, "Alas, Queen's daughter, there thou gangest. If thy mother knew thy fate, her heart would break with grief so great." Helen wasn't quite sure what gangest meant, or cambric, for that matter, but her own heart always broke on cue. Had she loved those stories because she was a miserable child? Or had they helped to make her that way?

When she did become pregnant, after ten years of marriage, she decided never to read those stories to her child. *Her child.* How extraordinary that a living creature could be made accidentally in darkness. That a reprieve could come so long after the end of hope. Helen experienced bliss that seemed dangerous. Jon was as happy as she was, although she knew he'd pretended acceptance of their childlessness out of a kind of gallantry, just as he continued to pretend she was the girl he'd meant to dance with.

One morning, in Helen's seventh month of pregnancy, there were a few drops of blood on the sheet, and Dr. Kelly ordered her to bed. He came to examine her at home each week, and it was like being a child again—his minty, medicinal smell in the room, the black leather bag gaping on the dresser top. Sometimes, after he'd listened to her belly with his stethoscope, he would put it to her ears. What a marvelous din! It denied what she had feared most about herself, that she was inferior and unfinished, incapable of this simple biological purpose. She rested, luxuriating in fantasy, as she used to do in the cedar closet, and willed her body to wait out its sentence. It didn't, though.

Two weeks into her eighth month, she woke during the

night with her waters flooding the bed. "Oh, Jesus," Jon said. "It's too soon!" While he went to fetch Dr. Kelly, their next-door neighbor came in in her nightgown. She worked dry blankets under Helen and crooned, "All right, dear. All right, all right."

It wasn't all right at all. Everything was happening so fast: the waters, and then the pain—accelerating, intensifying. Why had she ever thought she'd wanted a baby? The neighbor crossed Helen's legs tightly and said, "Don't push! Lie still!"

Dr. Kelly came, and he hoisted her from the bed, ordering Jon to take her feet and the other woman to carry his bag and throw the doors wide. They struggled down the stairs like barflies with a soused buddy, but they managed to get Helen to the street and into Dr. Kelly's car.

At Bellevue she was separated from Jon. The last thing she remembered of that night was his diminishing figure as she was wheeled down a hallway. When she woke, it was another day. Her mouth was sweet with ether and sour with sleep. They told her she'd had a daughter. They said that Jon had been to see her soon after, and that she'd spoken to him, but she didn't really remember that, either. She missed the baby in a physical way, with an emptiness that was not unlike hunger. Her breasts ached and leaked until a nurse came with a lethal-looking pump and expressed the milk. Helen was assured that the baby was alive, that this very milk would be fed to her soon in the nursery.

"Now you saw her, Helen," Dr. Kelly scolded, "just before we sent her down. You said she looked like a little drowned rat." And the nurse who gave her a sponge bath said, "Turn on your side for me now, Mother." They promised that she would be taken to the special nursery in the basement for another look as soon as she could tolerate a wheelchair ride. She'd lost a lot of blood, they told her, and she wasn't even ready yet to dangle.

An aide propped Helen up for supper and she found herself facing the grieving woman, who sat immobile over her own tray. They looked at one another in the cheerful clamor of silverware. The woman's eyes returned Helen's commiseration, like a mirror, and her mouth twitched into a bitter, conspiratorial smile. Helen couldn't eat her supper. She was almost glad when the babies were brought in again, and the three-sided screen came between her and that knowing gaze.

That evening, Jon was in the herd of visitors who carried the chill of winter in on their clothes. Helen questioned him about the baby and he said that she was doing well, breathing nicely and taking nourishment. "What did Dr. Kelly say?" she asked. Jon glanced nervously away before he said, "He told me she's holding her own." Helen knew that was only a partial truth, that the fate of premature infants was shaky, at best. They were meant to stay inside longer and develop. Their hearts and lungs might be too weak to sustain them, and they had no defenses against the slightest infection. She imagined the special nursery with its tiny, perishable occupants ticking away like home-made bombs.

"Well, what shall we name her, Helen?" Jon asked.

She had made up names, and even careers, for the unborn baby during those weeks in bed. She'd drawn up secret lists, under "Girl" and "Boy," but now she said, sullenly, "I don't know, I haven't thought about it."

"They need it for the certificate," Jon said.

She had a sudden, dreadful image of the small, toppled tombstones in the old churchyard near their house. Some of them were over the graves of infants whose chiseled names and dates could still be read. "I don't want to name her yet," she said in a rising voice, and Jon quickly said, "All right, dearest, don't worry about it," which only made her feel worse.

He sat at her bedside, helpless against her mood. He held her hand, and she was touched by the familiar sight of his ink-stained fingers. She thought of how he'd apologized for them the night of the dance, explaining that he'd come straight from work, that his hands weren't actually dirty. He'd worked so hard recently, and had never complained, even when she withdrew into the pleasure of her secret interior life. Yet there were times he'd enraged her with that glance of mournful sympathy he might have learned from her father. Now she felt a swell of love for him at the same time that she felt impatience and a desire for him to go.

At last visiting hours were over, and Jon was ushered away with the other outsiders. In a while the babies were brought in for their last feeding of the day. When they were taken out again, the overhead lights went off and a few of the bed lamps were switched on. Some of the women whispered together in the cozy dimness. Others combed their hair. This was the strangest hour, a time in the real world when only children are put to bed. Helen was very tired, but not sleepy. She couldn't find a comfortable position under the tight, starched sheets.

"Good night! Good night!" the happy mothers called to each other. One by one the lamps were shut off and the only visible light was outside the room at the nurses' station. The woman in the bed next to Helen's coughed and someone at the far end giggled. Someone else said, "Shhh!" Soon there was a chorus of slow, even breathing, the counterpoint of snoring. The shadow of the night nurse fell across the threshold as she stood and peered in at them.

After the nurse went down the hall, Helen sat up and worked her way out of the sheets' bondage. She turned carefully on the high hospital bed and let her legs hang over the side. She became dizzy, and had to sit still for a few moments. Then she slipped down until her feet were shocked by the cold floor. She found her slippers and stepped into them, and she put on her flannel robe. No one, not even the mother of the stillborn baby, stirred. Helen's bottom hurt and the thick sanitary pad she wore felt clumsy. She walked stiffly, sliding her feet along like someone learning to ice-skate. At the sink she paused and looked at herself in the mirror—a pale wraith with glints of silver in its tousled hair, as if childbirth had aged her. She peered more closely and saw that it was only the Kewpie dolls' glitter. She whispered "Mother," just to try it out, but it felt strange on her tongue, a foreign food for which she hadn't yet cultivated a taste. When she came to the doorway she stopped again, breathless from so much exertion, and leaned against the frame. The nurses' station was empty, and there was nobody in the corridor.

It took a long time to walk the few yards to the stairway. Behind her the phone on the desk rang and rang. In the stairwell Helen wondered what floor she was on. It didn't matter. They'd said the nursery was in the basement; she would go down and down until there were no more stairs. I've done this before, she thought, at the second or third landing. And then she knew it was school she was thinking of, the empty, echoing stairwell when she'd carried a note from one teacher to another while everyone else was in class. How privileged she'd felt, and free! But once she was punished in front of the whole assembly for talking when the flag was being carried in. She could never remember the joy without the shadow of humiliation. It was the danger of all happiness, and what she had willed to her mortal child. Alas, Queen's daughter.

There were two orderlies in the basement corridor, wheeling a squeaking stretcher and laughing. Helen waited until they'd turned the corner, and then she shuffled out in the other direction. She smelled something cooking, the strong, beefy odor of institutional soup or gravy. It made her feel hungry and a little sick. She looked through the glass panel of one of the swinging doors that led to the kitchen. It was as brightly lit in there as the delivery room—she remembered *that* now, the impossible glare. She'd tried to say something about the stingy light they suffered at home, and then the mask had come down, dousing her voice and the lights at once.

In the kitchen, witches' cauldrons were bubbling on the giant stoves. Three women in hair nets chopped onions and wept, and an angry chef attacked a slab of meat. It was the landscape of nightmares, and here she was in her nightclothes, but awake. Feeling lightheaded, she went past the kitchen and at the corner of the corridor found a sign, its arrow pointing the way to the *Laboratory, X-ray,* and the *Morgue.* The nursery had to be somewhere beyond them.

The locked laboratory door had a glass panel, too. There was no one inside; the small light might have been left on for the animals. She could see a few of them crouched in their cages: quivering brown rabbits, white rats squinting suspiciously back at her. She had surely never said that awful thing about the baby. It was only one of Dr. Kelly's silly bedside jokes. The rats scurried in their limited space, and Helen shuddered and moved on.

There was no one in sight, and she longed to sit for a moment on one of the wooden benches on either side of the door to the X-ray room. But she was afraid that if she sat down, she'd be unable to get up again. Instead she slumped against the black door. It felt cold and solid. Years ago, when she was about thirteen, Helen developed a bad cough that Dr. Kelly's syrups and tonics couldn't cure. Her father took her to the clinic of one of the big uptown hospitals to have a picture taken of her chest. It was a brand-new procedure, and she could still recall the anxious darkness, and the icy pressure of the machine against her beginning breasts. After she was dressed, the doctor invited Helen and her father into the consultation room, where the back-lit X-ray was hung. Astonished, she saw her own tiny, lurking heart, and the delicate fan of ribs that housed her lungs. With a pointer the doctor showed them a faint shadow he said was a touch of wet pleurisy. Her father was so relieved it wasn't pneumonia, he grasped the doctor's hand, making him drop the pointer. Helen should have been relieved, too, but she harbored a secret fury that there could no longer be any secrets. Her father could already read her evil mind, and now the last stronghold of privacy had fallen.

Later, she opened herself gladly to Jon, and then to the baby. Leaning against the door to the X-ray room, she was stirred by the memory of the child inside her, the thrill of its quickening. "Push!" the nurse in the delivery room had said, just as Helen's neighbor had ordered her not to push when her labor first began. And then her body had made its own willful choice. She could hear herself grunting, those deep animal grunts of colossal effort. You were never supposed to really remember the pain—that's what all the women she knew had said. They'd told her it was the worst pain in the world, and they said it with a kind of religious fervor. But they promised that she'd forget it afterward, as if it had all taken place in another life. Then why was it coming back to her here in the basement corridor, an echo of the pain and thrusting she'd believed she could not survive? Then she remembered *everything* that had happened under that brilliant sun: being shackled to the table, the grunts changing to screams, the mask she'd risen to meet as if it were a lover's mouth. The missing part was still the birth itself—that happened in a long tunnel of dreamless sleep—and the baby. Where was the baby?

A child was crying somewhere, and Helen's breasts ran. The crying got louder and closer, and she slid along the wall to one of the benches and sat down. But it wasn't an infant's sound— these wails smothered language, and there were footsteps hurrying toward her. There was no place to hide, no time to even stand up. Two people, a man and a woman, half-carrying, half-dragging the shrieking child between them, turned the corner. Helen shrank against the bench in terror of being discovered. The child banged his ear with his fist. The parents didn't seem to notice Helen's robe and slippers—the man shouted at her, "Where's the emergency room?" She was unable to answer him, although her mouth worked in spasms. They hurried past her, struggling with their struggling burden, their footsteps and the child's screams receding as they all disappeared at the next corner. God, she had wet herself! But when she looked down, she saw blood flowering her pink slippers and puddling the floor. She stood and stared down in amazement. The child with the earache still screamed in the far distance. "Help me," Helen said. "Help me!" she said, louder. Of course no one responded; she had to get back to the kitchen where there were people. She stood there in confusion before she was able to push off. Then it was as if the walls moved past her, and she walked on a treadmill. She was on fire, she was melting. "Papa," she whimpered. "Jon!" When she came to the morgue, she knew she had gone in the wrong direction. Her fists were soft against the door and they tingled with pins and needles, as if she had just woken and had to wait for them to wake, too. She thought she heard someone in there, or a radio playing, but she might have been hearing noises inside her own head. She was afraid to look at her slippers now, and she was shivering with cold. *"Please,"* she said, and turned to follow the drunken, slithery trail of blood. The first of it on and near the bench had already started to darken. It looked like the remains of an accident after the victims have been carted away. She staggered past the bench and went like a moth to the lighted window of the laboratory. The rats looked back at her. She gasped, as she had gasped during the last earth-shaking pain of her waking labor. When she'd emerged from the tunnel she saw the glistening blue-pink baby hung by its feet, girdled by the thick, pulsing cord. "Oh!" she had cried. "Oh! It looks like a little drowned rat!" That wasn't what she'd meant to say. She meant words of welcome and consolation for the terrible gift of the world. There thou gangest.

She fell through the double doors of the kitchen and saw the three women and the chef in a sudden, frozen tableau. She came to once more, somewhere else, with Dr. Kelly looming above her saying, "No! Oh, Christ, damn it!" Then she felt her soul folding end on end on end, like the flag from her father's coffin, like the wedding sheets in the cedar closet, until it was small enough to slip through the open mouth of the waiting black leather bag.

BRINGING THE NEWS

Ellen Hunnicutt

. . . .

In July my husband, Mark, harvests the first plump green beans from the garden and thins out the tiny carrots. The carrots are not large enough to save, but he saves them anyway. His large hands brush away the soil with small, scrupulous movements. Clad only in shorts and sandals, hunched above the garden foliage, his body looks powerful, tanned, and healthy. Only a few salty flecks of gray about the ears mark him as thirty-three and eight years married.

With his pocketknife, he carefully tops each tiny carrot, and hands the lacy greens to Amy, who stands beside him gathering them solemnly into a neat bouquet in the meticulous manner of a three-year-old who has been assigned an important task. The carrot tops will be a special treat for Bitsy, a plump brown rabbit who observes this Saturday morning idyll from the shelter of her cage, as I look on from the living room window. Watching, it occurs to me that Mark and Amy do not look like the family of a woman who has been raped. They look exactly like two people I knew a brief two months ago.

When the carrots have been topped, Mark rises a little stiffly, then brings his six-foot frame up to its full height, dwarfing Amy. He smiles and there is some exchange of banter I cannot hear. He picks up the pail of carrots and, with his free arm, lifts Amy. Safe in the bend of her father's arm, she rides serenely up into the air. Mark deposits her at the faucet beside the patio. He kneels, together they wash the small carrots. I grope for my customary Saturday contentment and find only a dull and empty sense of isolation.

Outside, Mark removes Bitsy from her cage. Clutched by her belly, the rabbit thrashes frantically, flailing the air with helpless legs. Her ordeal is over in one swift moment as Mark sets her free for a romp on the grass, a lunch of carrot tops, but I look away, sickened. I have commanded my mind not to play these tricks, but I seem ruled by some fretful stranger who wills what I should think and feel.

In the shadow of the patio, my husband's body moves like a cool, sleek machine. I discover that I am trying to understand him, as if he were a man I had just met.

I have no clear memory of Mark's presence in the hospital emergency room. I recall a clutter of voices, a shifting collage of faces. I remember, oddly, that my fingernails were caked with mud and that the palm of my left hand was streaked with blood. I believe it hurt Mark to learn that I did not remember more. I am sure he said courageous and comforting words to me, loving words. Later a nurse told me he had pounded his fists against a wall and then cried. I wish I could remember. Perhaps that memory would be the beginning of a bridge across the chasm that now separates me from my husband, an empty, silent space.

Amy and Mark return Bitsy to her cage and come into the kitchen for lunch with a grand sense of celebration. "Mama!" Amy summons me stridently. "We got theeese!" She tumbles the small, damp carrots onto the table and dances on her toes.

I mobilize some memory of myself and answer. "Marvelous!"

"They're delicious!" Mark's voice explodes in the small room. We are actors in Amy's drama. I search past noise and movement for the familiar fabric of our lives, and wonder if it ever existed.

Mark brings a warm washcloth and crouches on one knee beside Amy to wash her face. He pushes tousled hair carefully

from her forehead. She twitches and he murmurs encouragement, tilting her chin upward to wash her tiny neck, "almost
. . . just a touch more." The rising tone of his voice promises
that the task is nearly done. Mark believes he is the only father
who is raising a child in exactly the right manner. When he
sees children in shops, in the park, or in the street, his eyes
swiftly assess each one and catalog the parents' shortcomings.
He has appointed himself an authority on neglected diapering,
too-tight waistbands, dangerous toys, nutritious snacks. He
struggles to remain silent and be charitable toward adults who
take parenting lightly or who do not agree precisely with his
views. He is convinced that no father has ever loved a child as
intensely as he loves his daughter. I watch him and recall the
gentle touch of my own father's hand.

Amy participates fully in this venture and accepts without
question that she and Mark are unique human beings, set apart
from all other daddies and little girls in an important and
special way. She explores the latitude of her role and searches
out her boundaries with curiosity and delight, testing the limits
of both her power and her helplessness. To Mark's steadfast-
ness she is, in turn, petulant, generous, coy, selfish, fearful,
bold, courageous. In her father, a little girl seeks and finds
all men.

At her plate, Amy toys now with her half-eaten sandwich,
exhausted from the morning's excitement. She pulls the bread
apart and nibbles at a piece of lettuce. I set things away and
take her up for her nap. On the stairs she hums a tuneless tune
which, at the door of her room, becomes a fretful plea. "Sleep
with me, Mama!" I welcome the chance to lie down. I am
bone-tired with a weariness that sleep does not heal.

On the bed in her small, bright room Amy thrashes for a
moment, clutches me, murmurs about her rabbit. She looks at
the nursery figures on the wallpaper and yawns. In my own
memory I recall this process of going to sleep. These are the
rituals we carry out to be certain we are safe.

When Amy is satisfied that all the figures in her wallpaper
are in precisely their proper places, and that the silky coverlet

swishes against her bare legs with exactly the right sound, she closes her eyes and is instantly asleep. Her breathing is deep and regular. Tiny beads of perspiration appear on her forehead. In sleep, her small arm is raised and thrown against me.

When I was nine or ten, I belonged to the Camp Fire Girls. We met at seven in the evening in a basement room of our village library. One evening a girl named Lisa stayed after the meeting to discuss a project with Mrs. Hill, our leader. Later, as she was coming up the stairway alone, a man appeared from the shadows, clasped a hand over her mouth, and attempted to drag her away. Lisa managed to wriggle free and scream. Adults appeared. The man fled up the stairs and disappeared into the dark street.

This event became the subject of many furtive conversations among little girls, huddled in knots in backyards, clustered on the playground jungle gym, gathered behind closed bedroom doors. A chorus of fierce whispers: I would kick . . . oh, I would kick . . . very hard . . . and bite too . . . bite too . . . anybody would . . . because I would never . . . nobody would . . . oh, no . . . I'd scratch with my fingernails like this . . . I'd die . . . because you know . . . I know . . . everybody knows . . . because if you died you could go to heaven . . . I would definitely go to heaven.

When I was about to be raped, I discovered I did not wish to die. I wanted very much to live. The images that flashed through my mind at that moment were not really thoughts at all. I saw the afghan I had been crocheting. If I died, I knew my sister would complete it, and her stitch is tighter than mine. The result would be a sad, lopsided thing. Perhaps it would be given to Amy, a clumsy, botched object that would have to be cherished in my memory. And in time, my sister would teach Amy to crochet, in a fashion a little different from mine.

I recall quite clearly that my sister visited me in the hospital. The face of a nurse drifts into memory, efficient eyes looking down at me, a white world of soft, intermittent footsteps and the sharp odor of disinfectants. "Mrs. Warren . . . ? Sarah . . . ? Your sister is here."

My sister arrived like a hot wind, flushed cheeks, disheveled hair, breathless, agitated. For an instant she did not seem to know who I was. Then our hands locked in a familiar gesture, and she pressed my fingers so tightly they turned a bluish-gray and looked like useless dead things curled above the sheet. When she was able to speak, her voice was hoarse. "Sarah . . . you could have been killed." Trembling, she sat on the edge of the bed and pulled me to her. We held each other and cried, as we had cried so many times before, over a broken doll or a broken romance, as we cried when our mother died, as we cried when my sister's small son was stillborn. But these tears were different, I could feel distance between us. My sister's voice became a gentle, comforting hum. I listened to the words, and then past them, with growing disbelief. Her voice carried a note of rebuke. Although she did not say it, she believed, and continues to believe, that in some way I am responsible for what has happened.

On that night I did not alter my routine in any way, I performed no act to provoke another human being, I violated none of the rules for safe conduct. Yet, other women will believe I was somehow responsible for the attack upon me. I first learned this from my sister's voice.

Her words were really for herself. She believes that if she carries out certain precautions she will never be raped. It is easier for her to think I failed in some way than to believe she is vulnerable.

I have forgiven her. Until now I believed exactly as she does. Perhaps I still believe. If I had been able to think a powerful thought or say special words, could I have prevented the attack? I still want to believe in Amy's kind of magic, that the things we do will always keep us safe. Mark tries very hard to understand all these things. He listens intently to everything I say, as if I spoke a foreign language he must strain to understand. He assesses my words and keeps some invisible record where he charts the progress of my recovery.

There are two Marks now. A sane, clinical daytime man moves about with great control. In the morning, he ties his necktie with a neat little snap, as if to say, "See how well all this is going?" As if he might be called upon at any time to demonstrate the tying of neckties. He finds great hope in trivial things. "Look here!" he cries. "See how the grass is coming back on the west side of the lawn." When he performs small tasks, he speaks of himself as *we*. "We'll be finished here in just a moment." Giving me assurance.

The second Mark is the tentative man who lies beside me each night. In the privacy of darkness, gazing out at the distant, impersonal stars, does he ask the same questions I ask? Do they twist and turn upon themselves? Why has this thing happened to me and not to another person? Does it serve some purpose I cannot discern? Will my phone ring some morning and a voice say, "We are so pleased with what you are doing, Sarah, for all our sakes"? I have held this experience in my hand and turned it every way, like a dark gemstone that catches the light with each facet and reflects at a hundred different angles, searching for resolution, and there is none. I do not know if it is possible to live and love in an unsafe world.

Now I separate myself from Amy, cover her lightly, close the door softly behind me. Mark has showered and stands in our bedroom in a pair of light trousers, barefoot, examining the pine paneling above the fireplace. Although my steps are almost soundless, he is aware of me. "The wood is lifting," he says. "Moisture is getting through. Perhaps we should have someone look at this chimney."

Beside him, I touch the warped wood. This bedroom is like a summary of our marriage. We built this room ourselves, tearing out a partition and bringing two small rooms together, laying the fieldstone of the fireplace with our own hands, building enormous closets, setting in casement windows, paneling the fireplace wall and papering the others with a rich, textured wallpaper, laying the thick, soft ivory carpet. This room has been our only luxury.

A wall of deep shelves holds the mementos of our life together, our collection of Eskimo soapstone carvings, a Delft pitcher Mark's mother brought us from Amsterdam, our wedding photograph, a bouquet of dried weeds contributed by Amy, our two identical copies of Yeats from college years, cherished from the day we discovered we both read the same poetry.

Mark built our enormous bed, and Amy was conceived there. Beside the bed is the bentwood rocker we have dubbed Great Heaven, because my sister said, "Great heaven, how could you spend so much money on one chair?"

Mark's presence is sweet to me. His bare arms and shoulders smell faintly of soap, and his damp hair gleams in the light from the window. I touch his shoulder tentatively and feel a small ripple of desire begin in my stomach and, with it, fear, because the old pathways of easy, familiar feeling are gone.

Mark's hand drops from the wall, and he slips his arm around my waist. There is silence, tense, loving, confused. "What do you want?" he asks softly. And again, "Please tell me what you want."

And now words from the dark side of my mind come unbidden. I discover I am trembling. It is like the onset of labor, coming in its own ripeness, a birthing that follows its own necessities. "I'll tell you what I want," I say in a voice that does not belong to me, fierce, petulant. "I want all the world to be angry *with* me, all the people in the cities and in the country, riding in buses and flying on airplanes. I want some powerful act of retribution to occur . . . and that is not going to happen. I want to be like Amy again, full of myself, brimming with importance, happy, clean . . . instead of being broken . . . covered with a filth I can't wash off!" I am sobbing now. Mark grips my hand, as he did when Amy was born, and I descend into a strange room filled with brilliant light and gaudy color. It is my private hell of rage and shame, a place of mockery and degradation. My chest burns, and it is difficult to breathe.

"It's all right, Sarah. It's all right now."

Mark is holding me. Then the sudden fit is past, my sobs subside, and my ears ring in the great hollow of silence about my head. "I am so very tired of crying."

"It's all right." Mark's voice is a small, cool wind against my damp cheek.

"I feel a little better now." Vision clearing, the deep swell of my own breathing, the fist of muscle in my chest melting. *Sensations.* Bringing me the news . . . of my own juices, patient and persistent. Regeneration that happens out of sight, the dark work of the cell. Somewhere an old sweater is coming out at last at the elbows. "I feel better now."

"I know."

"Mark, I'll always remember. It will still be there ten years from now, twenty . . . and even when we are old."

"But it's going to be all right. Believe me."

"I believe you."

Mark strokes my hair with a small, clumsy gesture that makes him seem very young, vulnerable. "Let's have a glass of lemonade!" he says suddenly, brightly, as if he had just invented lemonade. A sluggish memory stirs, and before he can speak again I know he will say, "Just let me get my shoes and grab a shirt."

I move to the window and stand in the swath of afternoon sun that falls on the soft carpet.

"Look," Mark says, coming up beside me, "see how the grass is coming back?"

I see that it is true. The grass is returning. Each day the pale, fragile tendrils grow stronger, greener.

"Lemonade," says Mark, gently taking my arm. "Amy will sleep for a little while."

And this is also true. Amy will sleep a little longer, in her child's body, in her child's bed. Then she will wake and thrust herself eagerly into the next hour, with its unknown joys, its unknown misfortunes. I take Mark's hand and say a short, silent prayer for my daughter, that she will always be shielded by hope, that she will always trust love's courage.

MENTAL ILLNESS

. . . .

A SORROWFUL WOMAN

Gail Godwin

. . . .

One winter evening she looked at them: the husband durable, receptive, gentle; the child a tender golden three. The sight of them made her so sad and sick she did not want to see them ever again.

She told her husband these thoughts. He was attuned to her; he understood such things. He said he understood. What would she like him to do? "If you could put the boy to bed and read him the story about the monkey who ate too many bananas, I would be grateful." "Of course," he said. "Why, that's a pleasure." And he sent her off to bed.

The next night it happened again. Putting the warm dishes away in the cupboard, she turned and saw the child's grey eyes approving her movements. In the next room was the man, his chin sunk in the open collar of his favorite wool shirt. He was dozing after her good supper. The shirt was the grey of the child's trusting gaze. She began yelping without tears, retching in between. The man woke in alarm and carried her in his arms to bed. The boy followed them up the stairs, saying, "It's all right, Mommy," but this made her scream. "Mommy is sick," the father said. "Go and wait for me in your room."

The husband undressed her, abandoning her only long enough to root beneath the eiderdown for her flannel gown. She stood naked except for her bra, which hung by one strap down the side of her body; she had not the impetus to shrug it off. She looked down at the right nipple, shriveled with chill, and thought, How absurd, a vertical bra. "If only there were instant sleep," she said, hiccuping, and the husband bundled her into the gown and went out and came back with a sleeping draught guaranteed swift. She was to drink a little glass of cognac followed by a big glass of dark liquid, and afterwards there was just time to say Thank you and could you get him a clean pair of pajamas out of the laundry, it came back today.

The next day was Sunday, and the husband brought her breakfast in bed and let her sleep until it grew dark again. He took the child for a walk, and when they returned, red-cheeked and boisterous, the father made supper. She heard them laughing in the kitchen. He brought her up a tray of buttered toast, celery sticks, and black bean soup. "I am the luckiest woman," she said, crying real tears. "Nonsense," he said. "You need a rest from us," and went to prepare the sleeping draught, find the child's pajamas, select the story for the night.

She got up on Monday and moved about the house till noon. The boy, delighted to have her back, pretended he was a vicious tiger and followed her from room to room, growling and scratching. Whenever she came close, he would growl and scratch at her. One of his sharp little claws ripped her flesh, just above the wrist, and together they paused to watch a thin red line materialize on the inside of her pale arm and spill over in little beads. "Go away," she said. She got herself upstairs and locked the door. She called the husband's office and said, "I've locked myself away from him. I'm afraid." The husband told her in his richest voice to lie down, take it easy, and he was already on the phone to call one of the baby-sitters they often employed. Shortly after, she heard the girl let herself in, heard the girl coaxing the frightened child to come and play.

After supper several nights later, she hit the child. She had known she was going to do it when the father would see. "I'm sorry," she said, collapsing on the floor. The weeping child had run to hide. "What has happened to me, I'm not myself anymore." The man picked her tenderly from the floor and looked at her with much concern. "Would it help if we got, you know, a girl in? We could fix the room downstairs. I want you to feel freer," he said, understanding these things. "We have the money for a girl. I want you to think about it."

And now the sleeping draught was a nightly thing; she did not have to ask. He went down to the kitchen to mix it, he set it nightly beside her bed. The little glass and the big one, amber and deep rich brown, the flannel gown and the eider-down.

The man put out the word and found the perfect girl. She was young, dynamic, and not pretty. "Don't bother with the room, I'll fix it up myself." Laughing, she employed her thousand energies. She painted the room white, fed the child lunch, read edifying books, raced the boy to the mailbox, hung her own watercolors on the fresh-painted walls, made spinach soufflé, cleaned a spot from the mother's coat, made them all laugh, danced in stocking feet to music in the white room after reading the child to sleep. She knitted dresses for herself and played chess with the husband. She washed and set the mother's soft ash-blond hair and gave her neck rubs, offered to.

The woman now spent her winter afternoons in the big bedroom. She made a fire in the hearth and put on slacks and an old sweater she had loved at school, and sat in the big chair and stared out the window at snow-ridden branches, or went away into long novels about other people moving through other winters.

The girl brought the child in twice a day, once in the late afternoon when he would tell of his day, all of it tumbling out quickly because there was not much time, and before he went to bed. Often now the man took his wife to dinner. He made a courtship ceremony of it, inviting her beforehand so she could get used to the idea. They dressed and were beautiful together again and went out into the frosty night. Over candle-light he would say, "I think you are better, you know." "Perhaps I am," she would murmur. "You look . . . like a cloistered queen," he said once, his voice breaking curiously.

One afternoon the girl brought the child into the bedroom.

"We've been out playing in the park. He found something he wants to give you, a surprise." The little boy approached her, smiling mysteriously. He placed his cupped hands in hers and left a live dry thing that spat brown juice in her palm and leapt away. She screamed and wrung her hands to be rid of the brown juice. "Oh, it was only a grasshopper," said the girl. Nimbly she crept to the edge of a curtain, did a quick knee bend and reclaimed the creature, led the boy competently from the room.

"The girl upsets me," said the woman to her husband. He sat frowning on the side of the bed he had not entered for so long. "I'm sorry, but there it is." The husband stroked his creased brow and said he was sorry too. He really did not know what they would do without that treasure of a girl. "Why don't you stay here with me in bed," the woman said.

Next morning she fired the girl, who cried and said, "I loved the little boy, what will become of him now?" But the mother turned away her face and the girl took down the watercolors from the walls, sheathed the records she had danced to, and went away.

"I don't know what we'll do. It's all my fault. I know. I'm such a burden. I know that."

"Let me think. I'll think of something." (Still understanding these things.)

"I know you will. You always do," she said.

With great care he rearranged his life. He got up hours early, did the shopping, cooked the breakfast, took the boy to nursery school. "We will manage," he said, "until you're better, however long that is." He did his work, collected the boy from the school, came home and made the supper, washed the dishes, got the child to bed. He managed everything. One evening, just as she was on the verge of swallowing her draught, there was a timid knock on her door. The little boy came in wearing his pajamas. "Daddy has fallen asleep on my bed and I can't get in. There's not room."

Very sedately she left her bed and went to the child's room. Things were much changed. Books were rearranged, toys. He'd done some new drawings. She came as a visitor to her son's room, wakened the father and helped him to bed. "Ah, he shouldn't have bothered you," said the man, leaning on his wife. "I've told him not to." He dropped into his own bed and fell asleep with a moan. Meticulously she undressed him. She folded and hung his clothes. She covered his body with the bedclothes. She flicked off the light that shone in his face.

The next day she moved her things into the girl's white room. She put her hairbrush on the dresser: she put a note pad and pen beside the bed. She stocked the little room with cigarettes, books, bread and cheese. She didn't need much.

At first the husband was dismayed. But he was receptive to her needs. He understood these things. "Perhaps the best thing is for you to follow it through," he said. "I want to be big enough to contain whatever you must do."

All day long she stayed in the white room. She was a young queen, a virgin in a tower; she was the previous inhabitant, the girl with all the energies. She tried these personalities on like costumes, then discarded them. The room had a new view of streets she'd never seen that way before. The sun hit the room in late afternoon and she took to brushing her hair in the sun. One day she decided to write a poem. "Perhaps a sonnet." She took up her pen and pad and began working from words that had lately lain in her mind. She had choices for the sonnet, ABAB or ABBA for a start. She pondered these possibilities until she tottered into a larger choice: she did not have to write a sonnet. Her poem could be six, eight, ten, thirteen lines, it could be any number of lines, and it did not even have to rhyme.

She put down the pen on top of the pad.

In the evenings, very briefly, she saw the two of them. They knocked on her door, a big knock and a little, and she would call, "Come in," and the husband would smile, though he looked a bit tired, yet somehow this tiredness suited him. He would put her sleeping draught on the bedside table and say, "The boy and I have done all right today," and the child would kiss her. One night she tasted for the first time the power of his baby spit.

"I don't think I can see him anymore," she whispered sadly to the man. And the husband turned away, but recovered admirably and said, "Of course, I see."

So the husband came alone. "I have explained to the boy," he said. "And we are doing fine. We are managing." He squeezed his wife's pale arm and put the two glasses on her table. After he had gone, she sat looking at the arm.

"I'm afraid it's come to that," she said. "Just push the notes under the door; I'll read them. And don't forget to leave the draught outside."

The man sat for a long time with his head in his hands. Then he rose and went away from her. She heard him in the kitchen, where he mixed the draught in batches now to last a week at a time, storing it in a corner of the cupboard. She heard him come back, leave the big glass and the little one outside on the floor.

Outside her window the snow was melting from the branches; there were more people on the streets. She brushed her hair a lot and seldom read anymore. She sat in her window and brushed her hair for hours, and saw a boy fall off his new bicycle again and again, a dog chasing a squirrel, an old woman peek slyly over her shoulder and then extract a parcel from a garbage can.

In the evening she read the notes they slipped under her door. The child could not write, so he drew and sometimes painted his. The notes were painstaking at first, the man and boy offering the final strength of their day to her. But sometimes, when they seemed to have had a bad day, there were only hurried scrawls.

One night, when the husband's note had been extremely short, loving but short, and there had been nothing from the boy, she stole out of her room as she often did to get more supplies, but crept upstairs instead and stood outside their doors, listening to the regular breathing of the man and boy asleep. She hurried back to her room and drank the draught.

She woke earlier now. It was spring; there were birds. She listened for sounds of the man and the boy eating breakfast; she listened for the roar of the motor when they drove away.

One beautiful noon, she went out to look at her kitchen in the daylight. Things were changed. He had bought some new dish towels. Had the old ones worn out? The canisters seemed closer to the sink. She inspected the cupboard and saw new things among the old. She got out flour, baking powder, salt, milk (he bought a different brand of butter), and baked a loaf of bread and left it cooling on the table.

The force of the two joyful notes slipped under her door that evening pressed her into the corner of the little room: she had hardly space to breathe. As soon as possible, she drank the draught.

Now the days were too short. She was always busy. She woke with the first bird. Worked till the sun set. No time for hair brushing. Her fingers raced the hours.

Finally, in the nick of time, it was finished one late afternoon. Her veins pumped and her forehead sparkled. She went to the cupboard, took what was hers, closed herself into the little white room and brushed her hair for a while.

The man and boy came home and found: five loaves of warm bread, a roasted stuffed turkey, a glazed ham, three pies of different fillings, eight molds of the boy's favorite custard, two weeks' supply of fresh-laundered sheets and shirts and towels, two hand-knitted sweaters (both of the same grey color), a sheath of marvelous watercolor beasts accompanied by mad and fanciful stories nobody could ever make up again, and a tablet full of love sonnets addressed to the man. The house smelled redolently of renewal and spring. The man ran to the little room, could not contain himself to knock, flung back the door.

"Look, Mommy is sleeping," said the boy. "She's tired from doing all our things again." He dawdled in a stream of the last sun for that day and watched his father roll tenderly back her eyelids, lay his ear softly to her breast, test the delicate bones of her wrist. The father put down his face into her fresh-washed hair.

"Can we eat the turkey for supper?" the boy asked.

CRAZY LADY

Mary Peterson

. . . .

She had a Ph.D. in philosophy and two master's degrees, but they didn't stop her from being the town's crazy lady. Maybe they even helped. She was smart enough to be inventively crazy, and she always knew when they were going to commit her to the state hospital again. Perhaps there was a line she knew about, and she crossed it when she decided to.

She lived in a small white clapboard house with green shutters, on Main Street, tucked neatly between two larger colonial houses and directly down from Flo's Steamed Hot Dogs and Arnie's Real Italian Pizza. The house had a rickety rose trellis over the door. The houses staunchly on either side were really lawyers' offices.

Even with the bushes, and although her house was set back some distance from the road, people could still see the things she did to the lawn. She left the front door and back door wide open in any weather. She dressed the elm tree with a toga of sheet. She hung politicians' signs upside down in rows next to the front door. She found a blue sign that read "Bernie's Feeds" and nailed it over her window. She took the television set out to the side lawn and tried to bury it with a shovel, but there were too many roots and she couldn't dig deeply enough. So she left it there, antenna askew, the shovel stuck into the dirt upright.

Early in the summer, when she went bad crazy, her lawn was positively garlanded with toilet paper fluttering wildly from the tree branches, and balanced in one tree was a startling pink umbrella. People said, "What's the umbrella for?" But nobody knew. Then somebody said at Jimmy's Store that she was talking about the Viet Cong, and maybe she put things around her house for protection. But nobody knew what protection a pink umbrella would provide.

Townspeople saw her out walking every day, always heading in a new direction, and they avoided her when they could. If she saw a person she would stop and talk, and nothing she said made sense. Sometimes she chattered in Latin, or French. Sometimes she left notes for people on their doors, but even the town doctor—who understood Latin—could make no sense of the notes.

She usually wore a scarf and a trench coat, sometimes a long grey sweater. She was perhaps fifty-eight or sixty, but from behind she looked like a slim-hipped girl. Her walk had the forward urgency of someone on important business. She thrust her head and clenched her fists. She clenched her face within the babushka scarf, too; her face was lined and tight, tense with the pressure of whatever went on in her mind. A thin face, and old-looking. You could almost guess her age when you looked at her head-on. Perhaps she could have been beautiful. She had astonishing, insistent bones. Perhaps she could have been striking. She looked rather like an artist. Like a weaver. Her little thin legs had ropy muscles, and so did her arms.

The people who were most afraid of her were probably of two types: those who were so proper-polite they couldn't tell her to go away when she stopped them on the street; and the artists. There weren't many good artists in town—three writers, a sculptor, and only two good painters (the rest of the painters, and there were many, weren't good at all, and they were most outspoken about being artists, and they showed their work every summer in an open outdoor festival on the Meeting House lawn). The real artists were bothered by her in different ways that may have added up to the same way:

Perhaps the writers were reminded of their dreams. The dreams they couldn't shake when they woke first thing in the morning—when the house grew a tiller and set sail out of the harbor; when the tower spurted flames around the screaming family; when the swarthy rapist pursued from behind and clutched like a dog on the gravelly shopping center parking lot.

Perhaps the sculptor was reminded of the draped sheet of the covered object in his studio. It was unfinished. He was a practical worker and always finished everything, but that one tugged and nagged at him even when he had dinner with his kind, patient wife and his quiet, intelligent children. If he could only get the shape behind the drape to take form, then something very important would be finished. Formlessness was terrifying to him.

Perhaps the painters were uneasy about letting the public see their work, perhaps they were angry with poor attention that made people shake their heads and scratch their jaws and leave without noticing the quality of color in the foreground, the careful details that brought a subject coherently together in a frame. The crazy lady's lawn was like details without order; the eye skidded all over the place and never found a home. It was unbearable.

The artists in town were not very good friends, and probably never spoke to each other about it. They all had astonishing egos and bitter little insecurities, and they were loath to confess anything to anybody.

As for the proper-polite people, they let her stop and talk her gibberish while they looked around helplessly for rescue. Sooner or later somebody would come along and say to the crazy lady, "Harriet, knock it off. You're bothering people." Like magic she would shake her head and pull her grubby trench coat closer around her little bird body and shuffle off, muttering, down the street.

People in town had seen her do almost everything: walk into a restaurant and come quickly out again within a minute, as though somebody had thrown her out. Stand in the post office for three hours filling out change of address cards. Sneak home the back way through overgrown vacant property. Pick up things along the road and shove them into her pockets.

And everybody knew she smelled terrible. They were sure of that.

Her daughter, who lived in town but refused to try to do anything with her mother, said, "She's always been crazy, but worse the last few years. She has pills—just one in the morning and she's fine. But she won't take them. I don't know why. Maybe she likes being the town's crazy lady."

Somebody said, *A person ought to be careful of what they wish for, because of course it will come true.*

Her daughter said she hadn't known her father well either, and when he shot himself in that very little house five years ago, while her mother was institutionalized upstate, she wasn't even sad. "How could I be?" she said. "I didn't speak to him for years. He was a stranger." She said her brother felt guilty but was a weakling and wouldn't have anything to do with his mother. "He just pretends she doesn't exist," the daughter said.

Earlier in the summer, when the crazy lady was getting worse, she made friends with a halfwit in town and spent hours a day with her. But the halfwit finally couldn't stand her either, and threw her out. After that she took to wandering around town in her trench coat and finally she did not put on clothing under the trench coat, and walked into Jimmy's Store and the Economy Gas Station and the Mariner Bar and opened the coat and was picked up by the police within a day for "indecent exposure."

Later in the summer, when she was back from the state hospital, she was good for a while. Children stopped, for a while, calling her the witch. Mothers forgot to warn their children to avoid her house. But sure as the weather, in September she started to go off her nut again and began to redecorate the front lawn. And threatened a respectable woman in town with burning. And in a day was found on that woman's spacious front porch lighting little fires and smiling to herself. She was trucked off again by the police, who spoke afterward of the smell of her, and that she probably hadn't had a bath all summer.

Her daughter, who meant to leave town for California, stayed awhile to clean up the house. She saw the television on the lawn and the shovel next to it. She put them inside. Also the sheet around the tree and the upside-down political signs and the boxes set on end and the gatherings of tindery sticks and rotten vegetables. She took the knives out of the trees. She told people her mother must have known she was going away soon, because the kitchen was cleaned spotless, although the other rooms were a disaster.

Maybe when the artists drove past they noticed that the house was orderly again, and they felt something relax inside. They would never have to speak of it.

Maybe the polite people could finish a cup of coffee at Jimmy's in the morning, and walk on errands, since she wouldn't tag along embarrassing them. They were safe, too.

Somebody said, *Even a true story has a moral now and then.*

When the daughter was cleaning outside, she noticed a powerful and rancid smell. It took a long time to locate. Finally she saw a decayed cat's head—mostly bone, a little fur—lying in the bird feeder.

She threw it in the trash.

And made a mental note to tell her mother, if she saw her again, one should never feed cats to birds if one lives on Main Street.

PATIENTS

Jonathan Strong

. . . .

Tim was a thirteen-year-old fat boy, the youngest patient on the ward. I knew him after I had been at the hospital several weeks and had begun to get myself back in touch. We talked first in the lounge on a rainy afternoon, listening to a Donovan record.

"Jamie," said Tim, "that's your name, right?"

"Right," I said.

"You been here long?" His round face was red because it had been hard for him to start talking to me.

"Three weeks," I said. "Don't you remember?"

"I been here so long I don't remember who were here when. I been here eight months. Where you from?"

"Winnetka," I said.

"Is that your car, the turquoise-blue one?"

"Yep."

"You must be rich," he said.

"I wouldn't say so. Where you from?"

"Skokie." He had a bright voice that was starting to get lower but was mostly high-pitched still. His teeth stuck out a little, but otherwise he could have been handsome if he were not so fat. "I love rainy days," he said. "I hate sunny days. I love it when it's all gray and soggy."

"Are you kidding?" I said.

"Nope," said Tim, "I really do."

Our ward was in the basement of the building. The lounge was built of gray concrete blocks, and the windows at the ceiling showed clouds and the long grass that had not been clipped. There were about fifty of us day patients. A lot of guys were in for drugs, but there were all kinds—straight guys, suburban ladies with nerves, some messed-up girls, old ladies having shock treatments, two old men who played chess. I slowly made friends all around, but I mostly stayed with the guys my age with the same experiences.

I had sat with Tim once before at the O.T. table when he was drawing a bullfrog that turned out quite good. I had been working on a leather belt myself. We had not talked then, but now in the lounge we had. He sat back in his chair, and his T-shirt lifted up to show his round middle. We did not talk anymore for a while but listened to the Donovan record with the rain in the background. Tim had brought the record in. The lounge had a Victrola donated by someone, but we had to bring our own records. The younger patients were usually the only ones who brought records in, though sometimes we had to suffer through some lady's Dean Martin album.

"Hey, Jamie," said Tim, "you like this song?"

"Yep," I said. It was "Mad John's Escape," which I think is a cool song.

"I play the bass guitar, you know," said Tim.

"You do?"

"I couldn't get into a group yet, but I'm learning it."

"Great," I said.

"You play?"

"Some," I said. "Hey, how's the bullfrog?"

"Miss Hedrick wants me to enter it in the hospital art show." Miss Hedrick was the O.T. nurse.

"Great," I said.

"I love frogs," said Tim. "Except you know a funny thing? When I were little I used to dread lily pads."

"What?" He was sitting on the edge of his chair, and his friendly eyes were looking at me.

"I don't understand it," he said. "I actually dreaded lily pads, I dreaded them."

"How come, do you suppose?"

"I don't know. When I were little a wet lily pad blew onto my stomach when I were swimming up in Wisconsin. I couldn't get it off. I were really scared."

"How come you always say 'were' instead of 'was'?"

"I don't know," said Tim. "I just do."

Though he was seven years younger than me, I did feel like being his friend in a way. I found him a cool person. He was very bright for his age, not that he necessarily knew a lot, but he responded with a lot of feelings to things. I myself had been such a dead kid at his age. We went on talking most of the afternoon. I had nothing else to do, having got my work therapy out of the way that morning. We talked about his family and his lack of friends. He brought up his fatness, which I was going to ignore, but I should have known he would want to talk about it. He said Miss Hedrick told him he would look something like Donovan if he lost some weight.

I was a particular friend of Tim's for the rest of my time at the hospital. He said he did not have anyone he could talk to about his life except me and of course his doctor. Every day we sat and talked, particularly about the things he wanted to know about sex. He worried about getting excited seeing girls on the bus on his way to the hospital in the mornings. Once he went three stops beyond the hospital and had to take another bus back because he could not stand up without grossing-out the whole car, as he put it. He wanted to know all about my girl, Diane, and every morning he asked me if I had slept with her last night.

I made several other close friends too, but I do not feel like writing about other guys who were into drugs. I talked with them about drugs the same as if we knew each other on the outside. I was trying to get away from all that. My friends and I had spent the winter in one apartment or another turning on. They were still doing it. My doctor and I agreed that while I was in the hospital I would not hang around with my friends outside anymore. I only saw them for an hour or so in the evenings on the way home, and they thought it was very mystical and mind-blowing to be in the hospital. I spent most of my time at home and with some old straight friends from high school. I did not mind the quiet evenings, because my days were busier, and I slept a lot. I soon got sort of attached to the hospital. It was an experience I was having by myself which my friends could not share.

One Monday I wanted to talk to a girl who had just been admitted to the ward, but she was withdrawing, sitting with her head between her knees, rocking a little back and forth. While I was sitting beside her on the green plastic couch in the lounge, I heard the noise of a crash in the day room. I got up and went in, and it was Tim throwing things. He had tipped over the bridge table and thrown a chair. The ladies at the sewing table were all scared but trying not to notice what he was doing. Mrs. Fisk, the head nurse, was standing facing Tim with her hands on her hips. I realized that though I had thought of him as my friend I did not know him well enough to do anything at that point. I could not go up to him and try to calm him down because I was not his doctor and I did not know what was actually involved. That was the hard thing about making friends at the hospital.

They put him on restrictions for the rest of the week. He could not leave the day room to go to the gym or the grill or even the lounge, and the attendant had to go to lunch with him. The next day I tried to talk to him, but he did not want to talk. They had upped his dose of Thorazine, and that kept him pretty much subdued. He told me he wanted to go to sleep, but it was against the rules to put your head down or close your eyes, and the nurses kept making him sit up.

Tim spent the week at the O.T. table painting. His first bullfrog was so good he did more of them. He modified them till they were simple heart-shaped green things with one eye and feet. Then he started to do them in all colors. The last one he did was not even a frog but blobs of dark colors which he called "Frog at Night." While he was painting frogs, I wrote a poem about drowning which I hoped one of my friends outside could make into a song, and I submitted it to the hospital newspaper. The girl who had been withdrawing read it and said it was "a real trip."

The next week Tim was off restrictions, and we sat in the lounge again listening to records. I brought in the Cream and the Doors, and Tim brought Tim Buckley. He told me then what had caused his tantrum. He had gone with Lucille, a tough kid about his age, into the closet where they stored the gym equipment, and she had got him excited and unzipped his fly, and they had made love sitting on a chair. Tim had told his doctor because he thought he would keep it secret, but his doctor told the entire staff. Tim was so mad when one of the nurses talked to him about it that he started throwing things. It was a serious thing to him. It was the first time he had ever made love. Of course his doctor had to tell Lucille's doctor and the staff, but Tim did not understand. Now he wanted to know more about sex. It had not been very good, he said. He felt all funny about it. I told him that for it to be good you had to care something for the girl and you had to do it more relaxedly, in your bed, not in some closet.

That week Tim became troublesome again. Though he was still on Thorazine, he burped very loudly all the time and made the ladies at the sewing table cringe. In our talks he got more dirty-minded and talked about bathroom things a lot. I tried not to laugh and told him I did not want to talk to him if he would not be serious. He showed me a picture he had drawn of himself looking like a meatball standing behind his doctor, who was throwing up into the toilet, saying, "Tim, what a stupid, disgusting patient you are, you make me vomit!" I told him he should show it to his doctor. He said he already had.

My work therapy was changed from the shop to the grill, and Tim used to meet me on my break and have a milk shake. Once I told him to have a Diet Pepsi instead, but he said Diet Pepsi made him vomit, and he let out a burp. Everyone in the grill, mostly patients, looked at him.

"Jamie, why am I such a stupid baby?" he said to me.

"You're not stupid," I said.

"I know. You might not believe it. I have a very high I.Q. When I were tested they said my I.Q. were near genius level."

"I can believe it, Tim," I said.

"But I always act like such a baby. If I were only handsome like you."

"Cut out the milk shakes every day. Have a grapefruit juice if you don't like Diet Pepsi."

"Oh, puke," said Tim. "You know what that is you're eating?" I was eating a strawberry-rhubarb pie with powdered sugar.

"I hate to think," I said.

"It's bloody snots with curdles." I just kept eating and ignored him.

"I told you I want to talk to you without all that," I said.

"I can't help it. It just comes out. Like puke." He burped.

"Come on, Tim," I said. He looked at me with his friendly eyes.

"Why do you like to talk to me?" he said.

"I don't know. I can tell you about things. It helps me too, you know."

"But you'll be going soon, and you have all your friends and sexy Diane and your car. I'll be still here for years."

"It won't be years, Tim."

"Nothing will get any better."

"How do you know? Have faith in the place."

"They said I were getting worse."

"Well, I don't know, Tim."

"Why should some people be handsome like you and some ugly and fat?"

"Why don't you just try eating a little less each day?"

"You told me before I should starve myself for a couple of days so my stomach shrinks, and then I wouldn't want as much."

"Well, then try that. Doesn't your doctor give you a diet?"

"I'm mad at him now."

"Tim, you know, being thin doesn't mean you solve your problems." I felt bad saying that to him. To him being thin was a kind of solution.

The following week he was doing well enough to have work therapy. They assigned him to the grill with me, but he kept sneaking brownies and shakes. After a few days he had enough of work. When he was fooling around with the soda jet, it sprayed out onto some customers, and the manager of the grill sent him back to the ward.

I was going to be discharged, and I had told Tim about it. We were working at the O.T. table. I told him as casually as I could, and I immediately suggested that maybe I could still see him, maybe I could pick him up some afternoon and go to a movie. He said they would not allow it because patients cannot see each other on the outside. I told him I would not be a patient anymore, but he was still sure it would not be allowed. Anyway I felt better saying I would try to see him again. It was going to be a hard thing, leaving the hospital after so many weeks.

My own therapy had been going pretty well. I would still see my doctor once a week to keep me in line for a while. I planned to get a job and go back to college in the fall. I really felt I was through with drugs, at least acid and speed for sure. I am not going to get into that kind of thing again.

Tim painted a lot during my last week. He was on restrictions again and taking a lot of Thorazine. I decided to paint too, and I did a psychedelic painting of the bottom of the sea with creatures crawling around. It was an illustration of my poem. Tim drew in a little frog at the top, swimming.

Once I went into the bathroom to clean off my brush, and when I came back the paints on my palette had all been swirled around in a big mess, and VOMIT was written across my painting. Tim was not around. I did not see him the rest of the day.

The next day I was in the lounge listening to somebody's Donovan album, "Sunshine Superman." It was a beautiful day outside, but of course we could not go out. I was glad I was being discharged before the really good weather started.

Mandy, the girl who had been withdrawing, had become a pal of mine. She was sitting with me on the green couch making a string of beads. Tim came in and sat down across from us.

"Jamie," he said, "I'm sorry I wrote VOMIT on your painting."

"That's okay."

"I just had to get mad at you, for going."

"That's what I figured."

"I don't have any friends anywhere," he said. He looked up at the windows. "I wish it were gray and soggy out. I hate it like this."

"I asked my doctor about us getting together for a movie or something on the outside," I said. "He said he'd have to talk to your doctor, but it might be all right."

"It doesn't matter," said Tim. "When I get discharged from here I can see you whenever I like. They can't do anything about it." We sat and listened to the record, and then Mandy had to go, so Tim and I were alone. The side was over, and the needle lifted up and started at the beginning again.

"I lost three pounds," said Tim.

"Great."

"You know what this looks like?" He was eating a brownie.

"You don't have to tell me," I said.

"Don't you want to know?" he said, sitting on the edge of the chair.

"I know."

"What?" He was chuckling.

"You know. I'm not saying."

"Did you sleep with Diane last night?"

"Nope," I said.

"I wish I could meet her," said Tim.

"Maybe you will." Suddenly I felt sad, encouraging him. I did not know if I would come through. "Dreaded any lily pads lately?" I said.

"Nope. I really used to, though."

"You wouldn't make a very good frog."

"I know. But I wish I were a frog."

"Hey, Tim, I've got a present for you." I pulled off the belt I was wearing, the one I made in O.T., and gave it to him. "I'll make you a bet that when you're my age you'll be wearing this buckled at the same notch I do. That's this one." I took out my knife and scratched a cross on the next-to-tightest notch.

"Thanks, Jamie," he said, and leaned forward to hold the belt. He put it on, but it did not go around him at all. I had not thought he was that fat.

"Oh, boy," I said. "Well, that's incentive then."

He smiled. Then we said what was hard for us to say. He started. "I'll miss you, Jamie, I'll really miss you here."

"I'll miss you too, Tim," I said. I remember him as he was: he knew I was going outside and that I would change. It was like leaving him there.

The day I left the hospital it was very hard saying good-bye to everyone. I talked with Miss Hedrick for a while, and I wished I had got to know her better before. Our doctors still had not decided whether Tim and I could get together for a movie. My record as a responsible guy was a little fuzzy. Anyway I could not know all that was involved. Tim was a sick guy.

I promised to write him a poem on frogs, something about the Frog-who-did-a-wooing-go or the Frog Prince. My poem about drowning was printed in the hospital newspaper that week. I will put it at the end of this story.

De Oozy Bed

Layin in de oozy bed
Minners swim about me head.
Swarm o waterbug at play
Swim above me all de day.

Now me sinkin in de ooze,
Close me eye an take me snooze.
Do no hear de lates news,
Do no want an do no choose,
Nuttin here fo me to lose
Sleepin down among de ooze.

*　　*　　*

All dem fish no matter whose,
Comes in greens an comes in blues.
Crabbies crawlin by in twos,
Lobster grabbin at me shoes,
Crawdad an de octopooze
All a-livin in de ooze.

Sink into de oozy slime,
No mo place an no mo time.
All de oozy people knows
Here de place to close de eye.

HANGING

Steven Schrader

. . . .

I bought a bar with rubber ends that hung by its own pressure. As soon as I put it up I leaped on and swung. My arms
and shoulders hurt, but I felt exhilarated, freer than I had in
years. I began hanging before work and in the evening when
I came home. My arms and shoulders grew strong and my
hands became calloused.

My wife was amused. I would slam the door, kiss her cheek,
and leap onto the bar. My son begged to be put on also, and
when I was finished I would lift him up and let him hang. He
did very well, though he was only five.

Every day I hung thirty seconds longer than before, until I
could hang ten minutes. There seemed no limit to how strong
I could become. At first my wife called out to me from the
kitchen as I gripped the bar, but I didn't answer, not wanting
to ruin my concentration or upset my breathing. My son, too,
talked to me and pushed my legs to make me swing, but I
became angry and warned him not to disturb me.

I began learning tricks on the bar. Fortunately the ceiling
was high and I was able to whirl about. I bought a gymnastics
book and mastered the exercises. Then I bought rings, which
I could put my feet through and hang from upside down. By
twisting I could tighten the leather straps of the rings on my
feet and relax my body. I practiced simple tricks, swinging up

to grab the bar, but most of the time I just hung. Blood rushed to my head, and my eyes seemed ready to pop, but when I was finished I felt much better. My mind was clear, my sinuses drained. Everything became simple. I was able to hang longer and longer. Sometimes I would skip dinner and my wife would bring her plate and sit on the mat beneath me. My son would bring a book and I would read to him as he drank his bottle. Then he would kiss me good night. I began staying on the bar later and later, sometimes dozing, and when I did get to bed my wife would be asleep.

One night I didn't go to bed. Instead I hung on the bar. In the morning my wife gaped at me. My son didn't seem to notice. He rushed past me to eat breakfast and waited to be taken to school.

"Aren't you going to work?" my wife asked when she returned.

"No."

"Should I call in sick for you?"

"I'm not sick. I'm hanging."

She called the doctor, and he came in the afternoon. By then I'd been down to go to the bathroom and eat crackers and gone up again.

The doctor kneeled on the mat and examined me, made soundings with his stethoscope and looked up my throat.

He told my wife to call when I came down. But I stayed on the bar, dropping down only late at night to use the bathroom and eat.

At the end of the month, after my wife paid the bills we had nothing left in our account.

My father came to see me.

"This is what I raised you for, made sacrifices to send you through college?"

He stamped his foot and left.

The next day he sent a rabbi. The rabbi was my age and round, and had a little pointed beard.

"Frank, what's troubling you? You have a loving family, a car, your associates miss you. I know the world is difficult, but you must shoulder your responsibilities. God will help you. He understands. He will forgive."

My wife applied for welfare. The investigator was a young black girl with an Afro.

"Mr. Kaplan, you know you're going to have to go to Employment Rehab."

I shook my head. "I'm sorry, I can't come down."

She sent a psychiatric case worker to see me.

"Why are you depressed?" he asked.

"But I'm happy."

"Can you describe your happiness?"

"My head's clear. I can concentrate on things."

"Like what?"

"The wall, the molding, your knees. I think about things."

We shook hands and he left. Soon I began receiving temporary Home Relief. My son's friends grew used to me. They ran past me and no longer asked why I was hanging by my feet.

Every night my wife would leave food for me. Most nights she ate on the mat. A few times she kissed me and cried.

One night she was so lonely she invited everyone over—the doctor, the rabbi, the investigator, and the psychiatric case worker. They ate delicatessen and drank beer.

Come down, they all pleaded, but I refused. With a sigh, my father jumped onto the bar, followed by the doctor, the rabbi, the investigator, and the psychiatric case worker, and my wife and son. They were all pleased they had made it and they joked and shouted until the wall cracked from the weight of their bodies and the bar came loose and we toppled down.

THE PRISONER

Curtis Harnack

. . . .

Laura arrived on campus for her freshman year with a chipmunk in her bookbag. The dean of women, after a long consultation with the house president, decided to overlook the no-pets regulation, since crippled Laura, on crutches from polio, was such a poor thing, a special case. Unable to give her all the love she surely needed, they would let the chipmunk do what it could in their stead.

Daily I found Laura outside my office door, deliberately taking advantage of me, for she knew her special "gifted" status as one of my six students in a tutorial. She was a beautiful redhead with greenish hazel eyes, a long, arching neck, flawless white skin, and delicate hands and wrists. After listening to a lecture along with a couple of hundred other freshmen, she would discuss with me what she thought of it, and I guided her supplementary reading. The other privileged students were boys, relatively independent, who saw me only one hour a week. Laura seemed to dare me to turn her away. She knew I must be loathing the sight of her, and she was waiting—just waiting—for me to admit it. I always smiled when I opened the door to her and cheerfully set aside my other work. Neurotics imagine that their single-mindedness will get them exactly what they want. I try to put up a pretty good fight.

"I hope you don't mind my talking about myself," she said,

early in our acquaintance. "I suppose you've a file on me thick as a telephone book already."

"Not quite."

"Why I ever got a scholarship, I'll never know. I must have come under the cripples quota—blacks, dwarfs—you know."

"Your test scores on the College Boards were in the eight hundreds. *That* had something to do with it."

"I don't see where it comes from—the brains, I mean. Father's just an ordinary confused man with no education. My parents married while still in *high school*! Isn't it obscene? I was on the way. But most bastards in history turn out to be pretty interesting."

"You've made *that* romantic, too?"

"They're either the villains or the Tom Joneses, aren't they? Anyhow—we lived in an awful bow-front house near the brewery where Daddy worked. And Mother got a job as soon as she could—in order to save money, to leave him. I was locked in the apartment when she went off—each morning—since they couldn't afford a baby-sitter. I can't remember much about those years, except the darkness of the rooms, and trying all the doorknobs—and crying to myself."

"How was your father—toward you?" I was falling into my amateur therapist role.

"He'd stay away and drink beer most nights. You might say his whole *life* was beer! They never would've stuck together if it hadn't been for me. So . . . when Daddy got arrested, Mother was relieved, actually."

Picked up for shoplifting, sentenced to one year in the penitentiary: it was in her folder, part of her vital statistics.

"For a stick of deodorant—that's what they nabbed him with! Imagine!" Again, that shrill unhappy laugh. "Poetic justice or something. Wouldn't deodorant be just what he'd want? After all those days of sour malt smells."

I'd seen the newspaper story, which she carried in her pink Lady Buxton wallet, hauling it out (tattered, yellow, and nearly falling into separate squares at the folds) to show new associates just what an illustrious background she came from. He had been copping things from stores for some time, stashing away radios, watches, and stereo equipment. Her mother filed for divorce and later married a successful insurance executive. Soon Laura had a half-sister, then a half-brother. I wondered how she had caught polio, in this day and age. Probably picked it up on a trip to Greece with her family, she said. Her health-fadist mother had been against inoculations in general, believing they introduced poisons into an otherwise healthy body. But when Laura became ill, the two small children were quickly sent to the doctor for their polio shots.

"Don't you *ever* see your father?"

"I doubt Daddy knows where I even am—wherever *he* is. In some place like *that*, I suppose." She nodded toward the mental hospital across the lake. "In one kind of jail or another."

"That's not a prison. The patients are mostly voluntary. Complete freedom of the grounds, and they can—"

"The grounds, yes, but that ends with a gate and a guard, doesn't it? So where's the freedom?"

"Do you think *you're* so free now?"

"I'm free at least to decide—not to go *there*. That's something."

As soon as I learned of Laura's pet chipmunk, I brought the matter into our discussions on the nature of freedom, for we were reading existential philosophers. After exploring the classical arguments regarding will and circumstance, Laura found it increasingly hard to excuse the way she held that chipmunk prisoner, merely for her own company, pleasure, and entertainment.

"It isn't like an ordinary pet," I said, "—doesn't have even that much freedom. Why don't you take it out of your pocket right now?"

Nervously, Laura glanced around my office, searching for openings through which the animal might slip and escape her monitoring hand for good. Unlike a dog or cat, the taming of a wild creature, I knew from having had a pet crow in my boyhood, is effective only so long as the control remains immediate.

"I let her out in *my* room. But I've tested that."

"The chipmunk might find a haven behind Kant, is that it?"

"Oh, I suppose I could catch her again. But the experience would be so frightening for her."

"And for *you*." I felt it good that she examine her dependencies. There were few moments when she could get outside herself enough to view anybody—or anything—objectively. Twice before coming to the university she had tried to kill herself. The whips of white flesh on her wrists were a reminder, for both of us. Sometimes she rubbed them in my presence, as if half-regretting that the skin still held in her blood. She would touch the scars dreamily and brood upon the secret of her future.

As for the chipmunk's freedom problem, Laura got around it by saying, "She'd hibernate soon anyhow, wouldn't she? I mean, if she were out in the woods she'd curl up in a ball somewhere and simply be out of it till spring."

"It—or *she*—will probably do that in your room, too. Just to get away from you."

"She *does* seem to sleep more and more, in my dresser drawer."

"Lights on, the heat in the room—probably confused. Do you keep it in a cage, or what?"

"Oh, no, she occupies the same cell I do! She likes darkness and seclusion, just like me." It would come out to Laura's low whistle or the sound of rasping peanut shells; leap upon the bed, run up Laura's arm—the toes like prickles on the skin— and sometimes into her long red hair. Sitting on the windowsill, it would look out over the campus with sudden, wild eyes, as if oblivious to Laura and the room—but only for a few seconds. The chipmunk—perhaps it *was* female, as Laura insisted—liked to be stroked behind the ears. If Laura had a smear of butter on her fingers, which she frequently did, since she rarely went to the cafeteria but ate instead out of provisions kept in the room, the petal-shaped tongue would dart out and lap furiously, lovingly, up and down each finger. "Not a stickery tongue like a cat's, either. A smooth, velvet tongue."

In short, the animal was all life, movement, and gaiety:

things Laura was not. That's why all of us—the dean, the house president, and the staff psychiatrist who saw her a few times after she'd fainted from lack of food on a downtown street and was brought back to campus in an ambulance—thought the chipmunk was carrying her along. But it was an insubstantial crutch—and I use the word deliberately. Laura's real crutches were as sturdy as ironing boards, and she used them clumsily. Even now, two years after her polio attack, Laura might have tried muscular therapy, but she preferred to drag her limp, dead limbs along, defiant in her affliction. Leg braces would have helped, but she rejected them—ugly cages, which would imprison her limbs. For aesthetic reasons she almost always wore a pantsuit or slacks.

One autumn afternoon as she reclined on the library steps, the crutches out of sight behind her, a presentable young man tried to flirt with her, pressing for a date to the "mixer" dance coming up. Laura, when she could bear it no longer, reached behind her and pulled out the clublike crutches, a malicious smile on her face, a mad look in her eye. Without a word she struggled upright and hobbled away in her most ungainly fashion, leaving the boy to his embarrassment. "I'm sorry—oh, my God! I didn't—didn't . . ."

Laura herself told me this story, one of the many Laura anecdotes I passed on to friends and family in off hours. I found myself thinking about her altogether too much, mentioning her to my wife, who wanted to invite Laura to dinner—but I said no—and even dreaming about her, once a sexual dream, which for the life of me I couldn't reconstruct upon awakening. My children, especially John, the eldest, became interested in *her*, too, knew there was "something queer about her," and I realized I must stop my preoccupation if I could.

The blight of mental illness ran in my family, but its fell hand had not touched me, and to further distance myself from it, I now had four children, all escapees, apparently sound. My father, who like Laura's was a simple laborer—a carpenter— was a manic-depressive in the days before medication, with hard liquor his usual solace. One night careening home from the roadhouse on the highway, his foot got heavy on the gas pedal, his hands did not turn the steering wheel to make the curve. It had all been done respectably enough, in the small-town way. My mother went back to work, ending up as office manager of the Farmers' Elevator, and we three children excelled in college, just as she hoped. She never lived to know the full significance of my sister's tendency to crack under pressure and slink home from school rather than face final exams—or did she, but refused to accept those episodes for what they were? I was far away at another university and chose to tend to my own life, and yes, I have suffered guilt in the years since my sister's suicide. But I am realistic, too, and know that nothing I might have done could have made much difference. Perhaps I'm a better teacher as a result of it all. Discussions with students like Laura tend to become personal; I get involved as if my life depended on it.

I couldn't keep conference talk on a theoretical level, though each session with Laura started that way. The right of an animal to its own freedom of movement, its own life, was not a philosophical problem of endless ramifications. I wondered if bothering Laura with these questions were not my own neurotic reaction to her—my way of getting even for the trouble she was causing me: make her endure a little more, *she* who was already so miserable. Suffering in others sometimes produces these cruel inversions, perhaps out of self-protection.

Laura kept projecting herself into the life of the chipmunk. Instead of rejoicing in its limber movements, the grace of every leap, she felt instead only the boundaries she had imposed: the closed door, the shut window, the hand on its back while it crouched in her pocket. She sensed the misery of its confinement—she felt *herself* and knew herself to be the keeper.

And I, following the argument to its ultimate end, saw my chance to point out that psychiatric help was available just across the lake at the mental health clinic. "It's one of the best there is, because of the university connection." Why remain imprisoned in such a suffocating set of neuroses, I said: functioning, but only with half a life, getting along with whatever props came to hand—me, the chipmunk, the university. No reason why with proper help she couldn't eventually stand free of us all.

"Stand, yes—but walk?" A wry, self-pitying smile.

"Think you're the first ever to be afflicted?"

"No, but it's me. I *am*. You can't know what it's like." She stared scornfully at my gray flannel trousers, covering well-muscled legs; her slacks in contrast flapped around mere bones.

Soon after term began I had noticed her hobbling to the spectators' bench at the tennis courts, where she watched me for an hour through dark glasses—and thoroughly ruined my serve. I couldn't help but feel apologetic for my healthy body. I was also afraid that her initial hostility might suddenly turn into a schoolgirl's crush. I made it clear the next day that I was married, though such a fact might not deter her—some frumpy creature who'd snared me in graduate school. But the four children—yes, that settled her down a bit.

I needn't have worried. Laura never fell in love with me; she was too sick even for that. Any such longings would have been quickly translated into some poetic-tragic attitude—what things might've been like, had she not been struck down, had her mother not made a mess of her life before she even had a chance to live it.

Some of the dormitories were left open during Christmas vacation to accommodate the foreign students. Laura refused to go home for the holidays and perhaps hoped to join my family around the tinseled tree. But I could not inflict upon them what had become my professional burden—though it wasn't part of my job to expend upon Laura all the attention she needed, if I could have. The trouble is, such boundaries are difficult to see, and if you think of them you're already not much of a teacher. I pretended not to hear Laura's murmurings about how much she'd like to be in somebody's home on Christmas Day, in order to glimpse like a mouse—or chipmunk—in a corner, what true family happiness could be like. Her dormitory lounge had a decorated tree, and for Christmas

dinner there would be stuffed turkey, cranberry sauce, pumpkin and mince pies. The armed services, mental hospitals,
prisons, and boarding schools all purveyed food to cover an
absence of love.

I advised her to play Santa Claus to the sleepy chipmunk—
maybe give it a special holiday nut—but largely try to ignore
the folderol, considering her situation. "Or do you want to milk
emotion out of it and feel like a waif?"

"I'm *not* feeling sorry for myself."

"Good! You could always go home for Christmas. You said
your mother wrote, asking when you'd arrive. But you enjoy
giving her a rebuff, don't you? She winces when neighbors ask,
'Where's Laura?' "

"You see right through me sometimes."

"I only say out loud what you won't say to yourself. And
regret it's *me* doing this, not some qualified psychiatrist—over
there." I paused at the window to look across the frozen lake,
as Laura had done so often, purely for effect.

"You think I'm a candidate for the little men in white
coats?"

"I think you haven't decided yet whether to give yourself a
chance—for some kind of life. You're just using crutches—in
every way—and nothing about *you* changes. That's what I wish
you'd see."

"I need a job. I ought to be on my own—then people
wouldn't be always yelling at me. Quit school, find work somewhere. Take a cheap room where nobody knows me. I always
run through friends pretty quick and have to start fresh somewhere else. That's my pattern."

"What kind of job do you have in mind?"

"Companion for children, maybe. In somebody's home. I
could baby-sit, you know? I could baby-sit for *you*, for your
wife, I mean. Some night you might let me try it, when you're
out to a party. Just to see how it goes."

"Think you'd earn enough baby-sitting—to support yourself?"

"Maybe not, but something. Or I could learn to type and
take dictation. Isn't there a secretarial school downtown?"

"Yeah, but your scholarship's to *this* university. You'd have to move out of the dorm and pay them tuition."

"Maybe I should enroll in the school of commerce, instead. Switch to a business course—Mother'd like *that*! Something practical. Not all this philosophy and literature. You've no idea how bourgeois she is."

"Laura, Laura, you're trying on one dream after another. And getting nowhere."

For a while we didn't talk about her future, and I saw less of her because she found it difficult getting around on ice and snow. She stuck fairly close to a routine involving a minimum of movement from her dorm to the library to classrooms.

One day in January I spotted her being hauled on a sled by a girl—a most solicitous, freckle-faced, homely little thing, who wrapped the pull-rope around her waist as if it were a harness and bent low to her task, while Laura sat upright and queenly in her chaise, now and then shouting directions or urging her to go faster. The president of Laura's dorm told me that the two had developed a symbiotic relationship which was doing neither of them much good. But it relieved us for a time from the constant attention Laura demanded. In our conferences I was happy to concentrate on academic matters for a change. At the end of the first semester her grades were straight "A."

Just after Easter vacation, the snow still on the ground but the sun high and decidedly warm, Laura came to see me with the chipmunk in her pocket, its velvet nose poking out of a hole, like a pencil eraser. I knew we were heading for some kind of crisis. Laura had spent the holidays in her room, and the friend of winter, who'd gone home for Easter, would not be returning. "Our dear Laura wore that child out," said the dean of women later. The girl suffered what used to be called a nervous breakdown. "Only the chipmunk seems able to stand it," said the dean, with a grim attempt at a laugh. "We're not running a hospital here. We can't have Laura in the dorm next year." The question was, how could I prepare her for the news? She wouldn't be able to function in a room off-campus—she would have to quit school altogether. Certainly I had tried to help her, but after all, she did have a home—and family—

which she could go back to. In the final analysis it was their problem. However, the hours of close association had incapacitated me for such an easy out. There was still a month and a half before end of term, days and days of conferences with this girl, and the necessity of being honest with her. Evasion of the truth is one of the first things a sensitive student picks up on—is most upset by—since it gives the lie to the whole enterprise.

When she brought the chipmunk into my office that sunny day in April, before the ice on the lake had broken up, I thought it time to talk of her future—and I began with the animal. "You and the chipmunk are going to be turned out, come June. Have you planned the summer?"

"No."

"You said your mother wouldn't let you have the chipmunk. At least—that's why you couldn't go home spring vacation, wasn't it?"

"That's what I told the dean," she said, smiling, "but actually, there're three Siamese cats that have the run of our house. They'd grab her in a minute. Even if I kept her in a cage, my little brother and sister would soon unlatch the cage door. Just for the fun of it, you know?"

"So, how *will* you spend the summer?" I figured we could get into the matter of next year gradually.

"Maybe I'll just go off somewhere. I have a little money."

That didn't sound good. "How much?"

"By June maybe fifty dollars. I'm watercoloring—greeting cards, stationery. I sell 'em in the dorm. It's easier than asking for a handout. I charge exorbitant prices and everybody's conscience is eased."

"When your money runs out, then what?"

"I wouldn't go home."

"Where, then?"

"I suppose I'd just . . . do it again." She looked at her wrists. "This time good and proper."

"No, you wouldn't—think of the chipmunk! What would happen to it?"

"Oh . . . oh, she'd suffer! How she'd suffer . . . until at last . . ." Her eyes reddened with tears.

"Somebody came and opened the door—and let her run free?"

"Oh *yes!*" She looked at me with agonized hope, as if I'd reached out just in time and pulled her back from the edge. But what kind of rescue had it been, and where had I pulled her to?

She took the chipmunk out of her pocket, carefully supporting its stomach; tenderly, the way small birds are held. The chipmunk blinked its enormous eyes and wrinkled its nose. Its fingerlike paws clung to Laura's elegant hands; in its eye, the unmistakable look of the untamed, that wild wariness creatures of the wood never lose, no matter how closely they come in contact with people.

"Look at that mistrust—and fear!" I pointed at the chipmunk, my finger within a foot of its nose.

"Yes, of *you*! How her heart is beating! Like it's going to break!"

"Day after day, frightened out of its wits. What a horrible existence. I should think *you,* of all people, Laura, would have some compassion and see that—"

"Don't, please!" She wiped her cheeks with her sleeve. "Don't say anything more. You don't have to. I've made up my mind." A sob prevented her from going on, for a minute. "I can do the most glorious thing . . . anybody can do . . . for anybody," she said calmly. "And I'm going to! I'll set her *free.* No matter what happens to me, at least I'll always know—I've done some good with my life."

"There you go being melodramatic. You glory in the idea of the noble gesture, but you haven't done a thing. You never *will* set that animal free."

"I'll show you!" Her face was a maul of sudden hate—I was just another of her tormentors. Quickly, she moved her hand with its live treasure to the window ledge. The chipmunk fell awkwardly on the sill, looked at Laura, then at me. Neither of us moved. The window was wide open, roll-screen and all, since there were no bugs in the air. My office is on the ground level, which was how Laura had come to be assigned to me—she couldn't manage the stairs to other professors. Woodbine grew thick around the window, making it easy for a chipmunk to climb down to the grass and run away to the woods bordering the lake. But this chipmunk had been in captivity too long. Like Laura, it would have to be forced out of a set pattern. I picked up a newspaper, rattling it noisily. The chipmunk scurried to the outer ledge, leaped to the vine, and was gone.

Laura remained fixed in rigid, horrified grief. "What have you made me *do*? What have you made me *do*?"

"No, Laura, it's time you stopped asking the question that way. What've you yourself done? *You*, Laura."

Without looking at me, she pushed her crutches upright and swung into the rubber saddles of the armrests, as if mounting a horse. She left the room in vigorous, wooden strides, pulling her dead lower body after her.

I felt rather upset and worried all afternoon but refrained from calling Laura for fear of allowing her to sink into the old comforts. Somehow, I also didn't want to go home early, and so I was still in my office when the house president called at five o'clock. One of the girls reported that Laura had packed a suitcase, said she was leaving the university, and had gone off in a taxi.

Only one place she could have gone: I phoned the hospital across the lake. Yes, she had been admitted there two hours ago. They signed her in at once, for she said she felt like harming herself. She particularly requested a locked ward.

The very next week the ice on the lake turned under, the water astonishingly blue. Most of the trees were beginning to show leaves. I walked the campus with a delicious sense of ease and escape, as if a burden had been lifted. The chipmunks were all out of hibernation now—I could not possibly recognize which of them might be Laura's. But whenever I saw one quite near I would stop, whistle, and we'd stare solemnly at one another, as if something important needed to be said.

DISABILITY

· · · · · · · · · · · · · · · · · ·

AND THE CHILDREN SHALL LEAD US

Irving Kenneth Zola

. . . .

I t was freezing cold. I sat huddled behind the wheel of my car waiting, as I do every Wednesday, for Amanda to get out of school. The radio was blaring, the heater was rumbling, and I was absorbed in a paperback novel, so I didn't hear the first knock. With the second, I saw Amanda pointing to the window. Anything that let the cold in seemed outrageous, so I only opened it a crack.

"Daddy, you're such a silly," she said with a certain exasperation. "I meant the door, not the window!"

To me that seemed silly, and I told her so. "You know you can't climb over me that easily. Why don't you go in the back door . . . like always?"

With a patience that a nine-year-old develops to deal with the older generation, she gave me a benign smile. "I don't want to come in. I want you to come out." And then, acknowledging with her hand another snowsuited young girl, she explained, "I want you to show Kristin your leg."

"My what?" I stammered in surprise.

"Your leg, the one with the brace," she said offhandedly.

"My leg," I answered softly to no one in particular.

"Yes," she went on, "Kristin often asks me about you and about it. So when she brought it up today, I thought now was a good time."

292

Her matter-of-factness was almost hypnotic. And so turning in my seat, I first placed my left foot outside and then with my hands lifted my right to join it. And there I sat . . . a grey-bearded forty-four-year-old clad in an olive-drab parka jacket and his favorite blue jeans.

"Well there it is," said Amanda, pointing triumphantly at my leg. We all looked at it. Amanda, Kristin, and another friend who stopped on his way home. The only "it" that was immediately visible was the bottom of my brace, two pieces of shining aluminum attached to the heel of my shoe. Kristin nodded her head, and when she falteringly asked, "How, umm, umm . . . ?" I knew the question. "You mean, how high does it go?" She nodded again.

"It goes all the way up here," and I traced the brace from my ankle to my hip. Very young children want to touch it and say so, but this older audience said little and so I didn't offer.

"Why do you wear it?" asked the boy.

Amanda smiled, "I've told them about the polio, but,"—and she pursed her lips and shook her head as if she thought I'd like to tell it again—"you say."

And so I did, telling briefly about polio—a disease already to them a piece of history—something they knew about only indirectly by "the sips they once had to take in school" to avoid having it. But they were more interested in how the brace worked. And so I began to explain. "Because of the weakness in my leg . . . without the brace, my knee would keep bending and I'd fall. But this way"—and I patted it—"the brace keeps my leg stiff and unbending."

"You know, Daddy. Your leg doesn't look weak. I mean"—and she waved toward both of them—"they look the same to me."

"You're right." I laughed, a little nervously. This was a question I'd never been asked. "They are almost the same. But if you look close—someday when I'm not wearing the brace, I'll show you—the right leg is a little thinner than the left. And . . . if you look at me carefully in shorts, you'll see that I'm pretty big all around here,"—and I let my hands fall across my rather thick chest—"but that I'm much thinner below the waist."

This clicked off a memory in Amanda, and she turned to her two friends. "The other day my daddy and I were in a restaurant and we saw a waitress without a real leg." The two children gazed at her disbelievingly. "She had something else. I don't know what you call it. I think it was made of wood or plastic and looked sort of like a real leg but not exactly. I know you're not supposed to stare, but my daddy said it was better to be curious than be uncomfortable and look away . . . ." And then with a conclusive sigh, "It was amazing. She did real well," and nodded her head approvingly.

Her friends agreed and looked toward me.

"Do you have any more questions?" Amanda said in her most teacherly fashion. "No." They nodded and, smiling at both of us, whispered, "Thank you," and trotted away in the snow.

Amanda, with an air of satisfaction, settled in the back seat. I turned around and asked what that was all about. "Well, Kristin often asks me questions about you and your leg. And when she asked again today, I thought you could do it better."

"Better?"

"Yes, there's only so much I could say. Some things you have to see."

"Oh," I answered rather speechlessly.

"And besides, I knew you'd oblige."

"Oblige?" I laughed at her choice of words.

"Yes"—and she gave me a coy look, tilting her head downward—"I thought you'd be comfortable doing it. You were, weren't you?"

As I shifted the car to start, I nodded. "Yes." But to myself I added, "And every day I get a little more comfortable."

A PROBLEM OF PLUMBING

James M. Bellarosa

· · · · · · · · · · · · · · · · · ·

I like beautiful women with jet-black hair that tosses gently, and pearl-black eyes that entrance. I love them if they are witty, sensitive, educated, talk about literature, psychology, international politics, and laugh with equal hilarity over the Red Sox and Woody Allen. If they can play chess, that's the frosting.

Now there aren't many women like that around, but I found one recently at a seminar. Marcia taught English at a college in Worcester, Massachusetts. Sometimes. Other times she ran excursions to Bermuda on her own 90-foot sailing yacht. She was almost perfect; she couldn't play chess. I can't sail.

I'm a bit of a romantic, and impractical too, and friends tell me I spend too much time in my head and not enough caring about reality. They're right. I can get lost for three hours wondering about the psychological implications of Thomas Wolfe's obsession with October, forget a ten-pound prime roast in my oven and char it to a ten-ounce cinder. Ignoring practical realities and forgetting to plan ahead can complicate anyone's life, especially if he is confined to a wheelchair, as I am.

Marcia and I would talk after class. Later we met for lunch and then drove to the seminar. She liked my car, found the hand controls intriguing, asked me to let her drive with them.

She tossed her hair and laughed as she drove, and I imagined that was how she sailed her yacht. Flawlessly. With aplomb.

When we arrived, Marcia shut the car off and turned the black eyes on me.

"You adjusted quickly to those controls," I said.

She gazed at me for a few seconds, then:

"Would you take me to dinner Saturday?"

"Yes! Sure," I said. "The Town and Country?"

"Perfect," Marcia replied.

I'd been to the Town and Country only once, for a half-hour luncheon. There are elegant restaurants like the Town and Country because there are elegant people like Marcia.

I wasn't uncomfortable driving to Marcia's apartment, but I realized I'd forgotten to go to the bathroom. I should try to plan better.

Marcia wore a pleated black skirt and a soft yellow blouse that set off the sheen of her hair. When we arrived she attracted the glances of bored husbands sitting with uneasy wives.

I struggled through the deep carpeting to our table, which was padded with heavy embroidered linen and decorated with more silverware than you'd find in a Versailles banquet hall. We drank a glass of white wine.

"Teach me to play chess," Marcia said.

I looked around, whispered, "Not here. No one must know." More wine.

"Teach me to sail," I said.

Marcia leaned toward me. "It is written that one must learn to sail by starlight. You must wait."

We ate, drank more wine, talked about our favorite authors. Soft music purred from concealed speakers, and the Town and Country filled up with elegant people from the town. And before dessert I had to excuse myself.

Two-and-a-half feet inside the door to the men's room a floor-to-ceiling steel panel turned me away. I lingered in the hall for a couple of minutes, then returned to my table, feeling twice as uncomfortable and thinking unkind thoughts about people who don't plan for contingencies, and even worse thoughts about people who design men's rooms.

When Marcia got up a few minutes later, I asked our waitress where the accessible men's room was hiding.

"We have a larger one in the basement but—I'm sorry—we have no elevator."

She has spoken too loudly. A matronly lady at the next table hears, glances then to tell me she *knows*. Soon she whispers to her husband, who, hunching over to meet his fork, suddenly flashes his eyes up at me. He knows too. Oh, God.

I am trying to forget my embarrassment and trying to become invisible in the middle of the room during Marcia's absence. As I wait to vanish, I feel someone's presence. It is the man from the next table. He is fifty-five, a large man, who, with one hand on the table, the other on my wheelchair, droops over me like a willow.

"Is there any way I can help?"

He's sincere but, oh, my God, this should not be happening at the Town and Country.

"Oh, no," I say, "I'm fine, thank you."

That would be enough for most people, but this helpful, sincere man stays, and droops—and seems eternal. Finally he tosses his head. "I'm right over here if you need me." He straightens up and starts back to his table. Other diners are watching.

The waitress returns, with more concern in her voice.

"The manager would like to know if you'd care to use his private room. There's just two steps up."

The drooping man hears that and returns to confer again.

"I told him I'd help him," he says to the waitress. He's hurt. She smiles politely.

Our conference is attracting a growing audience. A young boy seated nearby seems especially curious, and speaks to his parents about me. Suddenly I see Marcia walking toward me across the room. Please, God, do not implicate this refined lady in my indelicate problem! Quickly I say: "Thank you both, but I really am fine. I'd like to finish my meal now."

The waitress nods. "Of course, sir." She leaves. The drooping man shrugs, shuffles back to his table, and mutters something to his wife.

Marcia smiles. "You make friends so easily," she says.

I'm ready. "Those people collect autographs of Hollywood
stars, but I told them you only accept such requests if they're
written on sailcloth."

"Or etched in whalebone!" Marcia's eyes brighten. "Shall
we continue the evening at the Blue Terne?"

"The Blue Terne?"

"There are no stairs," she assures me.

We cash out along with the family. The little boy looks at
me. He's five. He tugs his mother's sleeve, says:

"Mom, there's the man who needs to go to the bathroom."
His mother pulls his face into her skirt. Marcia missed it.

When I bend and lift to enter the car the pain explodes
through my abdomen, and as we drive across town I only half
hear Marcia's story of the crazed sailor who dived off her yacht
to attack a hammerhead shark.

The Blue Terne exists for quiet seductions—soft purples and
blues, lights that only glow . . . and a sultry lass who murmurs
and whimpers at a cylindrical mike, without a band. Marcia
orders a daiquiri, I a Manhattan. Then I excuse myself to find
the men's room. But can't.

"It's downstairs," a waitress says, "I'll take you on the elevator."

I'm trying not to move any more than I have to. Stiffly I push
through the door. Half-length vertical urinals to my left, stalls
beyond them. I push to the last one and see the handicapped
aid bar attached to the partition inside. This is it! No, the stall
jambs are too narrow—the chair does not fit, the pain claws at
my guts. I clench my teeth, then return to gauge the height
of the urinals on the wall. Too high.

I go out. The waitress has waited to take me upstairs.

"All set?"

"Lady, I can't get into the stall."

She rubs her palm up and down against the wall. "How
about the other . . . ?"

"They're too high!" I'm getting loud, testy.

"I'll see if the manager will come down to help you."

I wait outside the door for someone, anyone, to come along. A man, fortyish, balding, tiptoes down the stairs.

"Could you give me a hand in here?" I grunt.

"Sure, whatever I can do . . ." He's so eager to help. I'm not sure I like the way he walks, but there's no time to request a statement of honorable intent. I collapse the wheelchair just enough, and he pushes me into the stall. He stays, watches me.

"I'm all set now," I say, "Thank you." He doesn't move. I knew I didn't like the way he walks. "Get the hell away from me."

He jumps. "OK, mister, OK! I didn't mean anything, it's just that my brother-in-law's uncle is in one of these things, and I've had to help him out a few times. I didn't mean anything . . ."

"Everybody's got somebody who's in one of these things!!" I snarl.

He leaves, without going to the bathroom. That must have been the manager! Oh, God. The pain trickles away, and I close my pants. I try to back up. Oh, no! He's pushed me all the way in. The wheels are stuck. I scream for help. I bellow and rant and curse. Five minutes, ten. Finally I am on the elevator. I wonder how Marcia has been passing the time, wonder what she's concluded about my plumbing—twenty-five minutes in the bathroom. I hope she doesn't draw any incorrect conclusions.

She looks at me as I reenter the lounge, smiles as I reach the table. "Marcia," I begin, "I'm sorry . . ."

Her fingers lift off the table, touch my arm. "My yacht is parked outside," she whispers, "Tell me about it there . . ." The sultry lady moans, "In the Wee Small Hours of the Morning." We leave.

Over breakfast I decide to tell Marcia about my twenty-five-minute adventure in the basement of the Blue Terne.

"Imagine what Poe might have done with that," she laughs.

I saw Marcia for six months. Then she went to Bermuda. I haven't found anyone quite the same since she left, but if she comes back I'm going to tell her about a men's room I found in Boston. It's sunken. You go in, then down three steps. Someone said Kafka designed it. It could have been de Sade.

WHEELCHAIR

Lewis Nordan

· · · · · · · · · · · · · · · · · ·

W inston Krepps had been abandoned by his attendant, and the door was shut tight.

Winston pressed the control lever of his chair. The battery was low, so the motor sounded strained. The chair turned in a slow circular motion; the rubber tires squeaked on the lino-leum floor of the kitchen.

For a moment, as the chair turned, Winston saw two teen-aged boys on a bridge. Winston released the control lever, and the chair stopped. The boys were naked and laughing, and the Arkansas sky was bright blue. Winston recognized himself as one of the two boys. He pushed the hallucination away from his eyes. It was the day real life had ended, he thought.

The clock above the refrigerator said four—that would be Thursday. Harris, his attendant, must have left on Monday.

Winston turned his chair again and faced the living room. He saw a boy lying on his back on a white table. Winston turned his head and tried not to see. Doctors and nurses moved through the room. The prettiest of the nurses stood by the table and chatted with the boy. The boy—it was Winston, he could not prevent recognizing himself—was embarrassed at his nakedness, but he could not move to cover himself. An X-ray machine was rolled into place. The pretty nurse said, "Don't breathe now." The boy thought he might ask her out when he

was better, if she wasn't too old for him. He had not understood yet that this was the day sex ended. Winston looked away
and pressed the lever of the chair.

The motor hummed and he rolled toward the bedroom. The
tires squeaked on the linoleum, then were silent on the carpet.
The motor strained to get through the carpet, but it did not
stop. Monday, then, was the last day he was medicated.

Winston negotiated the little S-curve in the hallway. He
could see into the bathroom. The extra leg-bag was draped over
the edge of the tub, the detergents and irrigation fluids and
medications were lined up on the cabinet. Winston saw his
mother in the bathroom, but as if she were still young and were
standing in the kitchen of her home. He saw himself near her,
still a boy, strapped into his first wheelchair.

He closed his eyes, but he could still see. His mother was
washing dewberries in the sink. There were clean pint mason
jars on the cabinet and a large blue enamel cooker on the stove.
His mother said, "The stains! I don't know if dewberries are
worth the trouble." Winston watched, against his will, the
deliberateness of her cheer, the artificiality of it.

He stopped his chair in the bedroom. There was the table
Harris had built, the attendant who had abandoned him. Harris had been like a child the night he finished the table, he was
so proud of himself. He even skipped that night at the country-
western disco, where he spent most of his time, just to sit home
with Winston and have the two of them admire it together.
Winston resented the table now, and the feelings he had had,
briefly, for Harris. How could a person build you a table and
sit with you that night and look at it, and then leave you alone.
It was easy to hate Harris.

He looked at the articles that made up the contents of the
room—his typewriter, his lamp, and books and papers, a poem
he had been trying to write, still in the typewriter. His typing
stick was on the floor, where he had dropped it by accident on
Monday.

Then Harris stepped into the line of Winston's vision. Winston had not realized you could hallucinate forward as well as

back, but he was not surprised. It was the same worthless Harris. "I'm a boogie person, man," Harris seemed to explain. He was wearing tight jeans and no shirt, his feet were bare. He was tall and slender and straight. "I'm into boogie, it's into me." Winston said, "But you built me a table, Harris." Then he said nothing at all.

Winston's hunger had stopped some time ago, he couldn't remember just when. He knew his face was flushed from lack of medication. His leg-bag had been full for a couple of days, so urine seeped out of the stoma for a while. It had stopped now that he was dehydrated.

Winston heard cars passing on the paved road outside his window. He had cried out until his voice was gone. He imagined bright Arkansas skies and a sweet-rank fragrance of alfalfa hay and manure and red clover on the wind from the pastures outside town. He thought of telephone wires singing in the heat.

Winston looked back at the floor again, at his typing stick. The stick made him remember Monday, the day Harris left, and before Winston knew he was abandoned.

He had been in his chair at the kitchen table with his plastic drinking straw in his mouth. He was sipping at the last of a pitcher of water. The time alone had been pleasant for him—none of Harris's music playing, none of his TV game shows or ridiculous friends and their conversation about cowboy disco and girls and the rest. Winston sipped on the water and felt the top of the plastic tube with his tongue.

He pressed his tongue over the hole in the tube and felt the circle it made there. He thought he could have counted all the taste buds enclosed within the circle if he tried. He thought of his father holding a duck call to his lips to show Winston how to hold his tongue when he was a child, before the accident. Winston remembered taking the call from his father's hand, and he wondered if that touching were not the last touch of love he had felt—the last in the real world anyway, and so the last. The touching of the tube to his tongue brought his father back to him, the smell of alligator grass in the winter swamp, a fragrance of fresh tobacco and wool and shaving lotion and rubber hip waders, and more that he had forgotten from that world.

He had gone to his typewriter and had meant to write what he remembered. He had almost been able to believe it would restore him, undo what was done.

He had rolled up to the table, as close as the chair would take him. The stick with the rubber tips was lying on the table with four or five inches sticking out over the edge. Winston used his single remaining shoulder muscle to push his left hand forward onto the table. His fingers had long ago stiffened into a permanent curl. He maneuvered the hand until the typing stick was between his second and third fingers.

At last he dragged it close enough to his face. He clenched one end of the stick between his teeth and tasted the familiar rubber grip. He steadied himself and aimed the stick at the *on* button of his typewriter. The machine buzzed and clacked and demanded attention. For an instant, as he always did when he heard this sound, he felt genuinely alive, an inhabitant of a real world, a real life. And not just life—it was power he felt, almost that. Writing—just for a moment, but always for that moment—was real. It was dancing. It was getting the girl and the money and kicking sand in the face of the bully. He began, letter by letter, to type with the stick in his mouth.

When he had finished, what he had written was not good. The words he saw on the page were not what he had meant. What he had felt seemed trivial now, and hackneyed. He said, "Shit." He touched the *off* button and shut the typewriter down.

He tried to drop the stick from his mouth onto the table again, but the effort of writing had exhausted him. The stick hit the table, but it had been dropped hastily, impatiently, and it did not fall where Winston had intended. It rolled onto his lap, across his right leg, where he could not reach it. Finally it rolled off his leg and onto the floor.

That was on Monday. He could have used the stick now to dial the telephone.

*　　　*　　　*

There was a series of three muscle spasms. The first one was mild. Winston's left leg began to rise up toward his face. The spasm continued upward through his body and into his shoulders. For a moment he could not breathe, but then the contraction ended and it was over. His foot settled back into place. He caught his breath again.

When the second spasm began he saw the center of hell. A great bird, encased in ice, flapped its enormous wings and set off storms throughout all its icy regions. In the storms and in the ice was a chant, and the words of the chant were *Ice ice up to the neck.*

Winston's legs, both of them this time, rose up toward his face and hung there for an eternity of seconds. He watched the ice-imprisoned bird and listened to the chant. His legs flailed right and left in the chair. Now they settled down. They jerked out and kicked and crossed one another and flailed sidewise again. Winston's feet did not touch the footrests, and his legs were askew. His shoulders rose up to his ears and caused him to scrunch up the features of his face and to hold his breath against his will.

Then it ended. He could breathe again. It was easy to hate his useless legs and his useless arms and his useless genitals and his insides over which he had no control. He was tilted in his chair, listing twenty degrees to the right.

Winston felt an odd peacefulness settle upon him. He saw a swimming pool and a pavilion in summertime. The bathhouse was green-painted, and the roof was corrugated aluminum. He saw himself at sixteen, almost seventeen. For the first time he did not avert his eyes. A radio was playing, there was a screech of young children on a slide. The boy he watched stood at the pool's edge, a country boy at a town pool, as happy as if he had just begun to live his life inside a technicolor movie.

There was a girl too, a city girl. She told him she was from Memphis, her name was Twilah. There was a blaze of chlorine and Arkansas sun in her hair and eyes. No one could have been more beautiful. Her hair was flaming orange, and a billion freckles covered her face and shoulders and breasts, even her lips and ears. The radio played and the sun shone and the younger children screeched on the slide.

Outside his window, where he could not see it, a bird made a sound—a noise, really—an odd two-noted song, and the song caused the memory to grow more vivid, more heartbreaking. He wanted to see all the places Twilah might hide her freckles. He wanted to count them, to see her armpits and beneath her fingernails and under her clothing. He wanted to examine her tongue and her nipples and forbidden places he could scarcely imagine. It was easy to fall in love when you were sixteen, almost seventeen, and a lifeguard was blowing a steel whistle at a swimmer trespassing beneath a diving board.

The third spasm was a large one. It seemed to originate somewhere deep in his body, near the core. The tingle in his face that signaled it was like a jangle of frantic bells rung in warning.

He imagined great flocks of seabirds darkening the air above an island. He saw wildlife scurrying for shelter.

Motion had begun in his body now. His legs were rising as if they were lighter than air. Then, suddenly, and for no reason—it may have been merely the nearness of death—Winston did not care what his legs did. He watched them in bemusement. For the first time since the accident, they were not monstrous to him, they were not dwarfish or grotesque. They were his legs, only that. For the first time in seventeen years, he could not discover—or even think to seek—the measure of himself, or of the universe, in his limbs. He was in the grip of a spasm more violent than anything he had ever imagined, in which, for a full minute he could not breathe at all, could not draw breath, and yet he felt as refreshed as if he were breathing sea air a thousand miles from any coast.

He began to see as he had never seen before. He saw as if his seeing were accompanied by an eternal music, as if the past were being presented to him through the vision of an immortal eye. He was not dead—there was no question of that. He was alive, for a little longer anyway, and he was seeing in the knowledge that there is greater doom in not looking than in looking. He fixed his eye—this magical, immortal eye—on a swamp-lake in eastern Arkansas.

In the swamp he saw a cove, and in the cove an ancient tangle of briers and cypress knees and gum stumps. He saw water that was pure but blacker than slate, made mirrorlike by the tannic acid from the cypress trees, and he saw the trees and skies and clouds reflected in its surface.

The eye penetrated the reflecting surface and saw beneath the water. He saw a swamp floor of mud and silt. He saw a billion strings of vegetation and tiny root systems. He saw fish—bright bluegills and silvery crappie, long-snouted gar, and lead-bellied cat with ropy whiskers. He saw turtles and mussels and the earth of plantations sifted there from other states, another age, through a million ditches and on the feet of turkey vultures and blue herons and kingfishers. He saw schools of minnows and a trace of slave death from a century before. He saw baptizings and drownings. He saw the transparent wings of snake doctors, he saw lost fish stringers and submerged logs and the ghosts of lovers.

He saw the boat.

The boat was beneath the surface with the rest, old and colorless and waterlogged. It was not on the bottom, only half-sunk, two feet beneath the surface of the swamp.

The boat was tangled in vegetation, in brambles and briers and the submerged tops of fallen tupelo gums and willows. It was tangled in trotlines and rusted hooks and a faded Lucky 13 and the bale of a minnow bucket and the shreds of a shirt some child took off on a hot day and didn't get home with.

The world that Winston looked into seemed affected by the spasm that he continued to suffer and entertain. Brine flowed into freshets, ditches gurgled with strange water. The willows moved, the trotlines swayed, the crappie did not bite a hook. Limbs of fallen trees shivered under the water, muscadine vines, the sleeve of a boy's shirt waved as if to say good-bye. The gar felt the movement with its long snout, the cat with its ropy whiskers, the baptized child felt it, and the drowned man. The invisible movement of the water stirred the silt and put grit in the mussel's shell. The lost bass plug raised up a single hook as if in question.

And the spasm touched the half-sunken boat.

Winston was breathing again, with difficulty. He was askew in his chair, scarcely sitting at all. He thought his right leg had been broken in the thrashing, but he couldn't tell. He wasn't really interested. He knew he would see what he had been denied—what he had denied himself.

He watched the boat beneath the surface. The boat trembled in the slow, small movement of the waters. The trembling was so slight that it could be seen only by magic, with an eye that could watch for years in the space of this second. Winston watched all the years go past, and all their seasons. Winter summer spring fall. The boat trembled, a brier broke. Oxidation and sedimentation and chance and drought and rain, a crumbling somewhere, a falling away of matter from matter. In the slowness the boat broke free of its constraints.

It rose up closer to the surface and floated twelve inches beneath the tannic mirror of the lake.

The boat could move freely now. Winston was slouched in his chair, crazed with fever but still alive. He knew what he was watching, and he would watch it to the end.

Harris said, "I didn't know you would *die,* man. I never knew boogie could kill anybody." It was tempting to watch Harris, to taunt him for his ignorance, his impossible shallowness, but Winston kept his eye on the boat.

The boat moved through the water. It didn't matter how it moved, by nature or magic or the ripples sent out by a metaphorical storm, it moved beneath the water of a swamp-lake in eastern Arkansas.

It moved past cypress and gum, past a grove of walnut and pecan. It moved past a cross that once was burned on the Winter Quarters side of the lake, it moved past Mrs. Hightower's lake bank where the Methodists held the annual picnic, past the spot where a one-man band made music a long time ago and caused the children to dance, it moved past a brown-and-white cow drinking knee-deep in the Ebeneezer Church's baptizing pool. It moved past Harper's woods and a sunken car and a washed away boat dock. It moved past the Indian mound and past some flooded chicken houses, it moved past the shack where Mr. Long shot himself, it moved past the Kingfisher Café.

And then it stopped. Still twelve inches beneath the water, the boat stopped its movement and rested against the pilings of a narrow bridge above the lake. On the bridge Winston could see two boys—himself one of them—naked and laughing in the sun. Winston did not avert his eyes.

The boys' clothes were piled beside them in a heap. One of the boys—himself, as Winston knew it would be—left the railing of the bridge.

It was part fall, part dive—a fall he would make the most of. It lasted, it seemed, forever. Slow-arching and naked, sprad-dle-legged, self-conscious, comic, bare-assed, country-boy dive.

There was no way for him to miss the boat, of course. He hit it. The other boy, the terrified child on the bridge, climbed down from the railing and held his clothes to his bare chest and did not jump.

He only had to see it once.

And yet it was not quite over.

Winston's life was being saved, like cavalry arriving in the nick of time. This was not an hallucination, this was real. There was an ambulance team in the little apartment, two men in white uniforms. It was hard to believe, but Harris was there as well—Harris the boogieman, repentant and returned, still explaining himself, just as he had in the hallucinations. "Boogie is my *life*," he said, as the ambulance team began their work.

Then it began to happen again, the opening of the magical eye. It was focused on Harris. Through it he saw, as he always saw, even without magic, the bright exterior of Harris's physical beauty—his slenderness and sexuality and strength and straight back and perfect limbs, and also, somehow, beyond his beauty, which before this moment had been always a perverse mirror in which to view only his, Winston's, own deformity and celibacy and loss, beyond the mirror of his physical perfection and, with clear vision, even in this real but dreamlike room, filled with a hellish blue-flashing light from outside, and with I.V. bottles and injections and an inflatable splint for his leg and the white of sheets and uniforms and the presence also of the apartment manager who had come, a large oily man named Sooey Leonard, he saw past Harris's beauty to the frightened, disorganized, hopeless boy that Harris was. Winston understood, at last, the pain in what Harris told him. Boogie is my life. It was not a thing to be mocked, as Winston had so recently thought. It was not a lame excuse for failure. What was terrifying and painful was that Harris knew exactly what he was saying, and that he meant, in despair, exactly what he said. It was acknowledgment and confession, not excuse, a central failure of intellect and spirit that Harris understood in himself, was cursed to know, and to know also that he could not change, a doom he had carried with him since his conception and could look at, as if it belonged to someone else. The knowledge that Harris knew himself so well and, in despair of it, could prophesy his future, with all its meanness and shallowness and absence of hope, swept through Winston like a wind of grief. He wanted to tell Harris that it wasn't true, that he was not doomed, no matter the magnitude of the failure here. He wanted to remind him of the table he had built and of how they felt together that night it was finished, when they had sat at home alone together and not turned on the television but only sat and looked at the table and talked about it and then made small talk about other things, both of them knowing they were talking about the table. He wanted Harris to know that the table proved him wrong.

He could say nothing. The ambulance team bumped and jolted him onto a stretcher-table and held the clanking I.V. bottles above him.

The sunlight was momentarily blinding as he was wheeled out the door of the apartment and onto the sidewalk. For a moment Winston could see nothing at all, only a kaleidoscope of colors and shapes behind his eyelids.

And yet in the kaleidoscope, by magic he supposed, he found that he could see Harris and himself. They stood—somehow Winston could stand—in the landscape of another planet, with red trees and red rivers and red houses and red farm animals, and through all the atmosphere, as if in a red whirlwind, flew the small things of Winston's life: the typewriter and the failed poem in it, the battery charger for his chair, and the water mattress and the sheepskin, the chair itself and the leather strap that held him in it, his spork—the combination spoon-fork utensil he ate with—and the splint that fitted it to his hand, the leg-bag and the catheter and the stoma, his trousers with the zipper up the leg, his bulbous stomach, the single muscle in his shoulder, the scars of his many operations, the new pressure sores that already were festering on his backside from so long a time in the chair, his teeth, the bright caps that replaced them when his real teeth decalcified after the spinal break, his miniature arms and legs, the growing hump on his back, his hard celibacy and his broken neck. And the thought that he had, in this red and swirling landscape, was that they were not hateful things to gaze upon, and not symbolic of anything, but only real and worthy of his love. Twilah was there in all the redness, the long-lost girl with the freckles and the orange hair, who for so long had been only a symbol of everything Winston had missed in life and who now was only Twilah, a girl he never knew and could scarcely remember. It was a gentle red whirlwind that harmed no one. His father was there with a duckcall, his mother washing dewberries. The ambulance door slammed shut and the siren started up. Winston hoped he could make Harris understand.

OLD GLASSES

M. Thorne Fadiman

· · · · · · · · · · · · · · · · · ·

Monday. The Eyeglass Center in Cranston, Connecticut, has a big front window, and, inside, polished plastic frames, hard and bright, reflecting the glare of the sun.

I didn't want to come here. Millie insisted. Just like she insisted on the eye checkup. Millie is self-assured. No one expected us to have kids, for instance, but we did, two of them.

Not everybody in Cranston knows us. Even now. It's the looks you get that remind you of differences. Sideways glances as two people in wheelchairs roll out of a Chevy van into the store.

What's to see? Two middle-aged citizens—Millie, teased blonde, me, bald Bart Johnson. Both a little plump. Wrinkles. Casual clothing.

Is it the wheelchairs that block us out? People are uncomfortable until they get to know us, or hear about us, about the retail advertising business in Stamford we used to run.

We gave it up, sold out and moved North when the kids went off to college, started a weekly newspaper, the *Cranston Town Crier.*

It's something we always wanted to do. No big deal, but we don't need the money. Just a project to occupy us, involve us in the community. Something that lets us give ourselves back to Cranston—where we lived even when we worked in Stamford.

Seeing Dr. Neal Morton in the store is a surprise. He's buying sunglasses, peering at the dark lenses the way he might peer at a patient, quizzical upper lip thrust out.

Morton's wife is dead. He drives a convertible, plays jazz with the top down, filling up the car, driving the emptiness away.

We kid him. Morton is someone we've come to know better since starting the newspaper. We do what we can. Invited him to write a column, "Your Health."

He smiles at me, winks. While Millie is filling out the charge card, he and I conspire in a corner. Eyeglasses glint around us. We keep our voices low. We talk about the Boston operation.

An orthopedist has developed a new method of hip surgery for joint subluxation, the dislocation that keeps me from walking.

I've already had surgery to lengthen the muscle that pulled my hip out of joint, but it didn't help much. The operation Morton is talking about removes part of the bone shaft so the head of the femur pops back into the socket. It's secured there by surgical staples holding nearby tendons to the pelvis.

Morton says I'll be able to walk with crutches for several hours at a time. He wants me to meet the surgeon who'll explain the procedure in detail.

Morton's a good friend, but I think he takes my spastic paraplegia personally. He thinks I didn't get proper treatment as a child. He stares at the wheelchair spokes as if they're lancets ready to skewer him—or me.

He's got a kid at Tufts near Boston, which is why he's flying up there on Friday—convince his son to go to premed instead of predental. I should come with him.

I tell him I have to talk it over with Millie because we lay out the paper on Friday.

We talk on the way home. Millie had polio as an infant and it paralyzed her below the waist. The operation won't help her, but she's excited about it for my sake.

She says I must go. She'll take care of the paper.

Tuesday. I cover a Finance Board meeting at the dark paneled Town Hall meeting room. It's time for salary requests—predictable enough, everybody says what a good job he or she does, voices dark, heavy, wooden. Nobody does a bad job. As usual, everybody deserves a raise.

I drove the van back to the office at the edge of town, clapboard white ranch house, dark shingles, and bright windows. Ramped the way we want it.

Millie's got my eyeglasses. Sent one of the kids we hire for odd jobs down to get them. Morton called about the ticket. She didn't know what to tell him.

She gives me the glasses. I put them on and almost fall out of my chair.

Everything is so bright—makes me dizzy. Later I call up my opthalmologist, Dr. Bearn. He says it's normal. I'd waited too long for a checkup. That's why my prescription is so much stronger.

I can't drive. The road is too close. Cars seem huge. Home, I sit on the porch and listen to the birds on the lawn, but the notes are sour, skewed, as if I'm wearing a kind of fuzzy hearing aid along with the glasses. Cars whiz down the road beyond the hedge. I can see them. Feel them. The dark hedge was a moat separating the lawn from the road; now it seems to have shriveled, dried up.

Supper is a deli roaster. We eat on the porch.

With the kids gone, we can eat without having some kind of noise blasting at us—the TV or the newest teen hit.

Sometimes we put on something like the Magic Flute, horns, strings rising above the maples.

The dinner music is shoved away by headlights charging across the road, breaking into the porch. I'm uncomfortable.

Millie mentions the operation. She thinks it will be better for me. I'll be able to go up stairs. Won't have to hire so many students to do the reporting. Cut down on overhead.

I point out we're not strapped for money, and we're giving the kids a chance.

She goes on about it while she cleans off the table, stacks the dishes onto a big plastic tray on the front of her chair. She won't let me help. Does things like Mom, except she uses an electric wheelchair at home.

I should take advantage of the new technology, she says. Greater mobility means greater freedom. Even around the house, I'd be able to do things and reach things that had been beyond me.

After she's gone inside, I think about it, sitting there, listening to the crickets and the wind in the trees.

I like it there. I'm not the reflective type, but a wheelchair gives you time to think.

I'm a determined person, always went after what I wanted. Never felt sorry for myself. I've felt pretty good, as a matter of fact, most of the time.

Millie calls from the kitchen, "If you were on your feet, you could screw in this bulb over the sink."

That will have to wait. (The young man we hire for that kind of thing comes over once a week, on Saturday.)

I listen to night birds calling. I feel good, at peace. A good life. A business. A house. Who does better?

The call I have to make to Morton finally drives me off the porch, away from the moon and the maples.

I surprise Morton.

I tell him I'll pass on the operation.

He can't believe it.

When I get off the phone, I see Millie's upset too. She zips up a ramp into her study, slams the door so the air shivers.

I start after her, but going up the ramp is an effort without an electric chair.

Sometimes wheelchairs save quarrels.

I laugh.

After a moment I roll into the bedroom. Then out again to the porch.

I sit straight up, daring the moon to knock off my old pair of glasses.

Some things you just don't want to change.

PARTING

Michael Martone

. . . .

I stutter. Badly. I always have. Through therapy, I learned
that it all has to do with the way I've acquired language.
It is hard to explain, but it has to do with seeing. My eyes
really do roll up inside my head and I'm looking for the right
word or syllable or letter. I acquired language in a mechanical
age before the pulsing electronic models of the brain. I'm made
up of switches, gears, brushes, contacts, solenoid springs,
screws. I search by opening drawers, riffling files, sorting
through the trash, the business office of metals, green and gray.
My machines are the old machines.

I think it has to do with handedness, this stutter.

My father wanted a left-hander perhaps more than he
wanted a son. He was always throwing things at me—balls of
socks turned inside out, golf balls, Whiffle balls, Ping-Pong
balls, balls of string. They came at my face, my head, and my
father would project his face, his head along the path of flight.
He noted which hand I moved first, which finger of which
hand.

Now that I think of it, catching and throwing are the same
to me. I have a facility for both in both hands. I make no
distinction.

But this is a theory of mine, a hunch. The therapists didn't
say one way or the other. They were treating the outward
manifestation of how I acquired the language.

316

My father thought the movement of the left-handed more pure. Especially expressed in the asymmetry of baseball, left-handed was beautiful. I don't blame him. I don't blame him.

Writing this I am like those singers who stutter when they don't sing, whose stutter vanishes when the music begins. One word after another, like clockwork. I can stop my hand, either hand, before the long chorus line of *h*'s steps along this blue rule. What can I say?

There is that motto that circulates through the offices of the world, taped to typewriters and phones, photocopy of photocopy, with the other artifacts of the cute. The you-want-it-when keepers, comics that turn yellow, old postcards from bosses long gone. It says, "Be Sure Mind Is Engaged before Putting Tongue into Gear." Exactly. A type of poetry. Rebuild the drive train around the tongue, I say—the shaft of spine, the wires. Into the hand, the hands.

Martin, my friend, and I were in Indiana, Pennsylvania, once, looking around. We had stopped there on our way to somewhere else because we were from Indiana, the state, and we were aimless enough to stop, or maybe that was the whole aim of the trip. Did we imagine a Liberia, a colony of Hoosiers, a diaspora, families keeping alive the old ways, the slow ritual of team basketball? Nevertheless, we stopped and walked around the college they have there, saying we were from the other Indiana. There were few students, gone on the same holiday we were. But when we'd see a cop or a secretary in an office, we'd say we were from the other Indiana and they would always say the same thing: We get your mail.

"That's why we're here," Martin said, "for the mail."

We ended up talking to an African student, surprised that his classrooms were empty. We found him reading the bulletin boards for explanations. We told him, "We're from the other Indiana." It was clever, we thought. And he looked at us earnestly.

"Yes," he said, "my country is always sending its students to the wrong Indiana. It happens often. It's the case." He spoke English haltingly but well, searching for the words. I always marvel at anyone who knows more than one language. I could see he was the type that waited until everything was right, the grammar, agreement, before he spoke.

"We are sent away to one strange place. All we have is a name. And there are many known by that name. There is a California. A California, Pennsylvania."

I remember imagining a ship pulling away from the docks, flags popping. Everyone waves and waves. The sun sets in the wrong place. There's the dusty train station, the borrowed clothes and bag. Somewhere over there is Indiana. The end of the line.

"Why is that?" he asked. "Why is it that several places have the same name? That is not the case where I come from." His face was wide and his eyes. He wanted to know.

And Martin said without thinking, "America is so big we've run out of names."

We've run out of names. Martin.

Once, I took trips all the time with Martin, who never finished my sentences, who never knew where we were going. He waited until I was through talking and had thrown myself back in the seat. My eyes were closed and I was going through what I'd said, rubbing that place behind my ear. "What you mean to say," he would say, and tell me. And then, "Where are we?" and I'd look out, the navigator, and things would be flying by—disconnected signs, markers, arrows, signs that referred to other signs.

Martin calls the Indiana toll road the Bermuda Triangle of highway travel. It is disorienting. The cornfield, a visible magnetic field, changes intensity and color with the layout of the crop rows. The lines of cars and trucks spaced and stretched for miles. They don't move, because we're all moving at the same speed. The pull of the ditch, the siren. The main street of mid-America, the rest stops named after poets and coaches. It's a long sleep. Radios jam from all the iron dust. Time doesn't change. There are sudden sandstorms. Fog like mold on bread. Suddenly we are in Ohio, Chicago. The truck we'd been following—it bristled with antennas, its lights flicked each time it passed us—has disappeared.

This last trip I took with Martin, is it the last trip I'll take with him? I've always wondered. Will this one be? This one? The time we came back from New York—for a long time that was the last trip.

I've said good-bye to all of it, to going.

The truth is I can hardly accelerate up to the speeds necessary. I've found that I am repeating what I have just said. I haven't done that since I was a kid and the therapists suggested it as a way to make me conscious of what I was saying. Word for word, under my breath, an echo. After a while I didn't think about it. I want a glass of water. I want a glass of water. The second sentence was easier, slowed down, sorted out. I saw the hooks and eyes. It wasn't an echo. It was more like going over a signature slowly, staying in the lines. I can't possibly keep up anymore. I find I am often left speechless. The subjects are tattered paper under the wheel. The strange mailbox that is made out of the old plow, the pump, is behind me before I can even begin to begin to speak. It is not an echo. The sentences are not coming back. They bounce off the world. The radar of my own language closes in on me. There is a deer. A pig. A cloud. A tree. A car. These things are coming on too fast. These things are already gone too soon. No planned trajectory. No way to plot their courses.

I'm afraid, Martin. I'm afraid.

Long trips by car were the only times we had to talk. Phone calls, impossible. The stammer on long distance, the tick of a meter. That's it, isn't it? To be in a car is to be in a moving parlor, to leave an exhaust of words.

But this last trip could be the last trip. Because it is getting harder for me to speak, and the distance between us now, the space we shuttle back and forth in, is not great enough. What? I might utter a paragraph in an hour. And patient Martin could drive a Mack truck through the silences.

*   *   *

Martin likes to say that the job he does now for the Labor Department is the exact same thing Kafka did for Czechoslovakia. I don't know if that's true, but he says it often.

Martin works in the District in the government's own workers' compensation, an investigator. He is a GS-12 now, I think. His office is in one of those buildings downtown that can go no higher than thirteen floors because nothing in the city can be higher than Liberty or Freedom on the Capitol dome. That's why it's such a sad town, Martin says. It all ends at the thirteenth floor. Unlucky—no way around it.

In that building he reads files of claims government workers make, claims of injuries suffered on the job, in the line of duty, above and beyond the call. There are the things you'd expect, the usual accidents of the motor pool, the falls from buildings, office chairs that crumple, the chemical spills, the fires in warehouses. In this way the government simulates our world, its acts of God. But Martin must read about other accidents unique to the bureaucracy so large, the daily toll of service. The pale-green computer screen, the pastel shades of copies, the shades of language, the color of walls in offices that hum, the white lights and shirts, the colors of skin. What he hates is that he gets paid not to believe people who have headaches, undiagnosed lower-back pains. He must start from the position that the mumbling, the hand-washing have nothing to do with the job, that it's all unconnected or even faked.

Poor Martin—to work up ways not to believe, the advocate who punches holes in the cases for saints.

Maybe it's easy. I don't know.

It hasn't soured him on the species. His suspicion is professional. He leaves it on the thirteenth floor. But he carries around these stories. When he thinks of seeing, he is reminded of the blind man. When he hears, he knows he is hearing. And his limbs bud and grow all the other limbs that have been lost.

As we drive, he drives through my silences, between my words. The light is low from the instruments, just touches his cheek. The window behind him is black. Half his face is how I think about him now, his profile, round chin, the nose and mouth. That mathematical symbol, more than and equal to. And in the window, the other side of the face, milky. Skin. I remember remembering smearing white Elmer's Glue on my hand, letting it dry and peeling off long whole strips of fingers, the creases and prints, the topography and whorls of knuckles and nails. The other side of Martin's face in the cold window kept its eye on the road.

The road was in Ohio, wide Ohio. Or Pennsylvania wider still. And Martin was telling amputation stories.

Amputation stories are like ghost stories. There is nothing to them beyond the telling of them. The ghosts make you draw closer around the campfire. Amputation stories, too, make you want to wrap your arms around yourself.

How much of me goes before I'm gone?

Really the stories are about machines. Our marriage to them. Limbs are given *to* the machines, that comes up, to the machine, a type of marriage. Machines amplify our own body's levers—the legs, the arms, the fingers. These become ghosts, lost. Machines amplify the body, make it louder.

I remember remembering the time I sat on the copier in the office and the stripped-down picture of my butt emerging, what? like something being born or passed. The new workplace is all about light and language. I remember the cold glass and the green light rolling below me, my feet not touching the ground. I gave the copy to the woman I was with. Then she rested her white breasts on the glass. She liked me, she said, because I didn't say much, and turned away to look back over her shoulder at me and laugh as the light played over her and the fan came on and rumbled the machine and the little closet where we were. It's all high contrast, her nipples black and scratchy with toner, the depth all washed out, overexposed. The mole still floating there, too, with the dust and motes of the glass. It's on good bond. There was static in the room. Our life slipped into two-dimension, plane geometry, depth removed. But real amputations are still a matter of the solid and what Martin was saying sat there, something with a life of its own.

*   *   *

There was this man who lost all of his fingers to a machine. I think a machine that trimmed paper. It had a harness for safety that was supposed to clear the hands each time the blades descended. The device had been adjusted by the man working the machine the shift before. When the new man started this work he didn't check the play, and on the machine's first cycle, trusting it to pull his hands clear, the blades came down and all his fingers were off at once.

"Now the interesting part," Martin was saying. When the machine opened up again he could see his fingers where they had fallen perfectly as if they had been placed there, fanned out the precise distance apart from one another. "He then reached inside, he told me this," Martin said, "he reached inside to pick up his fingers. He forgot that he didn't have anything left to pick up his fingers with. And the machine was still going. But this time when the blades closed down his hands were pulled clear by the safety device."

It was Ohio. And it must have taken me a county at least to exclaim. "Really," and then under my breath again, really, a township at least. Really.

"Really," Martin said.

I remember thinking about the engine of the car, a Dodge, the old slant six. I thought how all those different operations were happening at once. The pistons all at different points in the cycle, the cam shafts timing and the rockers lifting, the valves, the flywheel flying, the distributor distributing. And if you froze it at one instant, the whole show was being run on only one cylinder and inertia, the tendency to remain at rest or to stay in motion.

It was night in Ohio. And the radio was talking, too. The talk shows of the clear-channel stations. I had a bet with a friend that there were more songs written about telephones than cars. I thought if you thought about it there would be hundreds of songs about wrong numbers and long-distance operators and information and late-night calls and arranging rendezvous and calls to repairmen to fix the phone, no answers, busy, dead lines, crossed wires. The song is just voice. And on the phone a disembodied voice at your ear, the privacy of the private line, the party on the party line. Besides, Bell was a therapist. To him the phone was a device that facilitated the acquisition of language. The instrument is a sentimental favorite, far more terrifying to the deaf and dumb than a speeding automobile.

That songs should be written about cars seemed like the conclusion everyone would jump to. It was a sucker bet.

Especially those songs about crashes, wrecks, accidents, death. Or traveling like I did with Martin, cruising on the road, a fabled love of motion and moving. You put poles and wires and miles between where you are and where you're going.

Now here at night in Ohio in a car with Martin there was a kind of nexus—the radio, the callers, the music, the road, the wires, the waves, all these connections. The voices talking on the show of talk were making a music, a song about singing. What was said meant nothing. Talk for the hell of it. Talk just to hear oneself talk.

"The new section of the drill pipe came down from the derrick too fast," Martin was saying. "This new kid had his foot over the hole, and when the pipe came down and sumped into the hole the kid started yelling, 'Get it off my foot! Get it off my foot!' and the diesel idled down. The local said, 'Step back, son. You ain't got no foot.' "

This is indeed like stories around the campfire. I remember the story of the lovers in a car telling stories, ghost stories, being afraid, wanting to hold each other, creating stories that gave them excuses to do so. And they are telling a story about a man with hooks, a murderer, a nut. The woods, the night. There is scratching at the door of the car. The lovers tease each other. Their imagination. Then they believe and tear out of there in the car. They travel miles with the hook hooked on the door handle. It dangles there. They discover it when they are safely home.

I was always quiet around campfires. To stutter is to sound afraid. No rounds for me, no verses. The night on those nights was vast. The sparks flew up. If I spoke I sounded as if I were afraid. I was afraid to speak.

Outside now I know are strip mines. There are crossed picks on the maps. I wish I could see the shovels, the pulleys and cables, the draglines, the little houses where the operator sits, runs the machine as big as an office building. The little crossed picks don't begin to represent what is going on outside our windows as we race along.

The lovers, the car, the man, are folklore. I have heard about them and so had Martin. Perhaps he is thinking about that very story now as I do.

If I could I would have told Martin my own story. I heard it first from one of my speech teachers. I would ask Martin if what happened was technically possible. I suspect it isn't, that what I have is another tale. But it is satisfying in some ways, especially when the wife comes to say good-bye. What would she say? Her husband alive somehow, but two grain hoppers coupled right through him in such a way, so tightly, my teacher said, that his insides are all packed in, his organs shoved up into his chest. There is so much violence suspended between those cars, and his legs are up off the ground. And so much loneliness, too, because he is still alive. I suppose there is shock, unconsciousness, if you can believe it at all. But the redemption, the reason I think of this, is that the man's wife works in an office near the tracks and the trainmen go and fetch her.

When I think about the story I think about the trainmen rushing in, the type clatter stopping, the women pivoting in their chairs. I think about the wife grabbing her purse from back of the big file drawer on the lower left-hand side of her desk. When I heard the story first, they held her by the elbows. She stood on her tiptoes, whispered in her husband's ear. What? Good-bye. There was steam and the bulk of the steel, its chill atmosphere, and way off the thrumming engine, the engineer trying not to make a move. This was supposed to have happened in Decatur, Indiana, in the Central Soya yards. My teacher worked there in the summers, picked up the story on a coffee break, told it to me years later after a lesson. If it were true, what would she have said? Could he speak at all? It would be too difficult, probably out of breath, in shock. He would know what was happening. There would be that look in his eyes if they were open, the privacy, the inarticulateness of death. And then later, much later, after the wife had been led away, they'd have to separate the cars, separate what's left of him from the cars. I can see the conductor, those mule-skinner gantlets, waving the all-clear signal.

The all-clear signal.

I was finally a very good baseball player. I batted left-handed. My father hid himself during the games in the lilac bushes bordering the park. There he smoked and tried not to watch me play. The bees circled above him in the flowers, the leaves. I was in the hole. I was on deck. He was nervous, I imagine, superstitious, embarrassed perhaps. Here I begin thinking of those microscopic pictures of chromosomes tearing themselves apart in cell nuclei; now it looks like iron filings lining up on a yellow piece of paper. Magnets are beneath the paper, and the slivers of metal are repelling, pulling away from each other. I was some half of him.

And there was grace. To swing left-handed, to hit the ball, to run were all one motion, the weight flowing from the left side of the body to the right as the foot steps into the pitch, then on a stride closer to first base, running, running.

And as I type this I realize, too, a slight advantage to that left hand. My *a*'s and *e*'s are strong clear strikes, no ghost images, no *z* floats below the line, the weak pinkie finger simultaneously hitting the big shift key. And the return, the big chrome spoon on this Royal manual, the twisted lever was made for the heel of my left hand. The return is effortless.

The return.
The return.

I remember the little boys out in the field in their baggy uniforms, the scratchy cotton overwashed, before the synthetic fabrics. The green grass and the redwood red outfield fence, snow fence that was rolled up at the end of the season, leaving an arch of tall uncut grass, a record of the summer. Those boys chattered insectlike while the pitcher thought on the mound. How to write it? Hey-bay. Hey-bay. Hey-bay. Swing batter swing batter swing batter swing. Fire hard fire hard. All one word. Seesawing and singing, building to the pitch and starting after it from nothing. And I was in the batter's box, the catcher chanting, the fielders babbling, none of it making sense. A stutter everywhere around me. I liked the sound of it. Its patterns. Its cadence. Its life.

At Breezeway we slowed and settled out from the turnpike, trying to read the yellow ticket with the boxes of numbers, the entrances and exits, and the tiny map of the road. We stalled at the booth trying to make the change.

There was still the trip through western Maryland then and one of the redundant roads that stretches from Baltimore to Washington. The trip was nothing but an excuse.

We wound up saying good-bye in that unlucky city, in Metro Center, where there is no place to sit and all the subway lines—red, blue, yellow, green—come together. Martin was on his way to work nearby. Above. I would go on to National Airport—I had my bag—and take one of those planes that shoots straight up in the air over the Potomac, that gets out of there fast, the whole trip home in silence, suspended, known by heart.

Along the edge of the platform green lights begin to pulse when the train approaches. Air begins to flow through the station. On some other level I can hear the doorbell warning of a departing train.

I remember the therapists counting the words in the sentences I spoke, long columns of numbers on the charts. I remember them waiting for me to finish, to be sure that the pause was a period. That there was a thought completed. They were trying to determine my mean length of utterance. Just how long could I go before ruin, decay, explosion, waste, disappearance, silence. They weren't really listening to me, to what was being said, but to its ending, the harmonics of closure, that falling off in voice. And I would want to string it out, add and digress both. It was no good.

This is the way I said good-bye to Martin. I could not have said good-bye in any other way, in any way that would make sense to you.

Martin rose out of the station on moving stairs to his desk, where a man is broken on the dry blue bottom of a motel swimming pool, where the whole office is inhaling the lethal fumes of correction, white-out.

I have another friend who has made an anatomical gift on the back of his driver's license. He is giving only his lips. The card is laminated. My friend loves to think of his death. The police trying to make heads or tails out of it. Doctors being told of the donation. My friend thinks of the harvest of his body, his smile.

As I type I am concentrating, forming the words with my lips: Flesh. And blood. And metal. And light.

CLOSE

Felix Pollak

. . . .

The eye doctor studied the chart of my just completed Field Test—a semiannual routine designed to show whether I had lost any peripheral vision since the last test. The doctor studied the chart and said nothing. The steps of the technician who had handed the chart to the doctor were diminishing down the hall. The papers rustled, as the doctor kept turning them back and forth. A faint whiff of cigarette smoke drifted unpleasantly from the corridor into the room. The pages kept turning—over and back. And over. My palms started to sweat, and I kept sliding them over the smooth plastic and metal of the armrests of the examining chair in which I was sitting. The doctor kept studying my charts and said nothing. I became conscious of the ticking of a clock somewhere on his desk or on the wall above it. I suddenly said, "Well?" The hoarse sound of my voice startled me. There was no response, except for the irregular rustling of the papers. The ticking of the clock grew louder, and there was a ticking also in my throat, only faster and soundless. "Close," said the doctor. The word was hanging in the air and I tried to grasp it. "Close—to what?" I said. Over and back. "Close to the last test, or close to . . . zero?" "Both," the doctor said. In a nearby office a telephone rang. Then it stopped. I looked in the direction of the lamp on the doctor's desk. Its light was soft and steady and had not changed at all.

CATHEDRAL

Raymond Carver

· · · · · · · · · · · · · · · · · · ·

This blind man, an old friend of my wife's, he was on his way to spend the night. His wife had died. So he was visiting the dead wife's relatives in Connecticut. He called my wife from his in-laws'. Arrangements were made. He would come by train, a five-hour trip, and my wife would meet him at the station. She hadn't seen him since she worked for him one summer in Seattle ten years ago. But she and the blind man had kept in touch. They made tapes and mailed them back and forth. I wasn't enthusiastic about his visit. He was no one I knew. And his being blind bothered me. My idea of blindness came from the movies. In the movies, the blind moved slowly and never laughed. Sometimes they were led by seeing-eye dogs. A blind man in my house was not something I looked forward to.

That summer in Seattle she had needed a job. She didn't have any money. The man she was going to marry at the end of the summer was in officers' training school. He didn't have any money, either. But she was in love with the guy, and he was in love with her, etc. She'd seen something in the paper: HELP WANTED—*Reading to Blind Man,* and a telephone number. She phoned and went over, was hired on the spot. She'd worked with this blind man all summer. She read stuff to him, case studies, reports, that sort of thing. She helped him organize his little office in the county social-service department. They'd become good friends, my wife and the blind man. How do I know these things? She told me. And she told me something else. On her last day in the office, the blind man asked if he could touch her face. She agreed to this. She told me he touched his fingers to every part of her face, her nose—even her neck! She never forgot it. She even tried to write a poem about it. She was always trying to write a poem. She wrote a poem or two every year, usually after something really important had happened to her.

When we first started going out together, she showed me the poem. In the poem, she recalled his fingers and the way they had moved around over her face. In the poem, she talked about what she had felt at the time, about what went through her mind when the blind man touched her nose and lips. I can remember I didn't think much of the poem. Of course, I didn't tell her that. Maybe I just don't understand poetry. I admit it's not the first thing I reach for when I pick up something to read.

Anyway, this man who'd first enjoyed her favors, the officer-to-be, he'd been her childhood sweetheart. So okay. I'm saying that at the end of the summer she let the blind man run his hands over her face, said good-bye to him, married her childhood etc., who was now a commissioned officer, and she moved away from Seattle. But they'd kept in touch, she and the blind man. She made the first contact after a year or so. She called him up one night from an Air Force base in Alabama. She wanted to talk. They talked. He asked her to send him a tape and tell him about her life. She did this. She sent the tape. On the tape, she told the blind man about her husband and about their life together in the military. She told the blind man she loved her husband but she didn't like it where they lived and she didn't like it that he was a part of the military-industrial thing. She told the blind man she'd written a poem and he was in it. She told him that she was writing a poem about what it was like to be an Air Force officer's wife. The poem wasn't finished yet. She was still writing it. The blind man made a tape. He sent her the tape. She made a tape. This went on for years. My wife's officer was posted to one base and then another. She sent tapes from Moody AFB, McGuire, McConnell, and finally Travis, near Sacramento, where one night she got to feeling lonely and cut off from people she kept losing in that moving-around life. She got to feeling she couldn't go it another step. She went in and swallowed all the pills and capsules in the medicine chest and washed them down with a bottle of gin. Then she got into a hot bath and passed out.

But instead of dying, she got sick. She threw up. Her officer—why should he have a name? he was the childhood sweetheart, and what more does he want?—came home from somewhere, found her, and called the ambulance. In time, she put it all on a tape and sent the tape to the blind man. Over the years, she put all kinds of stuff on tapes and sent the tapes off lickety-split. Next to writing a poem every year, I think it was her chief means of recreation. On one tape, she told the blind man she'd decided to live away from her officer for a time. On another tape, she told him about her divorce. She and I began going out, and of course she told her blind man about it. She told him everything, or so it seemed to me. Once she asked me if I'd like to hear the latest tape from the blind man. This was a year ago. I was on the tape, she said. So I said okay, I'd listen to it. I got us drinks and we settled down in the living room. We made ready to listen. First she inserted the tape into the player and adjusted a couple of dials. Then she pushed a lever. The tape squeaked and someone began to talk in this loud voice. She lowered the volume. After a few minutes of harmless chitchat, I heard my own name in the mouth of this stranger, this blind man I didn't even know! And then this: "From all you've said about him, I can only conclude—" But we were interrupted, a knock at the door, something, and we didn't ever get back to the tape. Maybe it was just as well. I'd heard all I wanted to.

Now this same blind man was coming to sleep in my house.

"Maybe I could take him bowling," I said to my wife. She was at the draining board doing scalloped potatoes. She put down the knife she was using and turned around.

"If you love me," she said, "you can do this for me. If you

don't love me, okay. But if you had a friend, any friend, and the friend came to visit, I'd make him feel comfortable." She wiped her hands with the dish towel.

"I don't have any blind friends," I said.

"You don't have *any* friends," she said. "Period. Besides," she said, "goddamn it, his wife's just died! Don't you understand that? The man's lost his wife!"

I didn't answer. She'd told me a little about the blind man's wife. Her name was Beulah. Beulah! That's a name for a colored woman.

"Was his wife a Negro?" I asked.

"Are you crazy?" my wife said. "Have you just flipped or something?" She picked up a potato. I saw it hit the floor, then roll under the stove. "What's wrong with you?" she said. "Are you drunk?"

"I'm just asking," I said.

Right then my wife filled me in with more detail than I cared to know. I made a drink and sat at the kitchen table to listen. Pieces of the story began to fall into place.

Beulah had gone to work for the blind man the summer after my wife had stopped working for him. Pretty soon Beulah and the blind man had themselves a church wedding. It was a little wedding—who'd want to go to such a wedding in the first place?—just the two of them, plus the minister and the minister's wife. But it was a church wedding just the same. It was what Beulah had wanted, he'd said. But even then Beulah must have been carrying the cancer in her glands. After they had been inseparable for eight years—my wife's word, *inseparable*—Beulah's health went into a rapid decline. She died in a Seattle hospital room, the blind man sitting beside the bed and holding on to her hand. They'd married, lived and worked together, slept together—had sex, sure—and then the blind man had to bury her. All this without his having ever seen what the goddamned woman looked like. It was beyond my understanding. Hearing this, I felt sorry for the blind man for a little bit. And then I found myself thinking what a pitiful life this woman must have led. Imagine a woman who could never see herself as she was seen in the eyes of her loved one. A woman who could go on day after day and never receive the smallest compliment from her beloved. A woman whose husband could never read the expression on her face, be it misery or something better. Someone who could wear makeup or not—what difference to him? She could, if she wanted, wear green eye shadow around one eye, a straight pin in her nostril, yellow slacks, and purple shoes, no matter. And then to slip off into death, the blind man's hand on her hand, his blind eyes streaming tears— I'm imagining now—her last thought maybe this: that he never even knew what she looked like, and she on an express to the grave. Robert was left with a small insurance policy and half of a twenty-peso Mexican coin. The other half of the coin went into the box with her. Pathetic.

So when the time rolled around, my wife went to the depot to pick him up. With nothing to do but wait—sure, I blamed him for that—I was having a drink and watching the TV when I heard the car pull into the drive. I got up from the sofa with my drink and went to the window to have a look.

I saw my wife laughing as she parked the car. I saw her get out of the car and shut the door. She was still wearing a smile. Just amazing. She went around to the other side of the car to where the blind man was already starting to get out. This blind man, feature this, he was wearing a full beard! A beard on a blind man! Too much, I say. The blind man reached into the backseat and dragged out a suitcase. My wife took his arm, shut the car door, and, talking all the way, moved him down the drive and then up the steps to the front porch. I turned off the TV. I finished my drink, rinsed the glass, dried my hands. Then I went to the door.

My wife said, "I want you to meet Robert. Robert, this is my husband. I've told you all about him." She was beaming. She had this blind man by his coat sleeve.

The blind man let go of his suitcase and up came his hand.

I took it. He squeezed hard, held my hand, and then he let it go.

"I feel like we've already met," he boomed.

"Likewise," I said. I didn't know what else to say. Then I said, "Welcome. I've heard a lot about you." We began to move then, a little group, from the porch into the living room, my wife guiding him by the arm. The blind man was carrying his suitcase in his other hand. My wife said things like, "To your left here, Robert. That's right. Now watch it, there's a chair. That's it. Sit down right here. This is the sofa. We just bought this sofa two weeks ago."

I started to say something about the old sofa. I'd liked that old sofa. But I didn't say anything. Then I wanted to say something else, small talk, about the scenic ride along the Hudson. How going *to* New York, you should sit on the right-hand side of the train, and coming *from* New York, the left-hand side.

"Did you have a good train ride?" I said. "Which side of the train did you sit on, by the way?"

"What a question, which side!" my wife said. "What's it matter which side?" she said.

"I just asked," I said.

"Right side," the blind man said. "I hadn't been on a train in nearly forty years. Not since I was a kid. With my folks. That's been a long time. I'd nearly forgotten the sensation. I have winter in my beard now," he said. "So I've been told, anyway. Do I look distinguished, my dear?" the blind man said to my wife.

"You look distinguished, Robert," she said. "Robert," she said. "Robert, it's just so good to see you."

My wife finally took her eyes off the blind man and looked at me. I had the feeling she didn't like what she saw. I shrugged.

I've never met, or personally known, anyone who was blind. This blind man was in his late forties, a heavyset, balding man with stooped shoulders, as if he carried a great weight there. He wore brown slacks, brown shoes, a light-brown shirt, a tie, a sports coat. Spiffy. He also had this full beard. But he didn't use a cane and he didn't wear dark glasses. I'd always thought dark glasses were a must for the blind. Fact was, I wished he had a pair. At first glance, his eyes looked like anyone else's eyes. But if you looked close, there was something different about them. Too much white in the iris, for one thing, and the pupils seemed to move around in the sockets without his knowing it or being able to stop it. Creepy. As I stared at his face, I saw the left pupil turn in toward his nose while the other made an effort to keep in one place. But it was only an effort, for that eye was on the roam without his knowing it or wanting it to be.

I said, "Let me get you a drink. What's your pleasure? We have a little of everything. It's one of our pastimes."

"Bub, I'm a Scotch man myself," he said fast enough in this big voice.

"Right," I said. Bub! "Sure you are. I knew it."

He let his fingers touch his suitcase, which was sitting alongside the sofa. He was taking his bearings. I didn't blame him for that.

"I'll move that up to your room," my wife said.

"No, that's fine," the blind man said loudly. "It can go up when I go up."

"A little water with the Scotch?" I said.

"Very little," he said.

"I knew it," I said.

He said, "Just a tad. The Irish actor, Barry Fitzgerald? I'm like that fellow. When I drink water, Fitzgerald said, I drink water. When I drink whiskey, I drink whiskey." My wife laughed. The blind man brought his hand up under his beard. He lifted his beard slowly and let it drop.

I did the drinks, three big glasses of Scotch with a splash of water in each. Then we made ourselves comfortable and talked about Robert's travels. First the long flight from the West Coast to Connecticut, we covered that. Then from Connecticut up here by train. We had another drink concerning that leg of the trip.

I remembered having read somewhere that the blind didn't smoke because, as speculation had it, they couldn't see the smoke they exhaled. I thought I knew that much and that much only about blind people. But this blind man smoked his cigarette down to the nubbin and then lit another one. This blind man filled his ashtray and my wife emptied it.

When we sat down at the table for dinner, we had another drink. My wife heaped Robert's plate with cube steak, scalloped potatoes, green beans. I buttered him up two slices of bread. I said, "Here's bread and butter for you." I swallowed some of my drink. "Now let us pray," I said, and the blind man lowered his head. My wife looked at me, her mouth agape. "Pray the phone won't ring and the food doesn't get cold," I said.

We dug in. We ate everything there was to eat on the table. We ate like there was no tomorrow. We didn't talk. We ate. We scarfed. We grazed that table. We were into serious eating. The blind man had right away located his foods, he knew just where everything was on his plate. I watched with admiration as he used his knife and fork on the meat. He'd cut two pieces of meat, fork the meat into his mouth, and then go all out for the scalloped potatoes, the beans next, and then he'd tear off a hunk of buttered bread and eat that. He'd follow this up with a big drink of milk. It didn't seem to bother him to use his fingers once in a while, either.

We finished everything, including half a strawberry pie. For a few moments, we sat as if stunned. Sweat beaded on our faces. Finally, we got up from the table and left the dirty plates. We didn't look back. We took ourselves into the living room and sank into our places again. Robert and my wife sat on the sofa. I took the big chair. We had us two or three more drinks while they talked about the major things that had come to pass for them in the past ten years. For the most part, I just listened. Now and then I joined in. I didn't want him to think I'd left the room, and I didn't want her to think I was feeling left out. They talked of things that had happened to them—to them!— these past ten years. I waited in vain to hear my name on my wife's sweet lips: "And then my dear husband came into my life"—something like that. But I heard nothing of the sort. More talk of Robert. Robert had done a little of everything, it seemed, a regular blind jack-of-all-trades. But most recently he and his wife had had an Amway distributorship, from which, I gathered, they'd earned their living, such as it was. The blind man was also a ham radio operator. He talked in his loud voice about conversations he'd had with fellow operators in Guam, in the Philippines, in Alaska, and even in Tahiti. He said he'd have a lot of friends there if he ever wanted to go visit those places. From time to time, he'd turn his blind face toward me, put his hand under his beard, ask me something. How long had I been in my present position? (Three years.) Did I like my work? (I didn't.) Was I going to stay with it? (What were the options?) Finally, when I thought he was beginning to run down, I got up and turned on the TV.

My wife looked at me with irritation. She was heading toward a boil. Then she looked at the blind man and said, "Robert, do you have a TV?"

The blind man said, "My dear, I have two TVs. I have a color set and a black-and-white thing, an old relic. It's funny, but if I turn the TV on, and I'm always turning it on, I turn on the color set. It's funny, don't you think?"

I didn't know what to say to that. I had absolutely nothing to say to that. No opinion. So I watched the news program and tried to listen to what the announcer was saying.

"This is a color TV," the blind man said. "Don't ask me how, but I can tell."

"We traded up a while ago," I said.

The blind man had another taste of his drink. He lifted his beard, sniffed it, and let it fall. He leaned forward on the sofa. He positioned his ashtray on the coffee table, then put the lighter to his cigarette. He leaned back on the sofa and crossed his legs at the ankles.

My wife covered her mouth, and then she yawned. She stretched. She said, "I think I'll go upstairs and put on my robe. I think I'll change into something else. Robert, you make yourself comfortable," she said.

"I'm comfortable," the blind man said.

"I want you to feel comfortable in this house," she said.

"I am comfortable," the blind man said.

*　　　*　　　*

After she'd left the room, he and I listened to the weather report and then to the sports roundup. By that time, she'd been gone so long I didn't know if she was going to come back. I thought she might have gone to bed. I wished she'd come back downstairs. I didn't want to be left alone with a blind man. I asked him if he wanted another drink, and he said sure. Then I asked if he wanted to smoke some dope with me. I said I'd just rolled a number. I hadn't, but I planned to do so in about two shakes.

"I'll try some with you," he said.

"Damn right," I said. "That's the stuff."

I got our drinks and sat down on the sofa with him. Then I rolled us two fat numbers. I lit one and passed it. I brought it to his fingers. He took it and inhaled.

"Hold it as long as you can," I said. I could tell he didn't know the first thing.

My wife came back downstairs wearing her pink robe and her pink slippers.

"What do I smell?" she said.

"We thought we'd have us some cannabis," I said.

My wife gave me a savage look. Then she looked at the blind man and said, "Robert, I didn't know you smoked."

He said, "I do now, my dear. There's a first time for everything. But I don't feel anything yet."

"This stuff is pretty mellow," I said. "This stuff is mild. It's dope you can reason with," I said. "It doesn't mess you up."

"Not much it doesn't, bub," he said, and laughed.

My wife sat on the sofa between the blind man and me. I passed her the number. She took it and toked and then passed it back to me. "Which way is this going?" she said. Then she said, "I shouldn't be smoking this. I can hardly keep my eyes open as it is. That dinner did me in. I shouldn't have eaten so much."

"It was the strawberry pie," the blind man said. "That's what did it," he said, and he laughed his big laugh. Then he shook his head.

"There's more strawberry pie," I said.

"Do you want some more, Robert?" my wife said.

"Maybe in a little while," he said.

We gave our attention to the TV. My wife yawned again. She said, "Your bed is made up when you feel like going to bed, Robert. I know you must have had a long day. When you're ready to go to bed, say so." She pulled his arm. "Robert?"

He came to and said, "I've had a real nice time. This beats tapes, doesn't it?"

I said, "Coming at you," and I put the number between his fingers. He inhaled, held the smoke, and then let it go. It was like he'd been doing it since he was nine years old.

"Thanks, bub," he said. "But I think this is all for me. I think I'm beginning to feel it," he said. He held the burning roach out for my wife.

"Same here," she said. "Ditto. Me, too." She took the roach and passed it to me. "I may just sit here for a while between you two guys with my eyes closed. But don't let me bother you, okay? Either one of you. If it bothers you, say so. Otherwise, I may just sit here with my eyes closed until you're ready to go to bed," she said. "Your bed's made up, Robert, when you're ready. It's right next to our room at the top of the stairs. We'll show you up when you're ready. You wake me up now, you guys, if I fall asleep." She said that and then she closed her eyes and went to sleep.

The news program ended. I got up and changed the channel. I sat back down on the sofa. I wished my wife hadn't pooped out. Her head lay across the back of the sofa, her mouth open. She'd turned so that her robe had slipped away from her legs, exposing a juicy thigh. I reached to draw her robe back over her, and it was then that I glanced at the blind man. What the hell! I flipped the robe open again.

"You say when you want some strawberry pie," I said.

"I will," he said.

I said, "Are you tired? Do you want me to take you up to your bed? Are you ready to hit the hay?"

"Not yet," he said. "No, I'll stay up with you, bub. If that's all right. I'll stay up until you're ready to turn in. We haven't had a chance to talk. Know what I mean? I feel like me and her monopolized the evening." He lifted his beard and he let it fall. He picked up his cigarettes and his lighter.

"That's all right," I said. Then I said, "I'm glad for the company."

And I guess I was. Every night I smoked dope and stayed up as long as I could before I fell asleep. My wife and I hardly ever went to bed at the same time. When I did go to sleep, I had these dreams. Sometimes I'd wake up from one of them, my heart going crazy.

Something about the church and the Middle Ages was on the TV. Not your run-of-the-mill TV fare. I wanted to watch something else. I turned to the other channels. But there was nothing on them, either. So I turned back to the first channel and apologized.

"Bub, it's all right," the blind man said. "It's fine with me. Whatever you want to watch is okay. I'm always learning something. Learning never ends. It won't hurt me to learn something tonight. I got ears," he said.

He didn't say anything for a time. He was leaning forward with his head turned at me, his right ear aimed in the direction of the set. Very disconcerting. Now and then his eyelids drooped and then they snapped open again. Now and then he put his fingers into his beard and tugged, like he was thinking about something he was hearing on the television.

On the screen a group of men wearing cowls was being set upon and tormented by men dressed in skeleton costumes and men dressed as devils. The men dressed as devils wore devil masks, horns, and long tails. This pageant was part of a procession. The Englishman who was narrating the thing said it took place in Spain once a year. I tried to explain to the blind man what was happening.

"Skeletons," he said. "I know about skeletons," he said, and he nodded.

The TV showed this one cathedral. Then there was a long, slow look at another one. Finally, the picture switched to the famous one in Paris, with its flying buttresses and its spires reaching up to the clouds. The camera pulled away to show the whole of the cathedral rising above the skyline.

There were times when the Englishman who was telling the thing would shut up, would simply let the camera move around over the cathedrals. Or else the camera would tour the countryside, men in fields walking behind oxen. I waited as long as I could. Then I felt I had to say something. I said, "They're showing the outside of this cathedral now. Gargoyles. Little statues carved to look like monsters. Now I guess they're in Italy. Yeah, they're in Italy. There's paintings on the walls of this one church."

"Are those fresco paintings, bub?" he asked, and he sipped from his drink.

I reached for my glass. But it was empty. I tried to remember what I could remember. "You're asking me are those frescoes?" I said. "That's a good question. I don't know."

The camera moved to a cathedral outside Lisbon. The differences in the Portuguese cathedral compared with the French and Italian were not that great. But they were there. Mostly the interior stuff. Then something occurred to me, and I said, "Something has occurred to me. Do you have any idea what a cathedral is? What they look like, that is? Do you follow me? If somebody says cathedral to you, do you have any notion what they're talking about? Do you know the difference between that and a Baptist church, say?"

He let the smoke dribble from his mouth. "I know they took hundreds of workers fifty or a hundred years to build," he said. "I just heard the man say that, of course. I know generations of the same families worked on a cathedral. I heard him say that, too. The men who began their life's work on them, they never lived to see the completion of their work. In that wise, bub, they're no different from the rest of us, right?" He laughed. Then his eyelids drooped again. His head nodded. He seemed to be snoozing. Maybe he was imagining himself in Portugal. The TV was showing another cathedral now. This one was in Germany. The Englishman's voice droned on. "Cathedrals," the blind man said. He sat up and rolled his head back and forth. "If you want the truth, bub, that's about all I know. What I just said. What I heard him say. But maybe you could describe one to me? I wish you'd do it. I'd like that. If you want to know, I really don't have a good idea."

I stared hard at the shot of the cathedral on the TV. How could I even begin to describe it? But say my life depended on it. Say my life was being threatened by an insane guy who said I had to do it or else.

I stared some more at the cathedral before the picture flipped off into the countryside. There was no use. I turned to the blind man and said, "To begin with, they're very tall." I was looking around the room for clues. "They reach way up. Up and up. Toward the sky. They're so big, some of them, they have to have these supports. To help hold them up, so to speak. These supports are called buttresses. They remind me of viaducts, for some reason. But maybe you don't know viaducts, either? Sometimes the cathedrals have devils and such carved into the front. Sometimes lords and ladies. Don't ask me why this is," I said.

He was nodding. The whole upper part of his body seemed to be moving back and forth.

"I'm not doing so good, am I?" I said.

He stopped nodding and leaned forward on the edge of the sofa. As he listened to me, he was running his fingers through his beard. I wasn't getting through to him, I could see that. But he waited for me to go on just the same. He nodded, like he was trying to encourage me. I tried to think what else to say. "They're really big," I said. "They're massive. They're built of stone. Marble, too, sometimes. In those olden days, when they built cathedrals, men wanted to be close to God. In those olden days God was an important part of everyone's life. You could tell this from their cathedral-building. I'm sorry," I said, "but it looks like that's the best I can do for you. I'm just no good at it."

"That's all right, bub," the blind man said. "Hey, listen. I hope you don't mind my asking you. Can I ask you something? Let me ask you a simple question, yes or no. I'm just curious and there's no offense. You're my host. But let me ask if you are in any way religious? You don't mind my asking?"

I shook my head. He couldn't see that, though. A wink is the same as a nod to a blind man. "I guess I don't believe in it. In anything. Sometimes it's hard. You know what I'm saying?"

"Sure, I do," he said.

"Right," I said.

The Englishman was still holding forth. My wife sighed in her sleep. She drew a long breath and went on with her sleeping.

"You'll have to forgive me," I said. "But I can't tell you what a cathedral looks like. It just isn't in me to do it. I can't do any more than I've done."

The blind man sat very still, his head down, as he listened to me.

I said, "The truth is, cathedrals don't mean anything special to me. Nothing. Cathedrals. They're something to look at on late-night TV. That's all they are."

It was then that the blind man cleared his throat. He brought something up. He took a handkerchief from his back pocket. Then he said, "I get it, bub. It's okay. It happens. Don't worry about it," he said. "Hey, listen to me. Will you do me a favor? I got an idea. Why don't you find us some heavy paper? And a pen. We'll do something. We'll draw one together. Get us a pen and some heavy paper. Go on, bub, get the stuff," he said.

So I went upstairs. My legs felt like they didn't have any strength in them. They felt like they did after I'd done some running. In my wife's room, I looked around. I found some ballpoints in a little basket on her table. And then I tried to think where to look for the kind of paper he was talking about.

Downstairs, in the kitchen, I found a shopping bag with onion skins in the bottom of the bag. I emptied the bag and shook it. I brought it into the living room and sat down with it near his legs. I moved some things, smoothed the wrinkles from the bag, spread it out on the coffee table.

The blind man got down from the sofa and sat next to me on the carpet.

He ran his fingers over the paper. He went up and down the sides of the paper. The edges, even the edges. He fingered the corners.

"All right," he said. "All right, let's do her."

He found my hand, the hand with the pen. He closed his hand over my hand. "Go ahead, bub, draw," he said. "Draw. You'll see. I'll follow along with you. It'll be okay. Just begin now like I'm telling you. You'll see. Draw," the blind man said.

So I began. First I drew a box that looked like a house. It could have been the house I lived in. Then I put a roof on it. At either end of the roof, I drew spires. Crazy.

"Swell," he said. "Terrific. You're doing fine," he said. "Never thought anything like this could happen in your lifetime, did you, bub? Well, it's a strange life, we all know that. Go on now. Keep it up."

I put in windows with arches. I drew flying buttresses. I hung great doors. I couldn't stop. The TV station went off the air. I put down the pen and closed and opened my fingers. The blind man felt around over the paper. He moved the tips of his fingers over the paper, all over what I had drawn, and he nodded.

"Doing fine," the blind man said.

I took up the pen again, and he found my hand. I kept at it. I'm no artist. But I kept drawing just the same.

My wife opened up her eyes and gazed at us. She sat up on the sofa, her robe hanging open. She said, "What are you doing? Tell me, I want to know."

I didn't answer her.

The blind man said, "We're drawing a cathedral. Me and him are working on it. Press hard," he said to me. "That's right. That's good," he said. "Sure. You got it, bub. I can tell. You didn't think you could. But you can, can't you? You're cooking with gas now. You know what I'm saying? We're going to really have us something here in a minute. How's the old arm?" he said. "Put some people in there now. What's a cathedral without people?"

My wife said, "What's going on? Robert, what are you doing? What's going on?"

"It's all right," he said to her. "Close your eyes now," the blind man said to me.

I did it. I closed them just like he said.

"Are they closed?" he said. "Don't fudge."

"They're closed," I said.

"Keep them that way," he said. He said, "Don't stop now. Draw."

So we kept on with it. His fingers rode my fingers as my hand went over the paper. It was like nothing else in my life up to now.

Then he said, "I think that's it. I think you got it," he said. "Take a look. What do you think?"

But I had my eyes closed. I thought I'd keep them that way for a little longer. I thought it was something I ought to do.

"Well?" he said. "Are you looking?"

My eyes were still closed. I was in my house. I knew that. But I didn't feel like I was inside anything.

"It's really something," I said.

SOCIAL ISSUES

....

HOW I CONTEMPLATED THE WORLD FROM THE DETROIT HOUSE OF CORRECTION AND BEGAN MY LIFE ALL OVER AGAIN

Joyce Carol Oates

. . . .

Notes for an essay for an English class at Baldwin Country Day School; poking around in debris; disgust and curiosity; a revelation of the meaning of life; a happy ending . . .

I. EVENTS

1. The girl (myself) is walking through Branden's, that excellent store. Suburb of a large famous city that is a symbol for large famous American cities. The event sneaks up on the girl, who believes she is herding it along with a small fixed smile, a girl of fifteen, innocently experienced. She dawdles in a certain style by a counter of costume jewelry. Rings, earrings, necklaces. Prices from $5 to $50, all within reach. All ugly. She eases over to the glove counter, where everything is ugly too. In her close-fitted coat with its black fur collar she contemplates the luxury of Branden's, which she has known for many years: its many mild pale lights, easy on the eye and the soul, its elaborate tinkly decorations, its women shoppers with their

excellent shoes and coats and hairdos, all dawdling gracefully, in no hurry.

Who was ever in a hurry here?

2. The girl seated at home. A small library, paneled walls of oak. Someone is talking to me. An earnest husky female voice drives itself against my ears, nervous, frightened, groping around my heart, saying, "If you wanted gloves why didn't you say so? Why didn't you ask for them?" That store, Branden's, is owned by Raymond Forrest who lives on DuMaurier Drive. We live on Sioux Drive. Raymond Forrest. A handsome man? An ugly man? A man of fifty or sixty, with gray hair, or a man of forty with earnest courteous eyes, a good golf game, who is Raymond Forrest, this man who is my salvation? Father has been talking to him. Father is not his physician; Dr. Berg is his physician. Father and Dr. Berg refer patients to each other. There is a connection. Mother plays bridge with . . . On Mondays and Wednesdays our maid Billie works at . . . The strings draw together in a cat's cradle, making a net to save you when you fall . . . .

3. *Harriet Arnold's.* A small shop, better than Branden's. Mother in her black coat, I in my close-fitted blue coat. Shopping. Now look at this, isn't this cute, do you want this, why don't you want this, try this on, take this with you to the fitting room, take this also, what's wrong with you, what can I do for you, why are you so strange . . . ? "I wanted to steal but not to buy," I don't tell her. The girl droops along in her coat and gloves and leather boots, her eyes scan the horizon which is pastel pink and decorated like Branden's, tasteful walls and modern ceilings with graceful glimmering lights.

4. Weeks later, the girl at a bus stop. Two o'clock in the afternoon, a Tuesday, obviously she has walked out of school.

5. The girl stepping down from a bus. Afternoon, weather changing to colder. Detroit. Pavement and closed-up stores;

grillwork over the windows of a pawnshop. What is a pawnshop, exactly?

II. CHARACTERS

1. The girl stands five feet five inches tall. An ordinary height. Baldwin Country Day School draws them up to that height. She dreams along the corridors and presses her face against the Thermoplex glass. No frost or steam can ever form on that glass. A smudge of grease from her forehead . . . could she be boiled down to grease? She wears her hair loose and long and straight in suburban teenage style, 1968. Eyes smudged with pencil, dark brown. Brown hair. Vague green eyes. A pretty girl? An ugly girl? She sings to herself under her breath, idling in the corridor, thinking of her many secrets (the thirty dollars she once took from the purse of a friend's mother, just for fun, the basement window she smashed in her own house just for fun) and thinking of her brother who is at Susquehanna Boys' Academy, an excellent preparatory school in Maine, remembering him unclearly . . . he has long manic hair and a squeaking voice and he looks like one of the popular teenage singers of 1968, one of those in a group. The Certain Forces, The Way Out, The Maniacs Responsible. The girl in her turn looks like one of those fieldsful of girls who listen to the boys' singing, dreaming and mooning restlessly, breaking into high sullen laughter, innocently experienced.

2. The mother. A midwestern woman of Detroit and suburbs. Belongs to the Detroit Athletic Club. Also the Detroit Golf Club. Also the Bloomfield Hills Country Club. The Village Women's Club, at which lectures are given each winter on Genet and Sartre and James Baldwin, by the director of the adult education program at Wayne State University . . . The Bloomfield Art Association. Also the Founders Society of the Detroit Institute of Arts. Also . . . Oh, she is in perpetual motion, this lady, hair like blown-up gold and finer than gold, hair and fingers and body of inestimable grace. Heavy weighs

the gold on the back of her hairbrush and hand mirror. Heavy heavy the candlesticks in the dining room. Very heavy is the big car, a Lincoln, long and black, that on one cool autumn day split a squirrel's body in two unequal parts.

3. The father. Dr. ———. He belongs to the same clubs as #2. A player of squash and golf; he has a golfer's umbrella of stripes. Candy stripes. In his mouth nothing turns to sugar, however, saliva works no miracles here. His doctoring is of the slightly sick. The sick are sent elsewhere (to Dr. Berg?), the deathly sick are sent back for more tests and their bills are sent to their homes, the unsick are sent to Dr. Coronet (Isabel, a lady), an excellent psychiatrist for unsick people who angrily believe they are sick and want to do something about it. If they demand a male psychiatrist, the unsick are sent by Dr. ——— (my father) to Dr. Lowenstein, a male psychiatrist, excellent and expensive, with a limited practice.

4. Clarita. She is twenty, twenty-five, she is thirty or more? Pretty, ugly, what? She is a woman lounging by the side of a road, in jeans and a sweater, hitchhiking, or she is slouched on a stool at a counter in some roadside diner. A hard line of jaw. Curious eyes. Amused eyes. Behind her eyes processions move, funeral pageants, cartoons. She says, "I never can figure out why girls like you bum around down here. What are you looking for anyway?" An odor of tobacco about her. Unwashed underclothes, or no underclothes, unwashed skin, gritty toes, hair long and falling into strands, not recently washed.

5. Simon. In this city the weather changes abruptly, so Simon's weather changes abruptly. He sleeps through the afternoon. He sleeps through the morning. Rising, he gropes around for something to get him going, for a cigarette or a pill to drive him out to the street, where the temperature is hovering around 35 degrees. Why doesn't it drop? Why, why doesn't the cold clean air come down from Canada, will he have to go up into Canada to get it, will he have to leave the Country of

his Birth and sink into Canada's frosty fields . . . ? Will the FBI (which he dreams about constantly) chase him over the Canadian border on foot, hounded out in a blizzard of broken glass and horns . . . ?

"Once I was Huckleberry Finn," Simon says, "but now I am Roderick Usher." Beset by frenzies and fears, this man who makes my spine go cold, he takes green pills, yellow pills, pills of white and capsules of dark blue and green . . . he takes other things I may not mention, for what if Simon seeks me out and climbs into my girl's bedroom here in Bloomfield Hills and strangles me, what then . . . ? (As I write this I begin to shiver. Why do I shiver? I am now sixteen, and sixteen is not an age for shivering.) It comes from Simon, who is always cold.

III. WORLD EVENTS
Nothing.

IV. PEOPLE & CIRCUMSTANCES CONTRIBUTING TO THIS DELINQUENCY
Nothing.

V. SIOUX DRIVE
George, Clyde G. 240 Sioux. A manufacturer's representative; children, a dog; a wife. Georgian with the usual columns. You think of the White House, then of Thomas Jefferson, then your mind goes blank on the white pillars and you think of nothing. Norris, Ralph W. 246 Sioux. Public relations. Colonial. Bay window, brick, stone, concrete, wood, green shutters, sidewalk, lantern, grass, trees, blacktop drive, two children, one of them my classmate Esther (Esther Norris) at Baldwin. Wife, cars. Ramsey, Michael D. 250 Sioux. Colonial. Big living room, thirty by twenty-five, fireplaces in living room library recreation room, paneled walls wet bar five bathrooms five bedrooms two lavatories central air conditioning automatic sprinkler automatic garage door three children one wife two cars a breakfast

room a patio a large fenced lot fourteen trees a front door with a brass knocker never knocked. Next is our house. Classic contemporary. Traditional modern. Attached garage, attached Florida room, attached patio, attached pool and cabana, attached roof. A front door mail slot through which pour *Time* magazine, *Fortune, Life, Business Week, The Wall Street Journal, The New York Times, The New Yorker, Saturday Review, M.D., Modern Medicine, Disease of the Month* . . . and also . . . And in addition to all this a quiet sealed letter from Baldwin saying: *Your daughter is not doing work compatible with her performance on the Stanford-Binet* . . . And your son is not doing well, not well at all, very sad. Where is your son anyway? Once he stole trick-and-treat candy from some six-year-old kids, he himself being a robust ten. The beginning. Now your daughter steals. In the Village Pharmacy she made off with, yes she did, don't deny it, she made off with a copy of *Pageant* magazine for no reason, she swiped a roll of Life Savers in a green wrapper and was in no need of saving her life or even in need of sucking candy, when she was no more than eight years old she stole, don't blush, she stole a package of Tums only because it was out on the counter and available, and the nice lady behind the counter (now dead) said nothing . . . . Sioux Drive. Maples, oaks, elms. Diseased elms cut down. Sioux Drive runs into Roosevelt Drive. Slow turning lanes, not streets, all drives and lanes and ways and passes. A private police force. Quiet private police, in unmarked cars. Cruising on Saturday evenings with paternal smiles for the residents who are streaming in and out of houses, going to and from parties, a thousand parties, slightly staggering, the women in their furs alighting from automobiles bought of Ford and General Motors and Chrysler, very heavy automobiles. No foreign cars. Detroit. In 275 Sioux, down the block, in that magnificent French Normandy mansion, lives ——— ——— himself, who has the C——— account itself, imagine that! Look at where he lives and look at the enormous trees and chimneys, imagine his many fireplaces, imagine his wife and children, imagine his wife's hair, imagine her fingernails, imagine her bathtub of smooth clean glowing pink, imagine their embraces, his trouser pockets filled with odd coins and keys and dust and peanuts, imagine their ecstasy on Sioux Drive, imagine their income tax returns, imagine their little boy's pride in his experimental car, a scaled-down C———, as he roars around the neighborhood on the sidewalks frightening dogs and Negro maids, oh imagine all these things, imagine everything, let your mind roar out all over Sioux Drive and DuMaurier Drive and Roosevelt Drive and Ticonderoga Pass and Burning Bush Way and Lincoln-shire Pass and Lois Lane.

When spring comes its winds blow nothing to Sioux Drive, no odors of hollyhocks or forsythia, nothing Sioux Drive doesn't already possess, everything is planted and performing. The weather vanes, had they weather vanes, don't have to turn with the wind, don't have to contend with the weather. There is no weather.

VI. DETROIT

There is always weather in Detroit. Detroit's temperature is always 32 degrees. Fast falling temperatures. Slow rising temperatures. Wind from the north northeast four to forty miles an hour, small-craft warnings, partly cloudy today and Wednesday changing to partly sunny through Thursday . . . small warnings of frost, soot warnings, traffic warnings, hazardous lake conditions for small craft and swimmers, restless Negro gangs, restless cloud formations, restless temperatures aching to fall out the very bottom of the thermometer or shoot up over the top and boil everything over in red mercury.

Detroit's temperature is 32 degrees. Fast falling temperatures. Slow rising temperatures. Wind from the north northeast four to forty miles an hour . . .

VII. EVENTS

1. The girl's heart is pounding. In her pocket is a pair of gloves! In a plastic bag! Airproof breathproof plastic bag, gloves selling for twenty-five dollars on Branden's counter! In her pocket!

Shoplifted! . . . In her purse is a blue comb, not very clean. In her purse is a leather billfold (a birthday present from her grandmother in Philadelphia) with snapshots of the family in clean plastic windows, in the billfold are bills, she doesn't know how many bills . . . . In her purse is an ominous note from her friend Tykie: *What's this about Joe H. and the kids hanging around at Louise's Sat. night? You heard anything?* . . . passed in French class. In her purse is a lot of dirty yellow Kleenex, her mother's heart would break to see such very dirty Kleenex, and at the bottom of her purse are brown hairpins and safety pins and a broken pencil and a ballpoint pen (blue) stolen from somewhere forgotten and a purse-size compact of Cover Girl Makeup, Ivory Rose . . . . Her lipstick is Broken Heart, a corrupt pink; her fingers are trembling like crazy; her teeth are beginning to chatter; her insides are alive; her eyes glow in her head; she is saying to her mother's astonished face *I want to steal but not to buy.*

2. At Clarita's. Day or night? What room is this? A bed, a regular bed, and a mattress on the floor nearby. Wallpaper hanging in strips. Clarita says she tore it like that with her teeth. She was fighting a barbaric tribe that night, high from some pills she was battling for her life with men wearing helmets of heavy iron and their faces no more than Christian crosses to breathe through, every one of those bastards looking like her lover Simon, who seems to breathe with great difficulty through the slits of mouth and nostrils in his face. Clarita has never heard of Sioux Drive. Raymond Forrest cuts no ice with her, nor does the C——— account and its millions; Harvard Business School could be at the corner of Vernor and 12th Street for all she cares, and Vietnam might have sunk by now into the Dead Sea under its tons of debris, for all the amazement she could show . . . her face is overworked, overwrought, at the age of twenty (thirty?) it is already exhausted but fanciful and ready for a laugh. Clarita says mournfully to me *Honey somebody is going to turn you out let me give you warning.* In a movie shown on late television Clarita is not a mess like this

but a nurse, with short neat hair and a dedicated look, in love with her doctor and her doctor's patients and their diseases, enamored of needles and sponges and rubbing alcohol . . . . Or no: she is a private secretary. Robert Cummings is her boss. She helps him with fantastic plots, the canned audience laughs, no, the audience doesn't laugh because nothing is funny, instead her boss is Robert Taylor and they are not boss and secretary but husband and wife, she is threatened by a young starlet, she is grim, handsome, wifely, a good companion for a good man . . . . She is Claudette Colbert. Her sister too is Claudette Colbert. They are twins, identical. Her husband Charles Boyer is a very rich handsome man and her sister, Claudette Colbert, is plotting her death in order to take her place as the rich man's wife, no one will know because they are *twins* . . . . All these marvelous lives Clarita might have lived, but she fell out the bottom at the age of thirteen. At the age when I was packaging my overnight case for a slumber party at Tony Deshield's she was tearing filthy sheets off a bed and scratching up a rash on her arms . . . . Thirteen is uncommonly young for a white girl in Detroit, Miss Brook of the Detroit House of Correction said in a sad newspaper interview for the *Detroit News;* fifteen and sixteen are more likely. Eleven, twelve, thirteen are not surprising in colored . . . they are more precocious. What can we do? Taxes are rising and the tax base is falling. The temperature rises slowly but falls rapidly. Everything is falling out the bottom. Woodward Avenue is filthy, Livernois Avenue is filthy! Scraps of paper flutter in the air like pigeons, dirt flies up and hits you right in the eye, oh, Detroit is breaking up into dangerous bits of newspaper and dirt, watch out . . .

Clarita's apartment is over a restaurant. Simon her lover emerges from the cracks at dark. Mrs. Olesko, a neighbor of Clarita's, an aged white wisp of a woman, doesn't complain but sniffs with contentment at Clarita's noisy life and doesn't tell the cops, hating cops, when the cops arrive. I should give more fake names, more blanks, instead of telling all these secrets. I myself am a secret; I am a minor.

*   *   *

3. My father reads a paper at a medical convention in Los Angeles. There he is, on the edge of the North American continent, when the unmarked detective put his hand so gently on my arm in the aisle of Branden's and said, "Miss, would you like to step over here for a minute?"

And where was he when Clarita put her hand on my arm, that wintry dark sulphurous aching day in Detroit, in the company of closed-down barbershops, closed-down diners, closed-down movie houses, homes, windows, basements, faces . . . she put her hand on my arm and said, "Honey, are you looking for somebody down here?"

And was he home worrying about me, gone for two weeks solid, when they carried me off . . . ? It took three of them to get me in the police cruiser, so they said, and they put more than their hands on my arm.

4. I work on this lesson. My English teacher is Mr. Forest, who is from Michigan State. Not handsome, Mr. Forest, and his name is plain, unlike Raymond Forrest's, but he is sweet and rodentlike, he has conferred with the principal and my parents, and everything is fixed . . . treat her as if nothing had happened, a new start, begin again, only sixteen years old, what a shame, how did it happen?—nothing happened, nothing could have happened, a slight physiological modification known only to a gynecologist or to Dr. Coronet. I work on my lesson. I sit in my pink room. I look around the room with my sad pink eyes. I sigh, I dawdle. I pause, I eat up time. I am limp and happy to be home, I am sixteen years old suddenly, my head hangs heavy as a pumpkin on my shoulders, and my hair has just been cut by Mr. Faye at the Crystal Salon and is said to be very becoming.

(Simon too put his hand on my arm and said, "Honey, you have got to come with me," and in his six-by-six room we got to know each other. Would I go back to Simon again? Would I lie down with him in all that filth and craziness? Over and over again

*   *   *

a Clarita is being betrayed as in front of a Cunningham Drugstore she is nervously eyeing a colored man who may or may not have money, or a nervous white boy of twenty with sideburns and an Appalachian look, who may or may not have a knife hidden in his jacket pocket, or a husky red-faced man of friendly countenance who may or may not be a member of the Vice Squad out for an early twilight walk.)

I work on my lesson for Mr. Forest. I have filled up eleven pages. Words pour out of me and won't stop. I want to tell everything . . . what was the song Simon was always humming, and who was Simon's friend in a very new trench coat with an old high school graduation ring on his finger . . . ? Simon's bearded friend? When I was down too low for him Simon kicked me out and gave me to him for three days, I think, on Fourteenth Street in Detroit, an airy room of cold cruel drafts with newspapers on the floor . . . . Do I really remember that or am I piecing it together from what they told me? Did they tell the truth? Did they know how much of the truth?

VIII. CHARACTERS

1. Wednesdays after school, at four; Saturday mornings at ten. Mother drives me to Dr. Coronet. Ferns in the office, plastic or real, they look the same. Dr. Coronet is queenly, an elegant nicotine-stained lady who would have studied with Freud had circumstances not prevented it, a bit of a Catholic, ready to offer you some mystery if your teeth will ache too much without it. Highly recommended by Father! Forty dollars an hour, Father's forty dollars! Progress! Looking up! Looking better! That new haircut is so becoming, says Dr. Coronet herself, showing how normal she is for a woman with an I.Q. of 180 and many advanced degrees.

2. Mother. A lady in a brown suede coat. Boots of shiny black material, black gloves, a black fur hat. She would be humiliated could she know that of all the people in the world it is my

ex-lover Simon who walks most like her . . . self-conscious and unreal, listening to distant music, a little bowlegged with craftiness . . . .

3. Father. Tying a necktie. In a hurry. On my first evening home he put his hand on my arm and said, "Honey, we're going to forget all about this."

4. Simon. Outside a plane is crossing the sky, in here we're in a hurry. Morning. It must be morning. The girl is half out of her mind, whimpering and vague, Simon her dear friend is wretched this morning . . . he is wretched with morning itself . . . he forces her to give him an injection, with that needle she knows is filthy, she has a dread of needles and surgical instruments and the odor of things that are to be sent into the blood, thinking somehow of her father . . . . This is a bad morning, Simon says that his mind is being twisted out of shape, and so he submits to the needle which he usually scorns and bites his lip with his yellowish teeth, his face going very pale. *Ah baby!* he says in his soft mocking voice, which with all women is a mockery of love, *do it like this—Slowly—*And the girl, terrified, almost drops the precious needle but manages to turn it up to the light from the window . . . it is an extension of herself, then? She can give him this gift, then? *I wish you wouldn't do this to me,* she says, wise in her terror, because it seems to her that Simon's danger—in a few minutes he might be dead—is a way of pressing her against him that is more powerful than any other embrace. She has to work over his arm, the knotted corded veins of his arm, her forehead wet with perspiration as she pushes and releases the needle, staring at that mixture of liquid now stained with Simon's bright blood . . . . When the drug hits him she can feel it herself, she feels that magic that is more than any woman can give him, striking the back of his head and making his face stretch as if with the impact of a terrible sun . . . . She tries to embrace him but he pushes her aside and stumbles to his feet. *Jesus Christ,* he says . . . .

* * *

5. Princess, a Negro girl of eighteen. What is her charge? She is close-mouthed about it, shrewd and silent, you know that no one had to wrestle her to the sidewalk to get her in here; she came with dignity. In the recreation room she sits reading *Nancy Drew and the Jewel Box Mystery*, which inspires in her face tiny wrinkles of alarm and interest: what a face! Light brown skin, heavy shaded eyes, heavy eyelashes, a serious sinister dark brow, graceful fingers, graceful wristbones, graceful legs, tongue, a sugar-sweet voice, a leggy stride more masculine than Simon's and my mother's, decked out in a dirty white blouse and dirty white slacks; vaguely nautical is Princess's style . . . . At breakfast she is in charge of clearing the table and leans over me, saying, *Honey you sure you ate enough?*

6. The girl lies sleepless, wondering. Why here, why not there? Why Bloomfield Hills and not jail? Why jail and not her pink room? Why downtown Detroit and not Sioux Drive? What is the difference? Is Simon all the difference? The girl's head is a parade of wonders. She is nearly sixteen, her breath is marvelous with wonders, not long ago she was coloring with crayons and now she is smearing the landscape with paints that won't come off and won't come off her fingers either. She says to the matron, *I am not talking about anything,* not because everyone has warned her not to talk but because, because she will not talk, because she won't say anything about Simon who is her secret. And she says to the matron, *I won't go home* up until that night in the lavatory when everything was changed . . . . "No, I won't go home I want to stay here," she says, listening to her own words with amazement thinking that weeds might climb everywhere over that marvelous $86,000 house and dinosaurs might return to muddy the beige carpeting, but never never will she reconcile four o'clock in the morning in Detroit with eight o'clock breakfasts in Bloomfield Hills . . . oh, she aches still for Simon's hands and his caressing breath, though he gave her little pleasure, he took everything from her (five-dollar bills, ten-dollar bills, passed into her numb hands by men and taken out of her hands by Simon) until she

herself was passed into the hands of other men, police, when Simon evidently got tired of her and her hysteria . . . . *No, I won't go home, I don't want to be bailed out,* the girl thinks as a *Stubborn and Wayward Child* (one of the several charges lodged against her) and the matron understands her crazy white-rimmed eyes that are seeking out some new violence that will keep her in jail, should someone threaten to let her out. Such children try to strangle the matrons, the attendants, or one another . . . they want the locks locked forever, the doors nailed shut . . . and this girl is no different up until that night her mind is changed for her . . . .

IX. THAT NIGHT

Princess and Dolly, a little white girl of maybe fifteen, hardy however as a sergeant and in the house of correction for armed robbery, corner her in the lavatory at the farthest sink, and the other girls look away and file out to bed, leaving her. God, how she is beaten up! Why is she beaten up? Why do they pound her, why such hatred? Princess vents all the hatred of a thousand silent Detroit winters on her body, this girl whose body belongs to me, fiercely she rides across the midwestern plains on this girl's tender bruised body . . . revenge on the oppressed minorities of America! revenge on the slaughtered Indians! revenge on the female sex, on the male sex, revenge on Bloomfield Hills, revenge revenge . . .

X. DETROIT

In Detroit weather weighs heavily upon everyone. The sky looms large. The horizon shimmers in smoke. Downtown the buildings are imprecise in the haze. Perpetual haze. Perpetual motion inside the haze. Across the choppy river is the city of Windsor, in Canada. Part of the continent has bunched up here and is bulging outward, at the tip of Detroit, a cold hard rain is forever falling on the expressways . . . shoppers shop grimly, their cars are not parked in safe places, their windshields may be smashed and graceful ebony hands may drag them out through their shatterproof smashed windshields, crying, *Revenge for the Indians!* Ah, they all fear leaving Hudson's and being dragged to the very tip of the city and thrown off the parking roof of Cobo Hall, that expensive tomb, into the river . . . .

XI. CHARACTERS WE ARE FOREVER ENTWINED WITH

1. Simon drew me into his tender, rotting arms and breathed gravity into me. Then I came to earth, weighted down. He said *You are such a little girl,* and he weighed me down with his delight. In the palms of his hands were teeth marks from his previous life experiences. He was thirty-five, they said. Imagine Simon in this room, in my pink room: he is about six feet tall and stoops slightly, in a feline cautious way, always thinking, always on guard, with his scuffed light suede shoes and his clothes which are anyone's clothes, slightly rumpled ordinary clothes that ordinary men might wear to not-bad jobs. Simon has fair, long hair, curly hair, spent languid curls that are like . . . exactly like the curls of wood shavings to the touch, I am trying to be exact . . . and he smells of unheated mornings and coffee and too many pills coating his tongue with a faint green-white scum . . . . Dear Simon, who would be panicked in this room and in this house (right now Billie is vacuuming next door in my parents' room: a vacuum cleaner's roar is a sign of all good things), Simon who is said to have come from a home not much different from this, years ago, fleeing all the carpeting and the polished banisters . . . . Simon has a deathly face, only desperate people fall in love with it. His face is bony and cautious, the bones of his cheeks prominent as if the rigidity of his ceaseless thinking, plotting, for he has to make money out of girls to whom money means nothing, they're so far gone they can hardly count it, and in a sense money means nothing to him either except as a way of keeping on with his life. *Each Day's Proud Struggle,* the title of a novel we could read at jail . . . Each day he needs a certain amount of money. He devours

it. It wasn't love he uncoiled in me with his hollowed-out eyes and his courteous smile, that remnant of a prosperous past, but a dark terror that needed to press itself flat against him, or against another man . . . but he was the first, he came over to me and took my arm, a claim. We struggled on the stairs and I said, "Let me loose, you're hurting my neck, my face," it was such a surprise that my skin hurt where he rubbed it, and afterward we lay face to face and he breathed everything into me. In the end I think he turned me in.

2. Raymond Forrest. I just read this morning that Raymond Forrest's father, the chairman of the board at ———, died of a heart attack on a plane bound for London. I would like to write Raymond Forrest a note of sympathy. I would like to thank him for not pressing charges against me one hundred years ago, saving me, being so generous . . . well, men like Raymond Forrest are generous men, not like Simon. I would like to write him a letter telling of my love, or of some other emotion that is positive and healthy. Not like Simon and his poetry, which he scrawled down when he was high and never changed a word . . . but when I try to think of something to say it is Simon's language that comes back to me, caught in my head like a bad song, it is always Simon's language:

> There is no reality only dreams
> Your neck may get snapped when you wake
> My love is drawn to some violent end
> She keeps wanting to get away
> My love is heading downward
> And I am heading upward
> She is going to crash on the sidewalk
> And I am going to dissolve into the clouds

XII. EVENTS

1. Out of the hospital, bruised and saddened and converted, with Princess's grunts still tangled in my hair . . . and Father in his overcoat looking like a prince himself, come to carry me off. Up the expressway and out north to home. Jesus Christ but

the air is thinner and cleaner here. Monumental houses. Heart-breaking sidewalks, so clean.

2. Weeping in the living room. The ceiling is two stories high and two chandeliers hang from it. Weeping, weeping, though Billie the maid is *probably listening.* I will never leave home again. Never. Never leave home. Never leave this home again, never.

3. Sugar doughnuts for breakfast. The toaster is very shiny and my face is distorted in it. Is that my face?

4. The car is turning in the driveway. Father brings me home. Mother embraces me. Sunlight breaks in movieland patches on the roof of our traditional contemporary home, which was designed for the famous automotive stylist whose identity, if I told you the name of the famous car he designed, you would all know, so I can't tell you because my teeth chatter at the thought of being sued . . . or having someone climb into my bedroom window with a rope to strangle me . . . . The car turns up the blacktop drive. The house opens to me like a doll's house, so lovely in the sunlight, the big living room beckons to me with its walls falling away in a delirium of joy at my return, Billie the maid is *no doubt* listening from the kitchen as I burst into tears and the hysteria Simon got so sick of. Convulsed in Father's arms, I say I will never leave again, never, why did I leave, where did I go, what happened, my mind is gone wrong, my body is one big bruise, my backbone was sucked dry, it wasn't the men who hurt me and Simon never hurt me but only those girls . . . my God how they hurt me . . . I will never leave home again . . . . The car is perpetually turning up the drive and I am perpetually breaking down in the living room and we are perpetually taking the right exit from the express-way (Lahser Road) and the wall of the rest room is perpetually banging against my head and perpetually are Simon's hands moving across my body and adding everything up and so too are Father's hands on my shaking bruised back, far from the

surface of my skin on the surface of my good blue cashmere coat (dry-cleaned for my release) . . . . I weep for all the money here, for God in gold and beige carpeting, for the beauty of chandeliers and the miracle of a clean polished gleaming toaster and faucets that run both hot and cold water, and I tell them, *I will never leave home, this is my home, I love everything here, I am in love with everything here* . . . .

IF THE RIVER WAS
WHISKEY

T. Coraghessan Boyle

The water was a heartbeat, a pulse, it stole the heat from
his body and pumped it to his brain. Beneath the surface,
magnified through the shimmering lens of his face mask, were
silver shoals of fish, forests of weed, a silence broken only by
the distant throbbing hum of an outboard. Above, there was
the sun, the white flash of a faraway sailboat, the weatherbeaten dock with its weatherbeaten rowboat, his mother in her
deck chair, and the vast depthless green of the world beyond.

He surfaced like a dolphin, spewing water from the vent of
his snorkel, and sliced back to the dock. The lake came with
him, two bony arms and the wedge of a foot, the great heaving
splash of himself flat out on the dock like something thrown
up in a storm. And then, without pausing even to snatch up
a towel, he had the spinning rod in hand and the silver lure was
sizzling out over the water, breaking the surface just above the
shadowy arena he'd fixed in his mind. His mother looked up
at the splash. "Tiller," she called, "come get a towel."

His shoulders quaked. He huddled and stamped his feet, but
he never took his eyes off the tip of the rod. Twitching it
suggestively, he reeled with the jerky, hesitant motion that
would drive lunker fish to a frenzy. Or so he'd read, anyway.

"Tilden, do you hear me?"

"I saw a Northern," he said. "A big one. Two feet maybe."

The lure was in. A flick of his wrist sent it back. Still reeling, he ducked his head to wipe his nose on his wet shoulder. He could feel the sun on his back now, and he envisioned the skirted lure in the water, sinuous, sensual, irresistible, and he waited for the line to quicken with the strike.

The porch smelled of pine—old pine, dried up and dead—and it depressed him. In fact, everything depressed him—especially this vacation. Vacation. It was a joke. Vacation from what?

He poured himself a drink—vodka and soda, tall, from the plastic half-gallon jug. It wasn't noon yet, the breakfast dishes were in the sink, and Tiller and Caroline were down at the lake. He couldn't see them through the screen of trees, but he heard the murmur of their voices against the soughing of the branches and the sadness of the birds. He sat heavily in the creaking wicker chair and looked out on nothing. He didn't feel too hot. In fact, he felt as if he'd been cored and dried, as if somebody had taken a pipe cleaner and run it through his veins. His head ached too, but the vodka would take care of that. When he finished it, he'd have another, and then maybe a grilled Swiss on rye. Then he'd start to feel good again.

His father was talking to the man, and his mother was talking to the woman. They'd met at the bar about twenty drinks ago, and his father was into his could-have-been, should-have-been, way-back-when mode, and the man, bald on top and with a ratty beard and long greasy hair like his father's, was trying to steer the conversation back to building supplies. The woman had whole galaxies of freckles on her chest, and she leaned forward in her sundress and told his mother scandalous stories about people she'd never heard of. Tiller had drunk all the Coke and eaten all the beer nuts he could hold. He watched the Pabst Blue Ribbon sign flash on and off above the bar, and he watched the woman's freckles move in and out of the gap between her breasts. Outside it was dark, and a cool clean scent came in off the lake.

"Un huh, yeah," his father was saying, "the To the Bone

Band. I played rhythm and switched off vocals with Dillie Richards. . . ."

The man had never heard of Dillie Richards.

"Black dude, used to play with Taj Mahal?"

The man had never heard of Taj Mahal.

"Anyway," his father said, "we used to do all this really outrageous stuff by people like Muddy, Howlin' Wolf, Luther Allison—"

"She didn't," his mother said.

The woman threw down her drink and nodded, and the front of her dress went crazy. Tiller watched her and felt the skin go tight across his shoulders and the back of his neck, where he'd been burned the first day. He wasn't wearing any underwear, just shorts. He looked away. "Three abortions, two kids," the woman said. "And she never knew who the father of the second one was."

"Drywall isn't worth a damn," the man said. "But what're you going to do?"

"Paneling?" his father offered.

The man cut the air with the flat of his hand. He looked angry. "Don't talk to me about paneling," he said.

Mornings, when his parents were asleep and the lake was still, he would take the rowboat to the reedy cove on the far side of the lake where the big pike lurked. He didn't actually know if they lurked there, but if they lurked anywhere, this would be the place. It looked fishy, mysterious, sunken logs looming up dark from the shadows beneath the boat, mist rising like steam, as if the bottom were boiling with ravenous, cold-eyed, killer pike that could slice through monofilament with a snap of their jaws and bolt ducklings in a gulp. Besides, Joe Matochik, the old man who lived in the cabin next door and could charm frogs by stroking their bellies, had told him that this was where he'd find them.

It was cold at dawn, and he'd wear a thick home-knit sweater over his T-shirt and shorts, sometimes pulling the stretched-out hem of it down like a skirt to warm his thighs. He'd take an apple with him or a slice of brown bread and peanut butter. And of course the orange life jacket his mother insisted on.

When he left the dock he was always wearing the life jacket—for form's sake and for the extra warmth it gave him against the raw morning air. But when he got there, when he stood in the swaying basin of the boat to cast his Hula Popper or Abu Relfex, it got in the way and he took it off. Later, when the sun ran through him and he didn't need the sweater, he balled it up on the seat beside him, and sometimes, if it was good and hot, he shrugged out of his T-shirt and shorts too. No one could see him in the cove, and it made his breath come quick to be naked like that under the morning sun.

"I heard you," he shouted, and he could feel the veins stand out in his neck, the rage come up in him like something killed and dead and brought back to life. "What kind of thing is that to tell a kid, huh? About his own father?"

She wasn't answering. She'd backed up in a corner of the kitchen and she wasn't answering. And what could she say, the bitch? He'd heard her. Dozing on the trundle bed under the stairs, wanting a drink but too weak to get up and make one, he'd heard voices from the kitchen, her voice and Tiller's. "Get used to it," she said, "he's a drunk, your father's a drunk," and then he was up off the bed as if something had exploded inside of him and he had her by the shoulders—always the shoulders and never the face, that much she'd taught him—and Tiller was gone, out the door and gone. Now, her voice low in her throat, a sick and guilty little smile on her lips, she whispered, "It's true."

"Who are you to talk?—you're shit-faced yourself." She shrank away from him, that sick smile on her lips, her shoulders hunched. He wanted to smash things, kick in the damn stove, make her hurt.

"At least I have a job," she said.

"I'll get another one, don't you worry."

"And what about Tiller? We've been here two weeks and you haven't done one damn thing with him, nothing, zero. You haven't even been down to the lake. Two hundred feet and you haven't even been down there once." She came up out of the corner now, feinting like a boxer, vicious, her sharp little fists balled up to drum on him. She spoke in a snarl. "What kind of father are you?"

He brushed past her, slammed open the cabinet, and grabbed the first bottle he found. It was whiskey, cheap whiskey, Four Roses, the shit she drank. He poured out half a water glass full and drank it down to spite her. "I hate the beach, boats, water, trees. I hate you."

She had her purse and she was halfway out the screen door. She hung there a second, looking as if she'd bitten into something rotten. "The feeling's mutual," she said, and the door banged shut behind her.

There were too many complications, too many things to get between him and the moment, and he tried not to think about them. He tried not to think about his father—or his mother either—in the same way that he tried not to think about the pictures of the bald-headed stick people in Africa or meat in its plastic wrapper and how it got there. But when he did think about his father he thought about the river-was-whiskey day.

It was a Tuesday or Wednesday, middle of the week, and when he came home from school the curtains were drawn and his father's car was in the driveway. At the door he could hear him, the *chunk-chunk* of the chords and the rasping nasal whine that seemed as if it belonged to someone else. His father was sitting in the dark, hair in his face, bent low over the guitar. There was an open bottle of liquor on the coffee table and a clutter of beer bottles. The room stank of smoke.

It was strange, because his father hardly ever played his guitar anymore—he mainly just talked about it. In the past tense. And it was strange too—and bad—because his father wasn't at work. Tiller dropped his book bag on the telephone stand. "Hi, Dad," he said.

His father didn't answer. Just bent over the guitar and played the same song, over and over, as if it were the only song he knew. Tiller sat on the sofa and listened. There was a verse—one verse—and his father repeated it three or four times before he broke off and slurred the words into a sort of chant or hum, and then he went back to the words again. After the fourth repetition Tiller heard it:

> *If the river was whiskey,*
> *And I was a divin' duck,*
> *I'd swim to the bottom,*
> *Drink myself back up.*

For half an hour his father played that song, played it till anything else would have sounded strange. He reached for the bottle when he finally stopped, and that was when he noticed Tiller. He looked surprised. Looked as if he'd just woken up. "Hey, ladykiller Tiller," he said, and took a drink from the mouth of the bottle.

Tiller blushed. There'd been a Sadie Hawkins dance at school and Janet Rumery had picked him for her partner. Ever since, his father had called him ladykiller, and though he wasn't exactly sure what it meant, it made him blush anyway, just from the tone of it. Secretly, it pleased him. "I really liked the song, Dad," he said.

"Yeah?" His father lifted his eyebrows and made a face. "Well, come home to Mama, doggie-o. Here," he said, and he held out an open beer. "You ever have one of these, ladykiller Tiller?" He was grinning. The sleeve of his shirt was torn and his elbow was raw and there was a hard little clot of blood over his shirt pocket. "With your sixth-grade buddies out behind the handball court, maybe? No?"

Tiller shook his head.

"You want one? Go ahead, take a hit."

Tiller took the bottle and sipped tentatively. The taste wasn't much. He looked up at his father. "What does it mean?" he said. "The song, I mean—the one you were singing. About the whiskey and all."

His father gave him a long slow grin and took a drink from

the big bottle of clear liquor. "I don't know," he said finally, grinning wider to show his tobacco-stained teeth. "I guess he just liked whiskey, that's all." He picked up a cigarette, made as if to light it, and then put it down again. "Hey," he said, "you want to sing it with me?"

All right, she'd hounded him and she'd threatened him and she was going to leave him, he could see that clear as day. But he was going to show her. And the kid too. He wasn't drinking. Not today. Not a drop.

He stood on the dock with his hands in his pockets while Tiller scrambled around with the fishing poles and oars and the rest of it. Birds were screeching in the trees, and there was a smell of diesel fuel on the air. The sun cut into his head like a knife. He was sick already.

"I'm giving you the big pole, Dad, and you can row if you want."

He eased himself into the boat and it fell away beneath him like the mouth of a bottomless pit.

"I made us egg salad, Dad, your favorite. And I brought some birch beer."

He was rowing. The lake was churning underneath him, the wind was up and reeking of things washed up on the shore, and the damn oars kept slipping out of the oarlocks, and he was rowing. At the last minute he'd wanted to go back for a quick drink, but he didn't, and now he was rowing.

"We're going to catch a pike," Tiller said, hunched like a spider in the stern.

There was spray off the water. He was rowing. He felt sick. Sick and depressed.

"We're going to catch a pike, I can feel it. I know we are," Tiller said, "I know it. I just know it."

It was too much for him all at once—the sun, the breeze that was so sweet he could taste it, the novelty of his father rowing, pale arms and a dead cigarette clenched between his teeth, the boat rocking, and the birds whispering—and he closed his eyes a minute, just to keep from going dizzy with the joy of it. They were in deep water already. Tiller was trolling with a plastic worm and spinner, just in case, but he didn't have much faith in catching anything out here. He was taking his father to the cove with the submerged logs and beds of weed—that's where they'd connect, that's where they'd catch pike.

"Jesus," his father said when Tiller spelled him at the oars. Hands shaking, he crouched in the stern and tried to light a cigarette. His face was gray and the hair beat crazily around his face. He went through half a book of matches and then threw the cigarette in the water. "Where are you taking us, anyway," he said, "—the Indian Ocean?"

"The pike place," Tiller told him. "You'll like it, you'll see."

The sun was dropping behind the hills when they got there, and the water went from blue to gray. There was no wind in the cove. Tiller let the boat glide out across the still surface while his father finally got a cigarette lit, and then he dropped anchor. He was excited. Swallows dove at the surface, bullfrogs burped from the reeds. It was the perfect time to fish, the hour when the big lunker pike would cruise among the sunken logs, hunting.

"All right," his father said, "I'm going to catch the biggest damn fish in the lake," and he jerked back his arm and let fly with the heaviest sinker in the tackle box dangling from the end of the rod. The line hissed through the guys and there was a thunderous splash that probably terrified every pike within half a mile. Tiller looked over his shoulder as he reeled in his silver spoon. His father winked at him, but he looked grim.

It was getting dark, his father was out of cigarettes, and Tiller had cast the spoon so many times his arm was sore, when suddenly the big rod began to buck. "Dad! Dad!" Tiller shouted, and his father lurched up as if he'd been stabbed. He'd been dozing, the rod propped against the gunwale, and Tiller had been studying the long suffering-lines in his father's face, the grooves in his forehead, and the puffy discolored flesh beneath his eyes. With his beard and long hair and with the crumpled suffering look on his face, he was the picture of the crucified Christ Tiller had contemplated a hundred times at church. But now the rod was bucking and his father had hold of it and he was playing a fish, a big fish, the tip of the rod dipping all the way down to the surface.

"It's a pike, Dad, it's a pike!"

His father strained at the pole. His only response was a grunt, but Tiller saw something in his eyes he hardly recognized anymore, a connection, a charge, as if the fish were sending a current up the line, through the pole, and into his hands and body and brain. For a full three minutes he played the fish, his slack biceps gone rigid, the cigarette clamped in his mouth, while Tiller hovered over him with the landing net. There was a surge, a splash, and the thing was in the net, and Tiller had it over the side and into the boat. "It's a pike," his father said, "goddamnit, look at the thing, look at the size of it."

It wasn't a pike. Tiller had watched Joe Matochik catch one off the dock one night. Joe's pike had been dangerous, full of teeth, a long, lean, tapering strip of muscle and pounding life. This was no pike. It was a carp. A fat, pouty, stinking, ugly mud carp. Trash fish. They shot them with arrows and threw them up on the shore to rot. Tiller looked at his father and felt like crying.

"It's a pike," his father said, and already the thing in his eyes was gone, already it was over, "it's a pike. Isn't it?"

It was late—past two, anyway—and he was drunk. Or no, he was beyond drunk. He'd been drinking since morning, one tall vodka and soda after another, and he didn't feel a thing. He sat on the porch in the dark, and he couldn't see the lake, couldn't hear it, couldn't even smell it. Caroline and Tiller were asleep. The house was dead silent.

Caroline was leaving him, which meant that Tiller was leaving him. He knew it. He could see it in her eyes and he heard it in her voice. She was soft once, his soft-eyed lover, and now she was hard, unyielding, now she was his worst enemy. They'd had the couple from the roadhouse in for drinks and burgers earlier that night and he'd leaned over the table to tell the guy something—Ed, his name was—joking really, nothing serious, just making conversation. "Vodka and soda," he said, "that's my drink. I used to drink vodka and grapefruit juice, but it tore the lining out of my stomach." And then Caroline, who wasn't even listening, stepped in and said, "Yeah, and that"—pointing to the glass—"tore the lining out of your brain." He looked up at her. She wasn't smiling.

All right. That was how it was. What did he care? He hadn't wanted to come up here anyway—it was her father's idea. Take the cabin for a month, the old man had said, pushing, pushing in that way he had, and get yourself turned around. Well, he wasn't turning around, and they could all go to hell.

After a while the chill got to him and he pushed himself up from the chair and went to bed. Caroline said something in her sleep and pulled away from him as he lifted the covers and slid in. He was awake for a minute or two, feeling depressed, so depressed he wished somebody would come in and shoot him, and then he was asleep.

In his dream he was out in the boat with Tiller. The wind was blowing, his hands were shaking, he couldn't light a cigarette. Tiller was watching him. He pulled at the oars and nothing happened. Then all of a sudden they were going down, the boat sucked out from under them, the water icy and black, beating in on them as if it were alive. Tiller called out to him. He saw his son's face, saw him going down, and there was nothing he could do.

END OVER END

Ron Carlson

. . . .

E veryone wanted to know what happened. The admitting
nurse or secretary, her pen cap chewed into a nasty spiral,
asked first, and then the real nurse asked. She took Cooper and
his wife, Day, back to one of the emergency cubicles and pulled
the curtain and looked closely at the baby's face and said,
"How'd this happen?" Cooper was holding the baby, and the
nurse stood behind him examining Billy's face, and she put her
other hand on Cooper's other shoulder to steady everybody,
and she said, "This looks odd."

"What do you mean?" Cooper said; his voice was thick as
if he were going to cry again, and he wanted to fight. Day put
her hand on his arm, and Cooper stopped and clenched his jaw.

"He fell off the bed and hit his eye on the end table. It was
an accident," Day said to the nurse.

"Could you just get us the doctor?" Cooper said, measuring
out the words.

When the nurse left, Day went around behind and stroked
Billy's hair. Billy held his head against the hollow in Cooper's
shoulder, not moving. He had stopped screaming when they
had removed the ice bag from his eye. Now the eye had swollen
entirely shut and flamed a dull red.

When the doctor came in, he nodded at Day and disappeared from Cooper's view to look into Billy's face. He did not

touch Cooper. After a moment he listened to Billy's heart and said, "How'd this happen?"

Cooper closed his eyes while Day talked briefly to the doctor. It had been one second. Billy was crawling over Cooper in the big bed while Cooper read part of the paper aloud to Day, who was sorting things in her closet. He was reading the article about the case Day was trying; the reporter had included dialogue. Billy was stepping experimentally on Cooper's stomach and laughing. Cooper loved Billy's laugh, a high snorty giggle which made everybody smile. And then Billy stepped back onto the mattress, bouncing already too far, and Cooper reached, and it all went slow motion. Billy turned and tried to put one foot down in air; he was swinging away off the bed. Cooper twisted, sitting up, and grabbed at the child, missing his wrists by an inch. Billy twisted once in the deep fall, and his face struck the corner of the end table.

Cooper's throat was closed and he knew he was going to cry again. The doctor was gone. Day was saying, "It's going to be all right," and stroking Billy's head. "Hey, Dad," she said to Cooper. "It's going to be all right. It was an accident. We'll get the X-rays and everything is going to be all right." She looked in Cooper's face. "Do you want me to take him?"

Cooper shook his head.

The X-ray technician was an Arab. He was a small, dark man, who Cooper thought didn't look clean. "Coober," the man said. He could be Iranian, Cooper thought. Cooper's R.A. in college had been Iranian.

"We're the Coopers," Day said.

The man looked at Billy and said in an alarmed way, "Ahh." Then he slid around and took the baby. Billy started to cry, his face contorted with the swelling. Looking at him made Cooper's eyes water.

"He looks like he's been hit," the X-ray technician said.

"Can we just get the X-ray," Cooper said.

Billy was screaming again, reaching wearily for his mother. "How did this happen?"

"Look . . ." Cooper stepped toward the man.

"It looks like a blow," the man said frankly to them both. He held Billy away from them and turned to speak.

"It was an accident," Day said.

They were not allowed in the X-ray room. Day sat with her arm on Cooper's outside the door and listened to Billy scream.

Cooper had his eyes shut. He was picturing clearly the X-ray technician falling through space end over end. In the luminous blackness of space, the man spun slowly. Cooper had pushed him out of their space capsule and the dark-skinned man turned end over end.

"End Over End" was the name of every bedtime story Cooper told. Billy went to bed easily, but especially so if Cooper promised him a story. They were all different: "The Football," "The Teddy Bear," "The Snowman," but they ended all the same: the football, or the teddy bear, or the snowman would have a few adventures and almost be home, flying *end over end over end over end.* Cooper would stand over the crib, sometimes collapsing his head onto his folded arms, whispering, "End over end over end over end over end . . ." The words would run together until it sounded like *dover-and-dover-and-dover.* And then there would be the bird-wing mix of Billy's breathing into sleep.

Billy's crying intensified in the X-ray chamber, and then the door opened and another young man in a lab coat carried Billy out and handed him to Day. "It will be a few minutes," he said. "You can wait in the examining room."

Cooper walked behind Day, looking into Billy's exhausted face. He looked like a prizefighter; his eye had mounted into a classic raw shiner. His other eye was open only to a squint.

"Want to hear a story?" Cooper said to him.

Billy stared back. Cooper took him from Day and walked softly around the examining room. He whispered, "Billy walked around and around the bed, around and around the bed and then he fell over and went end over end over end over end." Cooper closed his eyes too and walked in soft circles saying the words. He opened them once and Day was gone, and then he closed his eyes again and kept walking and talking.

Later Day took him by the arm. Billy was asleep. No bones were broken. When they walked out they saw the X-ray technician across the room.

Cooper headed over that way. "I want to say something to that guy," Cooper said to Day.

She took his arm and steered him back. "It's his job," Day said. "The guy sees nothing but trauma all day and all night."

"I'd like to smash his face in."

"Come on," Day said. "Save it for some worthy cause."

The X-ray technician was showing a clipboard to one of the doctors. Another case. Cooper snugged Billy into his shoulder. Day went on: "That guy saw you coming. He saw how scared you were for Billy, and you let him turn you upside down. We're all okay now. But I was surprised. You let that guy get to you."

PELICANS IN FLIGHT

Sheila Ballantyne

. . . .

This is California, the western edge, as far as you can go. The big quake, when it comes, will push the coastline back a bit and split this landfill down to its false core, and all these buildings with it. But for now everything's the same. I'm sitting on the beach, my Nikes by my side, my old jeans rolled up to the knees. Some smart-ass kids came by about an hour ago—cutting school and calling *me* a bum. "Hey, mister, you a *transient?*" Then they laughed. I laughed too, the way that they pronounced it; they must be from the private school on Fourth Street.

The old man is here, as always, standing with his shoes almost in the water, throwing crusts of bread to shorebirds. Every time he swings his arm they jump as one and land a little farther down the beach. Later, when the light begins to fade and he moves on, they'll return—pecking the bloated pieces as they bob with the tide. He reaches into his pocket's depths, broadcasting his crumbs with some deep faith—as though he'd been waiting all his life to feed something. He lifts his eyes as the pelicans fly over him in groups, unbent by their awkward weight and holding the air.

He's always here about this time. The bread is from his lunch, down at Bigger Better Burger on San Pablo. We see each other there, but rarely talk; I take my pictures, he throws his bread. He likes to listen to the conversations as he eats alone. You can tell he thinks of himself as not retired, but free. He has to cross the tracks to get to the shore, and I've seen him squinting between the ties in search of flattened pennies, as he must have in his youth. He was nodding in agreement with Al, the demolition foreman, at the counter just this morning: Things *have* changed. Al was saying, "I watch my daughter with her kids. She'll say, 'Jason, would you mind not putting your feet on the table?' Can you beat that? When I grew up, no one talked to us like that! It was, 'Ya want your head knocked off?' But I'm not complaining. I turned out okay." The guy who wipes the counter nodded too. I remember thinking, If it were nighttime, this could be a bar. It's old-fashioned, the way things used to be. The old man likes the stories the regulars tell, you pick this up by his expression as he listens. "I heard on a talk show about these franchises they've got in the South. You go in, rent a gun, and blow things away—just for recreation—the way you'd, say, go bowling."

Someone new came in the other day, but no one minded—we're cool. He struck up a conversation at the counter. He said, "I hate those restaurants advertising 'ambience.' I was in one yesterday and it was so plain, I felt ripped off—as if they'd used false advertising to get me in. I asked the waiter—I was baiting him, but I was pissed—'Where's the ambience?' and he said, 'It's in the back.'"

The talk this morning was of poisons. It came up over coffee: someone stared into his cup and started talking about the water. He wasn't a nut; he'd seen an article on conditions down in Silicon Valley. It claimed that all those microchip million-aires are bathing in toxic water, contaminated by their own greed; solvents from their companies have leaked into the groundwater and penetrate their skin now as they shower. People smirked, even as they recoiled, no one here has millions. Most of the regulars work, or worked before they were laid off or got old. Except for Ernie's wife: she buys products. It's her guiding inspiration.

Then Evelyn said, "Bet you don't know what goes on in that

warehouse over on the flats," and everyone looked up, their interest piqued. Conversation moves in themes here. Ike at the end knew; so did I. It's a place for freezing people when they die. She'd read about it in the paper. She's even seen their truck; she thinks it's used to transport bodies—what else could it be for, it's so big. It's white, with their slogan stenciled on the side in red: LIFE EXTENSION THROUGH CRYONIC SUSPENSION. People say, "Tsk!" and shake their heads. "They've got bodies in there, stored in cylinders of liquid nitrogen; it costs thousands of dollars a year. When they've found a cure for what they had, they'll unfreeze them and they'll live again."

"That money could feed the poor," someone inevitably remarked. But mostly they were silent; it seemed a possibility so beyond what they could comprehend, what they had ever known, that when the talk resumed, it drifted quickly back in old directions.

"Whatever happened to strontium 90 in milk?"

"Or mercury in fish?"

"I remember strontium 90; you'd go to nurse your baby and suddenly remember that what was keeping him alive was radioactive. It was everywhere, even in you—you were the agent of it. Some days, the thought was enough to stop the milk."

"I was nearly poisoned by my car last week—fumes from the exhaust were leaking through the floorboards. It's being fixed right now, over at Eddie's Muffler—he's the best. The proctologist of auto repair."

It could be a bar, the way they carry on. I was watching earlier when Rachel paused beside a booth to fish for a pill in her apron pocket. It was probably an upper, but you can never tell. Everyone's on something. For some, it's drink; others, Valium. Some do coke when they have money, or smoke grass when they don't. Rachel likes Ecstasy, when she can find it, but it's getting harder now. It seems strange to outlaw something with such a pretty name: a state that anyone would be grateful to be in. Some people I know have had to switch to lithium and stay there. I've stopped everything for now—as though to go back to a time when people were just themselves, and somehow managed that way.

Evelyn's bringing up the warehouse provoked a round of opinion on what happens after death. Nadine thought the soul moves on to another level, and what you do in this life determines if it's high or low. Rhonda agreed. But the young kid sitting by the door, he's too much. This was his theory: "You go to heaven and everything's just great. Just total happiness forever." He works over at the video-rental place. People were respectful, but you could see they didn't agree. Joe was more realistic ("Just live as best you can, after that, bye-bye"), but Patty—you can't say she wasn't predictable: "Your body decomposes and fertilizes the plants." Only Nick, who does the counter, had it right, if you ask me. He said, "On a deeper level, I'd like to think the soul lives on, but on an intellectual level, I think you're finished."

I'm down here now, watching him feed the birds. I just came from the warehouse; I wanted to see it for myself. It overlooks the bay, and if you didn't know what's in there, you'd think it was just another storage shed. They have a name: Trans Time, Inc. I just went in and asked around. It's for real. Out in the garage, where they store the chemicals, they have six capsules—two with bodies in them: a husband and wife in one, two heads and a disembodied brain in the other. I felt like running back to Bigger Better Burger to tell the folks; they won't believe it. But it can wait till morning; it's hard to sort your thoughts when you're given information like that, so I just walk the beach and think. The husband and wife have been in cryonic suspension for years. Storing a whole body until a cure for death is found costs from $80,000 to $100,000. There are living people on the waiting list; they've bought shares. They call it deanimation, by the way, not death. They've got heart-lung machines, respirators, and antifreeze; they prep them the minute they come in.

The old man is giving up on the birds; the sun is going down behind Alcatraz, a burning liquid red. I'm thinking of an article I read once on Walt Disney, how his life was devoted to searching for ways to make inanimate things move. He coined his own term for it, *audio-animatronics*. It's the guiding principle behind Disneyland. He had himself cryonically suspended when he died—which seems a contradiction, unless you think of him as visionary. I heard they did Roy Rogers' horse, Trigger, too. The two of them are probably down in Hollywood somewhere, chilled to the bone.

Another article comes to mind—a nutrition study at the university, using mice or rats—I think it was mice. It claimed that undernutrition fosters longevity, but I don't know. The undernourished mice lived longer than the ones who ate, but were they happy? Length isn't everything. What's the point of going on and on and always being hungry for something?

You have to imagine it; these people are serious. Deep inside that cinder-block building are the rockets with the bodies inside. And that solitary brain: bobbing in its liquid ice the way you'd picture pure intelligence pulsing in the farthest regions of space.

The old man was a professor; I found out accidentally; he doesn't talk much anymore. He was sitting on the stool next to mine and overheard when Rita poured my refill and asked if I'd ever gotten my graduate degree. It was so hard, that answer, because to say I'd dropped out explained nothing. In fact, it sounded like I *was* a bum—that's the way I'd hear it if it came from someone else. I cupped my hands around my mug, and the longer I stared at the steam the more complicated the answer became. I owe the old man. "Wisdom isn't found in degrees, son," he said softly, and that was all. But the air, so thick I couldn't breathe before, now lifted and the color returned to the room. Rita laughed. "He should know," she said. It's true I walk the beach these days; in every life there's a period for that, or its equivalent—like time out. Waiting table buys me freedom for now. Berkeley's full of waiter Ph.D.s; the conversation's first rate. I'm not on unemployment yet and don't intend to be. I observe the scene and develop my prints, and for the moment it's enough. It's my belief that nothing's wasted in this life.

I come down here to watch the pelicans in flight. Those birds! I shiver when I think of it: on the verge of extinction, the very edge. After DDT was banned, they slowly staged a comeback, contrary to every expectation. You see them differently after that. Ungainly things, more like beasts when on the ground. Prehistoric relics, weaving side to side, holding up those giant beaks. Yet when they fly, you're there too. I can't explain it any other way.

The wind just shifted, like a jolt; it nearly blew me over. I spread my hands against the sand for balance. I felt the earthquake, it's here at last. I hold my breath, but things seem calm. I must have had a vision, or a lapse—it wasn't a dream as we know them. Disney was there, lurching in his liquid nitrogen. I close my eyes, the after-image still before me, and it all begins again: his chamber shudders, bearing down. The walls of his tank begin to hiss, then finally crack. The rosy plastic corpse bursts through its boundaries and tumbles, buoyant, toward the sea. Behind us, the freeway buckles and the buildings go down like pins. Finally, there's the fire, all purity and light, and in its heat Walt Disney melts, and is reborn.

At times, it seems this pier stretches to infinity. I'm running down it now and breathing hard. The sun has given up—the Pacific just swallows it whole. The pelicans ride above me, lancing off the shades of wind, flying in place as though nailed to the sky, their beaks sharpened to dark points, waiting for conditions to change. My mouth opens on the cooling air and drinks it in. The way they move, they're not twelve, but one, not descendants, but the same pelican, throughout time.

RUNNING ON EMPTY

Edmund White

· · · · · · · · · · · · · · · · · ·

O n the charter flight from Paris to New York Luke sat on the aisle. Next to him, in the center seat, was a man in his mid-twenties from the French Alps, where his parents owned a small hotel for skiers. He said he cooked all winter in the hotel and then took a quite long vacation every spring. This year it was the States, since the dollar was so low.

"Not *that* low," Luke said when Sylvain mentioned he had only a hundred dollars with him for a five-week stay.

They were speaking French, since Sylvain confessed he couldn't get through even one sentence in English. Sylvain smiled and Luke envied him his looks, his health, even his youth, although that was absurd, since Luke himself was barely twenty-nine.

Next to Sylvain, by the window, sat a nun with an eager, intelligent face. Soon she had joined in the conversation. She was Sister Julia, an American, though a member of a French convent for a reason she never explained, despite their nonstop chatter for the seven and a half hours they were in the air. Her French was excellent, much better than Luke's. He noticed that Sylvain talked to her with all the grace notes kept in, whereas with Luke he simplified down to the main melody.

It turned out Luke and Sister Julia had both been in France for four years. Of course a convent was a "total immersion" undreamed of even by Berlitz. Nevertheless Luke was embarrassed to admit to his seat partners that he was a translator. From French to English, to be sure. It was pointless to explain to this handsome, confident Sylvain that a translator must be better in the "into language" than in the "out-of language," that a translator must be a stylist in his own tongue.

Sylvain was, in any event, more intrigued by Sister Julia's vows than by Luke's linguistic competence. He asked her right off how a pretty girl like her could give up sex.

"But I'm not a girl," she said. "I'm forty-six. This wimple is very handy," she said with a trace of coquetry, "for covering up gray hair."

She was not at all like the stern, bushy-eyebrowed, downy-chinned nuns who'd taught Luke all the way through high school. When Sylvain asked her if she didn't regret having never known a man—and here he even raised his muscular arms, smiled, and stretched—she said quite simply, "But I was married. I know all about men."

She told them her father had been a composer, she'd grown up an Episcopalian in Providence, Rhode Island, she'd taught music theory at Brown and built harpsichords. Her religious vocation had descended on her swiftly, but she didn't provide them with the conversion scene; she had little sense of the dramatic possibilities her life provided, or perhaps flattening out her own narrative was a penance for her. Nor was her theology orthodox. She believed in reincarnation. "Do you?" she asked them.

"I'm an atheist," Luke said. He'd never said that to a nun before, and he enjoyed saying it, even though Sister Julia wasn't the sort to be shocked or even sorrowed by someone else's lack of faith—she was blessed by the convert's egotism. There was nothing dogmatic about her clear, fresh face, her pretty gray eyes, her way of leaning into the conversation and drinking it up, nor her quick nods, sometimes at variance with the crease of doubt across her forehead. When she nodded and frowned at the same time, he felt she was disagreeing with his opinions but affirming him as a person.

Sylvain appeared to be enjoying his two Americans. Luke and Sister Julia kept giving him the names and addresses of friends in the States to look up. "If you're ever in Martha's Vineyard, you must stay with Lucy. She's just lost a lot of weight and hasn't realized yet she's become very beautiful," the nun said. Luke gave him the names of two gay friends without mentioning they were gay—one in Boston, another in San Francisco. Of course Sylvain was heterosexual, that was obvious, but Luke knew his friends would get a kick out of putting up a handsome foreigner, the sort of blond who's always slightly tan, the sort of man who looks at his own crotch when he's listening and frames it with his hands when he's replying. Certainly both Luke and the nun couldn't resist over-responding even to Sylvain's most casual remarks.

When the stewardess served them lunch, Sylvain asked her in his funny English where she was from. Then he asked, "Are all zee womens in Floride as charming like you?"

The stewardess pursed her lips in smiling mock-reproach, as though he were being a naughty darling, and said, "It's a real nice state. France is nice, too. I'm going to learn French next. I studied Latin in high school."

Sister Julia said to Sylvain, "If you can speak English like that you won't need more than a hundred dollars."

When they all said good-bye at the airport, Luke was disappointed. He'd expected something more. Well, he had Sylvain's address, and if someday Luke returned to France he'd look him up. Ill as he was, Luke couldn't bear the thought of never seeing France again, which suddenly seemed synonymous with some future rendezvous with Sylvain.

Luke changed money and planes—this time for Dallas. He was getting pretty ill. He could feel it in the heaviness of his bones, in his extreme tiredness, and he almost asked a porter to carry his bags. He had just two hundred dollars with him—he was half as optimistic as Sylvain. He'd never had enough money, and now he worried he'd end up a charity case or, even worse, dependent on his family. He was terrified of having to call on the mercy of his family.

He'd grown up as the eighth of ten children, all of them small if wiry and agile. His mother was a Chicana, but no one ever took her for Mexican—in any event she didn't appear to have much Indian blood and her mother prided herself on being "Castilian." His father was a mean little man with a tweezered mustache who'd worked his whole life as the janitor in a Lubbock, Texas, high school. He'd converted to Catholicism to please his wife and enrage his Baptist kin (Lubbock proudly called itself "the buckle on the Bible Belt"). Luke's father and brothers and sisters all shared a pleasure he'd learned how to name only years later—*Schadenfreude,* which in German means taking malicious pleasure in someone else's pain. Spite and envy were their ruling sentiments. If someone fell and hurt himself, they'd howl with glee. Their father would regale them with hissing, venomous accounts of the misfortunes of superiors at school. The one sure way to win the family's attention was to act out the humiliation that had befallen Mrs. Rodríguez after mass last Sunday or Mr. Brown, the principal, during the last PTA meeting. Luke's father grumbled at the TV, mocked the commercials, challenged the newscasters, jeered the politicians. "Look at him, he thinks he's so great, but he'll look like he's smelled a fart when he sees the final vote." Everyone would laugh except Luke's mother, who went about her work gravely, like a paid employee eager to finish up and leave.

In high school—not the public high school where his father worked, but the much smaller parochial school—Luke had emerged as the nuns' favorite. He'd been a brilliant student. Now that his brain was usually fuzzy—and had become an overcooked minestrone during the toxoplasmosis crisis, all swimming and steamy with shreds and lumps rising only to sink again—he regarded his former intelligence with respect. He'd once known the ablative absolute. He'd once read the *Symposium* in Greek without understanding the references to love between men.

Perhaps because of his miserable, mocking family, Luke had always felt unsure of himself. Nevertheless he'd done everything expected of him, everything. He'd been a cross-country champ, he'd stayed entirely virginal, avoiding even masturbation except for rare lapses, he'd won the statewide *prix d'honneur* in French, he'd once correctly and even humorously translated on the spot an entire *Time* magazine article into Latin, though the page had been handed to him only seconds before by the judge of the Cicero Club contest.

In another era he would have grown up to be one of those priests who play basketball in a soutane and whose students complain when he beat them at arm wrestling ("Jeez, Father Luke . . .").

He'd only narrowly escaped that fate. He'd found a job in a liberal, primarily Jewish private school just outside New York, and though he'd grown a beard and spouted Saint-Simonism, he hadn't been able to resist becoming the best beloved, most energetic teacher in the history of Dempster Country Day. The kids worshiped him, called him Luke, and phoned him in the middle of the night to discuss their abortions, college-entrance exams, and parents' pending divorces. Several of them had invited him to their parents' mansions where Luke, the gung-ho jock and brain—nose always burned from the soccer field and tweed-jacket pocket always misshapen from carrying around Horace's *Odes*—had had to study his own students to discover how to wield an escargot clamp, eat asparagus with fingers only, and avoid cutting the nose off the Brie.

What was harder was to keep up that ceaseless, bouncy energy that is always the hallmark of rich people who are also "social." Whereas Luke's father had beguiled his brutal brood with tales of other people's folly and chagrin, the Lords of Long Island looked at you with distrust the instant you criticized anyone—especially a superior. Envy proved your own inferiority. Since the parents of Luke's students were usually at the top of their profession or industry, they interpreted carping and quibbles as envy. They usually sided with the object of any attack. With them generosity—like stoicism and pep—had become signs of good breeding.

Luke learned generosity, too, as easily as he'd mastered

snails. The ingredient he added to the package, the personal ingredient, was gratitude. He was grateful to rich people. He was grateful to almost everyone. The gratitude was the humble reverse side of the family's taste for *Schadenfreude.* And yet Luke could express his gratitude in such an earnest, simple way, in his caressing tenor voice with the baritone beginnings and endings of sentences, that no one took it for cringing—no one except Luke himself, who kept seeing his father, hat in hand, talking to the district supervisor.

Luke had left the abjection and exaltation of Dempster and found work as a translator. Working alone was less engrossing than playing Father Luke, but the thrill of wielding power or submitting to it at school had finally sickened him. As a kid he'd managed to escape from his family through studies; he'd stayed in school to consolidate that gain, but now he wanted to be alone, wanted to work alone into the night, listening to the radio, fine-tuning English sentences. Luckily he had a rent-controlled apartment on Cornelia Street in Manhattan, and luckily an older gay man, the king of the translators, had taken him under his wing. He became a translator, joining an honest if underpaid profession.

By subletting his apartment for four times what he paid, Luke had had enough money to live in Paris in a Montmartre hotel on a steep street near Picasso's old studio, a hotel of just eighteen rooms where the proprietor, a hearty woman from the Périgord, watched them as they ate the meals she prepared and urged them to pour wine into their emptied soup bowls and knock it back. *"Chabrol! Chabrol!"* she'd say, which was both an order and a toast. She'd point at them unsmilingly if they weren't drinking. She liked it when everyone was slightly tipsy and making conversation from table to table.

He'd never enjoyed gay life as such. At least New York clones had never struck him as sexy. In turn they hadn't liked his look—wire-rim glasses, baggy tweeds, shiny, policemen's shoes—or his looks—he was small, his eyes mocking or hostilely attentive or wet and grateful, his nose a red beak, his slim body featureless under the loose pants and outsize jackets but smooth and well-built when stripped—the pale, sweated body of a featherweight high-school wrestler, but clones had had to work to get to see it.

Luke had sought out sex with workingmen, straight men, or close approximations of that ideal. He'd haunted building sites, suburban weightlifting gyms, the bar next to the firehouse, the bowling alley across from the police station, the run-down Queens theater that specialized in kung-fu movies. He liked guys who didn't kiss, who had beer bellies, who wore T-shirts that showed through their dacron short-sleeved shirts, who watched football games, who shook their heads in frustration and muttered, "Women!" He liked becoming pals with guys who, because they were too boring or too rough or not romantic or cultured enough, had lost their girlfriends.

In Paris he'd befriended a Moroccan boxer down on his luck. But very little of his time went to Ali. He spent his mornings alone in bed, surrounded by his dictionaries, and listened to the rain and translated. He ate the same Salade Auvergnate every lunch at the same neighborhood café. In the afternoons he often went to the Cluny museum. Luke liked medieval culture. He knew everything about Romanesque fortified churches and dreamed of meeting someone with a car who could take him on a tour of them.

At night he'd haunt the run-down movie palaces near Barbès-Rochechouart, the Arab quarter, or in good weather cruise the steps below Sacré-Coeur—that was where you met his type: men-without-women, chumps too broke or too dumb to get chicks, guys with girlie calendars tacked on the inner side of the closet doors, guys who practiced karate chops as they talked on the telephone to their mothers.

He didn't want to impersonate that missing girlfriend for them. No, Luke wanted to be a pal, a sidekick, and more than once he'd lain in the arms of a CRS (a French cop) who'd drawn on his Gitane *blonde* and told Luke he was *"un vrai copain,"* a real pal.

That was why he'd been surprised when he of all people had become ill. It was a gay disease and he scarcely thought of himself as gay. In fact, earlier on he'd once talked it over with an Irish teacher of English who lived in his hotel, a pedophile who couldn't get it up for anyone over sixteen. They'd agreed that neither of them counted as gay.

For him, the worst immediate effect of the disease was that it sapped his confidence. He felt he'd always lived on nerve, run on empty. He should have lived the dim life of his brothers and sisters—one a welfare mother, another a secretary in a lumber yard, two brothers in the air-conditioning business, another one an exterminator, another (the family success) an army officer who'd taken early retirement to run a sporting-goods store with an ex-football champ. He had another brother, Jeff, an iron worker who'd dropped out of the union, who lived in Milwaukee with his girl and traveled as far away as New York State to bend steel and put up the frames of buildings. Jeff was a guy who grew his hair long and partied with women executives in their early forties fed up with (or neglected by) their white-collar male contemporaries. The last thing Luke had heard, Jeff had broken up with his girl because she'd spent fifty of his bucks hiring a limo to ferry her and two of her girlfriends around Milwaukee just for the fun of it.

Luke had sprung the family trap. He'd eaten oysters with rich socialists, learned that a "gentleman" never takes seconds during the cheese course, worried over the right slang equivalents in English to French obscenities—he'd even resisted the temptation to strive to become the headmaster of Dempster Country Day. As the runt of his family, he'd always had to fight when he was a kid to get enough to eat, but even so as an adult he'd chosen free-lance insecurity over a dull future with a future.

But all that had taken confidence, and now he didn't have any. The translation he was working on would be his last. Translating required a hundred small dares per page in the constant trade-off between fidelity and fluency, and Luke couldn't find the necessary authority.

He never stopped worrying about money. He'd lie in bed working up imaginary budgets. When he returned to New

York, Dempster Country Day might refer students to him for coaching in French, but would the parents worry that their children would be infected? He'd read of the hysteria in America. If his doctor decided he should go on AZT, how would he ever find the twelve thousand dollars a year to pay for it?

When he landed in Dallas, his favorite cousin, Beth, was there. Growing up, he'd called her Elizabeth. Now he was training himself to call her Beth, as she preferred. She hadn't been told he was ill, and he looked for a sign that his appearance shocked her, but all she said was, "My goodness, you'll have to go to Weight Watchers with me before long." If she'd known how hard he'd worked for every ounce on his bones, she wouldn't joke about it; his paunch, however, he knew, was bloated from the cytomegalovirus in his gut and the bottle of Pepto-Bismol he had to swallow every morning to control his diarrhea.

Beth's husband, Greg, had just died of an early heart attack. She'd mailed Luke a cassette of the funeral, but he'd never listened to it because he hadn't been able to lay his hands on a tape recorder—not a problem that would have occurred to her, she who had a ranch house stocked with self-cleaning ovens, a microwave, two Dustbusters, three TVs, dishwasher, washer and dryer, and Lord knew what else. So he just patted her back and said, "It was a beautiful service. I hope you're surviving."

"I'm doing fine, Luke, just fine." There was something hard and determined about her that he admired. Beth's bright Texas smile came as a comfort. He told her he'd never seen her in such pretty dark shades of blue.

"Well, thank you, Luke. I had my colors done. It was one of the last presents Greg gave me. Have you had yours done yet?"

"No, what is it?"

"You go to this lady, she measures you in all sorts of scientific ways, skin tones and all, and then she gives you your fan. I have mine here in my purse, I always carry it, 'cause don't you know I'll see a pretty blouse and pick it up, but when I get home with it it doesn't look right at *all*, and when I check it out it won't be one of my hues. It will be *close* but not exact."

Beth snapped open a paper fan. Each segment was painted a different shade. "Now the dark blue is my strong color. If I wear it, I always get compliments. You complimented me, you see!"

And she laughed and let her smiling blue eyes dazzle him, as they always had. Her old-fashioned heart-shaped face made him think of Hollywood starlets of the past, as did her slight chubbiness and smile, which looked as though it were shot through gauze.

Her little speech about colors had been an act of courage, at once a pledge she was going to be cheerful as well as a subtle blend of flirting with him (as she would have flirted with any man) and giving him a beauty tip (as she might have done with another woman). She didn't know any other gay men; she wanted to be nice; she'd found this way to welcome him.

He'd been the ring bearer in her wedding to Greg. They'd been the ideal couple, she a Texas Bluebonnet, he a football star, she small and blond, he dark and massive. Now she was just forty-five and already a widow with two sons nearly out of college, both eager to be cattlemen.

"For a while Houston was planning to be a missionary," Beth was saying, "but now he thinks he can serve the Lord just by leading a Christian life, and we know there's nothing wrong with that, don't we?" She added an emphatic, "No sirree Bob," so he wouldn't have to reply.

Since Luke belonged to the disgraced Catholic side of the family, Beth was careful usually not to mention religion. Texans were brought up not to discuss religion or politics, the cause of so many gunfights just two generations ago, but Baptists were encouraged to proselytize. Beth was even about to set off on a Baptist mission to England, she said, and she asked Luke for tips about getting along with what she called "Europeans." Luke tried to picture her, with her carefully streaked permanent, fan-selected colors from Nieman-Marcus, black-leather shoulder-strap Chanel bag, and diamond earrings, ringing the bell of a lady in a twin set and pearls in a twee village in the Cotswolds: "Howdy, are you ready to take the Lord into your heart?" Today she was holding her urge to convert in check. She didn't want to alienate him. She loved family, and he was family, even if he was a sinner lost—damned, for he'd told her ten years ago about his vice.

The program was they were to visit relatives in East Texas and then drive over to Lubbock, where Luke would stay with his parents for a week before flying home to New York. He was so worried he might become critically ill while in Lubbock and have to remain there. He felt very uprooted, but New York— scary, expensive—was the closest thing to home. He was eager to consult the doctor awaiting him in New York.

Unlike some of his friends, who'd become resigned and either philosophical or depressed, Luke had taken his own case on and put himself in charge of finding a cure. In Paris he'd worked as a volunteer for the hot line, answering anxious questions and in return finding out the latest information and meeting the best specialists. He had a contact in Sweden who was keeping him abreast of an experiment going on there; through the French he knew the latest results in Zaire. He'd memorized the list of drugs and their side effects; he knew that the side effects of trimethoprim for the pneumonia were kidney damage, depression, loss of appetite, abdominal pain, hepatitis, diarrhea, headache, neuritis, insomnia, apathy, fever, chills, anemia, rash, light sensitivity, mouth pain, nausea, and vomiting—and those were just the results of a treatment.

The father of one of his former students at Dempster had promised to pay Luke's bills "until he got better." Luke felt getting well was a full-time job; he'd even seen all the quacks, swallowed tiny white homeopathic doses, meditated and "imaged" healthy cells engulfing foul ones, been massaged on mystic pressure points, done yoga, eaten nothing but brown rice and slimy or pickled vegetables arranged on the plate according to wind and rain principles. The one thing he couldn't bring himself to do was meet with other people who were ill.

They drove in Beth's new beige Cadillac on the beltway skirting Fort Worth and Dallas and headed the hundred miles south to Hershell, where Beth had just buried Greg and where their great-aunts Ruby and Pearl were waiting for them. Once they were out of the city and onto a two-lane road, the Texas he remembered came drifting back—the wildflowers, especially the Indian blanket and bluebells covering the grassy slopes, the men with the thick tan necks and off-white straw cowboy hats driving the pickup trucks, the smell of heat and damp lifting off the fields.

Hershell was just a flyspeck on the road. There were two churches, one Baptist and one Church of Christ, a hardware store where they still sold kerosene lamps and barbed-wire stretchers, a saddle shop where a cousin of theirs by marriage worked the leather as he sipped cold coffee and smoked Luckies, a post office, a grocery store with nearly empty shelves and the "new" grade school built of red brick in the 1950s.

Ruby's house was a yellow-brick single story with a double garage and a ceiling fan that shook the whole house when it was turned on, as though preparing for lift-off. The paintings—flowers, fruits, fields—had been done long ago by one of her aunts. Luke was given a bedroom with a double bed covered with a handsome thick white chenille bedspread—"chenille" was a word he'd always said as a child, but only now did he connect it with the French word for "caterpillar." Beth was given a room across the street with Pearl. Pearl's house had been her parents'. The house was nothing but additions. Her folks had built a one-room cabin and then added rooms on each side as they had the money and inclination to do so. She showed them pictures of their great-grandparents and their twelve children—one of the pale-eyed, square-jawed boys, named Culley, was handsome enough to step out toward them away from his plump, crazed-looking siblings. Pearl's Hershell high-school diploma was on the wall. When Luke asked her what the musical notes on it meant, she said, "Be Sharp, Be Natural but Never Be Flat."

Pearl said it right out. She was intelligent enough to recognize how funny it was, but as the local chair of the Texas Historical Society, she took pride in every detail of their heritage. The miles and miles of brand-new housing developments Luke had seen on the Dallas–Fort Worth Beltway, all with purely arbitrary names such as Mount Vernon or Versailles, had spooked him, made him grateful for these sun-bleached lean-tos, for the irises growing in the crick, for the "tabernacle," that open-sided, roofed-over meeting place above the town.

He and Beth sat for hours and hours with their great-aunts, "visiting" after their supper of fried chicken and succotash. They drank their sweetened iced tea and traded stories. There were solemn moments, as when the old ladies hugged Beth and told her how courageous she was being.

"That Greg was a *fine* man," Ruby said, her eyes defiant and sharp as though someone might challenge her judgment. Her enunciation had always been clear—she'd taught elocution for years in high schools all over the state—but she hadn't weeded the country out of her voice.

Then there were the gay moments, as when Luke recounted the latest follies of folks in Paris. "Well, I declare," the ladies would exclaim, their voices dripping from pretended excitement down into real indifference. He was careful not to go on too long about a world they didn't know or care about or to shock them. He noticed they didn't ask him this time when he was going to get hitched up: perhaps he'd gone over that invisible line in their minds and become a "confirmed" bachelor. They did tease him about his "bay window," which he patted as though he hadn't noticed it before, which made them laugh.

Beth and he went on a long walk before the light died. They had a look at the folks on the corner they'd heard about who lived like pigs; the old man had gone and shot someone dead and now he was in the pokey for life, and the old woman— didn't it beat all—had a garden sale going on every day, but who would want that old junk? He and Beth walked fast, with light hearts. He appreciated their shared views—they both loved and respected their aunts, and they were both glad to slip away from them.

They walked down to see the old metal swing bridge; earlier Ruby had shown them a photo of Billy Andrews, in their class of 1917, swinging from the bridge as a stunt, big grin on his face, fairly popping out of his graduation suit with the celluloid collar, his strong calves squeezed into the knickers.

Oh, Luke ached for sex. He thought that if he could just lie next to a man one more time, feel once more that someone wanted him, he could die in peace. All his life he'd been on the prowl, once he'd broken his vows of virginity—in French he'd learned there were two words for boy virgins, neither comical: *un puceau* and *un rosier*, as though the boy were a rose bush, blossoms guarded by thorns. He'd lived so fast, cherished so little, but now he lingered over sexy souvenirs he'd never even summoned up before, like that time he'd followed a Cuban night watchman into a Park Avenue office building and they'd fucked in the service elevator and stopped, just for the hell of it, on every one of the forty-two floors. Or he remembered sex that hadn't happened, like that summer when he was twelve, a caddie, and he'd sat next to one of the older caddies on the bench waiting for a job in the airless, cricket-shrill heat. He'd molded his leg so perfectly to the guy's thigh that finally he'd stood up and said to Luke, real pissed-off, "What are you, some sort of fuckin' Liberace?" And he thought of the cop who'd handcuffed him to the bedstead.

As he and Beth were walking out past a field of cows standing in the fading light, he started picking a bouquet of wildflowers for Ruby—he got up to twenty-nine flowers without repeating a single variety. Beth walked with vigor, her whole body alert with curiosity. She'd always struck him as a healthy, sexy woman. He wondered if she'd remarry. With her religion and all she couldn't just pick up a man in a bar. She'd have to marry again to get laid. But would she want to? How did she keep her appetite in check?

The next day was hot enough to make them all worry what the summer would bring. They were going to what was called the graveyard working ten miles east of Hershell. Once a year the ten or so families who had kin buried there came together to set the tombstones upright, hoe and rake, stick silk or plastic flowers in the soil—real ones burned up right away—and then eat. Ruby and Pearl had both been up since dawn cooking, since after the graveyard working everyone shared in a big potluck lunch.

They drove out in Beth's "fine automobile," as the ladies called the Cadillac. Ruby was wearing a bonnet, one she'd made herself for gardening. The cemetery, which was also named after Hershell since he'd donated the land, was on top of a hill looking over green, rolling farmland. There were ten or eleven cars and pickup trucks already parked outside the metal palings that guarded the front but not the sides of the cemetery. Big women with lots of kids were already setting up for the lunch, unfolding card tables and stacking them with coolers of iced tea and plates of chicken fried in broken-potato-chip batter, potato salad, pickled watermelon rind, whole hams, black-eyed peas, loaves of Wonder Bread, baked beans served right out of the can, and pecan pies and apple pies. There weren't more than a hundred graves altogether, and all of them had already been decently looked after, thanks to the contributions solicited every year by Ruby, who hired a part-time caretaker.

Luke felt a strange contentment hoeing his grandfather's grave. Pearl had to show him how to hoe and how to rake, but she didn't tease him about being a city slicker. He realized he could do no wrong in her eyes, since he was kin. Everyone here was kin. Several of the men had Luke's beaky red nose. He kept seeing his own small, well-knit body on other men—the same narrow shoulders and short legs, hairless forearms, the thinning, shiny hair gone to baldness here and there. Because of the rift in the family he'd met few of these people before, and he had little enough in common with them, except he did share the same body type, possibly the same temperament.

His grandfather had been a Woodsman of the World, whatever that was, and his tomb marker was a stone tree trunk. His wife was buried under a tablet that read, "She Did The Best She Could."

Beth was standing in front of Greg's grave, which was still fresh. Luke worried that her mission to England might shake her faith. Wouldn't she see how flimsy, how recent and—well, how corny her religion was once she was in that gray and unpleasant land? They were planning, the Southern Baptists, to fan out over the English countryside. Wouldn't Beth be awed, or at least dismayed, by Gloucester Cathedral, by the polished intricacy of its cloisters? Wouldn't she see how raw, raw as this fresh grave, her beliefs were beside the civilized ironies of the Church of England? It was as though she were trying to introduce Pop Tarts into the land of scones.

During the picnic Beth told Luke that her one worry about her son Houston was that he always seemed so serious and distracted these days, as though dipped and twirled in darkness. "I tell him, Son, you must be *happy* in the Lord. The Bible tells us to be happy in our faith."

Luke couldn't resist tweaking Beth for a moment. He asked her what she thought about the scandals—adultery, group-sex parties, absconded church funds—surrounding a popular television evangelist and his wife.

"I expected it."

"You did?"

"Yes, it's good. It's a good sign. It shows that Satan is establishing his rule, which means that we'll live to see the Final Days, the Rapture of the Church." She spoke faster and with more assurance than usual. Luke realized she probably saw his disease as another proof of Satan's reign or God's punishment. He knew the Texas legislature was considering imprisoning diseased homosexuals who continued having sex.

Ruby came up to them, energized by the event, and asked him if he'd marked off a plot for himself. "You can, you know. Doesn't cost a penny." She pronounced it "pinny." "You just put stones around where you want to lie. Up here it's all filling up, but out yonder we've got lots to go."

"No," Luke said. "I want to be cremated and put in the Columbarium at Père Lachaise. In Paris."

"I declare," Ruby said, "but you've got years and *years* to reconsider," and she laughed.

That night, as the ladies visited and told family stories, Luke felt trapped and isolated. Beth sat there nodding and smiling and saying, "Auntie Pearl, now you just sit and let me." But he knew she was lonely, too, and maybe a bit frightened. Other old ladies, all widows, stopped in to visit, and Luke wondered if Beth was ready to join grief's hen club. Girls started out clinging together, whispering secrets and flouncing past boys. Then there was the longish interlude of marriage, followed by the second sorority of widowhood; all these humped necks, bleared eyes, false teeth, the wide-legged sitting posture of country women sipping weak coffee and complaining about one another. "She wanted to know what I paid for this place, and I said, 'Well, Jessie, it is so *good* of you to worry about my finances, but I already have Mr. Hopkins at Farmers First to look after that for me,' and don't you know but that shut her up fast?" On and on into the night, not really vicious but complaining, spontaneously good but studiously petty, often feisty, sometimes coquettish, these women talked on and on. Those who couldn't hear nodded while their eyes timidly wandered, like children dismissed from the table but forbidden to play in their Sunday best.

Luke imagined he and Beth were both longing for a man—she for Greg, he for one of his men, one of these divorced cowboys, the sort of heartbroken man Randy Travis or George Strait sings about. . . . They'd met a man like that during their walk past the old bridge yesterday—a sunburned man whose torso sat comfortably on his hips as though in a big, roomy saddle. This sunburned rancher had known who they were; the whole town had been alerted to their visit. He didn't exactly doff his hat to Beth, but he took it off slowly and stared into it as he spoke. Without his hat on he looked kinder, which, for Luke, made him less sexy. When he left, he swung up into his truck and pulled it into gear all in one motion. He hadn't been at the graveyard working, although Luke had looked for him.

The next morning they drove a hundred miles west to Henderson, where Beth's mother, Aunt Olna, still lived. Her husband, now dead, had been a brother of Luke's dad's—estranged because Luke's dad had married a Mex and become an "old" Catholic (for some reason people hereabouts always smiled sourly, lifted one eyebrow, and said in one breath, as though it were a bound form, "old-Catholic"). Beth's mother had grown up Church of Christ but had converted to her husband's religion years after their marriage. One day she'd simply read a pamphlet about what Baptists believed and she'd said to herself, "Well, that's what I believe, too," and had crossed over on the spot.

Aunt Olna was always harsh to Beth, ordering her around: "Not that one, Elizabeth." "This one which, Mother?" Beth would wail. Beth's mother was too "nervous" to specify her demands. "Turn here," she'd say in the car. "Turn right or left, Mother? Mother? Right or left?" Olna was also too nervous to cook. She didn't tremble, as other nervous people did. Luke figured the nervousness must be a confusion hidden deep in a body made fat from medication. Because she couldn't cook she'd taken three hundred dollars out of the bank to entertain them. She named the sum over and over again. She was proud her husband had left her "well-fixed." When Beth drove to the store, Olna said, "Greg left Beth very well-fixed. House all bought and paid for. A big *in-*surance policy. She need never worry."

Aunt Olna liked Luke. She'd always told everyone Luke was about as good as a person could get. Of course she knew almost nothing about his life, but she'd clung to her enthusiasm over the years and he'd always felt comfortable with her. And she wasn't given to gushing. When he'd praised her house, she'd said, "Everything in it is from the dime store. Always was." She told him how she'd inherited a dining-room "suit" but had had to sell it because it was too fine for her house.

Even so he liked the shiny maple furniture in the front parlor, the flimsy metal TV dinner trays on legs used as side tables, the knubby milk glass candy dishes filled with Hershey's kisses. He liked the reproduction of the troubadour serenading the white-wigged girl, a sort of East Texas take on Watteau. He liked the fact there was no shower, just a big womanly tub, and that the four-poster bed in his room was so tall you had to climb up to get into it. Best of all he liked leaving his door open onto the night.

The rain steamed the sweetness up out of the mown grass, and the leaves of the big old shade trees kept up a frying sound; when the rain died down it sounded as though someone had lowered the flame under the skillet. He was surrounded by women and death, and yet the rain dripping over an old Texas town of darkened houses made him feel like a boy in his early teens again, a boy dying to slip away to find men. These days, of course, desire entailed hopelessness—he'd learned to match every pant of longing with a sigh of regret.

The next day the heat turned the sweet smell sour, as though spring peas had been replaced with rancid collard greens. Olna took them to lunch at a barbecue place where they ate ribs and hot biscuits. In the afternoon they drove to a nursing home to visit Olna's sister. That woman remembered having baby-sat Luke once twenty-five years ago. "My, you were a cute little boy. I wish I could see you, honey. I'd give anything to see again. My little house just sits empty, and I'd love to go back to it, but I can't, I can't see to mind it. I don't know why the good Lord won't gather me in. Not no use to *no*-one."

The waiting room had a Coke machine and a snack dispenser. One of the machines was making a nasty whine. The woman's hand looked as pale as if it'd been floured through a sifter.

"My husband left me," she was saying, "and after that I sold tickets at the movie thee-ay-tur for nine dollars a week, six days a week, on Saturdays from ten till midnight, and when I asked for a raise after ten years Mr. Monroe said no." She smiled. "But I had my house and cat and I could see."

In the past, when Luke had paid these calls on relatives in nursing homes, he'd felt he was on a field trip to some new and strange kind of slum, but today there was no distance between him and this woman. In a month or a week he could be as blind, less cogent, whiter.

He went for a walk with Beth through the big park the town of Henderson had recently laid out, a good fifty acres of jogging paths, tennis courts, a sports arena, a playground, and just open fields gone to weeds and wildflowers. On the way they passed a swimming pool that had been here over twenty years ago, that time Luke had served as Beth's ring bearer. Now the pool was filled, clean, sparkling, but for some reason without a single swimmer, an unheeded invitation. "Didn't they used to have a big slide that curved halfway down and that was kept slick with water always pouring down it?" Luke asked.

"Now I believe you are one hundred percent correct," Beth said with the slightly prissy agreeableness of Southern ladies. "What a wonderful memory you have!" She'd been trained to find fascinating even the most banal remarks if a man made them. Luke wasn't used to receiving all the respect due his gender and kept looking for a mote of mockery in Beth's eye, but it wasn't there. Or perhaps she had mockery as much under control as grief or desire.

They walked at the vigorous pace Beth set and went along the cindered jogging path under big mesquite trees; their tiny leaves, immobile, set lacy shadows on the ground.

That sparkling pool, painted an inviting blue-green, and the memory of the flowing water slide and the smell of chlorine kept coming to mind. He'd played for hours and hours during an endless, cloudless summer day. Play had been rare enough for him, who'd always had early-morning newspaper-delivery jobs, afternoon hardware jobs, weekend lawn-mowing jobs, summer caddying jobs as well as the chores around the house and the hours and hours of homework, those hours his family had ridiculed and tried to put a stop to. But he'd persisted and won. He'd won.

When he and Beth reached the end of the park, they turned to the left, mounted a slight hill, and saw a parked pickup truck under a tree. Two teenage boys with red caps on were sitting inside, and a third was standing unsteadily on the back of the truck, shirtless, jeans down, taking a leak. "Oh, my goodness," Beth said, "just don't look at them, Luke, and let's keep on walking."

The guys were laughing at Luke and Beth, playing loud music, probably drunk, and of course Luke looked. The guy taking a leak was methodically spraying a dark-brown circle in the pale dust. He was a redhead, freckled, tall, skinny, and his long body was hairless except where tufted blond. He looked like a streak of summer lightning.

"But they're not doing any harm," Luke said with a smile.

"You think not?" Beth spat out. "Some folks here might think—" But she interrupted herself, mastered herself, smiled her big missionary smile.

Luke felt a rage alarm his tired body, and tears—what sort of tears?—sting his eyes.

Tears of humiliation: he was offended that a virus had been permitted to win an argument. He'd been the one to learn, to leave home, break free. He'd cast aside all the old sins, lived freely—but soon Beth could imagine he was having to pay for his follies with his life. It offended him that he would be exposed to her self-righteousness.

Aunt Olna invited them out to a good steak dinner in a fast-food place near the new shopping mall. The girls ordered medium-size T-bones and Luke went for a big one. But then he suffered a terrifying attack of diarrhea halfway through his meal and had to spend a sweaty, bowel-scorching thirty min-utes in the toilet, listening to the piped-in music and the scrapings and flushings of other men. Aunt Olna appeared offended when he finally returned to the table, his shirt drenched and his face pale, until he explained to her he'd caught a nasty bug drinking the polluted Paris water. Then she relaxed and smiled, reassured.

When they left the restaurant, Olna told the young woman cashier, "My guests tonight have come here all the way from Paris, France."

He berated himself for having fallen away from his regime

of healthy food, frequent naps, jogging and aerobics, no stress. He was stifling from frustration and anger. When they returned to Olna's, it was already dark, but Luke insisted he was going jogging. Olna and Beth didn't offer the slightest objection, and he realized that in their eyes he was no longer a boy but a man, a lawgiver. Or maybe they were just indifferent. People could accept anything as long as they weren't directly affected.

He ran through the streets over the railroad tracks, past Olna's new Baptist church, down dark streets past houses built on GI loans just after the war for six or seven thousand dollars. Their screened-in porches were dimly lit by yellow, mosquito-repellent bulbs. He smelled something improbably rich and spicy, then remembered Olna had told him people were taking in well-behaved, industrious Vietnamese lodgers studying at the local college—their only fault, apparently, being that they cooked up smelly food at all hours.

The Vietnamese were the only change in this town during the last twenty-five years. Otherwise it was the same houses, the same lawns, the same people playing Ping-Pong in their garages, voices ricocheting off the cement, the same leashless dogs running out to inspect him, then walking dully away.

There was the big house where Beth had married Greg so many years ago in the backyard among her mother's bushes of huge yellow roses. And there—he could feel his bowels turning over, his breath tightening, his body exuding cold sweat—there was the house where, when he was fifteen, Luke had met a handsome young man, a doctor's son, five years older and five hundred times richer, a man with black hair on his pale knuckles, a thin nose, and blue eyes, a gentle man Luke would never have picked for sex but whom he'd felt he could love, someone he'd always meant to look up again: the front doorbell glowed softly, lit from within. The house was white clapboard with green shutters, which appeared nearly black in the dim streetlight.

On and on he ran, past the cow palace where he'd watched a rodeo as a kid. Now he was entering the same park where he and Beth had walked today. He could feel his energy going, his legs so weak he could imagine losing control over them and turning an ankle or falling. He knew how quickly a life could be reduced. He dreaded becoming critically ill here in Texas; he didn't want to give his family the satisfaction.

He ran past the unlit swimming pool and again he remembered that one wonderful day of fun and leisure so many years ago. On that single day he'd felt like a normal kid. He'd even struck up a friendship with another boy and they'd gone down the water slide a hundred times, one behind the other, tobogganing.

Now he was thudding heavily past the spotlit tennis court. No one was playing, it was too hot and still, but two girls in white shorts were sitting on folding chairs at the far end, talking. Then he was on the gravel path under low, overhanging trees. The crickets chanted slower than his pulse and from time to time seemed to skip a beat. He passed a girl walking her dog, and he gasped, "Howdy," and she smiled. The smell of honeysuckle was so strong, and he thought he'd never really gotten the guys he'd wanted, the big high-school jocks, the blonds with loud tenor voices, beer breath, cruel smiles, lean hips, steady, insolent eyes, the guys impossible to befriend if you weren't exactly like them. He thought that with so many millions of people in the world the odds should have favored the likelihood that at least one guy like that should have gone for him, but things hadn't turned out that way. Of course, even when you had someone, what did you have?

But then what did anyone ever have—the impermanence of sexual possession was a better school than most for the way life would flow through your hands.

In the distance, through the mesquite trees, he could see the lights of occasional cars nosing the dark. Then he remembered that right around here the redhead had pissed a brown circle, and Luke looked for traces of that stain under the tree. He even touched the dust, feeling for moisture. He wondered if just entertaining the outrageous thought weren't sufficient for his purposes, but, no, he preferred the ceremony of doing something actual. He found the spot—or thought he did—and touched the dirt to his lips. He started running again, chewing the grit as though it might help him to recuperate his past if not his health.

SOCIAL SECURITY

Norah Holmgren

· · · · · · · · · · · · · · · · · · ·

My mother and I were sitting in the Social Security office. It was on the eighteenth floor of an old building in the heart of the city, but I could still hear the *swish swish* of cars passing on the freeway below. If I stood up I could see them— long ribbons of them.

I don't live in the city anymore. The sight of ten thousand cars a day began to get me down. Where I live now, out in the country, I can distinguish each of my neighbors' cars by sound alone. In the evening when I come home from work, the children can hear me coming closer and closer. In the morning when I hear the rattles and explosions of the Ford truck next door, I know it's time to get up.

My mother had asked me to come with her to Social Security. She wanted me to speak for her and hear for her. She speaks English perfectly and her hearing is unimpaired. She simply can't believe what is being said. If I came with her, she said, we could talk things over later and try to make sense of them. It would be too late then, but it's better to try to understand anyway, isn't it?

In the waiting room we were among the Mexican families, the slim, young Chinese girls, the Filipino men, the gray old German men, and the old Swedish ladies like my mother who had been cooks and maids and seamstresses and bakery clerks. The music of these languages rose and fell. The clerks had to shout over the din. When it got too noisy, an armed guard would parade by us once or twice. We all had something in common: we were waiting for our names to be called.

The procedure was this: when we entered, a woman at the door questioned us about our business. If she couldn't turn us away, she gave us a number from 1 to 50. When that number was called, we turned it in and got a number from 51 to 99. When that number was called, our name was entered on a list. When our name was called, we could be shown in. We were told to expect to wait two or three hours for these transitions.

We sat side by side, not talking, observing the people in the room as they observed us.

When my mother's name was called, we stood up and were shown through a doorway into a vast room with rows and rows of desks. Our clerk beckoned to us. He was young, freckled, and dressed in a short-sleeved white shirt open at the neck and chest to reveal a spotless white undershirt. We sat down. I was going to do all the talking.

"I'm Mr. Sisk," he said.

"Ssss?" said my mother.

"Sisk."

"Yes," she said.

His last customer was still hanging around, though he had clearly been dismissed. He was a good-looking, tall old man who was standing very straight. He ignored us. It was Mr. Sisk he wanted.

"Why can't you be reasonable?" he said. "I'm an alcoholic. You know me. I never should have told you I haven't been drinking lately. It makes no difference at all. You know that."

"No, that's what I don't know," said Mr. Sisk.

We watched unashamed.

"You don't want to know."

"You aren't drinking now. Maybe you don't need a treatment program."

"I can't hang on much longer without help."

"The rules are clear. The key words are *currently* and *presently* and *at this time.*"

"Bend the rules a little. If I take a drink I'll be gone for months. Lost, lost, lost."

"Don't ask me to bend the rules."

My mother stood up. "The rules must be stupid and cruel," she shouted.

"Who are they for?"

Mr. Sisk looked at her. He didn't speak, but his eyes were blinking rapidly.

He stood up and led the man away.

"I couldn't help it," my mother said. "Do you think it will ruin our chances?"

"I don't think we have any chances to be ruined."

Mr. Sisk returned. He had buttoned up his shirt and put his jacket on. My mother handed him the letter she had gotten from Social Security. He looked it over and said, "What's the problem?"

I said, "What does it mean?"

"It means we paid her too much money, and now we have to get it back. We are going to suspend her payments until the money is made up. It will take nine months."

"Is there no alternative?" I said. "It isn't her fault you gave her too much money."

Mr. Sisk drew himself up in his chair. "We don't use the word *fault* here. She can fill out a hardship report, stating that she cannot live without her Social Security allowance." He found the form in his desk and handed it to me. I looked it over. Declare all your valuables. Declare all current sources of income. Declare possible sources of income. State names and addresses of family members. An inquisition.

My mother had a few old valuables. Her husband, my stepfather, had a pension. They could live without her money. It was just that she thought of her Social Security check as her own money, money she had earned by forty years of labor, money she could spend on herself with a clear conscience, not that she ever did spend much money on herself.

I said to her, "We don't want to fill out this form. All of this is none of their business. It seems that they have the right to withhold your money unless you tell them how much your wedding ring is worth and everything else."

Mr. Sisk addressed my mother in a very loud voice. "Are you willing to fill out this form?"

"I'm not deaf," she shouted at him.

He shuffled his paper. There was a commotion at the next desk. A redheaded clerk was yelling at an old woman in black. "Come back when you're sober."

"I'm not drunk. I've just had a little drink," she said.

"Sit down, then," the clerk screamed.

"Something about this place makes you want to yell," my mother said.

"It's because they think we're all deaf."

"I get so mad," my mother said. "Sure, that woman had a little drink. Sometimes you get so mad, sometimes you get so fed up, you just take a drink."

We got up to leave. "If you get a check from us by mistake, be sure to send it to me," said Mr. Sisk.

"You're going to make more mistakes? What's wrong with you people?" my mother said.

I took her out to lunch. I tried to minimize the loss of her money.

She said, "Stop trying to cheer me up. You're making me feel terrible." We sat in silence then.

After a while she started to talk. "I've worked and worked," she said. I sat very still. I hoped she would tell me her story. She rarely spoke about her early life. I knew only the generalities: Dad was good. Mother was a martyr, times were hard, you wouldn't believe it.

"When I was eleven—that was during the war—not much food then, the whole family got the flu at one time. There were seven of us children. Dad and I were the only ones who didn't get sick. Oh, how we worked. We cooked, we cleaned, we did the chores. I was so tired at night, I fell asleep in my clothes. My youngest brother died of pneumonia and was buried before the doctor got to us. My mother cried for months and months about that. It was just me and my dad doing all the work. We made soup, we dug potatoes, we fed the chickens. Oh, how we worked."

I waited but she didn't go on.

"What made you think of that story?"

"Mr. Sisk. I'd like to show him what work is."

We got up to leave. "I'm lonely," my mother said. "I'd like to go see Alice. Will you drive me over?"

Alice was a friend of hers I didn't care for. "I'll drive you, I'll wait for you, but I don't want to come in and visit."

"I don't want you to. I want to talk about places you've never been, times before you were born. You'd just be in the way."

After I'd dropped her off, I went into a little park near Alice's house and sat down with a book. There was an unexpected number of people in the park. A large table stood under the trees with paper cups full of water on it. People were watching the path expectantly. Soon tired men and women came running into the park. As each one crossed a chalk line, the bystanders would applaud and cheer. Friends would come forward to hug the runners. The event repeated itself over and over. The applause and cheers didn't diminish; they increased.

My mother soon came limping up the path. Runners passed her on either side. She paid no attention to them. I wanted to stand and applaud her, whose every race had been run without applause, but she would have been angry.

"Why are you smiling?" she said. "Are you laughing at me?"

"No. I'm appreciating you."

"Alice didn't remember the flu of 1917, but she was glad to see me."

Later that evening when I was back in the country and the children were in bed, I wrote a little note to myself. I planned to read it every now and then. It said: "Develop a terrifying persona for when you are old and at the mercy of systems. Save your money so you can always be independent. Never look as though you could be hard of hearing."

This morning when I was cleaning out my desk, I found it. I laughed first, then I called my mother to say hello.

MOTHER'S CHILD

David Shields

· · · · · · · · · · · · · · · · · · ·

Lilian Gurevitch lived alone now without ever leaving. An iron gate was swung back and chained open, exposing the garden. I walked up the high marble steps that led to her front porch. The harsh lights in the fancy chandeliers and antique lamps appeared to have been left on all night.

Double doors, which had shiny knobs and handles done in gold, and tinted glass windows serving as one-way mirrors gave onto the night. Straight up the staircase I went, taking two stairs at a time and gripping the banister while I made my way to Lilian's third-floor bedroom. Thick red carpet covered the stairs without an inch of bare wood. At the landing of each floor a chandelier, with pink flower petals floating in water in the hollowed-out glass in the center of the piece, hung down from the ceiling. I stopped at the third floor, caught my breath, turned right, and walked down the dark hallway to her bedroom.

The door was slightly ajar; I pushed it open and quickly walked in to see her fast asleep and flat on her stomach on top of the covers, dangling her withered feet over the edge of the bed and snoring. All the lights in the room were on. She had much less hair than when I had seen her last, as the crown of her head was nearly bald, and what was left along the sides and in back was white, snarled, and about to fall out.

Row after neat row of vials filled with pills and medicines, plastic bottles of lotions, wide cups holding water, and vases of white roses lined the sheet of glass on top of the bureau. Faded old pages of the newspaper and half-eaten, rotten pieces of fruit were strewn across a rug that was coming unraveled. Along the far wall hung gaudy portraits of Lilian's ancestors done in oil.

"Lilian," I said in a voice halfway between whispering and talking, but she didn't respond. I sat down next to her and, leaning over, shook her frail shoulders. "Wake up, Lilian," I called into her waxy ear, then lightly slapped her thighs and picked up her feet. She stopped snoring, and I heard her cough a little and suck up her breath before she finally shook herself awake and sat up in bed with two pillows supporting her. She looked straight at me down at the other end of the bed.

"Anything you want is yours," she said.

"What?"

"Take it. Take it all. Just leave me alone. Take everything you can find and get the hell out of here. Just don't touch me."

She raised her hand, in which she gripped used Kleenex.

"Are you all right, Lilian?"

"How did you know my name? How did you get in here?"

"Every door in the entire house is wide open."

I edged forward to boost up one of the pillows that was slipping.

"Stay right where you are."

"It's Walter, Lilian. Jane's son. Walter Bloom."

"You're lying."

"I've come to see you."

"Give me my glasses."

I found her case among the messy tubes and tall bottles on top of the bureau, and removed eyeglasses with lenses that must have been a quarter of an inch thick. I handed the glasses to her. Unfolding them, slipping them onto her face, she blinked a couple of times, then looked directly at me. Her eyes grew larger, rounder. She stared.

"You're not a robber."

"No."

"It is you."

"I came to visit."

"It's Walter."

"Do you remember me?"

"You've grown so much I hardly recognize you, but I remember you. Of course I remember you. Come a little closer. Let me have a look." I sat down next to her on the edge of the bed, and she took her warm hands out from under the blankets, feeling my face with her crooked fingers. "When's the next time you'll see your mother?"

"What do you mean?"

"Don't you visit her site on the High Holidays?"

"Usually."

"Next time you go you'll bring a flower to her for me."

"I'd be happy to."

She motioned to the vase of flowers on top of the bureau and asked me to bring her one of them. Lilian picked out the fullest flower in a vase full of white roses. She held the rose out in front of her, then handed it to me; I took it, thanking her and slipping the stem into the lapel of my shirt.

"Please get me some water," she said and then started coughing.

I poured ice water into a dirty glass and tried to get her to drink it, but she was choking and had raised her hands over her head and was waving them. She could scarcely breathe. Her face flushed, her eyes disappeared, and her mouth lost all its color until she brought up whatever it was that was lodged in the bottom of her throat and causing all the trouble. I patted her on the back and caused her to cough some more.

With a towel from one of the bureau drawers, I wiped her mouth. I held the back of her head and slowly poured water down her parched throat. She finally stopped shaking and got a hold of herself. I helped her back into bed, picking up those bony legs of hers, sliding her under the covers, fluffing up the pillows. I tucked her in and turned off all the lights in the room. She shut her eyes.

"Leave me be now. Let me rest."

"Okay."

"You must go now."

"I will."

"You're your mother's child, Walter."

"Thank you. Are you in pain?"

"Yes."

"Is there anything I can get for you?"

"Yes. I want you to spill the entire bottle of sleeping pills onto the bed and fill up the glass of water for me and place them on the bed stand. And then you can leave."

"No. I can't do that."

"Why not?"

"I'm afraid."

"Of what?"

"Doing harm."

Still whispering, with her eyes still shut, she said, "You mustn't be. You mustn't be afraid to do harm because I'm dying, Walter. Pour that bottle of sleeping pills onto the blanket or I'll take one of the pillows from behind my head and hold it over my face until the pain goes away. Please, Walter."

"Go ahead."

"You'll watch?"

"Yes."

"You won't stop me?"

"No."

"Then why won't you assist me?"

"I won't help you die."

"But I need an accomplice."

"Do it yourself."

"I'll do it."

"Go ahead."

"I can't. Do it for me. Empty the bottle and fill the water glass and then you can leave."

"No."

"You're cruel to leave me suffer."

"I'm sorry."

"You're afraid."

"Yes."

"Please. Walter."

"No."

"Have mercy upon me."

"No."

SINATRA

Susan Dodd

· · · · · · · · · · · · · · · · · ·

M y father, bent to peer into the lower shelves of the copper-brown refrigerator, resembles a snowy egret. His legs are thin and look twisted, like pipe cleaners. Hot air from a nearby floor vent billows his white nightshirt out above his knotty knees.

"Cripes," he says.

"What's the matter, Dad?"

"We were going to get prunes yesterday."

The "we" is subtle treason. This kitchen, this empty larder are his. I just flew in from Boston last night.

"You want me to cook your egg?"

"Break the yolk up a little," he says. "Now what am I going to do?"

"What?"

"One day without prunes, I'll probably pay for a week."

"You want me to run out and get some?" I look down at my flannel nightgown. I'm halfway to the stove, a skillet in my hand. It isn't eight o'clock yet.

"Ahh." My father forages deeper inside the cold interior, his stiff spine at a sharp angle. "Prune juice will do. For now." He straightens up and grunts. "I guess."

He slams the refrigerator door, pours himself a large tumbler, and drinks it down without seeming to pause for breath.

Just looking at the thick, dark liquid makes me feel slightly sick. The glass has Fred Flintstone painted on the sides.

"You like that stuff?"

"Blah," he says. Then he pours some more juice. He sips it as I fry his egg and put some whole-wheat bread in the toaster.

The kitchen, gleaming and barren, is not much more than a galley. We go sit at the glass-and-wrought-iron table in an alcove in the living room. Beyond sliding glass doors, a huge kidney-shaped swimming pool looks wan below a postcard sky. The Sangre de Cristo Mountains, mottled rose and terra-cotta, seem close enough to fall on us.

My father eats his egg in small, determined swallows, as if it were medicinal. "You never heard of salt?" he says.

"I salted it. You know you're supposed to go easy on the salt."

"What for?" he says. "How much longer you think I want to live?"

"Dad—"

"I'm kidding," he says. He gets up and goes into the kitchen. He returns, the tail of his nightshirt flapping, with a vial of salt substitute I sent him from a Cambridge health-food store. It's called The Spice of Life. When he twists off the cap, a sharp crack gives him away; the seal has never been broken. We both act as if we don't notice.

"I like your place," I say.

He has lived in this Santa Fe condominium for about a year. I haven't seen it before.

"It's all right," he says. "I get by."

There are two rooms, unless you count the kitchen and the bathroom. The place cost nearly two hundred thousand dollars. "Terrific view," I say.

"It's like everything," my father says. "You get tired of it."

"I wouldn't."

He waves a yolk-dipped crust at me. "Wait till you're eighty-nine," he says.

He won't be eighty-nine for three more months, but the point is not worth arguing.

"Maybe while you're here you could help me decorate," he says. "Pick out a couple plants or something?"

I catch my breath, try not to look startled. "Sure. O.K."

"You got any plans today—anything you want to do?"

I made it to New Mexico in less than twenty-four hours, on a moment's notice. His call seemed that urgent. I called my boss and dropped my son off at his father's place before dawn. Now my father is billing this as a leisure trip.

It was midnight in Boston, and I had been asleep for at least an hour when the phone rang. "I can't do this," he said. "I just can't keep this up."

"Dad?"

He was crying—a terrible, jagged sound. "Can you come get me?" he said.

"Daddy, what's wrong?" I sounded like my son, Jason.

"I don't know," he said.

"Where are you?"

"I forgot."

He was, I managed to learn eventually, at home, in his own place. He'd gone out for his usual after-dinner walk. Then suddenly he just didn't know where he was anymore.

A woman looking out her patio door happened to see him pacing in a tight circle around and around the pool. She came out because she thought he had lost something and she wanted to help him look. They were nodding acquaintances; she knew which door was his. She took him home, not a hundred yards away, and stayed until he was himself again. When she left, he called me.

"Beth," he said, "someone had better do something."

Beth, my mother, died six years ago.

"Just take it easy, Dad. I'll try to get out there tomorrow."

I heard him blow his nose.

"I'll call you in the morning and tell you exactly when, O.K.?"

"I didn't mean Beth," he said. "I meant Sharon."

"That's right, Dad. Listen, could you call somebody to come stay until I get there, maybe that lady who—"

"I'm not a child."

"No, Dad, I know, but—"

"I just said Beth by accident. *You* could do that," he said.

"I'll call you in the morning, Dad."

"If it's convenient," he said, and hung up.

I got out of bed and started packing. Then it was one o'clock in the morning. Jason hardly woke up. I carried him out to the car wrapped in a blanket. I was at Logan by six, prepared to take my chances. Even with a reservation, there's no guarantee these days that you'll get a seat.

"We can just take it easy today, if you want," my father is saying. "Too bad you couldn't come when the desert flowers were in bloom."

He glances quickly away when I look at him. He hasn't forgotten—he just wants to ease into it.

"What about you, Dad? Is there something you'd like to do?"

"You could meet my friend Gil," he says.

"Gil?"

"He used to live next door."

"He doesn't anymore?"

"Poor guy had a stroke. Got all flummoxed up." My father gazes casually at the mountains with what seems polite interest. The higher peaks are whitened, I can't tell whether by clouds or snow.

"He moved to this other place a few months back," my father says. "It's not a hospital or anything, but like a . . ."

"A home?" I say.

My father laughs softly. "Gil calls it a retirement village."

It's my turn now, but I can't think what to say.

My father stands and picks up the dishes. "Listen," he says, "when we go out, don't forget the prunes."

He won't let me wash the dishes. "I'm pretty good with the upkeep, don't you think?" He dismantles all four burners before he sponges off the stove.

✳   ✳   ✳

Up ahead, at the end of the corridor, two men stand in the arched entryway to a large, sun-flooded room. They are handsome, tall and straight as flagpoles. One wears paisley suspenders, the other an ascot and tapestry slippers. They look keyed up, as if they've been waiting for us. Their eyes are full of romance. They have got to be, between them, a hundred and sixty years old.

Half a pace behind me, my father's footsteps seem to mend the frayed edge of the corridor carpet with fine stitches. He is thin as thread. His dark clothes, grown too large, weigh him down.

His friend Mr. Gilhooly plunges ahead, telling me how he was a banker for more than fifty years. "Trust," he says, dropping his voice.

Mr. Gilhooly has acquired a merchant seaman's gait since his stroke. He lurches. He curses and hums as if sea chanteys come over him like afflictions. He has lived in the home for three months now. He shows us around with a proprietary pride. "Men only," he says. "But that's all right. We can have company. . . . Now, up here you got your whatchamacallit room," he says. "You know, where you do things."

"Recreation?" I say.

He looks at me slantwise, the left side of his mouth dragging him down. "How'd you know?"

"A lucky guess." I smile, declining to toot my own horn. In fact, my guesses are guided by no mean talent. Being a virtuoso at charades is excellent preparation for keeping company with ancient men.

"The recreation room, Daddy," I say, too loud. His hearing is fine—it's his attention span that is the wild card. "Up here. Look."

My father turns his head and peers instead through the doorway to a small, dim room we are passing, the last in a long row. Two skeletal gents catnap in the shape of question marks on top of the covers, their pink chenille bedspreads prudently turned down.

"Where is everybody?" my father says.

"Kinda tame around here today," Mr. Gilhooly tells him. Dad rolls his eyes at me.

"It can get pretty lively, though, Mike. On Sunday we have sherry."

"That's fine, Gil."

"At four, four-thirty."

Moving along beside me now, my father glances back once more at the darkened room.

We are nearly at the recreation room. The two handsome old men hover in the archway, their eyes ardent, expectant, the shade of maple syrup under the fluorescent hallway lights. One gestures: come hither. His elegant hand is all bone and manicure. The other's lips move, rhythmic and sensuous. Soundless. I imagine him singing "Begin the Beguine" as he beguiles me with dreamy glances.

The two men part so we can pass between them. The one who seems to sing bows slightly, his lips still keeping time to nothing I can hear. His friend reaches out with long, pale fingers and taps my father's shoulder, a dancing partner gallantly cutting in. Dad looks at him, juts out his chin, and nods curtly. "Hi, fellas," he says.

"Say, you got yourself a good one," the beautiful old man tells my father. "She looks like a real good one."

I smile. My father does not.

"What a shine on her." The second man sounds wistful.

Dad mutters something that sounds like "You bet" and ducks into the room after his friend Gil.

Mr. Gilhooly hums, lurching toward the entertainment center—a dazzling display of shelved audiovisual diversions and board games and paperback books. "We got everything we need," he says. "You can see that, right?"

On the far wall, beyond a battered Ping-Pong table, a large painting hangs between two windows. Its aluminum frame catches and makes much of the midday light. The painting, a portrait, is crude, overcolored, yet oddly compelling. A poor imitation of a Léger, perhaps. I cross the room to examine it.

I am very close before I discover that what I've taken for a painting is actually a collage. The man inside the frame is pieced together from poker chips, playing cards, Scrabble tiles, checkers and dominoes and Monopoly money.

I feel a displacement of air behind me and turn around quickly. My would-be swain, his paisley galluses slipping down the slopes of his shoulders, is at my side. He whispers, enclouding my face in sour but faintly anise-scented breath. "Our founder," he says. (Or does he? Since my father has grown somewhat tedious, I tend to ascribe unlikely cleverness and charm to other old men, trying to make of them an occasion my father might suddenly rise to.)

Smiling, I edge away, closer to Dad and Mr. Gilhooly, who is spreading out board games for our scrutiny. His voice is cool and persuasive, reassuring. No sea chanteys here, no gangplank, no brig. He is, again, a trust officer. "Not a piece missing anywhere," he says. "We hold depreciation to a minimum."

My father is gazing into the heart of a marble-studded star on a Chinese-checkers board, distant and absorbed as a sorcerer.

Mr. Gilhooly taps him on the chest, driving home a point. "You won't find a sounder alternative. Not in today's market."

"I know, Gil." My father, no stranger to safe bets and hard bargains, nods. He is staring now at me, waiting for the crucial move, the counteroffer. His eyes, blue as poker chips, reveal his hand: hope, falling short of the stakes, folds.

Then, with a terrible tearing sound, time stops. This moment, this roomful of harsh light have become a badly written page ripped from a tablet, these four old men and I mistakes being crumpled and furiously discarded.

Mr. Gilhooly jumps and winces. My father freezes, his startled eyes still caught on mine. "Good God," he says. I reach for him.

Then the tearing stops. I hear an abrasive ticking, as if time, rewound, had resumed. I realize it's only a phonograph; its needle has been dragged at top volume across a very old record. The volume is lowered as the scratchy music begins: "I'll get by . . . as long as I . . . have . . ." The recording is so old, the phonograph needle so worn that it takes several measures before I recognize the voice: Frank Sinatra, when he was very young. Then I hear another voice behind me, also youthful, yearning, stylish: "Please, if I may?"

At a light touch on my back, I turn. The man in tapestry slippers is holding out his arms to me. "Please," he says again. His topaz eyes are already dancing. Reaching for me, his hands hover between us, mettlesome and chalky.

I glance at my father, but he is looking away.

"Though I may . . . be far away . . . it's true . . . say, what care I, dear? . . . I'll get by . . . as long . . ."

I turn, and, smiling, step into the old man's arms.

Before we leave the home, Mr. Gilhooly takes us into the office to meet the Resident Director, Mrs. Fallows. Predictably matronly and cheerful, she wears a white lab coat over a dress printed with a dark crowd of flowers. She calls me "dear" but speaks mostly to my father, addressing him scrupulously as "sir."

We are given brochures with color photographs of private and semiprivate rooms, uninhabited. The cover shows the recreation-room portrait between two garish blue blanks of sky. Monthly rates are listed on the back, printed figures crossed out and upwardly adjusted in ballpoint pen.

Mrs. Fallows sees me studying the rates. "Everything is going up," she says softly. "Where will it end?"

As we rise to leave, she comes out from behind her desk to see us to the door. She has on white running shoes.

We say good-bye to Mr. Gilhooly at the elevator in the lobby. As the stainless-steel doors squeeze shut before his face, he calls out to my father in a hearty voice, "Be seeing you, Mike."

"Yeah," Dad says, but the elevator is already at the next floor.

We cross the lobby, picking up speed as we near the exit.

"Well," my father says. "It seems reasonable."

I smile, not quite looking at him. "Wasn't he something, though . . . the dancer?" I say.

At the revolving door my father stands aside, forcing me to lead. I step in, looking over my shoulder to make sure he's still with me. Just as I push the door ahead, I hear him say, "That bum."

"What?"

On the other side of the glass partition, his lips are moving soundlessly. Then the door hurls him onto the sidewalk next to me. He lurches, unsteady on his feet.

I take his arm. "What did you say, Dad?"

My father's sigh seems to summon up enough contempt to demolish the building, to stop sorrow in its tracks. "A real wiseacre," he says. "That Sinatra."

About the Editor and Authors

In addition to his M.D., **Jon Mukand** has earned an M.A. in English from Stanford University and is pursuing his Ph.D. in English and American literature at Brown University. Dr. Mukand has also compiled a book of contemporary poetry about medicine, *Sutured Words* (Aviva Press, 1987), and is the author of *The Rehabilitation of Patients with HIV Disease*, to be published by McGraw-Hill in 1991. Mukand is on the clinical faculty of the Boston University School of Medicine and the Medical College of Wisconsin, and is the medical director of rehabilitation at the Landmark Medical Center in Rhode Island. He lives in Providence, RI.

Margaret Atwood is the author of more than twenty volumes of poetry, fiction, and nonfiction, and is best known for her seven novels: *The Edible Woman, Surfacing, Lady Oracle, Life Before Man, Bodily Harm, The Handmaid's Tale,* and *Cat's Eye.* Born in Ottawa, she now resides in Toronto with novelist Graeme Gibson and their daughter Jess.

Sheila Ballantyne is the author of the novels *Imaginary Crimes* and *Norma Jean the Termite Queen,* and the short story collection, *Life on Earth.* She holds the W. M. Keck Foundation Chair in Creative Writing at Mills College.

Joe David Bellamy is the author of the novel *Suzi Sinzinnati,* winner of the Editors' Book Award. His other books include *The New Fiction, Superfiction, American Poetry Observed,* and two books of poetry, *Olympic Gold Medalist* and *The Frozen Sea.*

James Bellarosa lives in North Grafton, MA. He works three part-time accounting jobs and writes short stories in the free time he has left. He has been published in *Yankee, Time, American History Illustrated, The Saturday Evening Post* and other publications. In 1949, at age ten, he contracted polio and he has been in a wheelchair ever since.

T. Coraghessan Boyle is a native of Peekskill, NY, a graduate of the Iowa Writers' Workshop, a bon vivant, and as *The New York Times* has it, "a snappy dresser." He is the author of four novels, *Water Music, Budding Prospects, World's End,* and *East Is East* and several books of short stories, among them *If The River Was Whiskey.*

Anne Brashler's short story collection, *Getting Jesus in the Mood,* is due out from Cane Hill Press in 1991. Her poetry and short stories have been published in many literary magazines, including *The Transatlantic Review, Confrontations, Other Voices,* and *New Letters.*

Rosellen Brown is the author of six books: three novels (*Civil Wars,* 1984; *Tender*

430

Mercies, 1978; *The Autobiography of My Mother,* 1976), two books of poetry (*Cora Fry,* 1977; *Some Deaths in the Delta,* 1970) and a short story collection, (*Street Games,* 1974).

Gregory Burnham's short stories and humor have appeared in scores of journals and magazines across the United States. He lives on Vashon Island, WA.

Ron Carlson is the director of creative writing at Arizona State University. His work has appeared in *TriQuarterly, Carolina Quarterly, The Village Voice,* and other magazines and newspapers. His novels include *F. Scott Fitzgerald.* His most recent work is the short story collection entitled *News of the World.*

Pat Carr has published eight books, including *The Women in the Mirror,* which won the Iowa Fiction Award for 1977. She teaches at Western Kentucky University.

Raymond Carver was born in Clatskanie, OR, in 1939, and lived in Port Angeles, WA, until his death on August 2, 1988. The winner of many prestigious awards and fellowships, including the Guggenheim Fellowship, he was elected to the American Academy of Arts and Letters in 1988.

Diana Chang is the author of six novels and two collections of poems. She lives on Long Island, NY.

Kelly Cherry is the author of several novels, the latest of which is *My Life and Dr. Joyce Brothers: A Novel and Stories;* several books of poetry, the latest of which is *Natural Theology;* and a forthcoming book of non-fiction, *The Exiled Heart.* She has been the recipient of the Fellowship of Southern Writers Poetry Award. She is currently a professor of English at the University of Wisconsin at Madison.

E. S. Creamer's fiction has appeared in a number of literary journals including *The Antioch Review, The Alaska Quarterly Review,* and *The Missouri Review.* A senior editor at G.P. Putnam's Sons, Creamer is currently at work on a novel. She lives in Manhattan's Hell's Kitchen with husband Roger Finney.

Pamela Ditchoff's work has appeared in several literary magazines including *The Sonora Review, The South Florida Poetry Review, Negative Capability, Amelia, Slipstream,* and *Rhino.* She is currently with the Creative Writers in Schools Program in Michigan.

Stephen Dixon is the author of seven short story collections and four novels. His latest story collection was *Love and Will,* 1989; his latest novel was *Garbage,* 1988.

Susan Dodd is the author of two novels, *No Earthly Notion* and *Mamaw,* and two story collections, *Old Wives' Tale* and *Hell-Bent Men and Their Cities.* She is a Briggs-Copeland Professor of Fiction at Harvard.

Patricia Eakins lives in New York City.

Jeff Elzinga was born in Racine, WI, and is a graduate of St. Olaf College and Columbia University. He teaches writing at Lakeland College in Sheboygan, WI, has written a handful of screenplays, and has been working on his first novel. Before attending graduate school, he worked as an orderly in a hospital emergency room.

M. Thorne Fadiman has published fiction in regional and national publications, including *Kaleidoscope.* As a journalist, he has written for *Forbes, Manhattan, Inc.,* and *The New York Times.* He is the founder of the national quarterly health review, "SHR."

Tess Gallagher is the author of four books of poetry including *Instructions to the Double, Willingly,* and *Amplitude.* A native of the Pacific Northwest, Gallagher divides her time between Port Angeles, WA, and teaching English at Syracuse University.

George Garrett is the author of twenty-two books, including novels, stories, poetry, plays, biographies, and criticism—and editor of seventeen others. He is Henry Hoyns Professor of Creative Writing at the University of Virginia.

Reginald Gibbons is a poet and writer of fiction and criticism, the editor of *TriQuarterly Magazine,* and teaches at Northwestern University. His most recent books are *Saints* and *Five Pears or Peaches.* He is at work on a novel.

Gail Godwin was born in Alabama, grew up in Asheville, North Carolina, and now lives in Woodstock, NY. She is the author of two volumes of short stories and seven novels. Her most recent novel is *A Southern Family*.

Curtis Harnack is the author of three novels, two memoirs, a collection of short fiction, and, most recently, a history, *Gentlemen on the Prairie*, an account of English aristocratic settlers in nineteenth century Iowa. He lives in midtown Manhattan and rural upstate New York, and is currently at work on another memoir.

Robert Hass is the author of *Human Wishes* and other volumes of poems, and a collection of essays, *20th Century Pleasures*. He lives in Berkeley, CA.

Amy Hempel is the author of *Reasons to Live*, a collection of short stories. She lives in New York City.

Jim Heynen is the author of several critically acclaimed books, including *You Know What Is Right*, *The Man Who Kept Cigars in His Cap*, and *A Suitable Church*. He is currently writer-in-residence at Lewis and Clark College in Portland, WA.

Norah Holmgren lives in San Francisco, CA. She recently completed her first novel, *Driving North*.

David Huddle is the author of *Stopping By Home*, a collection of poems, and *The High Spirits: Stories of Men and Women*. He teaches at the University of Vermont and in the Bread Loaf School of English.

Ellen Hunnicutt was born and raised in central Indiana. Her stories have appeared in *Prairie Schooner*, *Wisconsin Academy Review*, and *Boy's Life*. She lives with her family in Big Bend, WI. Her first novel is entitled *Suite for Calliope*.

Bret Lott is the author of two novels, *The Man Who Owns Vermont* and *A Stranger's House*. He is an assistant professor of English and writer-in-residence at the College of Charleston, SC.

Michael Martone has published two books of stories, *Alive and Dead in Indiana* and *Safety Patrol*. He is the Briggs-Copeland Lecturer on Fiction at Harvard.

Bharati Mukherjee was born in Calcutta, India. She won the National Book Critics Circle Award in fiction for *The Middleman and Other Stories*, becoming the first naturalized American citizen to do so. Her most recent novel is *Jasmine*.

Tema Nason is a visiting Writer at the Bunting Institute, Radcliffe, and a resident at MacDowell Colony and Virginia Center for the Creative Arts. She is the author of *A Stranger Here, Myself* and the forthcoming *Ethel*, a novel about Ethel Rosenberg.

Lewis Nordan is a native Mississippian. He is the author of two collections of short stories, *Welcome to the Arrow-catcher Fair* and *The All-Girl Football Team*. He lives in Pittsburgh, and teaches creative writing at the University of Pittsburgh.

Joyce Carol Oates holds the Roger S. Berlind Distinguished Lectureship in Creative Writing at Princeton University. Her current novel is *I Lock My Door Upon Myself*.

Mary Peterson is a writer at the University of New Hampshire. She is a contributing editor to the *North American Review* and the Pushcart Prize Series. A collection of her stories, *Mercy Flights*, was published in 1985 by the University of Missouri Press.

Jayne Anne Phillips is the author of *Black Tickets*, *Machine Dreams*, and *Fast Lanes*.

Felix Pollak, a native of Vienna, came to this country as a refugee from Hitler; he died in 1987. A librarian and curator of rare books and special collections at Northwestern University, he was the author of several books of poetry, the last being *Benefits of Doubt*, 1987.

Scott Russell Sanders is the author of ten books—both novels and short story collections. He teaches in the English Department at the University of Indiana in Bloomington.

Steven Schrader is the author of several short collections, the latest of which is *Arriving at Work* (Hanging Loose Press, 1989). He lives in New York City where he runs Cane Hill Press, which publishes contemporary fiction.

Lynne Sharon Schwartz is the author of four novels—*Rough Strife, Balancing Acts, Disturbances in the Field,* and *Leaving Brooklyn,* and two short story collections, *Acquainted with the Night* and *The Melting Pot and Other Subversive Stories.* She lives in New York City.

Richard Selzer was a professor of surgery at Yale Medical School. His books include *Rituals of Surgery* (1974), *Mortal Lessons* (1976), *Confessions of a Knife* (1979), and *Letters to a Young Doctor* (1982). He lives in New Haven, CT.

David Shields's second novel, *Dead Languages,* is being published in April by Knopf. His first novel, *Heroes,* was published by Simon and Schuster.

Layle Silbert is the author of some fifty short stories published in a variety of literary magazines. A collection of his stories, *Imaginary People and Other Strangers,* was published by Exile Press in 1985.

Elaine Marcus Starkman lives, writes, and teaches in Northern California. She is currently editing a book of poetry, *The Lion Whose Mane I Groom.*

Richard Stern is the author of several books, among them the novels *Golk, Other Men's Daughters, Natural Shocks,* and *A Father's Words.* He is also the author of *Noble Rot: Stories 1949–1988.*

John Stone sees patients and teaches at Emory University School of Medicine. His books of poetry are: *The Smell of Matches, In All this Rain,* and *Renaming the Streets.* His short story collection, *In the Country of Hearts,* has recently been published by Delacorte Press.

Jonathan Strong has published two novels, *Ourselves* and *Elsewhere.* He teaches at Wellesley College.

Sandra Thompson is Assistant Managing Editor for Newsfeatures for the *St. Petersburg Times* in Florida. She is the author of a short story collection, *Close-Ups,* which won the Flannery O'Connor Award for Short Fiction in 1984. Her novel, *Wild Bananas,* appeared in 1986.

Rosalind Warren lives in Philadelphia, PA. Her stories have been published in *Seventeen, Fantasy and Science Fiction, Crosscurrents* and other publications. She is a bankruptcy attorney.

Robert Watson is the author of two novels and five books of poems. He has received an award from the American Academy and Institute of Arts and Letters. He lives in Greensboro, NC.

Edmund White teaches writing at Brown University. He is a frequent contributor to *The New York Times Book Review, Vogue,* and *Vanity Fair.* His works include *Forgetting Elena, Nocturnes for the King of Naples, States of Desire, A Boy's Own Story, Caracole, The Beautiful Room is Empty* and half of the stories from *The Darker Proof: Stories of a Crisis.*

Hilma Wolitzer lives in Syosset, LI. Her novels include *Silver* and *In the Palomar Arms.*

Irving Kenneth Zola is the Chair of the Department of Sociology at Brandeis University. His most recent publications include *Independent Living for Physically Disabled People* with Nancy Crewe and *Socio-Medical Inquiries: Recollections, Reflections and Reconsiderations.* He has edited and published the *Disability Studies Quarterly* since 1982.

Permissions

"The Wrath-Bearing Tree" by Lynne Sharon Schwartz. Reprinted from *Acquainted with the Night and Other Stories,* Harper and Row, 1984. Copyright © Lynne Sharon Schwartz, 1984. Reprinted by permission of the author.

"Going" by Amy Hempel. Reprinted from *Reasons to Live,* Alfred A. Knopf, 1985. Copyright © Alfred A. Knopf, 1985. Reprinted by permission of Alfred A. Knopf.

"In Search of the Rattlesnake Plantain" by Margaret Atwood, from *Bluebeard's Egg*